Kimberlin

Saxon DaRoxx

WARNING

This novel contains words and/or descriptive methods of its time, references to drug use, alcohol consumption, sex/nudity, violence and other 18+ adult themes which may offend those with a sensitive nature.

CONTENTS

This Mysterious Isle

Ello me little old tubular trumpets, good to see you, have you come for the weird and wonderful magical mystery tour of all the curious and bizarre shit that goes down here on the Isle of Portland, if so, you happened on the right place for sure.

Portland is one strange and quite often fucked up place, what with its gnarly cliffs, the desolate scenery, the windswept landscape and the secrets, oh so many secrets, plus of course, how shall I say it... the "peculiar" locals and some of the even more peculiar things that they get up too.

By the way, I'm talking about the *original* Portland, the great grand daddy of them all, the small tied island down on the South Coast of England in the United Kingdom, the one with the famous lighthouse called Bill, not one of the multitude of "knock-offs" over there in the good 'ole US of A.

Even that great demiurge of English literature, author Thomas Hardy, thought Portland and its inhabitants were a bit odd, he was a bit politer about it though and called Portland "The Isle of Slingers", mainly because its inhabitants love of throwing stones at Kimberlins (that's any non-Portland born and bred person to you and me), but whatever your thoughts of the place and its people, it cannot be denied that there's some really bizarre shit going down on the 4 mile by 1.7 mile lump of limestone that sits just off the coast of England.

A lot of the peculiar and strange things that go on can be traced back to a top secret hush hush institution called the Portland Environmental Trust, better known by its acronym P.E.T or just "the Trust", and you can be sure that the mysterious and covert organisation will have their dirty little fingers involved somewhere along the line.

In this anthology you will meet just some of the strange, weird and wonderful folk of this little island, you might even get a little history lesson about Portland (stop booing in the back!) and what drives it and makes its inhabitants so damn bonkers.

I'll be back every so often, especially if I have a new tale or something important to tell you, so keep your eyes peeled for me, you never know when or where I'll pop up.

So sit back, relax, grab a glass of wine, light a joint, stroke your poodle or whatever works for you, and get ready for the ride of a lifetime and lets get this trip of weirdiosity on the road.

Oh and one more thing – Never mention rabbi... Long eared furry things! phew, nearly had me there.

Andy, your new bestie and tour guide.

A Woman's Revenge, Portland Stylee

Alice Clayton awoke early and propped herself up on an elbow, she gazed lovingly at the sleeping man lying next to her and gave a contented sigh.

To Alice this was definitely the best part of her day, there was still a full hour to go before the alarm clock shattered this precious moment and woke her slumbering fiancée Sam, but this was her time, her secret time, time when she could just lay there without a care in the world and gaze at the beautiful face of the man she loved and adored.

Only twelve months to go, she told herself, her mind all dizzy with excitement at the thought of her and Sam taking their vows next August. *Only twelve months to go and we'll be Mr & Mrs,* she couldn't help breaking out into a big smile.

The couples wedding had been in the planning for almost two years now and Alice was close to busting with anticipation.

'Not long now darling and we'll soon be walking

7

up the aisle.' Sam would tell her every night before giving her a cuddle and making wild passionate love to her.

In the beginning, when she had first begun to plan their big day, she had been a little disappointed that "the aisle" would have to be a Portland aisle in a Portland Church, not in the vast cathedral of her childhood dreams, she had always wanted a wedding fit for a princess with a bishop and Cinderella coaches, but eventually she had come round to the idea of a Portland affair, after all, 'beggars can't be choosers, can they?' Sam would reassure her everyday and tell her not to be silly, 'A wedding is a wedding, at least we will be married and at the end of the day that's the important thing isn't it?' Of course he had been right, Sam was always right.

Eventually and all too quickly, the bedside clock bleated out its shrill alarm and Sam stirred and slowly awoke.

Even at this time of the morning he still looks gorgeous, Alice thought to herself as she gazed at his tousled hair and early morning stubble.

Through blurry eyes Sam saw Alice in her usual morning position perching next to him.

'Hi my lover.' his voice was thick with a Portland twang, he stretched and gave her a little peck on the lips.

She didn't even mind the quick waft of dragons breath.

'How did you get to be so good looking?' he smiled, studying her face.

Alice giggled and kissed him on the end of his nose.

'Come on you, none of that, you know what will happen if you carry on like that.' the sudden tent that appeared under the quilt confirmed that she knew *exactly* what would happen if she continued like that.

He laughed, 'See look what you have done now. That's your fault that is?'

'Oh really mister, is that so? Best I go and do something about it then.' with a sexy chuckle, Alice dived under the covers and didn't come up for air until Sam was thirty minutes late for work.

Alice and Sam were both twenty five years old and had grown up in the same village of Chiswell on Portland, they had been childhood sweethearts from the age of nine, they had both gone to the same school, they both had the same hobbies as each other, had both grown up liking the same music and bands and had both shared their very first intimate fumblings together at 16, the lovebirds were like two peas in the same proverbial pod.

Now though, after a long two year engagement, they were about to finally tie the knot and set up home as husband and wife.

It was a Tuesday morning and Alice was on her way to work, she had to stop off at the local print shop on the way so she could collect the wedding invitations that she and Sam had had made up, the invites would have to be sent out that week without fail.

Although there was only three weeks left until their impending nuptials, there were still a million things left to do, there was the final fitting for her wedding dress, a beautiful white satin number with matching veil, the caterers had to be visited to sort out the final seating arrangements, the bouquets and buttonholes had to be chosen, gifts for the bridesmaids had to be purchased, the list went on and on.

Alice was determined that this was going to be the wedding of the year, *no!* it was going to be *the* wedding of the century, this would be the best wedding that Portland had seen – *ever!*

As she walked up Fortuneswell high Street with the box of freshly printed invitations safely tucked away in her shoulder bag, Alice noticed Davey Dodds the butcher placing a sign in the window of his shop.

"Fresh in this morning – Local caught bacon!"

Alice stopped and did a double take and reread the sign again just to make sure that she hadn't imagined it.

'Oh my God!' She exclaimed once she realised that she had indeed read it correctly.

'PB is in!' Alice delved into her bag and reached for her purse, she had missed out on Portland bacon the last time it went on sale and she was determined to get some this time. She rummaged in her purse but realised that she didn't have nearly enough money on her.

Portland bacon was one of the few luxury items to be had on the isle for pure bloods only, and there was always a huge demand for it but supply was always short, if you were lucky enough to see the sign appear announcing fresh supplies, you bought it there and then as you knew that without fail stocks would all be gone within hours.

Well work or no work, this was too good an opportunity to miss and for the rare chance of buying some PB, she was even prepared to raid the wedding fund jar, so Alice about turned and scampered back home as fast as her legs could take her.

The return trip back to her cottage didn't take long, her mind was occupied with the thoughts of the juicy, succulent, slightly smoky flavour of Portland bacon and she shivered in anticipation.

Hey I wonder if I can get enough for the top table guests at the reception? she asked herself, w*hat a coo that would be, everyone would be so jealous.*

A little over five minutes later, Alice turned the key in the lock of the front door of the little pink cottage that she shared with Sam and let herself in. She went straight to the kitchen and counted out ten crisp £10 notes from the wedding fund jar and stuffed them in to her purse, it was then that she heard a thud followed by what sounded like footsteps coming from upstairs, her first thought was that it was Sam but realised that he had left for work ages ago and that he would be up to his elbows in grease and oil at the garage by now, the thud came again, this time followed by the distinctive sound of somebody tip toeing down the stairs... *creak, creak, creak.*

Alice held her breath as pin pricks ran up and down her spine, if she had been born with testicles they would surely have shrivelled with fear.

Burglar, thief, kidnapper, rapist, all these words and more spun wildly around her head, her eyes roved the kitchen for a defensive weapon and she quickly grabbed hold of the bread knife lying on the breakfast bar and clutched it tightly.

Alice forced her muscles to move and she made for the kitchen door, she held the knife aloft and listened, her ears straining for any sounds, a few seconds later the front door creaked as it opened and shut.

A rippling wave of relief washed over her from head to foot and she let out a long sigh, whoever it was was gone, or were they. The fear flooded back over her once again but this time her veins were awash with adrenalin.

Alice quietly made her way to the foot of the stairs and peered upwards, if there was someone still in the house they were getting a cold steel serrated enema. She began climbing up the stairs, with each step her fear abated and by the time she reached the landing all signs of anxiety were long gone.

Ahead of her was the bathroom, its door was ajar, a quick glance inside proved it to be empty, no rapists or burglars lurking in there, the next room was the spare bedroom., the door was shut and a quick twist of the handle and thrust of the door showed that the only occupants of the spare room were dust mites and a few spiders, that only left the main bedroom, her and Sam's room, their sacred space, if somebody was still lurking in the house waiting to perform nefarious activities on her body, then this is where the scumbag would be hiding.

Alice put her ear to the door and listened, silence, she gently took the doorknob in her free hand, tensed her muscles and listened again, still silence. As quick as lightning Alice shouldered the door and threw it open with a loud bang, she sprang gazelle like into the room and ran straight into the unmade bed, she caught her foot on one corner of its hard frame and went flying ass over tit, the knife she had been carrying flew out of her sweating hand and shot high into the air and lodged itself in the ceiling.

Alice landed on the bed in a tangle of arms and legs, coming to rest on her back, just as the knife decided that it didn't much like the ceiling and gave up its grip on the Artex, in vivid 3D slow motion, Alice watched a the knife performed a perfect 180 as it accepted the laws of gravity and came slicing through the air and straight towards her head below, Alice squeezed her eyes shut and watched her life flash before her, but had only got to her 10th birthday when a dull metallic thud made her reopen them, the knife was deeply embedded up to its hilt in the mattress just an inch from her face.

Picking the remains of her fibrillating heart from her teeth and plucking her sweat soaked thong from the crack of her arse, Alice crawled off the bed and laughed nervously, she looked down at the knife and realised just how lucky she had been, it had to be an omen, she wiped the sweat from her forehead with her sleeve, *Good luck for the rest of my life, that's what it means*, she convinced herself.

With the supposed intruder now long forgotten, Alice straightened her dress, exhaled loudly and composed herself, but suddenly, in the blink of an eye, her perfect little world came crashing down around her ankles.

Amid the debris of her life, looking as innocent as a discard beach towel, lay a pair of woman's oversized pink lace knickers and a still steaming used condom.

Daggers stabbed at Alice's heart, clawed hands then ripped it out of her body and cloven hooves ground the pulsating object into a red bloody mush, she stared at the shrivelled piece of rubber lying on the floor, in Alice's head, the condom taunted her, it looked up at her and laughed in her face, *I'm only a little sheath of rubber but I have destroyed your love ha ha. Cum see what I did. I took Sam away from you ha ha.*

Alice and Sam had never used condoms during their relationship, never, not once, she had been on the pill since she was fifteen and she'd had never had a lover bar Sam, so there was never a need to use them.

A used condom full of spent man juice and a barrage balloon sized pair of woman's underwear could only mean one thing, Sam was having an affair.

The scream echoed throughout the house making the sash windows rattle, birds in the garden squawked and took to the air in fright, neighbourhood dogs began barking and car alarms began shrieking, while passer-byers stopped to look in the direction of Alice's cottage with puzzled looks on their faces.

The hurt that flowed through Alice's veins was like molten lava, how could he have done this to her, why would he do this to her. Their sex life had always been great, she was always available to him whenever he had wanted it, even during the very few times that she wasn't interested herself, she never said no and had always enjoyed experimenting, she even did the pervy things that Sam had wanted to try, s*o why? Why would he do this?*

Alice went through the complete gamut of emotions, from enmity to fear, from indignation to loathing but slowly as hours of tears and torment and questions that were running around her mind began to subside, a serine calmness overtook her and she came to a decision about what she had to do, revenge, revenge was what she had to do, revenge like only a

14

scorned woman knew how to do.

Alice wasted no time putting her devious plan of revenge into action. She had vowed to herself that from that day forward she would be celibate, there would be no more early morning hanky panky for Sam, no more quickies in the car when they met up for lunch and no more two hour romps when Sam came home from work at the end of the day, in fact no more sex full stop, his filthy, probably disease ridden knob, was no longer going anywhere near her lady bits.

Alice spent the rest of the afternoon composing herself and getting her head straight, she didn't want Sam to get a whiff that anything was wrong and especially not a whiff of her fanny, and by the time Sam returned home from work later that day, Alice was ready to face him.

Sam had acted all innocent, like butter wouldn't melt in his mouth when he returned from work and had plonked himself down on the sofa, several times Alice had to restrain herself from strangling him with a tea towel or stabbing him in the neck with the pickling fork as he watched tv, but the few gins sloshing around in her stomach gave her resolve and she managed to resist the temptation.

Sam had quickly wolfed down his evening meal of Long Eared Furry Thing stew and licked his plate clean as usual, then had a quick shower, after which he had lain naked on their bed waiting for Alice to join him as she did everyday: work, home, food, shower, shag, it was his daily routine, for some reason though, tonight the shag part was slow in coming and after thirty minutes of waiting, Sam called down to his fiance.

'Oh honey lumps, Thor and his love hammer are waiting for you, come and get it while it's hard.'

Alice heard his repeated calls and thought, *this is it, if I can do this part then the rest will be easy.*

Under normal circumstances Alice could never resist the sight of Sam's dick and her juices would flow just at the thought of the thick veined slab of love muscle, but the image of that shrivelled condom full of the bastards fresh love custard had made her hole as dry as the Gobi desert.

She gulped down another double gin and walked up the stairs to the bedroom with her excuses at the ready, but as it turned out, not having sex with Sam had been a lot easier than she thought it would have been.

Alice had a very high sex-drive, somewhat akin to a turbo charged buzzing chainsaw would be putting it mildly, she could even orgasm just by squeezing her thighs together and thinking of Robbie Williams, but now even the glistening of his taught muscular body still damp with water from the shower, hadn't done it for her, she was truly repulsed by the idea of making love to the pig after what he had done.

'I'm sorry my little love noodle.' she oozed sexily, trying her best to rub his nose in it a bit.

'It's my time of the month, you'll have to party with Mrs Palm and her five daughters for awhile.' she knew that Sam hated masturbating himself and she giggled inside.

Sam begrudgingly accepted Alice's reasons for the first weeks lack of sex but as the ban stretched on, he started becoming more insistent, after all, he was a young healthy guy and he needed his hole.

He must be squirming in his underpants by now, Alice chuckled to herself as she made yet another excuse to avoid any nooky and left him alone to have one off the wrist.

By the end of the third week, Alice was still making excuses, "I have a headache." "I'm tired." "I'm just not in the mood."

By now Sam's nuts should be busting with blue balls. Alice rubbed her hands together with glee at the thought of how he must be suffering.

But then in the fourth week, Sam suddenly stopped pestering her. There was no more begging and pleading, no more childish crying saying that his balls would explode and no more emotional blackmailing for her to drop her knickers "or else."

Alice knew the reason why, he was still filling his boots elsewhere.

Wednesdays were Sam's half day at the Portland bus garage, normally he would get home from work at 12:30, then after a quick shower, he would just lounge around the house until Alice clocked off from her job at Tesco and joined him not long after 6pm, but today was going to be so different to any other day in both of their lives.

The couple shared their "lovers" breakfast of a dollop of Marmite on a bowl of hot porridge (pretences must be kept), then it came time for them to both leave for work, but this morning work was the last thing Alice had on her mind.

She had already arranged with her line manager to take one of her leave days and so instead of heading to the supermarket where every little helps, she walked around the corner and hid in the shadows until Sam had driven off and the coast was clear, she then returned home and let herself in via the back door.

Once up in their ex-love nest, Alice went straight to the airing cupboard at the foot of the bed and proceeded to remove all the blankets, sheets, towels and the other odds and ends that always seem to accumulate there, and stashed the lot in the spare room.

Now that the airing cupboard was completely bare, she set about making it as comfortable as possible by putting a few pillows inside to sit on, then she added a few supplies to sustain her during her long wait, in went a litre bottle of Volvic, two Mars bars (with wrappers removed) and a cheese string (she was partial to a bit of processed rubber), Alice also put in her fully charged Sony handicam, a present from Sam on her nineteenth, loaded with a 60 minute tape, and lastly, a one foot long chopping knife that she had spent hours in the shed honing to a gleaming razors edge.

Alice removed her shoes and climbed inside the airing cupboard and settled down in the confined cramped space the best she could, then pulled the door to, making sure that she left a little crack for her camcorder to peek out off, now all she had to do was wait.

Alice's plan was a simple one and practically foolproof, she couldn't imagine any way that it could go awry, after-all, all the best plans were simple ones weren't they.

She would sit in the dark confines of the airing

cupboard and wait for Sam to arrive with his flabby tart, the whore! she would then film the dirty bastard getting his hole, wait until he fell asleep as he always did after a shag, and the blobby slag to leave, then with the camcorder still running and placed on the bedside cabinet, she would proceed to castrate him and remove his dirty rancid bollocks from his body, she might even have them made into a pair of earrings.

The resulting video would then be given to that dodgy photographer from Fortuneswell, John Krocodile so he could publish it on one of his dirty websites and people would be able to watch and laugh as Sam was turned into a soprano, Sam's punishment would be then be complete.

Whilst she waited for what Alice hoped wouldn't be too long, she tinkered with the camcorder making sure that the tape was rewound, night mode was activated in case Sam drew the curtains and switched off the light, and that it was switched to standby so it was ready to begin recording as quickly as possible.

She cracked open the airing cupboard door just a smidgen more so that she could get a good angle of the bed without being seen and placed the chopping knife in her lap.

It was very hot and very dark inside the confines of that cupboard and after two hours Alice was beginning to think that maybe her instincts had been wrong and that Sam wouldn't be coming back with his bitch today, but she couldn't be wrong, women are never wrong, she reminded herself.

She debated whether she should go downstairs and make herself a brew and forget the whole thing, but eventually decided to wait a little while longer just in case. She checked the video camera for readiness again then leant back and continued waited.

Alice woke with a start and almost threw herself out of the airing cupboard, it took a few moments to remember where she was and what she was doing there but it all came back to her as her head settled, she hadn't meant to fall asleep.

Damn! what time is it? she looked at her watch and saw by the luminous hands that it was ten past two in the afternoon, that was it, she'd definitely had enough of this, her legs were knotted and her spine was stiff, her head throbbed and her feet were numb, *plus it was a stupid plan anyway.*

She rolled her neck from side to side with a satisfying crunch and gave it a rub, the feeling of relief that flooded through her as her joints popped and clicked was exquisite.

Alice swung open the door and crawled out onto the carpet on all fours, she had only gone two feet when her hand came down on an unopened condom still in its wrapper, it hadn't been there before, she looked up to the bed and suddenly came face to cheek with a pair over-inflated basketballs trapped in a frilly lace net.

Directly in front of her were the biggest pair of arse cheeks she'd ever seen in her life and they were bouncing up and down on top of her man!

Alice almost choked on her own tongue. She sat on her haunches totally stunned, her wide eyes latched onto the pair of enormous pimply buttocks and her head moved up and down in time with their beating rhythm, she was so close that she could feel the shock wave as the fleshy cheeks rippled and slapped together at the top of each stroke, Alice was mesmerised, it was only when the familiar cries of Sam reaching the vinegar stroke erupted over the squelching of the massive butt cheeks, that Alice snapped out of it and screamed, and screamed, and then screamed some more.

The ear piercing scream lasted for a full ten seconds before it ceased. Slowly, the shocked face of Sam peered over the huge fleshy bum bags and stared in her direction.

'Alice?'

Alice peeked over the now motionless but still wobbling bowls of pink jelly and stared at Sam, he was almost buried under a mound of quivering flesh.

'Sam!'

The bleached blonde bloater that was sprawled all over Sam, her flab still rippling as though suffering from aftershocks, turned and looked in the direction of the scream.

'Alice!!'

Alice's eyes flicked towards the face of the blubbery heifer.

'Mum!?'

Alice's mother scooped herself up and disengaged from Sam's fast receding sex pole with shluurp that sounded like a Wellington boot being pulled out of a bucket of mud, she was lost for words at what to say to her daughter.

'How could you mum?' Alice was nearly in tears.

'I'm… I'm sorry Ali,' she spluttered. 'it just sort of happened.'

Alice glared at her mother and lifted herself from

the floor.

'Just sort of happened? How the Hell can you shagging my fiancé, just sort of happen?'

Her mother looked shame faced. 'Well he was there and I was here. You know what Sam's like, he needs his hole.'

Alice was shell-shocked. 'But Mum... He's my fiancé!'

Alice's mum was by now, getting totally pissed off with this whole situation and decided that it was time to bring it to a close, the whole affair had been a bit unfortunate but it had happened.

'So what Alice? he's your fiancé and you're my daughter!' she started. '... And he's your twin brother and you're his twin sister! So let's just deal with it ok?'

Alice and Sam's wedding went without a hitch, although it was brought forward a little, there were smiles all round as the happy couple tied the knot in front of their friends and family.

The ceremony was held at the Portland Free Church and was performed by his Right Reverence Gambon Trite Gambon the third, of course his Reverence Gambon T Gambon the third wasn't an ordained minister of any recognised religion, not *off* the island anyway, an ordained minister would never in his wildest dreams have married siblings but this was Portland after all, and weird things happen on Portland.

A reception for 130 guests was held at the Portland Social Club where lashings of food and alcohol were provided (although unfortunately there was no PB available), and a disco ran into the early hours of the morning. Everybody that attended said that this was definitely the best wedding they had ever been to on Portland.

The newlyweds left the social club at 11pm to go on their honeymoon, the bride wore a two piece yellow and violet chiffon dress with matching accessories whilst the groom wore a pale blue suit with contrasting cummerbund. They posed for photos taken by Portland photographer Jack Krocodile and then left for two weeks abroad, over the sea in Weymouth, which was a typically weird Alice and Sam thing to do, after all, not many newlyweds take their pregnant mother with them on their honeymoon do they.

RolyPoly Crowley

Saunders nodded in the direction of an elderly woman as she hobbled along the street towards Chiswell, 'There goes old nurse Flannigan, weird old bird she is.'

Martin Samways who was sitting in the passenger seat agreed, 'Never been seen out of her nurses uniform she aint.'

'Thank fuck for that, the wrinkled old hag.' Saunders chortled .

He turned and looked at his buddy who was sucking noisily on a Starbucks latte.

'Not unlike Mandy Deacon. It's hard to keep her *in* her uniform' he laughed. 'Did you hear, she was giving Ellis Coleman a blowjob in the locker room yesterday,' Saunders giggled like an excited schoolboy.' she didn't give a toss that half of the day shift was watching her going down on him.'

'Ah bollocks, I missed that! You should have given me a shout, tidy bit of arse is Mandy Deacon.'

'Yeah right... As if, some stunner's on her knees working the purple python big time and you want me to stop perving and bell you on yer frickin mobile? I was next in the bloody queue for Christ sake!'

The men laughed and hi-fived.

Saunders and Samways, both 32, were sat parked behind a large advertising hoarding in Victoria Square, just like they did every day around lunchtime, it was a good place to sit and eat their lunch away from anyone's prying eyes and more importantly, away from their boss Crowley's big nose, *the bastard!*

The men's joking stopped as the cars two way radio cackled into life and the voice of Mandy Deacon herself drifted out of the speakers.

'Any cars in the area of Victory Road, Queens Road or Victoria Square, please respond.'

Samways winked at Saunders and picked up the handset.

'Hey sexy lady - PC1024 here, I'm in Vicky Square, I'm the man you're looking for, what can I do to you?'

The voice on the radio giggled, 'I'll tell you later big boy,' it cooed sexily. 'but... in the meantime can you please get your thrush infected dick over to Clements Lane, there's been a FATACC, one car involved.'

Saunders mouthed the word '*oops*' and keyed the mic again, 'Sorry dispatch, we're on our way.' he dropped the handset back onto its hook.

'A fatal accident eh, we haven't had one of those in awhile.'

As Samways gave the ignition key a twist and started the engine, he looked over at his partner.

'Let's just hope it's that fucker Crowley eh.'

He switched on the blues and twos and with siren blaring, the police car screeched off up the road in a spray of gravel and kerb dirt.

Detective Inspector Gary Crowley, or twat or wanker or shithead, take your pick of expletives, they all fitted, was the universally hated chief of the Portland CID unit. At the age of twenty four he became the youngest ever policeman in Dorset to be promoted to DCI, the boys in the locker room generally attributed this to the fact that he had a very long tongue and didn't care whose arsehole he stuck it up, but in reality, he rose through the ranks so quickly because he had in his possession some very explicit photos of a very important man, in a very compromising position, with a certain Luscious Lips McCree, the local whorehouse madam.

Crowley himself had arranged the sting and had photos and incriminating video taken by that other low-life, Portland photographer Jack Krocodile, a copy of which were sent to his very influential victim with a nice little note demanding promotion.

Crowley didn't have many friends, especially in the work environ where most people thought that he was a devious slimebag of the first order and it was best just to keep out of his way, outside of work he wasn't exactly flavour of the month either, generally the only people that ever willingly spoke to him were pushers and hookers and then it was only when he was paying for their services, usually with a flash of his ID card or a thump of his big fists.

Gary Crowley was born and bred on Portland

which made him a pure blood and he had an almost psychotic hatred for Kimberlins who he thought of as foreign muck that weren't even worthy of cleaning his toilet bowl.

He had attended Portland's Royal Manor School until the age of sixteen where he had been a straight A student with lots of promise and potential, but once he began attending Southampton University he began to change for the worse, especially after joining a society called the *De-Militarised Zone,* who debated the ethics of whether a fully anarchistic society would be, could be and should be, viable today in modern Britain, he was all in favour.

So here he was, Gary Keith Crowley, now 39 years old, detective chief inspector and God in his own head. He loved his job and the power it afforded him, he loved to see people cower in his presence almost as much as he loved food, especially his favourite sausage rolls, and he would usually been seen with flaky pastry crumbs on his shirt front, but even his love of elongated meat filled baked goods paled into insignificance compared to his love of opium.

Crowley had first gotten involved with the black sticky stuff three years previous when one of his regular hookers couldn't afford to pay him after he'd allowed her to have the privilege of him shagging her, he was rifling through her drawers looking for hidden cash but all he found was an ounce of opium tucked away in a bra, she pleaded and begged him not to take the opium as she was only holding it for her pimp, she cried that she would get a beating or worse if it went missing, but Crowley casually informed her that it wasn't his problem and left her to it sans the opium.

A few days later when Crowley heard that the girl had indeed received a battering from her pimp and was in hospital, he paid her a quick visit and warned her to keep his name out of any inquiries, he backed up the warning by pushing one of his sausage sized fingers deep into a knife wound on her arm until she passed out in agony.

Crowley had always been partial to the odd joint or two and the occasional snort of the old Bolivian marching powder but he'd never experienced anything like the high he got from the opium, and from his first pipe he was hooked, which created a problem.

The black wonderstuff was a specialist drug and was in very short supply on the island, which was more of a hash and pills kinda town than something as upmarket as opium, and you'd more likely end up being sold a lump of "long eared furry thing" shit than the beautiful Chinese Molasses.

Eventually, after exhausting all the supplies of opium on Portland, ironically provided by a scrote called Dace who was the battered hookers pimp, Crowley had to look further afield to sate his addiction, and to his horror had to travel across the water to Weymouth, but that just wouldn't do, the thought of going abroad and visiting those foreigners turned his stomach, so after a few phone calls he met up with a trustworthy acquaintance who was already well into the drugs scene and who just happened to run a large cannabis farm out of his factory at the top of the island.

Within the week, the two men had agreed on a mutually beneficial arrangement. The acquaintance, Tony Armstrong, agreed that if Crowley provided the premises, he in-turn would supply everything needed for the production of Crowley grade opium, he would also supply one of his chemists to run the place, a "genius" Armstrong told him, that could even make designer synths like Black Mamba and Spice and everything in-between.

The crooked copper informed Armstrong that he had the perfect place for the operation in mind, an innocent little electronics repair shop on Fortuneswell Hill who's owner, a country bumpkin called Andy, owed him a few favours for helping his son out of the shit awhile back, it had a large unused area out back that would be ideal for their nefarious needs.

It was agreed that in exchange for keeping Crowley supplied with opium, Armstrong could keep all the profits from any hash or other drugs that was produced there, and of course it went without saying, that Crowley would keep those twats in uniform and any other prying eyes away from the operation.

Armstrong was true to his word and within the month had provided everything needed and fitted out the large vacant area at the back of the repair shop and put his lad Billy in to run the place. The operation would mainly grow giggle weed but there would be space set aside especially to grow & cultivate Crowley's Papaver Somniferum opium poppies and a little lab area for making ecstasy and synths when required.

The traffic lights were red but DCI Gary Crowley sped through them without a care in the world, he powered his red Audi convertible, a present from Tony Armstrong, along Lerret Road at 60, hung a left at the roundabout and headed up Victory Road towards Fortuneswell High Street.

'Look at those lazy fuckers.' he said aloud as he spied a panda car tucked away behind a large billboard rising from the side of the road.

'They think I can't see them hiding there? I'll have those fuckers balls on a plate later.' he promised himself as he sped past.

Crowley pulled up outside the electronics repair shop, straightened his crimson tie and checked his ginger hair in the rear view mirror, 'Now that's sharp!' he announced to the empty car before stepping on to the pavement and entering.

The owner, a just over middle age guy called Andy, was sitting behind the counter with a soldering iron in his hand and went to stand up when Crowley entered but quickly sat down again and busied himself when he realised just who it was, Crowley's ego went up a notch as he saw the look of fear on the man's face but he completely ignored him and went out through the back door into a small storeroom lined with shelves, then through another door that led into the hash farm.

The fifteen by thirty meters "farm", was an unfinished breeze block construction that had been added to the rear of the shop some years previously and stood about ten meters high.

The large spacious room had been divided into three sections by thick black plastic sheeting, the first section contained a couple of kitchen type worktops that were covered in various pieces of lab equipment that included a Taylor Stiles electric press with cellophane wrapping attachment, there was also a small kitchenette area with the usual tea and coffee making facilities, stacked on the floor against one wall was a pile of ready to go, cellophane wrapped parcels each containing one kilo of cannabis resin, next to them were five black bin liners stuffed with fresh orange and purple cannabis buds.

Crowley walked through the lab area, casually taking in the scene and occasional picking up something to idly look at, he stopped in front of a desk where there was a large metal drum filled with some of the flowering parts of the cannabis plants, standing next to that was a fifty five gallon drum of murky looking acetone which was used in a process of evaporation to produce hash oil.

In the farthest corner of this area was where the cannabis soap was made, soap or slate as it's sometimes called, is probably the lowest form of cannabis and is made from the scraps of the plant, including the stems and leaves, occasionally you might find the odd plant bud (the part with the highest THC levels) had been thrown into the mix but that didn't happen very often. As soap is the weakest form of cannabis it's also the cheapest on the street, and to make it go even further, all sorts of shit is added into the mix, each manufacturer has their own favourite substance that they would add but usually something like beeswax, coffee, diesel or boot polish is used, Billy though preferred to add powdered milk as it had good bulking out properties, and as evidence of this there were three large catering sized tins of the stuff sitting on the workbench in readiness.

Crowley walked on over to a plastic sheet door and yanked it open, a surge of artificial heat hit him causing him to take a step backwards.

This area was by far the biggest, the walls were lined from floor to ceiling with Mylar reflective sheeting to help with light and heat distribution whilst from the ceiling hung twenty rows of Canatronics IEC reflectors that were hooked up to a five thousand watt Pro-Grow lighting system, the temperature this side was being kept under control by a massive Jetstream cooling pump and if that wasn't enough, just below the lighting rig dangled a complex array of water spray nozzles, one for each plant that automatically sprayed a fine mist into the air so as to keep the plants moist, some serious money had been spent here that's for sure.

On the floor under the hot bright lights, in long straight lines were two hundred large growbags, each growbag had two Rockwool growing media cubes inserted and each cube had a five foot tall marijuana plant growing out of it, in total there were four hundred Northern Light Purple Haze cross-bred marijuana plants reaching maturity.

The plants had been lovingly tended and each one was trimmed to perfection so that their height had been stunted allowing the plant to bush out, all the plants had been sexed so that only the Tetrahydrocannabinol (THC) producing females remained, the weaker male plants going into the soap drum in the lab, and as a result, each bushy plant was packed with huge orange and purple buds that positively dripped THC.

Crowley stepped up to the nearest plant and touched one of its buds, sticky juice oozed onto his finger and he took a lick.

'Hey! Don't touch the buds man!' a voice echoed out from amongst the plants at the far end of the room, which was swiftly followed by the appearance of a young guy in his mid twenties.

'You'll damage the...' the voice stopped abruptly.

'Ahh shit. I'm sorry Mr Crowley... Sir, I didn't know it was you. I thought that...'

Crowley stared at the younger man, *should I stomp this fucker?*

'Glad to see you're keeping your eyes open Billy.' he told the approaching man that was trying to hurriedly do up his trouser zipper with one hand whilst holding a Coke bottle that was half filled with golden liquid with the other.

'What the fuck were you doing behind there?' Crowley demanded to know with a quizzical look on his face.

'Eh?... Oh right, yeah sorry, you mean this?' the lad held up the bottle, 'I was having a piss like.'

Crowley decided that he should stomp this dirty bastard after all and gave the lad one of his famous scowls.

'Hey no man,' the youngster quickly stuttered, realising that Crowley hadn't understood what he meant. 'this is for the plants... for the plants, piss is full of nitrates, it's the best stuff to feed em on, they love it, honest truth like, honest.'

Crowley gave him a long, hard stare, it was a stare that made you feel like kneecapping yourself.

'Well I hope you don't put that fucking shit on my plants.'

'No no, there's no shit, just piss like man.' the lad laughed then gulped and a bead of sweat ran down the side of his forehead as he realised that it wasn't the time for humour. 'I mean like no way man, I'm under strict instructions about them ones, nothing but water and a drip or two of Baby Bio for them beauties.' he nodded over to the last black plastic sheet behind him.

The two men walked in silence through a large slit in the plastic wall and into a smaller room that was covered in a dense carpet of blue green poppy stems.

'How are they coming?' Crowley asked as he walked over to his babies.

'Excellent Mr Crowley Sir, I finished milking them yesterday,' the lad explained, 'they just need a few more days now and they will go to seed, then I can start over on the next batch.'

Crowley seemed pleased.

'You've got my tar ready?'

'Yes Sir Mr Crowley Sir, it's out here.' Billy dropped the half full Coke bottle, soaking his trainers in the process and darted back out through the plastic sheet door towards the lab room.

'Here you go Sir Crowley, Mr Sir.' he nervously picked up golf ball sized cellophane wrapped piece of pure black opium and handed it over.

Crowley wasted no time in peeling away a section of the wrapping and held it close to his nose, he shut his eyes as he inhaled that so familiar beautiful smell.

'Good shit eh?... told you it was good shit Mr Crowley.' Billy beamed from ear to ear.

Crowley pulled himself back from the brink of a pending smell induced flashback and leant towards the lad's ear and growled menacingly.

'Good shit! You're fuckin' right it's good shit, if it weren't good shit you'd be in deep fuckin' shit right now. Keep up the good work son.' then as quick as a flash, he flicked Billy in his right eye just for fun.

Just before exiting the lab, Crowley turned back towards the now sobbing man.

'And remember, don't piss on my poppies again or Ill suck your fuckin' eyeballs right outta your fuckin' head, okay!' and with that he was gone.

Billy danced around on the spot clutching his reddened eye as Crowley disappeared out the door.

'I'll get that bastard if it's the last thing I fuckin' do.' he hissed.

The following day, after a quick trip to the Portland hospital A&E department, Billy, now sporting the latest pink NHS eyepatch, was sat in his lab, daydreaming about how he could get his revenge on the sausage roll crumb infested scrote Crowley: rat poison in his opium, a bomb under his car, maybe he could hire a Ninja assassin to cut the bastards throat or he could just buy a gun and shoot the shitbag. In the end he decided that he would just keep pissing on his poppies instead.

It has to be stated that Billy was a genius, well almost a genius, in fact as close to a genius as you can get to being a genius without actually being one. He had graduated from Bristol university with full honours at the age of twenty one with a nice big fat petrochemical degree tucked under his belt, but his hopes and dreams quickly turned sour, mainly because no one would give him a damn job as he was over-qualified.

In the end, he turned to something where he could put his knowledge to good use and he decided he would help the unfortunates of this world, he would put his newly learned knowledge of the petrochemical industry to helping that oft overlooked and much maligned member of society - the pillhead.

Billy had quickly turned the kitchen of his flat into a little MDMA lab and began making ecstasy tablets. He didn't make many at first, just enough for himself and his friends and maybe a few to sell on in the nightclubs in Weymouth just to recoup some of his costs.

Things went well, very well in fact, until he sold a few pills to the wrong person who just happened to work for a local gangster and drug supplier, but Billy didn't know this at the time obviously, he found out this important bit of information when the gangster sent a few of his boys around to his flat, they kindly introduced themselves with the aid of a sledgehammer which they first used as a key to enter Billy's front door while he was still snoring in bed, and then as a massage aid on both of Billy's legs.

The two gentlemen informed him that they had a message from their boss, the message stated that Billy had had his private employment licence revoked forthwith and that he now officially worked for a guy called Armstrong, the two thugs kindly threw a handful of fifty pound notes at the screaming Billy as he rolled around clutching the broken remains of his legs and told him to buy himself a wheelchair.

Well obviously Billy had loved the idea of his new enforced employment and with only a tad of reluctance, he followed the thugs instructions and turned up at an engineering works at the top of the island in his new wheelchair two weeks later, luckily the wheelchair wasn't a permanent fixture to Billy's butt and as soon as his legs had healed enough to support his weight, it went scuba diving off the end of Blackbarge pier.

Strangely though, Billy quite enjoyed working for Tony Armstrong, the little bearded gangster turned out to be quite an affable fellow as long as you didn't cross him, the work was interesting and the hours were good, he even got paid holidays to the Bahamas twice a year, although strangely someone always stole his suitcase as soon as he arrived.

Billy quickly established himself as "the man that *can*" and was always using his chemistry knowledge to knock out a new type of high for Armstrong, some successful, some not quite so.

One memorable moment was when Billy created something he called Dragons Breath, it had all the good qualities of ecstasy, the best parts of a speedball and just for added fun, the horniness inducing qualities of good old Spanish Fly.

All went well and the drug sold like umm...drugs really, until one Saturday night when the revellers at a Weymouth nightclub, who had been stuffing their faces with Dragons Breath all evening, suddenly, en-masse, like a flash mob, stripped off all their clothes and started fucking anything that moved, some even started fucking anything that didn't move as well, it took the fire brigade two hours and three hoses of ice cold water to separate them all, oddly the next morning not one single partygoer could remember the event and it wasn't until photos and videos went viral that people began to remember what had happened. After that, Armstrong withdrew Dragons Breath from sale to the general public and began selling it to the sex shops in Soho as a mind blowing aphrodisiac instead.

Billy finished day dreaming about the many different and pleasurable ways that he could dispose of the ginger haired cockwomble Crowley and turned his attention back to his workbench in earnest.

He quickly pressed out some "Doves" using the MDMA that he'd knocked up during his lunch break, then went to another workbench that was covered in zany apparatus containing various bubbling coloured liquids and checked a timer, when he was happy with what he saw, he opened a vacuum cooker and stared inside at some newly created cream coloured powder that now filled it. Taking an empty catering sized powdered milk tin from a cabinet, he proceeded to fill it with the newly made powder, then sealed it with a red plastic lid and marked it with a small letter B. Glancing around the room for any hidden Crowley's that might be lurking in the undergrowth, he took his own private supply of illicit Dragons Breath to the storage room and mixed it with the tins already on the shelf, it would be safe there until he took it home a few days later.

After switching off the lights and shutting the door, Billy said goodnight to Andy out front and headed straight to the chemists to stock up on eye ointment and laxative.

Natural Born Loser

If there was ever such a person that could be described as a natural born loser, then it cannot be denied that Sam Bacon was most definitely that person. Sam was born on Friday the 13th 1966, during the month of July at exactly 11:11 in the morning.

His expectant mother, whose name remains unknown, went into labour at approximately 9:45am and was rushed by ambulance to the Portland Community Hospital down near Castletown. The journey was swift and within ten minutes she was dressed in a hospital gown and lay with her legs akimbo in a pair of birthing stirrups.

'*Pant! Pant!* - Don't push yet! That's it, *pant!*, remember your breathing exercises.'

The patient grimaced in pain as another contraction ripped through her abdomen.

'*Pant!* - Don't push... *Pant!...*'

The expectant mother snarled baring her teeth at the midwife and her knuckles whitened as she gripped the sides of the maternity table.

'You try panting with a demolition ball stuck up your vadge, bitch!!' she seethed, but the conductor of the birthing process ignored her, she'd heard it all before.

The 25 year old mum-to-be's eyes suddenly squeezed shut tightly as her baby's head abruptly crowned and made an appearance.

'This is it my lovely, now *push...*'

Boom!

At the very moment when the midwife finally gave the instruction to push instead of to pant, a hospital wide power cut plunged the maternity suite into total darkness.

What followed can only be described as a total nightmare for all those involved.

The medical room was engulfed in a sudden ink-black darkness causing a flurry of gasps and cries of shock from the assembled team, but the seasoned midwife recovered quickly.

She fumbled in her pockets and produced her Zippo cigarette lighter (yes kiddies, people were still allowed to smoke in those days, indoors too!), she leant forward and with a deft flick of the thumb, span the ignition wheel striking up a healthy flame, and under its flickering glow and as cool as a cucumber, she surveyed her patients condition.

'... And *push!*'

The midwife's eyes were concentrating hard on the quivering fanny in front of her and she didn't notice the flame was a little too close to the scene for comfort, the patient did.

'*Nnnnnnnaarghhhh!!!*'

'...This is it, now *puuuuuush!*'

The baby's shoulders began to appear and the woman screamed louder and longer, the scream rose in pitch and volume and quickly turned into an ear piercing shriek as the lighters flame made contact with her hairy patch, producing an acrid stench of burning pubes and singed lips.

'*Aaieeeee!*'

The panic stricken patient gave a final excruciating push and from behind a fiery wall of flame and crispy minge, baby Sam burst forth into the big wide world, his pinky red, 8.5 kg (19lb in old money) slippery body, blasted from between his mothers smoking legs in a scene that resembled an alien horror movie, as blood and placenta splattered the delivery table and speckled across the stunned midwife's face.

The new mothers first and only glimpse of her newborn son, was of him rocketing away from her like a cork shot from a Champagne bottle in a trail of slime and skidding off the edge of the delivery table.

Unfortunately the shock, stress and strain of the unfolding events were just too much for the poor woman and her entire body tensed and she grabbed her chest as a massive heart attack ripped through her. With her legs still unceremoniously strapped in the birthing stirrups and with wisps of smoke drifting up from her roasted lady garden, she died without making another sound.

Having one parent die on the day of your birth is a terrible thing, having two die on the day of your birth is nightmare territory, yet this was the fate of poor baby Bacon.

As Sam was being hauled legs first from the waste

bin that he had dive bombed in the maternity suite, his unaware father was rushing excitedly towards the hospital to be at his wife's side and to witness the arrival of his first born.

He was sat astride his Honda 250 motorbike, head down, giving it some revs along Weston Street, his mind was so full of anticipation and the exhilaration of soon being a new dad, that he didn't notice the squashed remains of a long eared furry thing lying in the road that someone had kindly left for an unwary biker to encounter. The motorbike skidded on a bit of backbone, lost control and careered off the road, demolished a small wall and took a nose dive into Tout Quarry Sculpture Park twenty meters below.

Sam's father was impaled on the horn of a cute unicorn statue made of Portland stone and died instantly.

All in all, not a great start to Sam's life, three minutes old and already an orphan.

With no living relatives to take him in and care for him, baby Sam was sent to the Portland orphanage where he was raised by a flock of nuns until he was eight years old

Unfortunately, on the day of his arrival, there were no spare cots at the orphanage, so Sam ended up sleeping at first in a small battered leather suitcase which had the words "Destination Unknown" stamped on its side, and then when big enough, in a broken MFI cupboard drawer in the orphanages boiler room.

On a bleak winters night in 1974, one of the worst storms in Portland's history battered the isle with the vengeance of a vegan that had just been served a Big Mac, it blew in from the East, the West, the North and the South, bringing with it torrential rain, snow blizzards, thunderstorms and hail stones.

Trees were uprooted and thrown across fields and roads, roofs were ripped from their gables and came crashing down all around, and lightning strikes caused numerous fires to break out in many houses across the island. Even the great Chesil Beach road, the only access on and off the island, took a pounding by mountainous waves causing it to flood for a good eight hours.

The orphanage didn't come out unscathed from the wrath of the storm either, it was struck by three huge lightning bolts in succession, the first blew a gaping hole in the roof and dislodged its chimney stack sending bricks and slates crashing to the ground below, the second shattered every window in the building showering the nuns in glass, which gave them the most excitement they'd had in years, and the third lightening bolt hit the outside fusebox causing a fire to break out in the boiler room. Luckily for Sam Bacon, the Mother Superior had been in the boiler room giving Henderson the gardener a special blessing, and she managed to rescue him from his cupboard drawer before he became Sam Crispy Bacon.

Flames quickly spread throughout the aged building as its old timbers fed the growing inferno until the fire became unstoppable. Panicked penguins gathered the terrified children together and as the flames licked around their billowing habits, the little mites were rushed from the burning building to the safety the orphanage bus at the far end of the car park. With tears in their smoke reddened eyes, the poor orphans watched as their home burnt to the ground.

Now, without even a roof over his head, eight year old Sam was sent to live with what was to become the first in a long long line of foster parents, in fact over the next eight years, Sam went through twenty seven different foster families, although he never stayed with any of the families for longer than a few weeks at a time, because in each and every case, Portland social services were called to take him away again after the families reported suffering strings of bizarre accidents and misfortunes, all of which began on the day Sam arrived in the family home.

One such family, John and Sarah Wilkinson from the Reforne area of Portland, reported that within minutes of Sam unpacking his bag their pets began mysteriously dying.

The dog Fluffy was the first to go, he was run over by Sam's social worker as she reversed her car out of the Wilkinson's drive two minutes after dropping him off, the following day the family cat Brian performed a perfect twelve foot leap from the back of the sofa, caught Scarface the parrot in its jaws mid-flight and by the time the cat had landed, Scarface was a parrot no more, Scarface got instant revenge on Brian though when his parroty wishbone stuck in the cats throat and it choked to death within minutes. Two days later, Sid and Nancy, the white mice belonging to the Wilkinson's daughter, ate ten of their own babies and then made a suicide pact and committed harikari by trapping their heads in the bars of their cage.

The mysterious events were to continue when a few days later, the glass bowl containing Mr

Wilkinson's beloved prize winning Samurai fighting fish, boiled dry after it inexplicably appeared on the cooker hob which was set to gas mark five.

All in all, these events were not conclusive proof that Sam was a bad omen, a bad seed or even a Jonah, but the final straw for the family came a week later when all on the same day, Mr Wilkinson was fired from his job of twenty five years for stealing an office pen, his wife Sarah broke both her legs when the brakes on her bicycle failed at a busy town junction and their fourteen year old daughter Sue, was arrested for selling crack cocaine in the school playground.

When Sam was the tender age of twelve, another very strange event happened, Mr and Mrs Darrow, Sam's fifth set of guardians, had just signed the adoption paperwork and left the social services office in Easton, their faces beaming with smiles, hand in hand with Sam. Graham Evans, the head of the social services team had managed to keep a straight professional face during the meeting until the family had left the office but couldn't hold it any longer.

'Yes! Yes! Yes!' he screamed joyfully fist pumping the air, this was the cue for the entire social services team to join him in the celebrations.

The five member team rose as one from their chairs and began cheering and slapping each other on the backs for a job well done, Graham proudly opened the bottle of Champagne that he kept hidden in the bottom of Sam's filing cabinet (yes Sam had his very own filing cabinet as his file was so big) ready for such an occasion as this, and with a huge grin on his face, began filling the teams eager waiting paper cups with fizz.

Suddenly and without warning, the office door burst open and the Darrow's rushed back into the office dragging Sam behind them, the mother was as white as a sheet and the father had a drip of spittle oozing from the corner of his mouth, both foster parents looked at each other with abject fear in their eyes.

The mother began sobbing hysterically and the father who had been babbling almost incoherently, suddenly made the sign of the cross over his chest, turned on his patent leather heels and in a cloud of Old Spice and tears the couple fled the office leaving young Sam, who looked as innocent as a cherub, standing all alone in front of Graham's desk.

With a heavy sigh, Graham re-corked the Champagne bottle, placed it back in the filing cabinet, lowered his head and began to sob, the rest of the team didn't notice though as they were too busy trying to stop Mavis the clerk throwing herself out of the office window.

Once again Sam was without parents and was homeless. The new Portland orphanage that had been built on the same site as its predecessor, had long since refused to have anything to do with the poor lad after blaming him for the events of its destruction, and social services couldn't find any new foster parents for the child as word had spread far and wide across Portland about unlucky albatross Sam, so the social services team took an unprecedented never before taken step, they adopted Sam themselves.

The photocopy room was cleared and converted into a nice bedroom, posters reminding you to check the copiers toner level regularly and warnings that making copies of your bum was strictly forbidden, were exchanged for posters of Starsky and Hutch and Charlies Angels, they even raided petty cash to buy a record player and tv from Andy's electricals in Fortuneswell.

The four strong team (Mavis had since taken early retirement on medical grounds) worked out a two days on two days off rota when they would take turns in being the boys guardian.

The system seemed to work well and no unlucky events befell any of them during their years as Sam's parents, unless of course you count the time when Graham got lost in the basement for nine days and only survived by eating old case files and drinking radiator water, or when Wendy the secretary, lost all ten fingers when her ageing Underwood Touch-Master 5 typewriter rebelled against her and ate them.

Eventually Sam left Royal Manor School at the ripe old age of nineteen, he should have of course left when he turned sixteen like all the other children but for some unknown reason the school lost his files and didn't know how old he actually was, so decided it best to hold him back three years just to be on the safe side.

When the school finally let him leave, he did so with zero qualifications, so was sent to college under the "*special student scheme*", a scheme devised by Portland social services especially for Sam, but six months later he was kicked out of college when his files were suddenly found and it was discovered that he was three years too old for the course.

If Sam had hoped that things would get better for himself when he finally got a job in the big wide world he was as foolish a man as he was an unlucky one.

His first ever job was as an ice-cream seller in a beach kiosk at Hallelujah Bay but that was the year of the crazy Arctic summer when everyone stayed at home and shivered, he didn't sell one single 99 cone and got frost bite in all of his his fingers and toes.

Another of his jobs was as apprentice light keeper at the lighthouse at Portland Bill, he absolutely loved that job, running up and down the three hundred steps kept him fit and healthy and polishing the fog horn was especially fun, he just loved to trigger it and laugh at the tourists as they jumped out of their skins and threw their chips and battered sausages into the air, unfortunately though, during his fourth week, Trinity House in their infinite wisdom, decided to computerise the lighthouse and Sam was replaced by a computer with all the power of a small pocket calculator and once again he was out on his ear and unemployed.

Eventually Sam got a break, when he was twenty three he met and fell in love with a girl called Sadie, they met in the Portland library on the same day that it was permanently closed down due to a mysterious bookworm infestation that scoffed all the books.

Sadie was a shy retiring little thing, she never did anything too exciting or adventurous, she never went to pubs or clubs, or ate any foods more exotic than shepherds pie, she preferred to keep herself to herself and to stay indoors and read or knit, Sadie really was the perfect girl for Sam, after all, what bad luck could befall a girl that never did anything.

The pair of love-birds had a whirlwind romance,

mostly spent in Sam's kitchen as they were both too afraid to go out, and after just five months, Sam bought himself a pair of knee pads, got down on them and proposed to her. Sadie happily and excitedly said yes to the marriage proposal and Sam slipped the engagement ring that he'd bought mail order onto her finger, unfortunately though the ring was three sizes too small and took the skin off her knuckle, as Sadie painfully removed it with the aid of a tub of marg, the ring slipped from her grasp and with a quiet tinkling sound followed by a loud metallic crunching, it disappeared down the sink waste disposal unit.

Sam and Sadie's wedding ceremony was meticulously planned to the minutest detail so nothing could go wrong and it took place on the wettest August day in living memory.

Unfortunately none of the guests arrived at the church as the coach driver got lost and took them to the wrong venue and the vicar was scarily late after some yobs stole the wheels from his pushbike and he had to run to the church with his cassock flapping around his ankles, but eventually the wedding service was performed and Sam and Sadie became husband and wife.

The happy couple left on their honeymoon that afternoon, two weeks of quiet relaxation five miles away on the mainland in exotic Weymouth awaited them (Sam didn't trust public transport enough to travel too far from Portland).

On the first evening in the hotel, Sam ate a bad packet of cheese and onion crisps and went to bed alone with a dodgy stomach, Sadie decided to stay in the hotel lounge talking to twenty five year old Katie from Dunstable and they chatted and giggled constantly until the early hours. The next morning as Sam struggled to keep down a bowl of cornflakes in the hotel restaurant, Sadie and Katie packed their respective suitcases, held each other's hands and skipped off into the sunset never to be seen by Sam again.

Sam returned to his hum-drum existence back on Portland where his bad luck continued it's seemingly never-ending run.

He spent the next nine years flitting between the unemployment line, the occasional part time job which he could never keep for more than a week and the hospital casualty department being patched up after suffering yet another completely random accident, walking into closed doors and tripping over pavements seemed to be his preferred method of injury.

On what would have been the tenth anniversary of his very short marriage to Sadie, Sam decided he would do something extravagant, he would spend all his life savings and buy a brand new car.

Sam paid in full in cash when he picked up the new metallic green Ford Capri from the garage at Tophill, he collected the keys from the reception desk and proudly sat behind the wheel of his new car beaming from ear to ear, he felt good, he felt great. He ran a hand across the genuine imitation leather covered passenger seat, inhaled the new car smell and produced a pair of fake Ray-Bans bought mail order and placed them over his eyes, he wound down the window and placed an elbow on the sill, started the engine, put the car into gear and pulled away, only to reverse over the salesman two seconds later.

Throwing the Ray-Bans into the glove box, Sam started again. This was the life, this is what he'd been missing all these years he decided, the wind in his hair, the open road, the world was his oyster, it was then that he realised that apart from the salesman incident, which was obviously the salesman's own fault as he shouldn't have been standing behind the car, he hadn't actually had any bad luck for nearly four days, the last time was when he was cleaning his bedroom window and the pane of glass fell out and killed the neighbours dog that was peeing in the garden below. Maybe his luck had finally changed he thought to himself.

Sam's excitement grew and grew, he was wearing the new green (he had a penchant for green) satin suit bought especially for the occasion and his new, hopefully lucky, purple polyester shirt, he glanced at his reflection in the rear view mirror and liked what he saw, he had even dared to unbutton the top two shirt buttons showing off his chest and its three lonely hairs.

The car purred as he pulled out of the showroom and headed along the road, he neared the zebra crossing half way along Fortuneswell High Street and stopped for an old lady who was for some reason pushing a shopping trolley piled high with pineapples, suddenly, out of the blue, a squawking seagull flew in through the open car window, no doubt attracted to his 'Mr Stud' aftershave.

Sam yelped in surprise and his muscles tensed, his foot slammed down on the accelerator pedal and his new car leapt forward across the zebra crossing narrowly missing the old woman, but slamming straight into the back of a stationary number 1 bus waiting at the bus stop, surprisingly Sam was unharmed but unsurprisingly, the car was a total right-off and had to be towed to the scrapyard where it was crushed into small metal cube, to add insult to injury, the insurance company refused to pay out on his claim because Sam had forgotten to mention that he didn't actually have a driving licence.

At the age of forty nine, after years and years of the most terrible luck you could ever imagine, things were about to change for Sam.

It was a cold miserable Saturday morning, Sam had just been fired from his job as a waiter in a small bistro in Chiswell after misjudging the distance between his hand and a blind customers teacup and he poured scalding hot water over the customers seeing eye dog, the dog howled in pain and scarpered out of the door dragging the blind man behind it in a tangle of chairs, scones and strawberry jam.

Sam walked home to his flat in East Weare (he wished he had a car) and stopped to buy a newspaper at the newsagents and as an afterthought he used his last pound coin to buy himself a national lottery ticket, he chose the lottery numbers that meant the most to him, the date that he broke his arm for the first time, the date he met Sadie, the date Sadie left him and ran away with *that* woman, the day he used Vicks instead of Vaseline (his eyes still watered at the memory) and the date Sam had taken a stray dog he'd found to the veterinary surgery and it turned out to be an escaped wolf and ate the vet.

That evening Sam settled down in front of the tv to

watch the week's National Lottery draw, he balanced a plate of baked beans on his knee and held a fork in one hand and his lottery ticket in the other.

The opening credits danced across the screen and Phil Schofield pranced across the stage, after the usual welcomes and general prattling, Schofield announced it was time for the big draw and to excited clapping from the audience he pushed the red button on lottery machine Guinevere.

The multicoloured balls began tumbling around and around in the drum building the tension, a few second later with a computerised *ding*, pink ball number 13 dropped down the chute, Sam examined his ticket, wow*!* he had that number, the balls continued rumbling. *Ding*, the next ball dropped down the chute, blue 43.

Sam's eye widened, he had that number too, his luck hadn't been this good since a seagull pooed on his head back in 1973, he couldn't believe it. Another *ding* made him look back at the tv and there was another of his numbers displayed, yellow number 8. he had won a tenner.

Sam fist pumped with a loud '*YES!*' and an even louder '*woop woop!*' causing the fork in his hand to dislodge, shoot upwards and embed itself in the ceiling with a twang, he hadn't been this lucky since 82 when he bought a pair of shoes and one of them had actually fitted him.

The balls continued tumbling around and around, Sam held his breath, *ding*, white 26, he swallowed hard, it was his.

Sam's mind was beginning to spin faster than Guinevere in the studio, *What the Hell is going on?*

Ding announced yellow 14 swiftly followed by blue 33, more of his numbers.

Sam's eyes bulged and a bead of sweat formed on his brow, he had six numbers! six bloody numbers! he couldn't believe it, he knew he had won some serious money, maybe even a thousand quid.

The balls rumbled around in the machine preparing to deliver the bonus ball down the chute, he kissed his ticket and closed his eyes, the loud *thud thud thud* of his heart pounding in his ribcage was all he could hear, the balls span for a lifetime.

'And the bonus ball is…' Schofield drew it out long and hard, the wait was agonising.

'…White 29!'

Slowly Sam opened one eye and peered at his ticket then shut it again quickly, he did the same thing with his other eye, then even slower, he opened both eyes together and stared hard, then all Hell broke loose.

Sam screamed for joy and leapt up from the sofa splattering his beans on toast across the carpet.

'I did it!! I bloody well did it!! – My God I did it!!' he screamed, he laughed, he cried and he danced.

Sam hopped from one foot to the other with excitement and began running around the room like a chicken that's head had rudely been removed by a big axe, he stopped in front of the tv, bent and kissed it.

'Thank you tv.' he shrieked.

He ran to the table and picked up his only photo of his long lost love Sadie, taken in the A&E when she was having a skin graft on her ring finger.

'Thank you Sadie.'

He jumped across the room to his bookshelf.

'Thank you books.' he cried.

On the tv, the cameras turned to Phil.

'Our computers show that there is only one jackpot winner of this incredible five week roll over,' the audience oohed.

'That lucky winner has just won an incredible, get this...£42 million pounds!' the studio audience cheered and clapped and roared with excitement, Sam's knees buckled, he felt sick, he felt nauseous, he felt fucking terrific.

Sam was having a party, a one man party right there in his living room, his rapturous screaming yelling and shouting continued for as long as his lungs would let him, all the while he was skipping and jumping around the room like a gazelle on heat. The coffee table went flying with a crash, he banged into the sideboard causing cups and plates to smash to the floor but he didn't care.

'*Yes Yes Yes!!*' he kept screaming as he laughed with tears of delight in his eyes, he ran around the room a few more times like a puppy chasing its tail, he even began pummelling on the walls, only stopping to perform a quick two step shuffle like a boxer that had just defeated Ali at the Rumble in the Jungle - Well you would wouldn't you.

Gradually exhaustion began to overtake the euphoria and Sam collapsed back onto the sofa, he was pouring with sweat and his mind was whirling. He began thinking of all the new things that he would do and buy with his new found wealth. Firstly there's a trip around the world, first class of course, he chuckled. Then obviously there's a new house, I think a nice little thirty room pile in the country should do it

- Oh, and maybe a Ferrari or two in the drive just to balance out the Lamborghini, he whooped loudly again and laughed at his own humour.

A sudden loud hammering on the front door interrupted Sam's revelry and with his head still full of the wondrously expensive spending spree that was to come and the even more wondrously expensive women he was going to rent, Sam 'Grande Cabrioled' in full Rudolph Nureyev mode out into the hallway and opened the door, it was Crowley, his ginger haired downstairs neighbour.

'Grumpy!!' in his excitement Sam let his secret nickname for his neighbour slip.

'Oops sorry... Hi.' he gulped and hoped that his little faux pas hadn't been heard, and better yet, that Grumpy didn't still bear a grudge about the window and his dog incident.

'You're not going to believe this, I've only just gone and won the…'

Grumpy raised a large sausage of a finger and silenced him.

'What have I told you about making a racket? I'm trying to fuckin' sleep down there!' he poked his sausage at the floorboards.

'But but... listen to this, you wont believe it. I've just won the National bloody Lottery! I got all the numbers *and* the bonus ball' Sam emphasised the word, it made all the difference to the jackpot, but Grumpy Crowley wasn't in a listening mood, he reached into his back pocket and pulled out something long and shiny.

Before Sam's brain had time to register what the object Crowley held in his hand was, Sam's brain had a personal encounter with it as Crowley rammed the pointed end of a large sharpened screwdriver straight into Sam's right eye socket and gave it a wiggle.

Sam's last ever thought on this planet was "Bloody typical, just my luck." he died instantly.

Sam Bacon was buried the following week at St Georges Church on Portland, it was a beautiful ceremony, there were lots of flowers and lovely music was played, but unfortunately nobody witnessed any of it because all the mourners went to the wrong church by mistake.

Sam was gone but not forgotten though. On the very same day that the body of Sam Bacon was interred, or more aptly, his coffin was unceremoniously dropped into a hole by a drunken gravedigger, a brand new £2.5 million luxury cruiser called "Ole Grumpy" chugged its way lazily around the Algarve, its skipper, a ginger haired copper called Crowley from Portland, complete with a pair of plastically enhanced floozies called Sadie and Katie, raised their glasses of ice cold Cristal (infused with 24 carat gold flakes of course), and drank a toast to 'lucky' (for Crowley) Sam Bacon.

Never Smile for the Krocodile

Ello me slippery digits, your host with the toast 'ere again.

Young Billy from out the back was in 'ere just now, just 'avin a chat and whatnot, anyways, he asked me if I wanted to borrow a movie and pulls this little silver disk out his pocket and calls it a DVD, but I think he was having a laugh with little old Andy cuz I'm all high tech in 'ere I is and I never seen these weird things before.

'Dunno what your little disk is *but* it's VHS these days mate.' I tells him.

Anyways, he chuckles and tells me it's a bluey and puts it on me counter, I said to him that I'm not into politics much but thanks anyways but he laughs again and says it's a "porno".

Well why didn't he just say that it was rumpy pumpy in the first place, kids eh, what are they like.

But anyways, it put me in memory of that porno photographer from down the bottom of Fortuneswell, he was into the mucky stuff too, I hear he made a fair living from it he did. Thinking about it though, I aint seen or heard of him for yonks now.

So here's a little warning for you, this next tale is a bit mucky, so skip it if you don't like that sort of thing, like Timbo Tanner from the "Three Goats", he hates anything to do with rumpy pumpy, wont even watch Coronation Street anymore cuz Hilda Ogden once appeared in her dressing gown. What a prude!

Now then, what exactly do I do with this little silver disk thingy...

'C'mon, move it baby, shake it darlin', let's see what ya mumma gave ya. Yes baby that's it, give it to me, work it work it, yes yes yes!'

This atypical one sided conversation was coming out of the adrenalin fuelled mouth of sixty two year old photographer extraordinaire, Jack Orlando Krocodile. He was well into the middle of the hour long photo-shoot, his victim was a twenty year old wannabe glamour model called Sally.

'That's it baby - Do it, do it, shake that ass!'

By day, Jack was Portland's answer to David Bailey, he was a highly respected portrait photographer who owned his own studio and gallery in Underhill. Locally he was best known for his family and wedding photographs but it wouldn't be uncommon to see varied shots of landscapes, sports or even aerial scenes adorning his gallery walls.

If you were a pure blood Portlander and were planning your wedding it would be taken as read that you would hire Jack Krocodile to take the photos, but at night, when the gallery doors shut and excited newlyweds were off consummating their marriage, Jack became a different kind of photographer.

'Yes baby – Spread those cheeks, give it to me, let me see your chocolate starfish!'

The silver haired cameraman was born on the island in 1959 where until the age of sixteen he attended the the Royal Manor School (later to become the famous Royal Manor Arts College). After a couple of years working part-time jobs he went on a self financed trip to Myanmar to photograph the temples using a second-hand Pentax ME SLR, after a three month stint shooting the Stupas of Bagan, Jack returned home and entered the resulting photos into a competition in a national photography magazine and won the twenty five grand first prize.

Using his winnings, he bought himself better camera equipment and financed another trip, this time to Bromo Tengger Semeru National Park in Indonesia, where he continued to fill his ever increasing portfolio.

Over time Jack built up his reputation and finances until he could afford to become pro and the rest as they say (to use that much over used cliché) is history.

'Mmm baby – Shake those titties! – Work it! Work it. Pinch the nipples!'

Jack clicked away with his pride and joy, a Leica SL2 single lens reflex, he twisted it this way and that way, left, right, up and down, he jumped around the room in an animated flurry of excitement while shouting demands at the poor beleaguered model who was completely overwhelmed by the whole experience.

This was Sally Fletchers first ever "glamour" shoot

and she had already decided that it would be her last, this wasn't what she wanted to do with her life, the clothes modelling and the brochure work had been fun but this was just downright degrading.

'Yes, beautiful darling! – Spread the lips just a little wider, C'mon let's see the pink!'

Grabbing another roll of film from his pocket, Jack slotted it into the camera as quick as he could, he didn't want to lose momentum now the girl was obviously enjoying herself. To be honest Jack thought that she was a bit of a heifer and he doubted that she would ever make a name for herself in the business, she would probably end up in the low budget wank mags or as just another slag in the under-the-counter hardcore skin flicks, she didn't have the looks or the aptitude to make it to the big names like Climax or Sweetmeats, her only redeeming features were her long flowing red hair, pale skin and big boobs, the mags liked that look for some reason.

No doubt it had probably been her parents or maybe a close friend that had told her how pretty she was and had persuaded her that she would be a good model, so of course she had come to see him, *the* famous Jack Krocodile and have her portfolio taken, poor deluded cow, but what the Hell, it was her money, and who was he to shatter a girl's dreams.

'Oh that's so sexy baby! – Use the dildo, yes, push it right in like you love it!'

Even though she was a little overweight for her height, had a boring personality and cried a lot, the girl had the most enormous set of knockers he had seen since Chesty Morgan, *these puppies could be worth some serious wonga,* he knew the cock-

61

stroker's on the net would love her fleshy bags of fun and would pay good money for a piece of *her* action.

He had decided on his first meeting with her, that she would be the next month's "Shag the Hag" centerfold on his website, lambtotheslaughter.port.uk.

'Come on now baby, rub that little clitty, oh yeah baby – That makes me so hot!'

Jack could see from the girls teary eyes that she wasn't happy or ready to do the things that he was encouraging her to do, but he could smell the wads of money he could make from this photo shoot and that was much more important than this silly bitch's feelings. He continued pushing her.

'That's good baby, I love it. Stroke your bum-hole baby - Mmm tickle your mud whistle.'

When Sally stopped and broke down in floods of tears Jack tossed her a packet of wet wipes and carried on clicking, he couldn't let her finish now, not before the money-shot.

Whilst she dried her eyes, he screwed his camera down onto a tripod and loosened the zipper on his trousers.

'Ok baby, now don't be shy, I'm just gonna put my cock in your mouth for the final shots.'

The girl looked horrified. More tears ran down her face smearing her mascara into long streaks, *mmm nice* thought Jack, *adds to the 'I'm a victim look.*

He ordered her to stop being childish and to get on with the job, 'I don't pay for half finished shoots dear and you don't wanna lose out after all your hard work, do you?'

Sally pinched the soft flesh between her thumb and forefinger and stopped the tears before reluctantly opening her mouth and letting Jack do as he wanted.

'Oh yeah that's bloody good baby, run your tongue around the head, nice.'

He griped the camera remote control and began clicking again - *The stupid cow fell for it, shows she's a bloody amateur. I'm gonna make a mint out of this old bag.* He reeled the photos off one after another, *click click click.*

'C'mon baby, suck it hard and start wanking the stalk, Mmmm yes that's it!!'

The tears began again, the watery black fluid ran down her cheeks and mixed with the fresh saliva coating his man meat. Jack tingled with excitement and chuckled to himself as he thought of all the money that would soon be swelling his bank account, his knob throbbed in agreement.

'You're gonna be a star baby, you're fantastic... don't stop!... Oh Christ yes!... *Unnnnnngh!'.*

'Now just swallow my baby gravy and we're done for the day.'

Sally gagged as the thick hot salty fluid hit the back of her throat and she reluctantly swallowed it all down, it tasted disgusting, like a dead badgers vomit, she could feel herself starting to heave.

This was her first time performing fellatio on a man, in fact she had never had any sort of sex with a man before, she was a twenty year old virgin and had been proud of it.

Normally Sally was the shy retiring type and would run a mile if a man had even looked in her direction, that was one of the reasons she had decided to do photo modelling, to gain a little more confidence with the opposite sex, she had stupidly dared to dream that with the extra confidence gained that she would meet Mr Right, fall in love, marry, buy a house, have 2.4 children, get a cat, get a dog, grow old and die at peace with the world, but her dream was now forever ruined.

Jack looked on horrified as the girl gagged once more and squirts of warm vomit issued from between Sally's clenched lips, but his brain was already working out how much photos of vomit sex could make on the net.

'Don't stop! Keep going – lick it clean baby! Swallow it all back down.'

She couldn't hold it back any longer and huge guttural sobs broke forth from within her, Sally crumpled to the floor and cried her heart out.

Jack stared down at the scene unfolding at his feet with a look of pure disgust in his eyes and tutted as he realised that he'd missed out on a good little earner, there was no way she was going to continue with the shoot now.

'Ok now pull yourself together girl, get cleaned up and get your clothes back on, I'm off out to the pub for a pork pie and a beer in a minute.'

Now that Jack's rampant desire had been sated, Sally was just another stupid wannabe model again, he turned around and wiped his spunky vomity cock on her yellow knickers that had been folded neatly on a chair, then reached for his wallet.

'Hurry up Sarah, I gotta go.' He threw down three fifty pound notes at her feet and zipped his fly, the three fifties were the same three fifties that Sally had paid him for the privilege of having her portfolio photos taken by the famous Mr Krocodile, it would be cruel to keep the fee, *I'm not that much of a bastard* he chuckled to himself.

'It's Sally.' she suddenly wailed, her voice trembling, 'My name is Sally!'

'Sarah, Sally, Sid, who cares?' he shrugged his shoulders and sneered back at her before scooping up the used rolls of film and putting them into a Jiffy bag.

He entered his darkroom through a door at the side of the studio and locked the envelope in his safe then returned.

'You still here Sonja?... Jeez girl, get a shift on will you.'

'I was... I was thinking Mr Krocodile.' Sally had dressed and was pulling on her overcoat, her long red hair was dishevelled, her face was a mess and she was wearing wet sticky knickers.

'I think I made a mistake really, you know, having the pictures taken, could I please have them back?' she swallowed hard.

Jack looked her over for a moment and smiled warmly. 'Have them back? Of course you can baby.'

Sally sighed with relief.

'Thank you Mr Krocodile, I knew you...'

Jack cut her short. 'Just write me a small cheque for 20k and I will give you the negatives.' he reached for a pen as Sally began crying again.

Jack was buttoning up a fresh white shirt, one of the many that he kept in a small wardrobe in the back of the studio, Sally was sitting on the chair with her head in her hands, her cries had died down to occasional small sobs. He walked up to her and put his hand on her shoulder.

'Look Sandra. I'm not a complete shit, I know how you feel, really I do.'

Her eyes had a glimmer of hope in them as she raised them towards him.

'Listen, you're a nice girl - this is what I'll do for you.'

He was a nice man after all, the kind nice sweet lovely adorable Mr Krocodile, her heart cheered immediately.

'When you visit me next week, we will just stick to straight fucking ok. I had planned to ream your arse out but that will wait for another time.' he smiled a thin wry smile.

Sally's world vanished in a blink of an eye, all her hopes and dreams smashed into a million pieces, her mascara streaked face ran cold.

'But but I'm a virgin!!' she stammered, she felt weak, sickened and abused, 'I'm not coming back here ever again!'

Jack laughed at the silly girls distress. 'You don't understand how it works Sabrina, I have the negatives of all the disgusting and vile things you've just done, if you don't come back next week and every other week after that until I say otherwise, copies of the disgusting filth will unfortunately find their way into your parent's letterbox.' he pulled a sad face at her and then laughed as she screamed, rushed past him and fled out the door in a whirlwind of tears.

Jack roared with laughter as her rapidly disappearing figure bolted out into the night, 'Wait until I get the donkey involved, then you'll have something to cry about.' he laughed as he locked the door behind her.

Sally ran, she didn't know where to and she didn't care, she just had to get as far away from Jack Krocodile as she could, she ignored the worried look on people's faces as she rushed past them on the street, she darted across roads in front of the traffic ignoring their horns and the screeching of brakes.

Eventually she found herself outside her house, the house she shared with her parents and the place she called home. Sally unlocked the font door and rushed up the stairs two at a time and slammed the bedroom door behind her.

Sally was mortified, her life was ruined, everyone would find out what a disgusting whore she really was, she would never be able to show her face in public again, *the photos will kill mummy and daddy*.

After awhile, her heartbeat began to slow and she began to gather herself together, she stripped off her clothes and entered her on-suite shower room, span the hot tap to max and scrubbed until her skin was red raw, but the dirt and degradation didn't want to come off under the almost scalding water and after thirty minutes Sally gave up and began crying again.

The house was empty, Sally's parents were nowhere to be seen, they were probably at the wine bar having a few afternoon drinks, she told herself, so she raided daddy's booze cabinet and dug out the strongest liquor she could find, ironically, the bottle she found was her father's pride and joy, it was a bottle of Saint Magdalena Single Malt and was the exact same bottle of Malt that he had purchased on the day she was born twenty two years previous, he was saving it for a very special occasion, it looked like today was that day.

Sally sat on her bed naked as the day she was born and took a tentative gulp of the whiskey, it burned her throat but wasn't too bad, she then opened her clenched fist to reveal twenty small white pills courtesy of her mother's legalised drug addiction.

She stared at the pills, the innocent white pills, they looked almost virginal in their whiteness, *virginal, she was virginal, until next week when that bastard Krocodile was goi... Oh my God*, she wailed as images of her naked body suddenly flashed in front of her eyes, she saw Jack Krocodile abusing her over and over again in a non-stop tirade that would last her entire lifetime, she saw her friends her family and even complete strangers pointing at her and laughing when they found out.

Sally shook her head in a vain attempt to clear the images from her mind but it was too late, they had taken root. Fresh tears began streaming down her cheeks, with a sudden lift of her head she stuffed her mouth with the tablets and washed them down with a large swallow from the whiskey bottle, she turned and picked up a small photo of her parents that stood on her bedside cabinet. 'I'm sorry mummy I'm sorry daddy.' she sobbed, 'Please forgive me.' she hugged the little photo to her chest and slowly closed her eyes as the sedatives took effect.

Sally's lifeless body was discovered the following morning by her father who immediately called an ambulance, he felt a huge relief when the attending paramedics detected a very faint pulse and she was rushed straight to the hospital in Fortuneswell.

Forty minutes later he was joined by Sally's mother and the two distraught parents comforted each other as the doctors and nurses did their best to save her life.

An hour later saw Sally's parents sitting in the consultants office while he explained the situation.

'We've pumped Sally's stomach, given her a blood transfusion and managed to stabilise her, but she's had a huge dose of powerful Ativan and it's already done lots of damage,' he told them, 'unfortunately Sally slipped into a coma at 11:13 exactly. We've done all we can do for her, now it's in the hands of God.'

Sally's parents sat vigil by her bedside for two days, they were holding hands for the first time in years as a machine sighed quietly and pumped oxygen into their daughters lungs. They couldn't understand what had happened, why had their beautiful girl done such a terrible thing.

'She has everything to live for. She has a good job, has good friends has good prospects, why?' her mother sobbed. Sally's father remained silent.

'My beautiful beautiful girl – Why??' she stared at her husband, her eyes pleading for an answer but he let go of her hand, took one long look at his daughter and without a word, left the room.

Back home, Sally's father paced around his daughter's bedroom, he just couldn't come up with an answer to his wife's question that was still ringing in his ears, as far as he knew Sally had been happy, she was a bit off about being a little overweight but aren't all girls, surely she wasn't upset about it enough to try and kill herself though, he felt tears well up in his eyes and as he sat down on her bed.

His eyes scanned over her bedside cabinet and noticed Sally's personal dairy lying on her bedside cabinet, he knew he shouldn't read it but he couldn't resist, maybe there was a clue in there. A few minutes later his blood ran cold and he wished he hadn't.

Jack Krocodile sat in the Eight Kings pub laughing with a couple of pals, he was regaling them with a humorous tale of how he had taken a shy retiring fat cow called... what's her name, and turned her into a hardcore porno star and how she was going to make him a mint of cash.

'A cash cow!' he laughed at his own humour.

He was so happy about the thought that he bought the next round even though it wasn't his turn.

Sally's father sat in a state of shock at what he'd just read, this cannot be true, he thought, not Sally, not my daughter! He re-read the contents of the last few pages of her diary again in disbelief.

3rd May 7pm – Met Mr Krocodile for the first time, he took photos for my new portfolio. They look good.

4th May 8pm – Did my first proper shots for Mr Krocodile today. He's a nice man. I modelled wedding dresses and saris.

8th May 7pm – Modelled swimwear today. Was scared at first but Mr Krocodile gave me a few drinks and things got easier.

9th May 7pm – Mr Krocodile says I'm one of the best models he has ever had. He gave me more drinks and I did my first nude shoot. My god I was petrified, but it was sort of fun, I think.

15th May – Mr Krocodile called this morning. He said he had a very special shoot lined up for me - Something completely different, he said and there could be big money in it for me. I'm sort of excited but scared as well. I wonder what it is that he wants me to do. I can't wait to find out.

The last entry in Sally's diary was dated the very day that Sally had tried to kill herself, it was written in a trembling scrawl.

17th May – Krocodile is a disgusting pig, I hate him, I hate him, I hate him. Please forgive me Mummy and Daddy, I love you both.

It didn't take long for Sally's father to figure out what had probably happened, he knew Jack Krocodile and his reputation only too well, his mind span. *Jack Krocodile! That fucking Jack fucking Krocodile!!* he dashed downstairs, grabbed the phone and made a few calls.

Jack checked the time on his genuine Rolex Submariner, it was five to eight, he just had time for a quick shower, a nuked lasagne and a large mug of Rocket Fuel coffee, his staple diet nowadays.

After towelling himself off and throwing on his favourite white linen trousers and open necked shirt, he was soon speeding off in the direction of Weston in his Land Cruiser, he had a date, a date with a potential client, and although it was only to give a quote for a simple wedding shoot, moneys money and he never turned that down.

The meeting went well, the client had told him that he had liked his spiel and his quote was good, so he booked him there and then on the spot, he also told Jack, in hushed tones that his private members club was having its annual Spring Ball in a few days time, and that their usual videographer had let them down at the last minute, for a hefty sum, could Jack take his place to capture the events for posterity.

Jacks eyes had lit up at the thought, he knew what sort of "events" these private members clubs held, he tried not to sound too keen as he said yes to the deal.

Jack was pleased with himself, *another few quid in the bank account and the chance of something very interesting,* he smacked his hands together at the thought before climbing into his Land Cruiser.

He was about to start the engine when a hand came through the open window and grabbed his shoulder in an iron grip that he had met many times before, a deep voice drifted in after it.

'Well well - if it isn't the great Jack Krocodile!'

Jack looked out towards the voice to see a familiar figure, the venous plexus in his forehead throbbed and a bead of sweat rolled down his temple. Not many people could have this effect on Jack but this person was one of them, the shadow that loomed into the car window was none other than DCI Crowley, Portland's very own answer to Bergerac.

'Jesus, you made me jump Crowley.'

He hadn't seen the copper in about a year and hadn't particularly wanted to see him ever again, he was as bent as they come and the last time Jack had encountered him was when he got into a spot of bother with a seventeen year old whore, that meeting had cost him five grand to get the creepy copper to turn a blind eye.

'So what you up to these days then Crowley, you still arresting the scumbags?'

The ginger haired policeman leaned in through the window in a cloud of sausage roll crumbs and showed his white teeth in a large grin.

'You know me Jack, do it to the bastards before they do it to you, pre-emptive strikes and all that.' he squeezed Jacks shoulder tighter.

'But nah, not so much at the moment really, I've just come back from my hols, cruising around the Algarve on me new boat.' he breathed stale cigarette breath in Jacks face.

'It's funny though that I should bump into you, are you still in the photography business? still making those dodgy vids?'

'I...' Jack was cautious, you had to be very cautious with any info you volunteered to Crowley.

'Yeah still dabbling occasionally, actually I've just been to visit a client in there.' he nodded at the house he'd just left.

Crowley grinned, the trap was set.

The German Connection

Schuldig! (*Guilty!*)

The gavel fell with a resounding wooden thud onto the judge's bar. The packed crowd of ragtag townsfolk waiting anxiously up in the spectator's balcony jumped to their feet and cheered and yelled with ecstatic joy, the older women amongst them began crying with happiness and hugged each other while the men folk threw their hats high into the air and shook hands with each other in jubilant celebration.

Every one of the fifty people that had been watching the trial with bated breath, sighed with relief and felt the weight of a thousand horses lift from their shoulders.

The judge, clearly annoyed at the sudden outbreak in his courtroom, rapidly banged his gavel in quick succession bringing a hushed silence once more to the courthouse in Kollnburg, Germany.

Casting a stern gaze at the rejoicing spectators, the judge reached into a drawer under his bench and produced a black square of cloth which he placed on his head, he cleared his throat and turned his attention to the wiry prisoner with piercing blue eyes that was standing in the dock.

'Leon Bergman.' he addressed the twenty seven year old, bone thin man.

'You have been found guilty by twelve of your peers of the most heinous crimes imaginable to man.'

A few cries of bastard and scum rang out from the balcony but the judge ignored them and continued.

'On the 8th February 1939 or thereabouts, you did wilfully murder Herr Otto Mayer, Herr Oskar Schmidt and Herr Bruno Schafer by various means as previously detailed by the court, you then proceeded to deny your victims right and proper burial by mutilating and desecrating their corpses and...' the judge, who looked visibly distressed, paused and took a deep breath before continuing.

'And then... did consume their lifeless corpses.'

More shouts and obscenities echoed around the courtroom quickly followed by urgent shushing from other spectators who were perched on the edges of their seats awaiting the completion of the sentencing.

'Leon Bergman, you will be taken from here to a place of imprisonment, where seven days from this date, you will be hanged by your neck until you are dead, your body will then be buried within the prison walls in unconsecrated ground. May God have mercy on your rotten soul.'

Once more the judge brought his gavel down hard

against the bar bringing an end to this most harrowing of cases.

Rapturous shouts of jubilation once more reverberated around the small courtroom and the hugging of people and the throwing of hats resumed with renewed vigour, at long last "The Beast of Kollnburg" was to die.

With the sounds of celebration ringing in his ears, the monstrous cannibal with piercing blue eyes was taken away to the cells, he showed zero emotion or remorse.

The incessant sound of constant dripping water was the only thing he hated about his tiny 8 by 6 cell. Leon Bergman had grown up with nothing, not even a roof over his head, so this little room if anything was luxury, it had a feather mattress and an electric light bulb, what more could a man want, but the *drip drip drip* of a leaking gutter outside the barred cell window really made his head hurt.

Leon Bergman, The Beast of Kollnburg, sat on the edge of his bunk staring at the concrete floor, he really didn't understand what all the fuss was about or why he had been sent to this place, all he had done was to kill a few bastards that would surely have killed him if he hadn't done it to them first, they weren't even good men like that stupid ignorant judge fooled everyone into thinking, a burglar, a rapist, a child abuser, what the Hell, he had done everyone a favour, ok so eating their flesh was a bit much he guessed, but why not, he was hungry and it would have been a shame to let the lovely tasty meat go to waste, mind you, if the judge had known the true figure of how many he had killed and eaten he would probably have been shot in the head right there and then in the courtroom.

The slatted grill that covered the view port on the cell door creaked then clanked open and the face of a stern prison guard appeared behind it.

'Herkommen! *Come Here!* Herkommen!'

Bergman rose to his feet and dutifully approached. *Here we go again.*

The guard slowly studied the killers features and peered deep into his piercing blue eyes as though trying to read his innermost thoughts, then spat a thick wodge of phlegm into his face and laughed.

'Dreckiges tier!' *Filthy animal!*

Not much was known about Leon Bergman's life before the events that brought him to cell number four in Kollnburg prison, although if anyone had bothered to ask he would gladly regale them with tales of his life on the streets, of how he had been dumped at the age of seven in the middle of the town marketplace by his prostitute mother, with no food or money, of how he had survived by eating discarded rubbish that he found in the gutter and if lucky might find a rotting piece of fruit or a vegetable that had fallen from one of the market stalls, there were even times while he was growing up that he would have to boil a discarded shoe or a found broken belt to soften the leather just so he could eat them.

By the time Bergman had reached the age of nine he was killing rats, dogs and cats, although it would be a lucky day indeed if he found a source of fire so that he could cook them instead of eating them raw.

Bergman consumed his first human being when he was just fourteen years old and it happened during the worst winter in his memory.

There had been no market for weeks due to the fields being frozen solid so nothing was taken to the market for him to steal from its stalls, all the stray animals were dead already from the evil winter cold, and even the usually plentiful supply of vermin had dried up as they kept undercover in the sewers.

The only things he had eaten in the previous week were a few cockroaches and spiders that had strayed too far, a piece of an old blood stained leather apron which he sucked clean and a frozen dog turd that he thawed in his hands and mixed with some chopped up straw from his bedding.

At that time in his miserable woeful life, Bergman's accommodation consisted of a flimsy wooden packing crate that had probably once contained clay pots or the like, that he had dragged out of the biting wind of the market square into the backyard of one of Kollnburgs hostelries, here he would wrap himself in a stinking dog skin peeled from a kill the previous summer.

The morning of his first human kill had been exceptionally cold, slushy ice laden rain had been pouring for most of the night and icicles hung from every surface. Bergman's face was frozen and numb and he could no longer feel his legs, he was probably just hours from death and he knew it.

The sound of a door opening across the yard drew his attention and he raised his weak head above the parapet of the crate to see an unsteady figure enter the yard from the tavern opposite, the man drunkenly staggered towards Bergman's crate and stopped less than a two feet away.

Bergman's eyes widened as a hot stream of piss created a cloud of steam in the biting air and the drunk let out a satisfying sigh as he began urinating. Bergman shuddered at the sight of the wasted heat.

The drunk continued his seemingly never-ending satisfying call of nature, all the while blue eyes studied him from the darkness like a hawk studying its prey, then with a sudden energy surge and using his last reserves of adrenalin, Bergman pounced.

'Was zur Holle?' *What the Hell?*

In the blink of an eye, Bergman vaulted from the wooden crate and launched himself at the stranger like a coiled waiting viper, he collided with the drunk and they both hit the icy ground in a tangle of limbs, without even thinking and on automatic pilot, Bergman sank his teeth deep into the man's windpipe and tore it from his neck.

Now running on pure survival instinct, the starving child hurriedly chewed on the gristly flesh and gulped down mouthfuls of hot salty blood, the sensations that ran through his body were exquisite, his body flooded with tingling warmth as the flesh and blood reached his stomach, he squeezed his eyes shut tightly as he bathed in the almost erotic experience.

Bergman slept like a newborn baby following the attack, the warm blood had saved his life and it had given him a new vigour the like he had never experienced before. The life giving properties of the blood had given him a new strength, it had given him the fresh energy needed to take his little honed blade, fashioned from a belt buckle, and to begin de-fleshing

79

the corpse right there in the back streets of Kollnburg.

He had stripped the body of its clothes and immediately put them on over his own tattered rags then started to cut the man's flesh from its bones, firstly he sliced his kills calf muscles from its legs, followed swiftly by the meaty rump and loin, in Bergman's mind, this wasn't the flesh of a human, it was meat from an animal, it was life sustaining food and he would eat like a king.

Bergman looked at his growing pile of delicious freshly warm meat and realised now what he must do to survive. For the first time in his entire abysmal and wretched life, he smiled, and the Beast of Kollnburg was born.

It was day seven of the killers imprisonment as he awaited his execution, today was to be his last day on this mortal coil.

It won't be long now he had conceded, but Bergman didn't care, death didn't frighten him, he had experienced much more frightening things than death already.

Flakes of grey paint fell to the floor as the heavy prison door was abruptly opened and two armed prison guards rushed into the cell, the sudden unannounced entry was designed to catch prisoners off-guard and not give them any time to think or react, but prisoner number 2141 Bergman, didn't bat an eyelid anyway.

'Heraus schnell!!'

The two guards, working in well rehearsed tandem, took hold of the prisoner by his armpits, lifted him to his feet then locked a pair of cuffs around his wrists and frogmarched him out of the cell and out into the bright sunlight of the prison parade ground.

Outside it was disorganised chaos, prison guards rushed around barking orders at anyone that would listen, lines of chained prisoners were being herded at double time in and out of different side rooms while others were loaded into the backs of six big military trucks that were parked next to the prison gates, the only sense of order in the parade ground came from the far right corner where a handful of guards encircled a wooden gallows towards which Bergman was dragged.

A German soldier with stripes on his arms was heatedly talking in a loud voice to the most officious looking guard in the circle of men, while another with a swastika on his arm made notes in a big leather bound book, but Bergman's attention was fixed on the long dangling rope that hung from the gallows.

'Schnell die stufen hoch!' *Up the steps quick!*

Once more, no thinking time was given, Bergman received a hard push from behind ushering him up the five steps to the gallows.

'Schnell Schnell!'

It was obvious that the guards wanted his death to be over and done with as quickly as possible.

He climbed the wooden steps that led to the execution platform and was told to stand on a red painted cross before a rope noose was placed over his head and around his neck. Bergman watched calmly as his executioner took hold of a long lever and waited for the order that would release the trapdoor under his feet, the seconds passed like an eternity.

'Senken sie diesen gefangenen!' *Bring that prisoner down!*

The guard holding the drop-lever looked confused and peered down at the army officer that had shouted the order, it was the one wearing the swastika arm band.

'Senken sie diesen gefangenen!' he repeated.

'But but... this is the *Beast of Kollnburg*! You can't take him, he is to be executed immediately.' he looked to his superior for clarification, the army officer held up a sheet of paper and waved it above his head.

'Here read it!' he barked, but he read it aloud himself instead.

'ALL prisoners are to be immediately transferred to Gardwald labour camp, this man is still alive, so he's still a prisoner is he not? Now get him in to the truck!'

On cue, the prison guards began protesting shouting and yelling just how dangerous the Beast of Kollnburg was but their remonstrations fell on deaf ears, as far as the officer was concerned he had an order signed by Waffen-SS Reichsführer Himmler himself and he was going to carry it out to the letter, even if he had to get his men to shoot these stupid prison guards one by one.

The Gardwald labour camp was located fifty miles north of Berlin, it was originally constructed in March 1936 to house mostly political prisoners, but by the time the 40's came around, the German prison system was being emptied into the Nazi camps and so it was here that Leon Bergman the "Beast of Kollnburg" and his fellow convicts from Kollnburg prison were taken.

The forced labour camp was a sprawling complex of brick built buildings, comprising of separate barracks and workshops. The barracks area, which was designated Sector B1, held the prisoners in a multitude of buildings that were designed to hold about seven hundred prisoners in each one, but in practice they housed up to one thousand two hundred.

When Bergman had first arrived, he and the other prisoners had to sleep on straw-stuffed mattresses laid on an earth floor, but in 1941, a layer of concrete was poured over the ground and three-tiered bunks began appearing in the barrack rooms, which although were designed to only hold three people each, would be crammed with up to fifteen of them.

Aside from the bunks, the only furniture in each building were a dozen wooden wardrobes, several tables and handful of stools. There was no heating, nor was there any windows, instead there were a row of skylights on the roof to see by, until 41 when a string of bare bulbs were fixed to the barracks ceiling.

In Bergman's first few months as an internee, he and his fellow inmates had to draw water from an outside well which stood next to a small toilet building, that was until an extension was built at the end of each of the barracks which contained twenty toilets and washbasins and forty water taps, these had to be shared amongst the one thousand two hundred other prisoners in the barracks.

Although the Kapo's (work supervisors) were prisoners themselves, they held the power of life and death over other prisoners and dished out extremely harsh treatment. A daily line-up took place every morning after being woken up to the loud metallic rattle of a triangle being hit with a metal bar, or by a Kapo's truncheon to the soles of your feet.

After the morning roll call, most prisoners were marched to work in their allocated workshops where they worked for up to twelve hours a day.

The only break was at lunchtime for the one meal a day, which consisted of boiled rutabaga and cabbage soup and a chunk of stale bread, it was served hot but was always cold by the time prisoners got to the place were they were allowed to eat it. This of course meant that starvation was rife in the camp, but if you were lucky, you could catch a rat to add some protein, something that Bergman excelled in, rats attracted rats it seems.

In 1942, the SS added what they called "Station Z" to the camp, this was built specifically for the extermination of the prisoners, killing capabilities of the camp were increased a year later when a gas chamber was added to Station Z.

The camp had a design capacity of five thousand but at the time of Bergman's incarceration, the Nazis had already crammed it with over twenty thousand men women and children and more poor souls were arriving everyday.

Conditions in Gardwald were incredibly barbaric. A death strip ran around the perimeter of the camp and if a prisoner stepped a foot into it they would be shot immediately without warning, the guards would often order inmates to enter the death strip or be shot, a lose lose situation for the prisoner.

There were daily executions by shooting, hanging and beating for absolutely no reason at all except that you were in the wrong place at the wrong time, and sometimes, just for fun, the guards would pick a man woman or child at random and suspend them by their bound hands from a wooden post and proceed to use them as a punch bag until they were dead. Another favourite was to force a prisoner to stand naked out in the snow for days on end until they froze completely solid.

Bergman had remained silent on his journey from the prison in Kollnburg, firstly in the back of the military truck then after being loaded on to a packed cattle train with other prisons from around Germany.

On disembarking at the sidings at Gardwald and entering the camp, Bergman had been deloused with pesticide to kill any typhus bearing lice and was asked what his occupation had been before being sent to prison in Kollnburg, Bergman could have told the truth and said that he had no occupation whatsoever, that he had lived on the streets, but he was smarter than that.

'Ich war schneider.' - *I was a tailor*

The SS guards had no reason to disbelieve him.

After being issued with a grey striped uniform that had a green triangle sewn onto its chest which announced to everyone that he had once been a prison inmate in another life, Bergman joined a long line of new interns and a serial number was tattooed on his left forearm.

This was the first time that Bergman had encountered a tattooing machine, he was fascinated as its fine needle pierced his epidermis and left its indelible mark and as he watched the buzzing machine scribing his skin, he vowed to himself that one day he would find out more about this amazing device and how it worked.

Bergman had been one of the luckier ones and he had been given a job in one of the tailors workshops outside sector B1 in the complex of workshops and factories where the prisoners were assigned to work.

He spent twelve hours a day stitching together soldiers uniforms but he could easily have been put on what was called "boot duty" involving the breaking in of brand new army boots before they were issued to German troops, this entailed a forced non-stop walk of twenty five miles a day around the camp perimeter, the death rate was extremely high.

At the end of the work shift it was back to the barracks where the Kapo's would force the inmates to perform the "Gardwald salute" making them squat with their arms outstretched for an hour at a time, if you dropped an arm, even for a second, you would get the Kapo's whip across your back and his boot in your face, or shot in the head if a guard happened to be watching.

Bergman kept himself to himself and avoided trouble as much as possible for the following two years, his ability to blend in and not be noticed helped keep him alive during this time, although he wasn't totally immune and suffered the random beatings, whippings and punishments at the hands of the brutal guards and Kapo's just like many of his fellow inmates.

One time Bergman coughed whilst standing at attention during the daily head count and was dragged out of the line, after receiving thirty lashes of the whip he was forced to do the Gardwald salute for twelve hours, bizarrely, his experience of crouching in his small wooden crate back in Kollnburg probably saved his life, on another occasion he was pulled out of a line and made to do boot duty everyday for a week for no other reason than he looked at a Kapo when he should of kept his head down.

The promise of finding out more information about the incredible tattooing machine that had fascinated him so much on his first day at the camp, came about eight months after his arrival.

As fate would have it, Bergman discovered that a fellow inmate in his barracks, Polish Michal Dabrowski, had been a tattooist in the old life.

Early that Spring, Bergman had noticed that the Pole was using a sewing machine needle to give very basic tattoos in exchange for food and favours and on questioning he learnt that Dabrowski, who hailed from the port of Gdansk, had owned a small tattoo parlour on the docks catering to the Polish navy.

The man had been a fountain of knowledge and had taught Bergman everything he knew about the subject of tattooing, but the price had been high and had cost him his food ration and his arse many times.

Dabrowski taught his eager pupil all about pressure control, skin drag, colour lay-down, coil wrappings, needle gauges and more, but what the tutor couldn't teach Bergman was real practical experience, it was all well and good sitting on his bunk at night using a needle and wet ash to slowly prick a design into his own thigh but it didn't give him the results he was looking for, what Bergman needed now was a fully working tattooing machine, but the only tattooing machines in the camp were owned by the Nazis and he doubted that they would let him borrow one anytime soon.

They say that necessity is the mother of invention and in Bergman's case it definitely was. Working in the tailors workshops as he did, it had been easy for him to collect the parts he needed to construct a basic working tattooing machine, most of the parts came from the many broken sewing machines that were dumped in a corner and after a few days he had managed to collect a motor, springs, wire, screws and the various small pieces of metal required and he'd soon constructed himself a rudimentary tattooing device.

Although very basic and crude, the new machine was a vast improvement on hand pricking with a needle and would serve his purposes for the time being.

Using a new ink that he formulated from finely ground charcoal mixed with at first piss and then with home-made potato vodka, which again, had cost him his arse, Bergman honed his skills by laying down dozens of tattoos on his skin.

Each night he would plug his machine into the dangling light socket above his bunk and tattoo a new part of his body, legs, arms, feet and genitals were soon completely covered in black artwork, only his face remained tattoo free, yet Bergman's desire was still to be sated.

Like an unscratched itch under a plaster cast, the need to tattoo was driving him crazy and with every stroke and every drop of ink that Bergman etched into his skin, he sank further and further into his own dark twisted madness.

The psychotic killer Bergman, continued with his nefarious new hobby for a further six months until the following September. Now out of blank space on his own body for his tattoos, he began removing the skin from the backs of the bodies that lay scattered around the camp to feed his new addictive habit.

Undercover of night, Bergman would prowl the compound and its ditches and slice the skin from the backs of the fresher corpses that had been left to rot by the Nazis. Occasionally, when the mood took him, the disgusting fiend would also cut a chunk of foetid flesh from the body and pop it into his mouth to savour when back in his bunk, old habits die hard.

That same year, as the prisoners shivered in their barracks eating watery slops and the Nazis stuffed their bellies on Christmas meats and wine, Bergman changed his modus operandi yet again.

Forgotten now were the waxy yellowing skins of the rotting dead, he had quickly discovered that without special treatments, the paper thin skin began to degrade within days of being peeled from their hosts, rendering them useless for his diabolical needs, and that frustrated him beyond belief, what he desired now was living tissue.

It was just as easy to obtain living skin in the camp as it was to cut it from a decaying corpse but it was a lot more satisfying for the crazy cannibal. It was a simple task to get his selected victims alone, and it only took a hard rock to the back of the head or a few minutes with his garotte around their necks, to render them unconscious, then he had all night to do as he pleased with their comatose body and his pleasure was to tattoo them from head to foot.

The following summer, now with his drawing and needle skills honed to an evil perfection, Bergman, who was almost constantly living in his own perverted paradise, took things to the next level of depravation.

He decided that he was going to redesign and

rebuild his tattooing machine from the ground up, he would construct a tattooing machine to surpass all tattooing machines and he would put his very heart and soul into the creation of such a magnificent device.

This tattooing machine would be constructed from body parts taken from living humans, bones would replace metal, veins and arteries would replace wiring and his own blood would replace the ink.

Construction began with Bergman de-fleshing the little finger of his own left hand to get to his distal phalanx bone, the pain as he stripped the skin and muscle was unbelievable but eating the blood dripping flesh helped ease the agony. Using a pair of tailors scissors smuggled out from the workshops, Bergman sharpened the little bone to a sharp vicious point, this would be the needle of his new machine.

Seventy two year old Weizenbaum from barrack number six, donated his first and second cervical vertebra bones along with a handful of metatarsals from his feet, Bergman had ensured that the poor fellow stayed alive as he carved the needed parts from his body, he needed his victims agony to soak into them and give them power.

Blumenthal, one of the camps cooks, provided three ribs, his trachea and many veins, sinews and muscles, again, the parts were removed while the man was still alive.

Most importantly in Bergman's foul deranged plan was obtaining a human heart, the twisted insane killer would of used his own if it had been possible, but four year old Eliana Drachman provided the necessary cardiac muscle when her mother averted her gaze for a few minutes. Bergman chuckled to himself as he heard the child's distraught mother anxiously calling her name as he slashed at her tiny body with one hand and stifling her screams with the other.

It took Bergman all of two days to assemble his macabre tattooing device once his vile collection of human skeletal and body parts was complete. He used sinews to hold the bone parts together and he stitched in veins and arteries to act as ink channels, he stitched strips of human skin and fat together and wrapped it around the machines handle grip and used a length of spinal cord for the rear spring and armature bar, he even used an optic nerve, ripped from one of his victims eye socket, as the tension band.

Finally, Leon Bergman's tattooing machine was complete. He sat on the corner of his bunk at the back of barracks number nine in the Gardwald forced labour camp somewhere near Berlin Germany, and cuddled his atrocious invention, he had never been happier.

He kissed his machine gently and his tears began to fall over it, he ran his hot sticky tongue along its disgusting curves and let his saliva drip into its crevices.

Giving the revolting object a loving kiss, Bergman held it aloft above his head and with his decrepit heart pounding with excitement, he offered it to Satan, Beelzebub, Astaroth and Azazel, the four Gods of Hell.

As loud thunder-cracks reverberated in his ears and sheet lightning illuminated the barracks through the skylights, Bergman, the vessel of pure-evil in human form, recited the Lords prayer backwards and then in one sudden movement brought his tattooing machine, created out of agony, torture, blood and death, down towards himself and plunged the sharp bone needle straight in to his own heart and smiled for only the second time in his repugnant life.

Gardwald labour camp was liberated by a unit of the 47th Soviet Army on April 22nd, 1945. The Soviet soldiers only found a few hundred survivors in the camp, strangely almost every single one of them had unusual tattoos on their bodies, mostly featuring ghoulish creatures and devilish marks and symbols.

It was noted that all the tattoos appeared similar in design and style but when questioned by their liberators about the source of the tattoos, the prisoners became extremely scared and agitated and refused to talk about it.

The surviving inmates of Gardwald were taken by train to hospitals in and around Berlin, all had been skeletal thin, starving and too weak to walk, only one seemed better fed than the others, he told his liberators that his name was Samuel Goldstein, that he was a German Jewish tailor and that he had only been in the camp for two months after being taken there from the ghetto, and this was the reason that he looked healthier than the others. Who were the Soviets to disagree.

Samuel Goldstein was given a quick check over by medics and apart from being slightly malnourished and missing the little finger of his left hand, he was deemed well enough to travel so was issued a new ID card and sent on his way out in to the big wide world.

The queue seemed to stretch on forever, excited men woman and children stood in huddled groups awaiting their turn to board HMS Portland. The British naval transporter was docked on the river Elbe at Hamburg patiently waiting to take its passengers, who were mostly refugees fleeing the death camps of Europe, to a new life in the United Kingdom.

A lone figure with strikingly blue eyes stood quietly watching a father cuddling a small child in front of him, the blue eyed man looked haggard and tired and aged beyond his years.

A loud blast from the large ships horn broke his thoughts and he knelt down and opened his suitcase, he rummaged through his meagre possessions until he uncovered a small mahogany box with brass corner pieces, he stroked the box tenderly with a heavily tattooed hand before covering it and shutting the suitcase again.

The queue shuffled forwards.

Sofa so Good

Ello again me little Swordfish Trombones, welcome to me little shop, don't think I seen you in 'ere before.

If you didn't already know it, I repair things I do, well electrical things that is, don't be bringing in yer pet rover and ask me to repair him, unless he's a robot dog of course.

Anyways, I is Andy as you already know and I'm a pure blood Portlander, born and raised on this 'ere little island I was. Hey do you know that you can always spot a pure blood just by looking at their legs, cuz theys got one leg longer than the other aint they, it's to make it easier to walk up and down all dem bloody hills.

To be honest, I shouldn't really be talking to you cuz us pure bloods are spossed to hate you Kimberlins, that's what we call anyone that can't prove their Portland heritage for at least ten generations, but I don't go in for all that shit like, it's a bit of nonsense if you ask old Andy, but don't tell dem

94

nutters up at the Trust that I told you that or they'll
have me in the Chop Shop faster than you can say
'How many holidaymakers go missing on Portland
every year?'

Being the "number one" go to guy 'ere on Portland
for anything that you've got that's broke, like a tv or
radio, or if you need a new light bulb, or a screw – ere
not that type, you needs the Doghouse down in
Castletown for that type of screw, or even just some
sucky suck bags for yer hoover, people comes to see
old Andy, so I gets too see and hear lots of weird shit
that happens here on the island.

If you ever wanna hear a yarn or two just pop in
and if I aints busy I'll tell you a few of 'em.

Anyways, I'm about to have me lunch, got me a
nice meal deal from down the Co-op, a tuna salad
sarnie and a bottle of Coke for only a quid, check it
out cuz you also get a free pot of lime jelly with it, not
bad eh.

So anyways, if you don't mind a few crumbs 'ere
and there, I got a weird little tale for you, it's a bit
close to home this one cuz it involves me little red
sofa right there, yep that one in the bay window, and
its about somethin' old Ma Jessop did on it this very
mornin'.

Well what happened was this: Ma J had previously
dropped her ancient old radio in for repair like and I'd
had it here for a week or so. I dunno if you know old
Ma J but she's a nice old dear, she's gotta be in her
late seventies, maybe eighties by now, but she still
gets around okay.

Anyways, she had popped in to see old Andy 'ere
this morning, just on the off chance that I'd managed

to repair her radio already, luckily for her I was in the process of putting the beast back together again at that very moment and only had a few more screws to go.

It had been a real bugger to repair it this one, cuz it was made back in the 40's before transistors were invented even, and was full of glass valves instead, just finding replacements had taken me yonks but luckily I found some in the end on that interweb thingy.

I told Ma J to go and have a seat while I finished up as it would only take me about ten minutes and she might as well wait as she was already here like.

As you can see, its a bit cluttered in here but it's workable like. So Ma J wanders over and plonks her old bones down on me sofa for awhile and picks up a magazine from the little table there, it weren't none of that smut type stuff, cuz I keep that hidden away under the counter, for my more discerning gentleman customers when they's waiting for something or other.

Anyways, I keep this 'ere coffee machine full of fresh java on the end of me counter so customers can make themselves a cuppa if they likes that sort of thing, although I never touch the stuff myself, far too much caffeine for my liking, I just stick to me Coke Cola thanks, by the way, the coffee machine was an old repair job that the customer never collected, so if it's yours and yer wantin' it back, well tough titties, you're too late mate, its mine now so hands off, I got this policy see, if a customer don't collect their equipment within six months I send dem a letter stating they got another two weeks or I'll sell it to recover me costs for fixing it, I can't say fairer than that can I.

But I'm digressabating, back to the story.

Anyways, out of politeness, I asked Ma J if she fancied a coffee, and she surprised me when she said yes please, I'd put her down as a tea gal meself, but hey ho there you go. I don't keep any fresh milk in the shop cuz I don't have a fridge like, I guess I should get one really but whatevers. I use powered milk instead of fresh but me tin was all empty, so I quickly nipped to the stockroom where that weirdo Billy keeps his tins of powdered milk and I grabbed one off the shelf, why buy from the Co-op when there's always a stack of them in the stockroom just collecting dust, Billy uses far too much of it anyway, it can't be good for him, I'll pay him for it later.

Within minutes the coffee was hot and steaming so I poured old Ma J a cup and added two extra large heaped teaspoons of powered milk, gave it a nice long stir for her then placed it on the table next to her, she took a sip and gave a satisfied sigh.

'Ooh nice, that hit the spot Andy, you make a lovely cuppa.'she smiled at me and took another big sip then leant back on me sofa to relax again, and I continued finishing up on her radio.

Now I don't know if there's something special about me sofa, I know it's well padded and really comfortable like but every time people sit on it they start to talk, I don't mean just talk, I mean *really* talk, they start jibber jabbering like there's no tomorrow, it's weird.

I had Mr Browning the Chippy in 'ere a few weeks ago, just dropping off 'is missuses hairdryer for repair he was, he'd played a joke on her and poured talcum powder inside it so when she turned it on – *Ploooff!*

she got a face full of the white stuff, now after a two week nooky ban, he was here to pray that I could fix it, or it was the divorce courts next.

He took a seat on me sofa and had a hot cup of milky java and within minutes he was telling me all about the steamy affair he'd been having with his window cleaner called Gerald, I mean, like I don't even know the chap really, only from him coming in the shop a couple of times, once to buy a reel of satellite cable and the other to purchase a packet of 13amp fuses.

A week before that, some girl that I didn't know from Adam, or Eve, popped in and asked if she could do some photocopying on me old Canon photocopier, she paid for two hundred copies of something or other and sat down on me trusty sofa to wait for them to be done. Being the gent that I am, I made her a cup of java just to be friendly like you do, she asked for extra milky so in went an extra spoonful of me powered milk, and within minutes she was telling me about the time when it was her twenty fifth and how she had returned home from work that day exhausted, but very horny.

Her house was in darkness she told me, and she dashed in to the kitchen for a glass of orange juice, unbeknown to her though. was that in the lounge was all her family and friends who had gathered to give her a surprise party.

All the guests had heard her come home and go into to the kitchen, so they stifled their laughs and waited with their party streamers and balloons and confetti bombs in their hands, and waited, and waited some more.

After ten minutes or so, she still hadn't come into
the lounge so they decided to sneak in to the kitchen
to surprise her there instead, if the mountain wont
come to Muhammad and all that, anyways, the guests
tiptoed quietly to the kitchen door and on the count of
three they burst in shouting.

'Surprise!'

Surprise is bloody right, they never been so
surprised in their entire lives, cuz there was the
woman lying naked on the kitchen floor, she had only
gone and smeared dog food all over her fanny aint
she, and there was Buster the pet Labrador busy
licking it all off with a very big smile on his face I'm
sure.

What the 'ell, I thought, I didn't wanna to be
hearing this from a complete stranger, although I gotta
admit I did find it kinda sexy in a weird Portland
kinda way.

Anyways, by the time the woman had finished
telling me this tale, or should it be "tail" ha ha, her
copying was done so she picked it up, gave me a sexy
little giggle and a tenner and left the shop, although
she did trip over her own feet on the way out the door,
flashed her red knickers and dropped all the
photocopies that went blowing away down the street,
silly mare ha ha.

So see what I mean about me sofa? There's
something going on with it I'm sure, and to back up
me suspicions, old Ma J who I was just telling you
about, suddenly started laughing aloud to herself.

I looked at her to see what she thought was so
funny but got such a shock at what I saw that I went
and stabbed meself with me bloody screwdriver, for

there, sitting on my sofa, as happy as Larry, giggling like a schoolgirl, was Ma J, stark bloody naked!

Now I'm as red blooded as the next man and if she was five years younger I would have been straight in there tucking five quid notes into any crack I could find, but I mean, the woman's ancient, and there she was getting down and dirty in me bloody shop.

'Whoa whoa whoa there Ma J.' says I as I rushed around the counter and threw her clothes over her, I needed to cover as much of that wrinkly elephant skin as I quickly could, the sight of it was makin' me eyes bleed. 'This aint the time or the place for this sort of thing old gal.'

'Isn't it my dear?' she said as her false teeth rattled in her mouth. 'Isn't this the Doghouse? Where's Luscious?... I I I...' she stammered looking confused the rubbing her head. 'Ooh sorry Andy, I don't know what come over me.'

Then she goes and does somethin' so disgusting that I don't think I'll ever be able to erase the memory of it from me mind.

Ma J only goes and puts her hand between her still naked legs, wipes around her shrivelled up bits for a second, then put her fingers under he nose and sniffed deeply.

'You're right my dear, it wasn't you that come over me.'

I gagged and dry heaved and nearly tossed up me free Co-op jelly right there and then.

The little old woman rocked sideways laughing like it was the joke of the century, and I'm sure I could hear her bones rattlin' in her loose skin. You wont believe 'ow close she come to leaving me shop dressed only in me lime jelly flavoured yawn.

Bollocks! I've just gone and put meself off me sarnie now. I need a sit down and have a glass of Coke so I'll say adiós for the time bein', let yerselves out won't you.

TaTa for now, your new pal, Queasy Andy, the repairman.

The Devils Scribe

The twenty four year old lad's constant nervous
pacing was slowly wearing a groove in his blue
bedroom carpet.

Adrenalin pulsed through his veins as he lit yet
another cigarette and deeply inhaled the calming
nicotine, he was smoking like there was no tomorrow,
he couldn't help it, he always got like this before
going out on a night rob.

John Halliwell was a part time sociology student
and full time layabout that still lived with his parents
in what was once the Royal Waterfront public house
down in Castletown. He knew that he should have
probably left home by now and got himself a little flat
somewhere, but he also knew when he was onto a
good thing, the rent was as cheap as chips and his
parents gave him space and never hassled him, so why
change it if it aint broke, was his philosophy.

John stopped pacing and sat on the edge of his bed
and began bouncing his feet on the carpet like he had

restless leg syndrome, then hastily stubbed the cigarette out into the overflowing ashtray, he checked his watch and instantly lit up another smoke before resuming pacing the room once more, he really should give up the bad habit he thought to himself.

A few minutes later John peeked through his bedroom window curtain for the fourth time in ten minutes and was happy to see that it was still a full moon, he stubbed out the cigarette and picked up an open rucksack from his bed.

'Pry bar check, torch check, rubber gloves check, lock picks check and Balaclava check', he secured the backpack and lit another cigarette.

The Poundland watch peeped boringly on his wrist announcing it was finally eleven o'clock and time to leave, but only after he had another quick smoke just to calm his nerves.

In theory tonight's job was going to be an easy one, a simple in and out no messing around, the kind of job that he had done dozens of times before, but knowing that didn't quell his nervousness.

The planned target of tonight's raid was a small tailors shop that he had discovered purely by accident earlier that very day. He had been walking up Fortuneswell Hill towards the Co-op, minding his own business, when he looked up and saw that bastard Crowley, the ginger haired knobstalk of a cop, was standing on the pavement ahead, no doubt he was threatening some old lady with imprisonment for having the wrong tint of blue in her hair or something.

Suddenly panicked, his eyes darted around seeking a quick exit before he himself felt the strong arm of the crooked coppers attention, and that's when he spied what had to have been the narrowest alleyway on Portland, possibly in the whole of Dorset.

The alley which was really just a crack between two houses, was so small that he'd never noticed it before, even though he'd lived on the island his whole life and there was even a sign attached to one wall naming it Needlers Walk.

The alleyway had been the proverbial lifesaver, if Crowley had spotted him and got his hands on him again... Well, he knew that jail-time would be coming or knowing Crowley as he did, a long hospital stay would more likely be the outcome.

John ducked into the safe shadows of Needlers Walk and hugged a wall as he waited until he heard the distinctive sounds of Crowley's Audi pulling away, or the terrified screams of a blue rinse biddy, to tell him it was safe to continue.

It was while he waited, with his back to the wall, that John peered down the alleyway and saw that it opened up a lot wider half way along its length and he could see windows.

John liked windows, windows meant easy access for his grubby little hands to do their thieving, so never one to miss an opportunity, John decided that while he was in the tiny alley he might as well scout it out and see if there was anything worth his further attention.

The first thirty feet or so of the alley was just unrendered brick walls and it wasn't until he had walked past them that a line of grimy windows on both sides began, disappointedly John saw that most of the windows had been boarded up from the inside with what looked like metal security blinds which were beyond his particular skill set.

He walked on for another fifty feet hoping to find at least one window that he could force but they all appeared the same and he'd just about given up hope when he noticed something interesting right at the farthest end in the darkest shadows.

Unlike all the other buildings, which had only offered their rears to him, the building that he now faced, blocked the end of the ally and looked like a small retail unit.

An odd place for a shop, he noted to himself as he went up to the plate glass window and peered inside.

John felt a little disheartened when he saw that it was just an old clothing shop and looked like it had closed down many years ago.

He wiped away a circle of dried on street grime and peered in to the darkness inside, but the place was definitely abandoned, whatever the shop had once stocked had long been removed just leaving bare floorboards and stained walls, although he did spy something that might just be of interest to him, and if he was correct in his thinking, might just be worth a few pennies to the right person. That's when he decided to revisit the shop under the cover of darkness for some nocturnal larceny.

John stubbed his latest smoke into the over-flowing ashtray and pulled the rucksack over his shoulders and quietly left the house, he chuckled to himself at the irony of double locking his front door, he didn't want any dirty bastards burgling him while he was out on the rob did he.

Outside, the moon was full and illuminated the

quiet streets with a blue white glow.

John made good use of the shadows to retrace his steps from earlier that day, along Castle road, Past Victoria Gardens and up Fortuneswell Hill, within fifteen minutes the cautious cat burglar was once again standing at the end of the narrow alleyway in front of the little empty shop.

The place really was tiny, the frontage which spanned the entire width of the alleyway, was just a two meter wide plate glass display window and a half glazed door that led into its interior.

John panned his torch around the outside of the shop and illuminated a tarnished brass plaque screwed to the door frame: Goldstein – Bespoke Tailors, how he hadn't noticed it on his earlier reconnoitre he didn't know.

The door was secured by a bog standard single lever mortice and it took less than three seconds to yield to a Bogota scrubbing pick from his lock pick set. Before crossing the threshold, John aimed his torch carefully around the room paying special attention to the corners near the ceiling for any infrared motion detectors but he just knew that this particular shop wouldn't have anything so sophisticated.

Taking a breath, John stepped inside and quietly closed the door behind him. His first impression was that the place just didn't feel right, that there was an almost clawing, grabbing atmosphere, he felt a shiver as a feeling of foreboding ran down his spine and made him tremble, it was like someone had died here and had left an evil presence behind, or that he was walking on a haunted grave, *this is a bad place* he thought as a strong desire to turn around and flee washed over him.

It was only the thought of his prize that he had seen earlier in the day that kept him leaving and he briskly crossed the expanse of dusty floorboard to a rack set in an alcove. It was here that he'd seen what at the time had appeared to be two suits hanging on the rack and he knew that bespoke vintage suits could fetch a lot of money.

John reached out a hand and took hold of a lapel but disappointment hit him as he ran his fingers over the once fine material and they came away coated in a green mildewy stickiness, the suits were beyond saving and were worthless.

After muttering a few expletives under his breath and trying to remove the green stuff from his hand, john panned the torch around the rest of the empty shop.

Now, being able to see things much closer, it was so obvious that the tailors shop had definitely been abandoned many many years ago, maybe even thirty of forty. The majority of the shelves that ran around the perimeter of the room were completely empty save for some scraps of material and a few ancient reels of thread that were covered in dust and the same green sticky goo.

The feeling of dread suddenly returned and something inside him told him he really shouldn't be there and to get away as quickly as possible and he was only too happy to oblige, that was until his torch caught sight of an object that piqued his interest.

The shop counter at the far side of the room facing the door, stood at waist height and was constructed from old carved wood and thick glass, there was nothing behind the glass except what looked like a few old hat boxes, spiderwebs and more horrible green stickiness, but on its top stood a very dusty antique National Dayton cash register, now this *was* interesting, he knew that the probability of there being any cash inside was less than zero and even if there was it would probably be useless pre-decimal money, but it wasn't the thought of some old coins that excited him, it was the till itself.

The cash register was an elaborate antique brass affair, it looked Victorian in design with huge press lever buttons, it was covered in fancy engravings of birds and flowers and intertwined vines, he'd seen old cash registers like this on Antiques Roadshow and some of them could be worth thousands.

John's index finger pushed gently on the green coated NO SALE button but it didn't budge, he tried again, a bit harder this time but it still wouldn't move, on the third try, the machine vomited a cacophony of noise, a loud bell chimed twice followed by a long dry squeal and finally a loud clunk as the cash drawer sprang open.

John gritted his teeth and instinctively his hands went to his ears which coated them in the strange green sticky stuff from his fingers. The din reverberated around the empty shop for what seemed like minutes before it echoed into nothingness. He was sure that someone would come bursting through the door any second, but no one appeared and he relaxed once more.

Shining the torch around inside the cash drawer revealed exactly what he was expecting, a lot of nothing, not a single coin or note was to be seen, except right at the back, hidden under a thick layer of green sticky dust, which he almost missed, was a small key.

John had been in the thieving business for a couple of years now and he knew about locks and he knew about keys, he also knew without a doubt that this particular key was a safe key and that where there was a safe key, there was usually a matching safe to go with it.

He flicked his beam of light around the shop looking for a likely hiding place for a safe, the only candidates were a very small door behind the counter that led to an even smaller alcove, which was more like a built in wardrobe really, or a large framed picture hanging on the wall next to it.

A quick search of the alcove proved fruitless, there were no hidden panels or false floorboards in it, so he turned his attention to the picture on the wall, which on closer inspection turned out to be a hand-drawn map of Germany, more specifically, the Bavaria region. There were several notations written in German around its edge with arrows pointing to various spots on the map, but none of it made any sense to John.

He ran his fingers around the edge of the wooden frame, a habit learned through his nocturnal trade and felt no hidden reed switches or alarm triggers, so he lifted the picture gingerly away from the wall and peered behind.

The young cat burgler smiled to himself, buried in the wall was an old Burg-Watchter wall safe, he had seen pictures of these before and knew that they were quite rare, but rare or not, the small key fitted perfectly in its keyhole and the mechanism inside the door made a satisfying metallic click when turned.

The small but heavy door swung open silently and smoothly as if its hinges had only just been oiled, although it was more likely to be the quality engineering of the Germans than anything else. Like the cash register, there was no money at all to be seen inside the safe but there was something there at least.

Lying on the bottom shelf of the safe was an ornate box the size of child's shoebox, John carefully lifted it out and weighed it in his hand, *about a kilo* he guessed. He could see that the box was made from mahogany or some speciality wood and that its corners were braced by brass straps so it could be worth something in its own right, he would of attempted opening there and then but decided against it as he didn't want to spend a second longer than necessary in the eerie shop, so he put it into his rucksack and turned his attention back to the cash register, which it turned out weighed a tonne and try as he might there was no way he could lift it on his own.

John was about to contemplate going to get a mate to help shift the till when a sudden weird tingling sensation ran through him, it strangely began in his ears which he immediately began rubbing but all that did was to spread the weird green stuff all over them even more.

At the same time, the sense of foreboding returned and hit him straight between the eyes, the feeling totally unnerved him, the incredible desire to flee and to get out of there immediately was so overwhelming that all thoughts of the cash register were quickly abandoned and like a scared little girl, he grabbed his gear and he fled out of the shop as fast as he could go with his heart pounding like a taught drum in his chest.

The weird sensations didn't stop as John slowly made his way back home, in fact they intensified, every footstep felt as though Thor's Mjölnir was pounding on his heart and every breath felt like it would rip his lungs from his ribcage. The sense of fear he had felt turned into a terrified dread and his mouth filled with the taste of his own death and his head span with viscous thoughts of his own mortality.

John all but collapsed onto his bed when he finally staggered home, but as he lay down panting and sweating the intense sensations in his mind and body began to ebb.

As he slowly began to regain his sense of self and normality began returning, he reached for a cigarette and sat on the edge of his bed.

What the Hell was all that about, he asked himself as he quickly lit the smoke.

The experience had been the worst he had ever felt in his life. He'd had a few panic attacks in his life before, most notably when his sister had been diagnosed with cancer, but the feelings and sensations he'd just suffered went far beyond any of those and were off the scale for sure.

John stubbed out the fifth cigarette in as many minutes and finally felt well enough to get a glass of water from his en-suite bathroom, he also grabbed the rucksack that he had dumped by his bedroom door when he'd entered.

Sitting back on the bed, John opened the rucksack and removed the mysterious wooden box and after giving it a clean with a few tissues, he examined it further.

The box was indeed as he had thought and was made from a deep red mahogany type wood, it had an aged patina but unfortunately there were no markings to help identify a maker or year of manufacture, along with eight brass corner protectors there was a keyhole set in the center of a brass scratch-plate on the box's front face.

The last thing that John wanted to do was to break the lock and devalue its potential worth, especially as his nights work had so far been an abstract failure, so he reached for his lock pick kit, courtesy of Ebay, and with a jiggle of his Bogota and a twist of the tension bar, a little click announced the box was ready to give up its secrets.

Cautiously he lifted the lid and studied the contents then a look of disgust began to slowly spread over his face as his eyes absorbed the view that confronted him.

'What the...??'

John's immediate thought was that it was some sort of sick joke, that someone had realised that one day the box could get stolen and so put this horrible thing into it just to say *thanks and fuck you very much you thieving bastard.*

Inside the box, nestled on a black velvet cloth, was what appeared to be at first glance, a grotesque gnarled and well chewed dog bone complete with clumps of rotting meat attached to it.

'Yuk!!'

John was about to toss the gross thing into the wastepaper bin when he noticed that there was something even weirder about it, something not quite right, that this thing was no ordinary chewed dog bone.

Curiosity peaked further, John reached for his rucksack again and grabbed a latex glove which he threw on to his right hand, there was no way he was going to touch this nasty looking thing without protection. He poked and prodded the grim article it in its box and yes he was right, this was most definitely no ordinary half chomped dog bone, for one thing, it had some sort of defined shape to it and if he used a very far stretch of his imagination, it could possibly look like a gun or pistol.

One end of the object curved downwards and was fused with other smaller bones which if you thought outside the box, could almost be a pistols hand grip, the other end of the rank object was intertwined with what looked like veins and dried sinews and narrowed in to what could almost be a gun barrel, at the end of this barrel part protruded what could possibly be a viscously sharp slither of bone.

With extreme caution and fighting the urge to vomit, John warily picked the object up in his hand and rotated it left and right and up and down, he raised it to his nose and took a sniff, but it was odourless, instinctively he gently ran a finger tip over the sharp bone point and yelped when it pierced the glove and drew blood, *that's it, this hideous thing is definitely going in the trash now.*

John turned to throw the gnarly and gross object across the room and into the bin, when a curious thing happened. The drop of blood from his finger that had been left behind on the sharp bone tip began to vanish right in front of his eyes, the blood seemed to soak into the bone as though it was being absorbed by a dry sponge, fascinated, he squeezed his finger to get some more blood, once again the thick red fluid was absorbed into it.

John was examining the mess of what appeared to be intertwined sinews and veins to see if there was a reason that his blood was seemingly being absorbed in to the object, when suddenly it pulsed in his hand, not once but twice. A look of repulsive horror flittered across Johns face and in normal circumstances he would of dropped it but instead he felt compelled to grip the object tighter and make it more comfortable in his hand, it felt good, so so good.

That's when an inner desire washed over him, like a drunk needing a whiskey or a junkie needing his next fix, he had an overwhelming desire to feel the disgusting object against his bare skin.

Trance like, John ripped off the latex glove with his teeth and placed the objects sharp tip on his left forearm. In the same way that a newborn butterfly unfurls its wings for the first time when it breaks out of its cocoon, the bone device seemed to expanded and inflate like it was breathing, like it was coming alive, it pulsated in his grip and took on a reddish rusty hue, and just like an early morning ground fog slowly rising, or the final jigsaw piece fitting into place, a veil lifted inside Johns head and everything became crystal clear in his mind.

He stared at the hideous creation in his hand with a new insight and a new admiration, he knew now what

114

it was, this horrendous but beautiful thing, a thing that must surely have been forged in the sewers of Hell, was the Devils own tattooing machine.

It buzzed and vibrated in his hand and an unworldly power seemed to rush through him, tingles of electric current ran from his head down to his feet as the tattooing machine buzzed again, it felt incredible.

Without even questioning the thought, John brought the buzzing machine towards his left arm again and pressed the sharp bone needle into his skin, there was no pain but he shut his eyes tightly as a wave of pure bliss caressed him.

His right hand began moving as if on some pre-planned flight course as the tattooing machine skipped and danced across his skin leaving a trail of multicoloured ink behind it.

Within moments, the outlines of a picture began to appear on his arm, it looked like a bird. The sensations that coursed through his body as the tattoo was being laid down were as sweet as honey and John's entire body pins and needled as a warm orgasmic fire flushed through him, he squeezed his eyes tighter and embraced the feeling, his heart thumped happily in his chest and his mind swam in a soup of sexy deliciousness, and then, as quickly as they had started, the sensations were gone.

All fell silent as the machines buzzing ceased. John opened his eyes just in time to see the last few drips of his blood being absorbed into the now fleshy looking tattooing machine, but he didn't care about such trivia anymore, *if it can make me feel like that*, he mused, *it can have all the blood it wants.*

Gently, with new found respect, John placed the machine back on its black velvet pad in its wooden box and turned his attention to the tattoo of a multi-coloured bird that now adorned his body. A huge smile crept on to his face and like a first time heroin user, his eyes rolled back in their sockets and he let out a huge contented sigh, then in slow motion, fell backwards into the waiting embrace of his cloud like bed which happily swept him away into a world full of dreams.

John awoke late the next morning, the sun had long crept over the skyline and he was late for college but he didn't care, he gave a yawn and a little stretch then smacked his lips, he felt good, really good, actually he hadn't felt this good in years, the usual lower back pain that he had suffered since a rugby accident in school was non-existent and he didn't even feel the need to reach for his customary morning packet of smokes.

John didn't know why he felt this good but he wasn't complaining, it was great, he swung his legs out of the bed and was just considering if he should go to the local swimming pool for fifty laps or to the gym and having a full workout, weights and all, when he noticed his left arm, he had completely forgotten about the previous night's weirdness but it all came flooding back to him now in a rush of memories.

He studied the fresh tattoo in awe, the detailing was incredible, the bird literally shone with vivid colours, the blues, red, and greens of its feathers were almost luminous, it looked so life-like that it could have been a photograph instead of a tattoo, undeniably a better tattoo couldn't have been found in any tattoo studio anywhere in the world, it was truly stunning, but then something so extraordinary and unbelievable happened that it almost caused John to have a coronary right there in his bedroom.

He was still admiring the amazing piece of skin art and wondering how he had actually managed to draw it so perfectly as his eyes were shut tight through most of the incident, when the tattoo began to blister, strangely there was no pain as a large puffy bulge appeared under the tattoo and it began to rise from his skin, the swelling continued like a small balloon being inflated until it got to the stage where it looked like it would pop in a pus explosion, but instead, the tattoo blister peeled itself off of his arm and dropped to the floor with a little splat, it hadn't hurt in the slightest.

John sat stunned as the pus filled skin balloon quivered on the floor like a jelly fresh out of a mould, then it contracted a little, almost like taking a small breath, before suddenly expanding and morphing into a 3d representation of the tattoo, no longer was it just a flat one-dimensional piece of skin art, now it had metamorphosed into an actual real bird.

Johns heart was beating as fast as a hammer drill inside his ribcage, he couldn't believe what he had just witnessed, he stared wide eyed at the what was, for all intense purposes, a dead multi-coloured bird lying on his carpet where no dead multi-coloured bird had a right to be, but this multi-coloured bird wasn't dead, far from it, first one wing twitched and flickered, then the other wing followed suit, then both of the birds wings began to flutter in unison like a cold engine trying to start on an even colder morning.

The bird bounced and jittered around on the carpet

117

for a few seconds and then with a little chirp it flew into the air and began flying around the room, it circled the bedroom twice and then stopped in mid air and hovered just inches away from Johns face, a pair of small dark eyes seemed to study him, almost as if it were looking into the depths of his soul, then as he stood watching, the little bird gave a series of loud chirps, turned towards the open window and disappeared into the morning sun.

John stood stunned, he didn't know what to do or what to think, he just stared out the window after the little bird, the incredible bird that shouldn't exist but did, the little bird that was once a tattoo but was now a live living creature.

John sat down hard on the edge of the bed with a dazed, confused and baffled look on his face and reached for a cigarette.

Missing Persons Case File #7

Prty 2nt ghst tnnlz - gd&r

It was a foreign code to most people, but to sisters Hailey and Jenny Williams and others of her generation, the text message was simple - Party tonight Ghost tunnels - Grinning Ducking and Running.

The two girls crowded around Jenny's Nokia 6111, a seventeenth birthday present from her mother and giggled excitedly, the girls had both been waiting desperately for this text message for what had seemed like years but in reality it had only been eight months since the girls had moved to the Isle of Portland from Birmingham as part of a council housing exchange program.

They had tried their hardest to be liked at school by integrating themselves in the local youth scene as much as they could and although they had both made many friends, they had not as yet been invited to one of the raves that the *in crowd* held at the ghost tunnels once a month, now it seemed that Jenny at least, had received that all important invite.

Hailey rummaged around in her Adidas rucksack for her own phone.

'Just checking its switched on.' she glared at her sister who watched her with an amused look on her face.

'Don't worry sis, I expect you'll get an invite soon.' Jenny knew that it was unlikely because her sister was still only fifteen and a little too young for one of *the* raves but she didn't want to see her upset so the fib was justified.

'Come on Hails, let's choose what I'm gonna wear tonight.'

Hailey pulled a sad face but knew deep down that her sister was correct, who would want a little kid like her hanging around at one of the Ghost Tunnel raves, so reluctantly she followed her sister upstairs to their shared bedroom.

The Ghost Tunnels as they were known locally were in actuality part of the High Angle Battery at New Ground, a large Victorian gun emplacement and associated support buildings built to protect Portland harbour from enemy ships, although the guns had never been fired in anger.

The tunnels themselves were a labyrinthine network of underground tunnels that ran from where the guns stood over-looking the bay, to the shell stores and magazines and everywhere in between, the guns themselves had been removed at the end of World War 2 and now the buildings had been left to decay just as many of the historically important sites on

Portland had been by the ever incompetent town council.

Now the site had taken on a new lease of life and had been commandeered by the local teens of the Island, who swiftly put the place to good use and what better use could there be than partying.

The ever resourceful teens had "acquired" an old electrical generator from one of the local quarries to provide power, fixed up a home-made lighting rig and fitted it with a couple of Gobo flower effects, a Stormbird laser unit, a magma oil projector and an Aqua Haze smoke machine. A steel shed, again purloined from a disused quarry, was fitted with a huge padlock and used as a safe lock-up to store the Kam KXR600 2000 watt amp and speakers, the decks were provided by whoever was to be DJ on the night, usually this was Slick Pete because he had a pair of very nice Technics SL1210's at his disposal.

The police were aware of the monthly raves up at the battery but they turned a blind eye and kept their distance, after all, there was bugger all else for the kids to do on Portland, there were no amusement arcades, no youth clubs or any cafes for them to hang out in, so the rave scene continued to flourish.

If you were a Portland pure blood, admittance to a rave was a given but to go to a rave if you were a Kimberlin (non Portland born) was a different story, Kimberlins were allowed admittance by invitation only and you only got invited if you knew the right people, now at last, Jenny's dreams had come true and she had finally met the right people.

The girls spent almost four hours sorting through Jenny's clothes, it wasn't that Jenny had that many but trying on different combinations of skirts, tops and shoes, putting on different shades of lipstick and eye shadow and styling and restyling Jenny's hair time and time again takes a while.

Finally, both girls were happy with their choice of white low-rise phat pants, red crop top showing Jenny's belly button and a nice Von Dutch trucker hat, once she had put on her Vans trainers both agreed that Jenny looked stunning and was ready to paaar.....tay!

Darkness can fall quickly sometimes and before long it was almost time for Jenny to set off for the rave, a few more dabs of lipgloss and a run through with a hairbrush and she would be ready. The ever hopeful Hailey rechecked her mobile for missed calls for the thousandth time that day although she knew now that she wasn't going anywhere with Jenny.

'Don't worry sis, I expect they had enough people going this time that's all, just you see, you'll be first on the list next time.' she gave Hailey a hug. 'Oh and if mum asks why you aren't staying the night with me at Karen's like we told her, just say that you had unexpected homework to do or something. OK?'

Hailey gave a non committal shrug.

'Come on Hails, you know I would do the same for you.' she gave a well practised sulk expression and pushed her bottom lip out, her sister responded with a poked out tongue and smiled.

'Go before I change my mind.'

'You're the best Hails, you know that.' Jenny hugged her sister again and with a flick of her bright red hair she dashed out the door and headed off out into the evening.

The rhythm of the bass throbbed in her chest as she

entered the disused gun emplacement at New Ground, instantly adrenalin began to pump around her veins in musical simpatico with Rave Alert by Praga Khans, *my fav toon – a good start*, she began nodding her head to the beat as she walked.

'Hey Jen!' a voice rang out from the darkness.

'Over here.'

She turned and saw a familiar face coming out of the night. 'Hiya Rainey, good to see ya.'

'You got my text then?'

Jenny laughed, 'It was you that sent it huh?'

'Duh! Who else would be stupid enough to invite you anywhere you skanky ho?'

'You Bitch!' Jenny shot back.

'Slut!'

'Whore!'

Both girls began laughing and at each others banter and then hugged.

'Come on you old slapper, I'll show you where everybody is.'

Rainey grabbed her friend's arm and dragged her off towards the swelling music. In the distance a lone figure stood watching and waiting.

Jenny was well and truly knackered, she had been dancing for two and a half hours solid, she had been offered an E several times but declined them politely, she didn't do drugs and although every single muscle in her body ached it was great, she felt so alive, she didn't need drugs.

This was the best night of her entire life and she wanted it to go on forever, but for the moment, forever would have to be put on pause as her tired legs couldn't take it any more and she had to go and sit down, forever could continue after a bottle of water and a seat in the chill-out room.

Luckily the chill-out room wasn't very far away; it was just a few turns down one of the well lit tunnels which had been painted in a cool shade of blue and had large red arrows pointing the way so that no one could get lost. She reached the room and flopped down in a large comfy sofa and glugged hard from the plastic water bottle, the soft soothing sounds of Enchanted by Delirium filled her ears and her racing heart stepped down a gear, she sighed but was so happy, she sat back and closed her eyes for a few minutes and re-ran the nights events over in her head a few times.

'Oi! – Wake up sleepy head.'

An elbow dug her in her ribs, 'Wake up, its time to go.' Rainey and some boy Jenny half recognised as Paul Creighton from the chippies at Easton were sitting beside her on the sofa.

'How long you been asleep girl?' Rainey enquired.

'I saw you leave the floor over an hour ago, haven't seen you since.'

Jenny was a little sleep confused and checked her watch, it was 2am.

'Uh yeah, a couple of hours I guess.'

'Well were all heading back to Paul's for some drinks and a spliff or two, you wanna come?' she lent over and whispered in Jenny's ear, 'You know Billy Johnson from 5A, well he fancies the arse off you and asked me to invite you back to Paul's, he'll be waiting for you there, if you're interested.'

Jenny's face reddened with embarrassment, *Billy Johnson! Friggin 'ell! Oh my God!!*

She tried to remain cool and unfazed, 'I uh - Yeah I guess so but first I got to go to the loo or I'll pee me knickers.'

Rainey pointed towards an exit on the other side of the chill-out room. 'It's through there, You'll see it, we will meet you out front in five ok?'

Jenny nodded and got up and as coolly as she knew how and walked out through the door that had been indicated, once out of sight of her friend, Jenny began bouncing along the tunnel excitedly.

'My god I can't believe that Billy Johnson fancies me'. she had to fan her face with her hand to cool it down.

'Oh My god, oh my god, oh my god!'

This evening was turning into the greatest event ever, this beat all her Christmases and birthdays rolled into one, it beat the time when she won the school Spelling Bee championship and got a huge gold cup, it even beat Aunty Sue having baby Charlie last year.

'Oh my god this is so cool' then a thought struck her, *What if Billy wants to have sex with me?*

Thoughts of safe sex, condoms, STDs and losing her virginity all ran around in her mind like a washing machine on its spin cycle.

'Oh my god this is even cooler.'

The tunnels were almost empty by now, the music had been turned right down to just a trickle of sound and people were leaving or had left already. Jenny was about to enter a small room that had a spray painted picture of a matchstick girl on the outside when she heard a soft voice calling her name from behind her.

'Jenny… Jenny…'

The voice was female but too quiet to be recognised.

'Jenny… Jenny…' the voice came again.

The blue painted walls and red arrows she had followed had stopped at the toilets and didn't continue to the farthest unlit end of the tunnel where the voice was coming from.

'Jenny it's me, come here.' the voice was louder this time and this time she did recognise it.

'Hailey??'

She jogged down into the dark towards her sister's voice, 'Hailey what the Hell are you doing here?' she demanded of the blackness but only got silence in return. 'Have you been hiding down here in the dark all night?'

Silence

'Hailey where are you?'

Silence.

The blackness was beginning to get claustrophobic, her voice rose up a pitch. 'Hailey where are you?'

'I'm here Jenny.' the voice came drifting softly out of the abyss.

Jenny faced a wall of blackness. 'I can't see you...'

There was a sudden tap on her shoulder which made her jump, 'I'm here Jenny!'

'Bloody Hell sis, you scared the shit out off me.' Jenny turned to face her sibling but it wasn't her sister standing there.

A shocked look of confusion spread across Jenny's face as a metal claw hammer arced through the air and smashed against her temple, she crashed to the ground and the darkness enveloped her still body.

The music ended and the tunnels became silent

once more.

Cutting from Portland Daily Echo:

The disappearance of seventeen year old Portland girl Jennifer (Jenny) Williams continues to baffle local police.

Jennifer's sister Hailey told the Echo that Jenny was last seen setting off to a rave being held at the High Angle Battery complex on Portland, known locally as the Ghost Tunnels, but her friends deny knowing anything about any raves being held in the area.

Detective Chief Inspector Crowley of the Portland CID told reporters that it was most likely that the seventeen year old went for a walk up on the cliffs and tragically went over the edge, he added that the investigation would now be handed over to the coastguard who would commence sea searches around the island.

The Problem with Alchemy

Please God, Let today be the day.

An old and rusting wind-up alarm clock rattled wearily but was hardly audible even in the early morning peace. A man lying on a camp bed nearby opened his eyes and stared up at the wooden rafters above him, he had been awake a few hours already, he didn't sleep much these days although he was tired beyond words.

Please God, Let today be the day.

The man offered up his prayer once more, although he had stopped believing in any God years ago, a God wouldn't have been so cruel, he knew that, what God would have done this to him.

He sat up and and perched on the beds edge, there was no cliched stifled yawning or rubbing of sleepy eyes, there was no stretching of night stiffened limbs, not even the scratching of a stubbly chin, he just sat still and thought back to *that* day, that terrible terrible day so so long ago. His mind began to drift down into the thick fog of depression that constantly lay in his peripheral vision waiting to grab him and take him even lower, he knew he must fight it, he had spent too many wasted years deep in its evil clutch already.

Henry Mitchell battled the darkness and desperately searched for some happy memories, they were the only things that could save him now, it was becoming harder each day to fight, the struggle seemed endless.

Suddenly, out of the mire, an image floated up to him, a woman, a familiar woman, a beautiful woman, but from so long ago, how long had it been now since he'd last seen his beautiful wife, it felt like many lifetimes for sure. Henry's tired mind brought the image into focus and the terrible blackness began to fade, he drew power from the memory of his beloved wife, just enough power to enable him to continue his desperate daily search for her.

The howling wind created an ominous droning as it rushed to the shore and echoed around Church Ope Cove, bringing with it a fine white mist of sea spray that seemed to hover over Henry's rickety beach cabin, it seemed that even nature was against him.

As the cabins loose window rattled in its frame, Henry emerged and slammed the door behind himself and pulled the collar of his tatty and dirty yellow raincoat high up his wrinkled neck. The weather didn't bother him so much any more, he had seen worse, but it was that endless drone, it mocked him mercilessly, if only it would stop and give him peace so that he could concentrate on his mission. Peace! he didn't deserve peace and he knew it.

Henry looked up at the high cliffs that surrounded

the cove, at their sheer rock faces that glistened with rain in the early morning light as they soared skywards, he remembered that many years ago he and his wife Elisabeth had owned a magnificent Georgian house right at the top looking out to sea. That's where *it* had happened. Now though, the house stood as a ruinous reminder of his utter stupidity and recklessness.

'Elisabeth!'

The power of saying her name aloud gave him a renewed hope once more.

Repeating her name over and over as though it was some sort of spell-breaking mantra, and with wet pebbles crunching under his old leather boots, Henry began to make his way up the shingle beach toward the base of the cliffs

The year was 1854, a young fourteen year old gentleman whooped with delight as he witnessed his first ever horseless carriage puttering down the street, the billowing white smoke cloud that followed in its wake made his mother erupt in a fit of unladylike coughing.

'Disgusting things, they will never catch on.' his mother was adamant as she dabbed her nose with a fine but useless lace handkerchief.

'Oh mother, you are so old fashioned, these machines will be everywhere one day, you will see.'

She responded with her famous glare that could turn a navvy to stone, 'Heaven forbid.'

The young gentleman stayed motionless watching awhile longer as the wonderful contraption with its dripping oil and sulphurous stench slowly trundled away, turned the corner and disappeared out of view.

'One day I will be inventing things like that, mark my words.' he enthused.

'Yes of course you will Henry darling, but first come inside and have some lunch, tea and sandwiches in the orangery will be nice today I think.'

It's 1864, Thames embankment was bustling with people, elegantly dressed women wearing the latest French fashions hung onto the arms of men wearing dress suits, top hats and silk cravats, all of whom were taking advantage of the warm evening to walk to the theatres or one of the many restaurants in the locale, all that is except for our now not so young twenty four year old gentleman.

Henry Mitchell was briskly walking along the embankment on his his way to the great Savoy on the Strand, where a meal was being held in his honour and as usual he was late, but it didn't stop Henry from halting for a minute or two as he admired the latest auto-cars coughing their way along the road, *one day I will be inventing things like that* he thought to himself.

As the autocar turned the corner out of sight Henry resumed his fast pace. He would usually of course taken one of the new underground trams but the pollution in the tunnels was so bad that it would have turned his white silks black with soot, he made a mental note as he moved off to take a look at electrifying the underground tram system one day.

It had taken eight long hard years of constant learning at the Royal Academy in London before Henry was finally awarded his science and engineering doctorates and had been deemed a genius by his peers.

In his final two years he had been mentored by Lord Kelvin himself and it was during his time under the eminent physicists tutelage that he met his two heroes, Charles Babbage, who was making great strides with his revolutionary analytical engine with the help of genius mathematician Ada Lovelace, and physicist Galileo Ferraris, inventor of the induction motor, who was making great strides with the development of alternating current with Tesla. 'Edison and his Direct Current be damned, it's AC all the way', he had laughed after meeting Ferraris for the first time.

Little did he know then, that although it was these incredible people that had fuelled his yearning for experimentation and discovery, they would also ultimately change his life forever in a way that no man could have possibly foreseen.

In the year of our Lord eighteen hundred and eighty, Henry Mitchell left the bright glittering lights of London academia and returned to his beloved Isle of Portland way down on the South Coast of Dorset in England. With financial support of mater and pater, he set up a research laboratory in an old warehouse on the docks in Castletown, where he began his own personal voyage of discovery.

It didn't take long before Henry had made a host of very important inventions, some of which were of great interest to the Royal Navy, such as the Mitchell Mylox Equivalator and the Mitchell Valvex Comparator, both now being successfully used in underwater communications, another of his great successes had been the highly regarded Mitchell

Magnowav Beam Shaper which was currently revolutionising medicine and finding uses in the new science of electricity generation, if his old friend Ferraris and that charlatan Edison hadn't already been dabbling with AC and DC respectively, then his MC current would have been a household name by now.

Of course holding the patents for his inventions created great wealth which made Henry a very sought after bachelor with a number of lady admirers, but only one woman had caught his heart, twenty two year old Elisabeth Curtis of The Grove Portland, whom he met at the Portland Mayors annual Ball and had fallen head over heels in love with during their first waltz.

Within two years Henry and Elisabeth had married in Portland's grandest church, St Georges, and within five, had their dream house built high up on the cliffs at Church Ope Cove. Life was good.

Ironically, it had been the discovery of something very strange by the workmen digging the foundations of his house that had spurred Henry on to his next achievement.

Like most inventors, scientists and philosophers of the period, and indeed ever since man first gazed at golds wondrous glow, Henry was interested in and tinkered with alchemy.

Alchemy was split into two distinct groups, there was the search for what was called the Philosophers stone, also known as the elixir of life and said to provide immortality, the theory was built on the works of Zosimos of Panopolis and Byzantine alchemist Paracelsus, but it was the other group that Henry was particularly interested in, the ability to transmute a base metal like lead or mercury into precious 24 carat gold, he would leave the search for the philosophers stone to the quacks.

Like one of his idols, Sir Isaac Newton, Henry was fascinated with the idea of being able to perform the miracle of miracles, he like those others, were well aware that dense lead was only one molecule different in composition to that of pure gold and it was the search of a way to convert that one molecule that alchemists sort.

Even though by the 1800's alchemy was mostly frowned upon by the scientific fraternity and it had long been decided that it was something for the crackpots to meddle with instead of bonafide scientists, Henry liked to dabble and to this end, he had a fully equipped laboratory and mechanical workshop built down in the cellars of his new house.

He had wasted no time in designing and constructing what was to be his most wonderful machine to date, a machine that he proudly named the Mitchell High tailed Plasma Inducer, it could, once perfected, induce extremely high voltages over a magnetic field and would be revolutionary, indeed it could even kickstart the third industrial revolution, but Henry hadn't invented this machine for the good of mankind, he had invented it for purely personal reasons, the machine would form the central hub of his magnum opus, his great alchemy device.

For three years Henry had slowly constructed and assembled his machine from the ground up, using theories and formulae derived from the likes of Tesla, Johann Friedrich Bottger, Hennig Brand and Ge Hong himself, the machine was growing spring by spring, coil by coil and magnet by magnet in his cellar laboratory and he knew that without a shadow of a doubt, it would be capable of morphing that one solitary molecule and turn lead into gold.

Now at long last, on the fourth anniversary of its initial conception, Henry's alchemy machine was almost complete, he had burnt the midnight oil connecting the final pieces of the machine and by the time the sun arose the following morning it was at long last ready for its first initial test.

Although married life had been wonderful for the Mitchell's in every way imaginable and the house was constantly filled with laughter, never an argument was heard or a cross word said, never a voice was raised in anger or a tear shed, an underlying sadness ran through Henry and Elisabeth's hearts, they were unable to bear children and no matter how many times they tried, Elisabeth couldn't conceive, whether the problem was down to Henry or Elisabeth neither of them knew, but as the question of fertility was never raised or spoken about, all they knew was that no babies were forthcoming.

Henry closed the labs main power breaker causing equipment and gauges to spring into life with various clicks and hisses.

Elisabeth woke early that morning and wasn't surprised to see Henry missing from the marital bed, he was often either working in his lab until late or starting really early before she had woken. After ablutions were complete and a light breakfast, Elisabeth wrote a note to her husband and left it on the desk in his study, donned her coat and then left the house.

An excited Henry made some final checks and adjustments to the machine and when happy took his seat on the plush red padded chair in front of its control console, he flexed his fingers and shivered with anticipation.

Elisabeth had hated writing that note, she had never lied to her husband before and she felt mortified, in her note she had explained that she was heading in to the village to pick up a few skeins of fabric for a dress she was to make, in truth she had no intention of going to see the haberdashers, instead she had a secret liaison arranged and was going to visit another man.

Henry donned the pair of thick safety glasses that had been resting on his forehead and rotated a large brass dial on the console in front of him, the alchemy machine on the other side of the lab groaned as its plasma inducer began to glow and its many vacuum tubes lit up.

Elisabeth gaily strolled along the road with a skip in her step, she breathed in the warm morning sun and enjoyed listening to the birdsong in the trees, she gazed at the various shop windows at all the wonderful things they had on display and even stopped outside the haberdashers and admired the latest materials draped in the window display. Elisabeth could feel her cheeks flush with guilt at the lie she had told her husband that morning and quickly moved on. Four minutes later, she arrived outside her destination.

With his sleeves rolled up to the elbows and his starched collar removed, Henry flicked a few more switches and pulled a large lever, a motor somewhere deep inside the machine began to spin and a soft mechanical whine filled the lab.

Elisabeth stood nervously outside the garden gate and stared up the path that led to *his* front door, *Do I really want to go through with this? It could change things forever,* she nibbled a fingernail and thought about the question for awhile and almost scared herself out of going ahead, but she took a deep breath, walked along the path and knocked on the door.

This was it, finally after years of head scratching, hard-work, blood sweat and tears, everything was ready. Henry flexed his nervous fingers again and mopped his sweating brow. A quick flick of a red toggle switch in the center of the console initiated the spinning of four large coils mounted at the bottom of the machine which produced a soft whine that increased in pitch with their acceleration, a button was pressed and a large cylindrical plasma flask containing a strange green liquid, sparked into life casting an eerie glow around the room, dancing ghostly shadows bounced from the walls as the liquid boiled.

Metallic clicking sounds of circuit breakers and solenoids opening and closing echoed around the laboratory as the magnetic coils span faster and faster. Henry resembled a maniacal pianist playing a tumultuous overture of weird electronic sound and light as he flicked switches, turned control knobs and pulled various levers on the control console.

Bright purple and blue arcs of plasma began to spew from the electrically excited flask causing a red warning light to begin flashing indicating that it was time to activate the high-tailed plasma inducer control, if the Gods were with him, then this would be the time for them to prove it. He pulled a heavy lever on the power circuit.

The green door clicked quietly behind her as Elisabeth left the man's house, she smoothed down her skirt hoping to remove any unsightly tell tell creases and half ran half skipped along the street in the opposite direction.

Elisabeth's heart was pounding like a child's toy drum and she was dizzy with an excitement the like of which she had never felt before, she couldn't believe she had actually done it, she couldn't believe that she had had the nerve to see it through, but she was so glad that she had, Elisabeth now felt like a real woman, a huge grin spread across her red flushed cheeks.

Sparks began to fly around the laboratory as various different potions and compounds combined inside the alchemy machine, static electricity began forming around the coil conduits and created little blue arcs of energy that cracked and fizzed in a frenetic dance.

Elisabeth had entered through the man's front door with a nervous trepidation in her step, her nerves were stretched like over-tuned violin strings. Coy pleasantries were quickly uttered between the man and woman, and once out of the way, she followed him to a room that contained no furniture except a bed. Shyly, Elisabeth obeyed the man's instructions and had removed her skirt and her undergarments and lay down on the bed as told, she shut her eyes tight and said a silent prayer as the man's cold hands had gently parted her lilly white thighs and crept towards

138

her private parts making her face burn with embarrassment, a heavy pressure on her abdomen caused her gasp as his weight squeezed down on her. Elisabeth counted the minutes as the man did everything that he wanted to do to her, which thank the Lord didn't take too long, and before she knew it, she opened her eyes to see him washing himself in a small sink. The deed was done.

Another heavy lever clunked as it locked into place producing more bright sparks that erupted across the lab with a roar of white noise. Henry span what resembled a ships wheel and the volume suddenly increased by over a hundred decibels, he had to quickly clasp his hands across his ears as the high-tailed plasma inducers power level ramped up and caused large yellow forks of man-made lightning to spit out in a frenzy across the room.

The plasma flask began to emit ribbons of violet, pink and blue plasma which spilt over its sides and flowed into the collecting chamber below. Glass conduits began to fill with a molten hot rainbow of liquid electricity that poured into the very heart of the machine, every hair on Henry's body stood to attention as the huge magnetic force being exerted by the machine became stronger and stronger.

A large arc of magnetic lightning cracked through the air with a loud static boom charging the laboratory with more and more electrons, another crack of lightning erupted and then another, the entire laboratory was fast becoming an inferno of Hellish lightning bolts and red hot burning plasma.

Elisabeth kept repeating the man's words over and over in her head, she still couldn't believe what she had heard.

'Congratulations Mrs Mitchell, I can happily confirm that you are with child and you're into your second trimester, I would say that you are about four months pregnant.'

The laboratory stank of burning ozone as huge lightning sheets, electric sparks and plasma scorched the air. A green neon light flickered on the face of the power control board announcing that the machine was now at maximum and was ready to release its energy on the cauldron full of lead bricks standing next to the machine and transmute it into pure gold.

Elisabeth ran her hands across her belly, she could almost feel the baby in her stomach, *was that a kick,* she giggled at herself for being so silly, she couldn't wait to tell Henry the good news.

She knew that the subject had never been discussed between them but knew that he would dearly love to be a father, *a little Henry Junior running around the place would make him so happy.*

Elisabeth let herself in to the house and excitedly called out to her husband as she removed her coat and hung it on a peg.

'Darling are you here?' she was met with a wall of silence, she called out again before realising that he would be in the laboratory, she headed towards the cellar stairs.

The alchemy machine shimmered through the heat haze that it generated, blue smoke emanated from the whirling magnetic coils as they span at their maximum, the purple and blue plasma boiled in the flask and lightning arcs exploded across the room, all was going well.

Henry studied a brass dial and waited for its needle to reach the indicated mark on its face, *any second now...*

He grimaced through the deafening volume of noise as more and more sparks erupted from within the depths of the machine while fingers of plasma leapt high into the air.

Out of the corner of his eye, he noticed a movement that shouldn't have been there and on turning his head in its direction he saw the door to his laboratory opening, quickly followed by his excited wife.

'Darling darling, you'll never guess what... We're pregn...'

Elisabeth's smile vanished in an instant and her hands went to her ears as she was assaulted by the dreadful noise.

Henry shouted an unheard warning for her to get out of the lab immediately but it came too late as an enormous bolt of lightning exploded from the machine and snaked towards her, a massive cracking roar rocked the room as the energy bolt made contact, the woman's scream was lost amongst the onslaught as another huge bolt of lightning leapt from the machine and twisted and thrashed around the workshop like a headless snake trapped by its own tail, it hit the plasma flask and shattered it into a thousand pieces.

A huge shockwave hit Henry, ripped him from his seat and threw him across the room like he was a rag doll. Suddenly a violent storm of boiling plasma and highly charged electrons exploded in an incredible flash of blinding light which illuminated the lab as a final deafening boom destroyed Henry's eardrums.

The alchemy machine exploded with such force that it was heard a mile away in Easton Square.

Silence… Calm… Serene Silence. No sounds, no sights, no feelings, no nothing.

So this is death.

Wafts of white smoke drift gently upwards unaware of the destruction that caused their coming into being, burnt and shattered pieces of a once magnificent machine lay scattered around the remains of Henry Mitchell's laboratory, little orange flames danced across the broken surfaces while an acrid nose clogging stench filled the air, it smelled of ozone and seared meat.

The chequerboard black and white tiled cellar floor was now littered with rubble, broken masonry, charred wood and ash, so much ash, torn wires and cables dangled, sparked and fizzed as they hung in coils from the remnants of the ceiling.

At the far end of the lab where the door once stood, there was nothing except a large ragged hole that let in the bright sunlight from the world outside.

It was the fresh salty sea breeze drifting in the through the ripped wall that brought Henry back to the land of the living. He tried opening his eyelids but they refused to move, he lay still, the pain wracked through him, he tried again, his head span, but slowly, almost impossibly, Henry's senses began to come back to him and he tried opening his eyes once more, this time they flickered open and gradually sight returned through his blurred retinas and the sounds of

142

sparking and hissing creaking and snapping of his destroyed laboratory returned to his bleeding ears.

Henry willed himself to stand up and then vomited. God alone knew how he was still alive, he checked himself for broken bones but apart from a multitude of cuts and scratches and burns he seemed to be still in one piece, he surveyed the damage around the wrecked room, it was total.

He was stunned and in shock, he didn't know what to make of what had happened, *what did I do wrong? surely the power couplers were up to the job, I designed them specially so, maybe the coil windings weren't thick enough? no, that can't be it...*

Suddenly, like a lump hammer to the temples, the full memory of everything that had just happened came rushing back, he spun around on the spot and stared at where he had last seen Elisabeth, a look of total disbelief spread across his face as the reality dawned, he screamed her name.

'Elisabethhhh!'

Henry screamed his wife's name over and over as he scrambled towards the gaping hole where the laboratory door once stood and came skidding to a halt, there was nothing on the other side, no wall, no corridor, no floor and no Elisabeth.

He teetered on the edge of the precipice and looked down into the void where his wife once stood, all that he could see was the small beach of Church Ope Cove and a scattering of the remains of what was once his laboratory far below.

Precariously he dropped to his knees and balanced on the edge of the drop, he didn't care if he fell, his world had ended, and Elisabeth was dead.

The hours passed and the sun began to set in the distance, Henry was still perched on his heels and was rocking to and fro, time meant nothing to him any more. What life could he have without Elisabeth, without his beloved he could no longer face the world, he didn't want to, he knew what he must do.

Henry wiped the tears from his blackened filthy face and rose to his feet, he would join Elisabeth in oblivion. Taking a deep breath he calmly stepped forward, 'I'm coming my darling.' he sobbed and took another step, his foot now dangled in mid-air. 'I'll be with you very soon.'

The still warm evening zephyr lapped around his body and made his ripped and burnt shirt billow like a ships sail, his sore fingers gripped the rough walls edge, far below him the hard pebbles and rocks of the beach waited to welcome him, they called to him, they wanted him and they were going to get him.

Henry peered out to the calm sea that licked the shore and tensed his muscles, then he leapt in to the abyss.

Or at least he would have leapt if not for at the very instant his muscles thrust him outwards into the nothing, something far below on the beach suddenly caught his eye. Henry quickly re-grasped the edge of the broken brickwork and pulled himself to a stop and clambered back inside the building, *Oh my God, it can't be! It can't be!* he rubbed his eyes and forced them wider trying to getter better focus on what it was that the setting sun was glinting off of far below.

Confusion turned to realisation and realisation turned wonderment.

Henry took to his heels and forcing his wracked

body through the pain, he climbed the remnants of the basement staircase, out of the wrecked house and on to the path that led towards the pebble beach at the base of the cliffs.

It was the end of another long long day of searching, the tired old man returned to his ramshackle wooden shack on the stony beach of Church Ope Cove. He sighed heavily as he sat on the side of his bed and just stared ahead at nothing for what seemed like an eternity.

He was so so tired and very very old and wasn't sure how much longer he could keep this up, the daily searching, the daily digging, the daily disappointment and the daily heartbreak, even the knowledge of knowing that his alchemy machine had actually worked all those years ago couldn't lift the depression that knifed at his soul.

Eventually, Henry slowly got back to his feet and took a battered wooden cigar box from under his bed, checking over both shoulders that he was alone, he flipped up the box's lid and peered inside, his heart rejoiced and skipped a beat, a wry happy smile spread across his lips as a warm golden glow reflected in his face.

'Forever! That's how long I can keep this up.'

He blew a kiss into the box and re-shut its lid, then clutched it tightly to his chest in a loving embrace, he felt a renewed vigour coursing through him and the years of toil and despair recede as he placed the box back under the bed.

Henry knew that tomorrow he would be out there on the beach again no matter what the weather, this tired and ancient old man that had somehow, miraculously defied the laws of physics and live to over two hundred years old, knew that his timeless search would continue for more missing pieces of his 24 carat solid gold wife.

Angela the Angel

Nurses are supposed to save lives aren't they, so why was Nurse Flannigan currently fattening up a patient ready to be eaten?

Nurse Angela Flannigan is the archetypal old age pensioner, pink rinse, thick bifocals, lots of wrinkles and the ability to remove her teeth at will, she could have passed for anyone's little old granny.

Although now looking every one of her ninety years, Angela was once as strong as an ox, both physically and mentally. During World War II when she had been a mere slip of a girl, she had been a nurse on the front line in North Africa and had loved every minute of it. She had not long finished her nurses training in England when in 1941 Rommel took back the axis of power in North Africa for the Germans, and as the Allies were being blasted to Hell and back, Angela volunteered for service in the army medical corps and was posted to the Kasserine Pass in the Atlas Mountains.

She was in her element in Africa looking after the dying and wounded and up to her elbows in blood and guts with shells and bullets flying left right and center, she knew that this was what she was born to do.

The war ended when Hitler cowardly blew his brains out in his bunker in Berlin but it came far too soon for Angela and she went into a spiralling three year depression lasting until 1948. She spent those three years in a clinic being treated for what they called "shell shock", but eventually she was deemed fit again and entered back into mainstream society.

Angela didn't hang around on her laurels for long and by 49 she was working as a nurse at the Royal North Sussex Hospital in Chichester where she stayed for almost ten happy years, but as she grew older a yearning for home began in her heart and she decided to return to the place of her birth, the Isle of Portland in Dorset.

In 1958 Angela moved in with her mother at Whiskey Row, in the small village on the island called Chiswell, and found a job in the local community hospital, where she worked on Kelspar ward, looking after people with blood disorders.

It was during this period that her mother became ill with diabetes and was taken to Angela's ward at the hospital, unfortunately though she died of complications three days later with her daughter at her bedside.

Life went on. Angela worked at the hospital for the next twenty five years doing what she loved to do and it wasn't until 85 when she should be thinking about retiring that another dramatic change occurred in her life once again.

The hundred bed Portland Community Hospital where Angela had been working had been lucky enough to receive a government grant to improve its services, they decided to buy much needed hospital equipment and to have a new admin wing built which would house the latest computers that were becoming very popular and all the hospitals paper documents and patient files would be transferred over to them.

It took almost two years to complete the building phase and another year to transfer all the hospitals files to the new computer system by a band of volunteers. It was one of those volunteers that noticed something very peculiar and immediately contacted the hospital administrator.

One Wednesday morning in December that year, not long after her shift had began, Angela was in the process of treating an old man who had just been admitted to her ward with diabetes complications, when she was approached by a junior nurse who told her that a note had been left saying that she was to report immediately to the administrator's office in the new admin wing.

At first Angela brushed the messenger aside and told her that she was busy and he can wait, the junior nurse tried repeating the message but she got shot down again as Angela all but physically pushed her aside and continued with the patient.

A few minutes later, the ward Sister appeared with the younger nurse by her side and told her the same thing, 'You must immediately report to Sir James in his office.' this time when Angela went to walk away, the Sister grabbed her arm.

'Now Nurse Flannigan!'

Angela turned puce with rage, but she was a professional and knew that the ward was no place for emotions, so she held herself in check, placed the fully loaded syringe that she held in her hand back on to a tray, gave a deep sigh and promptly left the ward.

Angela coughed and brushed away a thick fug of cigar smoke as she brusquely entered Sir James Monkton's office without knocking.

'James James, what's all this nonsense, pulling me off the ward when I'm in the middle of treating a patient, couldn't it have waited!' she was annoyed to say the least. If she was nothing else, one thing Angela was, was assiduous. 'You don't just pull a nurse out of the ward like that, it's just not right!'

The hospital administrator who was waiting for her behind his big oak desk, looked up and removed his glasses and gave a long drawn out sigh.

'Well man, spit it out, what was so damn important that it couldn't wait until the end of my shift?'

Sir James looked tired and weary, he could feel a vein in his temples throb, there weren't many people that he would let talk to him like that.

'Please sit down Angela.'

'No, damn it man, tell me what was so...'

Just then, a man that who had been sitting on a chair at the side of the room unnoticed by Angela, coughed and stood up, which surprised the nurse in to silence.

The grey haired stranger who wore a dark brown suit and had a very serious and stern look on his face, looked at Sir James, who gave a small cough and resettled himself on his thick office chair.

'Uh... Yes yes, please sit down Nurse Flannigan,

something extremely important has come up.' he composed himself and now looked solemn but nervous.

Angela now realising that something serious was afoot, remained silent as she took the chair in front of the desk.

There were no formal introductions between the stranger and the nurse before Sir James cleared his throat and went on to explain that some extremely grave discrepancies had been found in the patient records as they were being transferred to the new computer system, and that heinous crimes had been discovered.

It transpired that over the last fifteen years an unusually high number of patients had of died from cardiac arrests, nothing suspicious about that at the time as heart attacks in hospitals are very common, but after collating the records, it had been discovered that each patient had been under Angela's own personal care, each had been admitted with diabetic complications and that each had been given very high doses of insulin prior to their deaths, more importantly though was that it had been Angela herself that had administered the drug.

The administrator shut the paper folder that he had been reading through and then stared hard at her for a full thirty seconds before speaking again.

'You know that all it will take is one suspicious relative to make a complaint, there would be an exhumation and you'll be facing life in prison.'

Angela turned pale while the administrator wearily sighed and rubbed his eyes.

'What are we going to do with you Angela?

You're an extremely good nurse I won't deny that but I really can't believe you have done this this...' he shook his head and sighed again.

'So far we have discovered...' he rechecked the file before continuing, 'So far we have discovered at least eighty four deaths directly linked to you.' he slammed the folder down on to his desk with a sudden burst of rage.

'*EIGHTY BLOODY FOUR!* Christ woman, what were you thinking? Were you trying to start your own personal undertaker business?' he shook his head and calmed slightly and then looked over at the stranger who had remained silent and emotionless throughout.

'This gentleman is... well you don't need to know his name, he is from a very *special,'* he emphasised the word special, 'establishment on the island. I took the liberty of calling him and we've discussed this... problem.' he rubbed a temple, 'This whole damn mess will ruin the hospital! Damn it woman, your despicable activities will ruin me!' he almost shouted it, 'But we think we may have a solution to all our problems'.

The stranger approached and placed a sheet of paper on the desk in front of Angela.

'Sign this form and cooperate fully with this gentleman and comply with all his requests and he will make sure that all the...' he struggled to find the words, 'The "incriminating" evidence against you, how shall I say it... disappears permanently.' he offered her his fountain pen.

Angela wasn't a stupid woman, far from it, she was as smart as they come, she had to have been to be able to get away with her crimes for so long, but she knew when all the cards were stacked against her.

In silence, Angela took the pen, paused awhile as though she was running some thought around in her head and then made her mark.

It's twenty years later that we catch up once more with Nurse Angela Flannigan, her once luxurious brunette hair has been replaced by a cool pink rinse and she occasionally needs the aid of a cane to walk on her bunion inflicted feet, but one thing that hadn't changed in all this time was that she still wore her starched nurses uniform.

Angela checked the fob watch that hung from her chest, it had just turned 6:30am. She pulled on her heavy wool coat and stepped out in to the brisk early morning as a weak daylight was just beginning to punch its way skywards.

Angela was on her way home to her little cottage down on Whiskey Row, she had just spent the graveyard shift working after having been called out on an emergency the previous evening. She didn't work much these days, she was far too old for it, but sometimes, as in the case last night, her special abilities had been required.

Angela's cottage, the same one that she had inherited from her long dead mother, was tiny compared to modern equivalents, it had been constructed in the early 1700's when it seemed that people were only half the height they are today, the top of Angela's front door frame was only five feet from the ground and just wide enough to squeeze through if you turned sideways. Built out of huge chunks of the famous Portland stone, these particular cottages were a reminder of one of the less salubrious activities that happened on the Isle of Portland between the 16th and 18th Centuries.

The row of five little cottages, including Angela's, are ex pirate cottages, that were designed and built purposefully for buccaneers and smugglers, and unbeknown to anyone but their occupants themselves, each cottage had a secret tunnel built into their cellars. One end of the tunnels led to the small beach at Hallelujah Bay where the pirates would unload their illegal booty under cover of darkness, the other end, which was connected to a long winding tunnel, led to what was later to become the Portland underground hospital.

Ironically the tunnel passed right through the cellars of famed pirate hunter Admiral Percy Prescott's mansion house in Fortuneswell, the idea was that if Prescott ever came looking for pirates at Whiskey Row, the pirates would use the tunnel and hide out in Prescott's very own cellars - Ingenious.

Angela pulled her thick woollen overcoat tight around herself as the early morning wind bit into her ageing bones, she knew she had been a bit silly to take this route rather than use the tunnel to get home, this time of year it could get bitterly cold out especially at this time of day, still, it wouldn't be long until she had a hot mug of tea with a dash of brandy to warm her cockles and would be sitting in front of her blazing fire.

It felt as though the wind was trying to take big bites out of her skin as she crossed the exposed ground of the common up by the Verne prison, and she quickened her step, but she was mindful to keep to the right and away from the huge drop of the Verne moat on her left, a fall here meant certain death.

The Verne moat is what's called a dry moat that was never designed to contain water but as its two hundred feet deep and surrounded by sheer Portland stone walls on both sides, it was as good a deterrent to escaping prisoners as it was to invading armies.

The moat encircles the Verne citadel which was built on the site of an iron age hill fort in 1847 to protect Portland harbour from French invasion, but just over 100 years later it was handed to his majesty's prison service and put to use as a high security facility housing some of the worst criminals in the British penal system.

Angela moved away from the edge of the precarious drop and continued walking along the narrow path, she hadn't gone far when she heard a strange noise ahead of her, it sounded like it could be an injured animal, maybe a fox or even a badger, little high pitched yelps and a soft whimpering drifted towards her. Angela loved animals and if there was one in distress she would have been straight over to help it.

She looked about but there was nothing to be seen, the whimpering sound came again but louder this time, yet she still couldn't see its source, it must have been her ears playing tricks on her or the wind carrying the sound from elsewhere she thought and continued walking, but a few steps later and the sound came to her a third time, a lot louder and a lot nearer..

Angela began moving towards the sound but suddenly came to an abrupt halt as a dark shape materialised in front of her as it unbelievably slithering up over the lip of the moat.

Angela watched in shocked horror as the form of a man came scrambling up over the edge of the shear two hundred foot drop that was the Verne prison moat, and with bloodied fingers digging deep into the top soil, gave a final weary groan and heaved himself up onto the safety of the flat grassy earth.

If this vision had shocked her, it was nothing compared to the sight that she witnessed next.

Another groaning sound took her eyes back to the edge of the moat and again another shape slowly rose from the impossible climb, this second apparition was a huge bald headed behemoth of a man with shoulders the size of a bus, he came scrabbling and clawing up onto the flat ground and rested on his hands and knees.

If the old woman hadn't already been trembling with fear and shock by now, then she surely would as the huge man lifted his head skywards and ruptured the still morning with a wolf like howl that seemed to never end, before he staggered to his feet, took a handful of stumbling steps forward and promptly collapsed in an unconscious heap next to his companion.

No doubt any normal man or woman would have called an ambulance, or maybe even taken flight at the frightening spectacle that had just transpired on the bleak, windblown edge of the Verne prison moat, but not Nurse Flannigan, her brain thought quickly and it was mere seconds before she had formulated a plan.

The first man that had so shockingly dragged himself up over the edge of the moat lay on his back gasping for breath, his face was almost black with dirt and grime and streaks of blood.

As far as Angela could tell he looked to be in his thirties, his hair was matted with dirt and mud that clung to his scalp but she could see wisps of light brown in amongst the matted mess, his hands were thick with red tinged dirt and it looked like most of his fingernails were either missing or hanging on by threads of tissue.

Her nurses eyes travelled down the man's body, scanning for wounds, she paused at the mud caked end of a broken rib that protruded from his chest and tutted quietly, then continued down to his legs, the bulge of the tibia under the man's left trouser leg told her all she needed to know to realise that it was horribly broken, she looked him over again and noted how very thin he was, almost stick like she thought.

The man groaned as she knelt next to him and carefully touched his shoulder, the man turned his head and looked at her through blood-shot pleading eyes.

'Please help me.'

'Don't worry, everything will be ok, I'm a nurse.' Angela gently took hold of the man's hand and began standing slowly, 'Try to stand if you can, lean on me it'll help.'

The injured man cried in agony as he slowly managed to stand on his one good leg then wrapped an arm around her shoulders for support. Now taking the man's full weight, Angela took a few delicate steps but the man suddenly let out a blood curdling scream as she knocked the protruding rib bone, she shut her eyes as the tormented cry echoed around her and brought back so many memories from the war.

When she opened her eyes again she looked hard at the wretch standing next to her.

'I'm sorry.'

Her eyes really did show sorrow as she gave the man a thrust backwards and he went flying off into the abyss of the moat, surprisingly he didn't make a single sound as he fell the two hundred feet and smashed into the rocks far below.

Angela turned her attention to the unconscious bald headed man.

The long cold winter, finally gave up its battle and let the spring in. Daffodils and crocus flowers were already blooming as nurse Angela Flannigan paid for her meagre shopping at the Co-op in Fortuneswell, tonight was a special night though, so she had used the last of her pension to buy a half pint bottle of brandy for the purpose, that's if she survived the journey home, as a police car with its blues and twos suddenly appeared from nowhere and almost knocked her over.

As an electronic reminder alarm peeped, Angela put down her coffee cup and checked the fluid level in a saline solution drip pouch, she noted the figure and wrote it down on a clipboard hanging from the end of a hospital bed, she then read through some of the other handwritten notes that were already written there: Anterior dislocation of right shoulder, laceration of the neck into the sternocleidomastoid muscle, subluxation of the right glenohumeral, Colles fracture of the right wrist, effusion of multiple joints, dislocated left patella and severe trauma to both hands. It read like a shopping list.

'My my, you were in a bad way young man, it looks like you've been in a car crash?'

The male patient chuckled and sat up in the bed.

'I don't know what I would have done without your help Nurse Flannigan, I really don't.'

The nurse's cheeks flushed with mild embarrassment, 'I was only doing my job, you know that Eric.'

She lifted the patients right hand and inspected the scarring on the stump remains of where three fingers should have been, 'They've healed up very nicely, it shows you have a marvellous healing system my dear.'

Angela walked towards the door but stopped before leaving and turned back to the man, 'Oh and by the way Eric, you are being discharged today and can leave this evening after tea.' she smiled warmly and closed the door quietly behind her.

The big burly man was overjoyed at this news, he was fed up to the hind teeth with all this laying in bed and was eager to get on his way. Nurse Flannigan was a sweet old bird but he couldn't wait another minute to meet up with his younger brother again.

The old nurse had been very very understanding after she had found him and Trev up by the prison that morning, she hadn't even called the cops even though it was so obvious that they had just broken out.

Actually, now he thought about it, Nurse Flannigan had been truly amazing about the whole thing, she had nursed him and Trev back to health, and when Trev was better she had found him a little place to stay while he waited for him to gain consciousness and recover himself, she'd even fed him like he was a

King with huge home-made meals and the stickiest of cakes, what a woman!

The kettle whistled excitedly and Angela switched off the gas, she poured the water into a teapot and placed it on the tray before her.

Eric was daydreaming again, he did a lot of that lately, this time he had been daydreaming about finally meeting up with his brother Trev after all these months. His brothers absence had been hard to take at first, but Nurse Flannigan had told him that it was vital they remained separated, less they aroused suspicion, she could just about fool the neighbours that Eric was some distant relative but she couldn't make excuses as to why there were two men living in her little cottage, she had told him, and of course she was right, he should just be thankful that she hadn't gone to the police and that she had taken care of them both herself instead of taking them to the hospital where the game would have been up for sure.

Nurse Flannigan bumped Eric out of his daydream as she appeared by the man's bedside with a tray of food and happily reminded him that as soon as he had eaten he could leave and that he would be meeting Trev really soon.

'But first, you need to take your last dose of medicine.'

Angela put her hand into her tunic pocket and removed a small glass bottle, 'As it's a special occasion, here's a special dose of medicine,' she smiled as she showed Eric the bottle of brandy in her hand.

Eric clapped his hands together as Angela poured him a double shot into a plastic medicine cup and handed it over. Eric thanked her and downed it in one.

'Damn! that hit the spot.' he groaned as the alcohol burnt its way into his stomach.

'Language!' Angela joked, 'Now eat your tea and you can go my dear.'

Eric could hardly contain his excitement as he tucked into the food on his plate.

'Thank you again for everything Nurse Flannigan.' he repeated for the hundredth time, between mouthfuls of a thick bacon butty whilst grease dribbled down his chin.

'No need to thank me dear, as I've said, I'm just doing my job.'

'This bacon is delicious by the way, I've never tasted anything so good.' he told her as he demolished the food and wiped his chin clean with a paper napkin.

'I know dear.' she replied, 'We have a special breed of pig here on Portland, they're very rare, we even have a special name for them dear.'

Eric nodded losing interest in the conversation already, she said something about the breed of Portland pig being called Camberling or Kimberling, or something like that, but his attention was already on other matters, he leant back on his pillows and rubbed his full stomach.

'What about Trev? Can I see him as soon as I leave here?' Eric asked after a few minutes silence.

The nurse remained silent for awhile longer as she filled out a form and clipped it to the clipboard at the end of the bed.

'Well...' she looked at Eric, 'Remember how I told you that you'd meet your brother again *really* soon?'

she smiled and placed the empty plate back on the tray then looked at the greasy remains, 'Well you just have my dear.'

A look of confusion spread over Eric's face and he started to ask her what she meant, but he began to feel a little light headed and his vision began to blur.

'What do you... Where's... What's going... I don't feel...' suddenly he couldn't move his lips or mouth and he began to panic.

Eric tried to shout and get up but he was paralysed and couldn't move a muscle.

Just then, right on queue, the door opened and in walked two men wearing green surgical gowns and face masks, all Eric could do was evacuate his bowels.

In March 2022, Nurse Flannigan, who had all but retired from nursing and spent her days watching American murder mysteries on Freeview and knitting, got a call on her mobile phone, her special skills were required once again.

The patient that required Nurse Flannigan's attention was a middle aged pregnant woman called Ruth, she had been taken to the underground hospital near Castletown instead of the NHS Trust hospital in the same vicinity because Ruth was a very central cog of an ongoing scientific experiment that was due to come to fruition very very soon.

The patient had been admitted to BreakSpear ward four days previous and was an incredible fourteen months pregnant, the extended gestation was fully expected though and was the result of many years of research and experimentation by the doctors at the

Portland Environmental Trust, who had a special purpose for the hybrid that grew inside her.

Ruth gave birth at 23:54 on the Friday night by caesarian section, the 20lb infant was removed and immediately taken to another room deeper in the complex for use with project X12. A newborn baby from the Portland orphanage was placed in the incubator at the end of Ruth's bed in its stead ready for when she awoke from the anaesthetic.

Nurse Flannigan was in a small operating theatre ready and waiting to receive Ruth's placenta, its recipient was prepped and ready on the operating table in front of her.

As she waited for the arrival of the specially bred chemically enriched afterbirth, she took a good look at the unconscious body lying before her, its name escaped her now but she remembered the day it came clambering out of the Verne moat and those bus sized shoulders, it was a lot thinner these days but that wasn't surprising as it had been held in a comatose vegetative state for nine years.

The body's face was completely unrecognisable now as most of it had long since been removed, along with most of its skull the day that the Trust took him, in their place was some sort of biological organism that had been grafted to his brain stem and if one was to look hard enough at the organism, they might have seen the little stumps where tiny arms and legs used to be and what could once have been a little human head.

The human hybrid organism pulsed and shuddered and gave a little cry that sounded almost like a newborn baby.

Angela knew from experience that the things six month feeding cycle meant that it was now hungry again, she leaned in close to what resembled a tiny ear.

'Don't worry little one, food is on its way.' she lovingly stroked a gloved hand over the quivering jellied flesh just as the theatres door opened and lunch of fresh chemically enriched placenta arrived.

From Russia with Sisterly Love

In 1957 during the height of the cold war, the USSR stunned the world and kick started the space race by launching the first ever living creature into space onboard the Sputnik 2. While Laika the dog floated around space looking for the nearest lamp post, back on Earth in the poor animals home country, a harsh stinging wind howled across frozen lake Labaz, icicles hung like daggers from wind blasted trees, while a dirty mix of snow and grit sandblasted car paintwork and etched unprotected windscreens, welcome to Petrekovia somewhere deep inside the Eastern Bloc.

Yelena Kushnova shivered as she hurriedly double locked the heavy steel security door of the state run research laboratory behind her, she wrapped her thick scarf tightly around her neck and pulled her rabbit ushanka down over her ears, a few wisps of her blonde hair bristled as she stepped out into the minus twenty two centigrade blizzard.

Work was done for the day, it had been another long twelve hour shift and as usual she was too late for any public transport.

The ice crunched under the thirty five year olds boots as she began a long forty minute trudge through the packed snow, she was tired and hungry and longed to get home, home, now there's an oxymoron, home should be a happy place, a place where you can rest your weary head comfortable in the knowledge that your home is your castle, a place where you felt safe, but Yelena's home was none of these things, home for Yelena was a one bedroom flat on the 43rd floor of tower G, Rimmschovec Street, just one of the many dark grey imposing tower blocks built in the early 50's by the state for the people, a place where the powers that be could keep an eye on the comings and goings of everyone.

The one hundred and fifty towers stood sentinel like, soaring high into the sky blocking out what weak sun there was, the pavements are in continuous shadow on Rimmschovec Street.

A dog began snarling and barking in one of her neighbours flats as Yelena opened the door and entered her dank dominion, the window glass creaked nervously in its rusting metal frame as a sharp wind whistled through a spiderweb of cracks in the dirty glass. She had filled in a form at the town hall for the windows to be repaired but she was near the bottom of the list and was told that a repair would be at least two years away yet.

The paper thin walls did nothing to block the incessant howling as the dog barked on, the flat was as cold inside as it was outside.

Yelena Kushnova's job as one of the countries leading animal research scientists made no difference in Petrekovia, everybody was equally a nobody here, the state let you exist only as long as you had a use and that was it.

She grabbed a threadbare black jumper and pulled it over her head and wished there was some heating in the flat but she knew that she would need to be a full party member and be promoted at work to be able to get the necessary licence for a small one-bar fire.

The 'studio apartment' as it was listed in official documents, consisted of just two rooms, an open plan living room come kitchen come bedroom and a toilet and shower room, there was nothing more.

Yelena picked up the last tin can from the table, the label only had one word on it "soup", she hoped that it was tomato and not meat soup, she hated meat soup, meat can mean so many things. Yelena pierced the can top with her pocket knife (all women in Petrekovia carry a knife), and placed it directly on the gas ring to heat. Five minutes later she poured its contents into two chipped mugs, thankfully it was mushroom.

Carefully, so as not to spill a drop of the precious fluid, Yelena carried the mugs through a heavy cloth sheet slung over a rope that ran from wall to wall and walked into to the bedroom area, this part of the room was devoid of any furniture except for a double bed, a broken wardrobe and a large pot to piss in when it was just too cold to get out of bed and go to the bathroom.

A svelte figure with the most vibrant natural red hair lay huddled under the bedsheets and watched the woman enter, her arm reached out to unburden Yelena of one of the steaming mugs of soup and mumbled a thank you, Yelena climbed in next to her and kissed her on the lips.

'It's the last for today.' she looked at her sister and smiled.

The nourishing soup was soon devoured and the mugs licked clean sending a comforting glow through both their bodies, but it wasn't enough to sate them and the sisters began to hug and devour each others bodily warmth as their hands explored each others thin bodies, their soup warmed lips kissed each other passionately, their tongues intertwined as the fervour built and within minutes the siblings started making love, the sex between them was base and animal but it served both their purposes.

A water weak tepid sun, tried to creep through the ragged curtains of the flat on the 43rd floor of tower G, Rimmschovec Street but failed miserably.

Yelena reached out for her discarded clothes and got dressed under the bedsheets as it was far to cold to stand naked in the room, she kissed her still sleeping sister gently on the forehead.

'Tatty, Tatiana, its time to wake up, you'll be late for work.'

The twenty one year redhead stretched and rubbed sleep from her eyes and smiled at her sister, she longed for a shower but it was Tuesday and the hot water wouldn't be back on until Friday, she wanted to stay in bed and savour its warmth.

Tatiana hated her job in the tinning factory but knew that she was one of the lucky ones and if it wasn't for her job and the occasional chance to steal a few cans, neither she or Yelena would have eaten lately. She just *loved* Socialism.

Slowly, Tatiana dressed under the bed covers and reluctantly joined her sister who was huddled by the one ring gas burner stove in the kitchen area.

A sudden loud hammering on the door startled them both, a loud voice with a distinct British accent startled them even more.

'Dr Kushnova! This is the British Consulate, open the door please, I need to speak to you.' the deep voice resonated from the other side of the thin sheet of wood causing a sprinkle of dust to fall to the floor.

The knocking came again.

'Open the door please Dr Kushnova, it's most urgent that I speak to you.'

Yelena hesitated a moment and a worried look spread across her face. She knew only too well that it could be the MVD, the ministry of internal affairs, everybody in Petrekovia knew that people vanished mysteriously from their homes never to be seen again, no reasons were needed, guilty or innocent made no difference here, at any moment night or day your door could be kicked in and you would never be heard from again.

Yelena steadied her nerve and took a deep breath then opened the door wide. A brown suited man stood before her, he wore wire spectacles and his greying hair was as thin as his face, Yelena knew instantly that the stranger wasn't the MVD, no MVD agent could be that thin, they stuffed their bourgeois faces at the expense of the people, plus no MVD agent would be seen dead in a brown three piece suit.

The man smiled at her warmly and offered her his

ID card and then held out a thick brown envelope which had a single word stamped on its front in red ink – P.E.T. He leant in close and began whispering in her ear.

Dawn was breaking, the flaccid sun wept its way over the horizon like a dry tear and the cold morning air bit deeply into the two sisters pale skin. Yelena and Tatiana stood in the shadows of a large shipping container blowing into their hands, a small beaten suitcase stood between them which contained their entire worldly goods, Yelena stamped her feet to keep herself warm and Tatiana checked her government sanctioned watch.

'It's almost time sis.'

They looked out across the small shipyard to where the steel grey sea lapped at the icy dock and shivered some more.

Twenty minutes later, an ageing fishing trawler spluttered into life as it fired up its diesel engine creating a blue grey plume of exhaust fumes which spread lazily upwards. A bright torch was shone through one of the boats cabin windows and flashed on and off three times in quick succession.

'That's it, that's the signal.'

The two girls gave each other a hug before ducking out of their cover and sprinting across the open space in front of them, up the gangplank and onto the boat, where they were greeted by a short stocky man wearing a thick black moustache and a woollen hat, he eyed them up and down and held out a stubby hand.

'Money?'

Yelena pushed her hand deep into her pocket and withdrew a rolled up wad of roubles, they were just one of the items from the envelope she had been given days before.

The man licked a tobacco stained finger and flicked through the notes with a well practised agility, he coughed and spat a mouthful of green phlegm over the gunwale into the sea and his mood lightened.

'Anatoly will show you to your quarters, stay out of sight until you are called ok.' it wasn't a question, it was an order.

The girls quarters turned out to be a small storeroom below decks that they shared with some stinking old nets, fishing lines and other detritus from the sixty year old clinker built boat.

Food, if and when it came was mostly plates of fried fish and hard salt bread along with mugs of hot tea which kept them warm in the cramped space during their eight day journey.

Eventually the trawlers engine slowed to a coughing splutter and the sisters felt the boat banging against concrete.

Yelena and Tatiana both blinked in the bright light as they were escorted topside and onto the deck an hour later, the moustachioed sailor was waiting for them.

'Welcome to your new home.' he laughed and coughed as he pointed out towards the foreign vista then he thrust a handful of coins into Yelena's hand.

'English money... Now go, wait in that building there, drink tea, someone will contact you.' the man nodded to a small inviting looking building on the quayside, it had a large sign above its door, The Bluefin Cafe.

'Go now, drink tea and wait.' he repeated, then added, 'And don't mention rabbits.' the sailor laughed and coughed at his own humour, then disappeared below decks.

Yelena and Tatiana Kushnova, sisters, refugees from Petrekovia, had travelled 1800 nautical miles and had arrived on the isle of Portland in the United Kingdom.

True to the sailors word, an hour later, a brown haired middle aged man walked in through the cafe door, he knew exactly who he was looking for and sat at their table, he stared at Yelena, his face was stern.

'You have paper sheath?' his broken Russian was bad and just barely understandable.

Yelena rummaged through her small suitcase and handed the stranger the crumpled envelope with the word P.E.T stamped on its front in red ink, he opened it and peered inside then looked back at Yelena.

'Good hello to Portland gentlemen.'

The man's pock marked face broke into a wide warm smile and he stood and offered out his hand, 'My implement is Coombs, Jonathon Coombs, you can rust me.'

The weary travellers rolled their eyes and contained sniggers as they did their best to understand the man's odd language. After he had bought them all a few more cups of tea, and a small interruption when one of the waiters caused a ruckus by pouring hot water over a blind man's dog and it scarpered out the door dragging the poor man with it, they all climbed into Coombs' car and were driven up through

Fortuneswell to the top of the island, only stopping briefly at a set of electrified security gates where a guard checked the man's ID and waved them through. The sisters looked at each other and both had the same thought *it's not much different here to back home.*

On the journey, Coombs had tried his best to explain that when the trio reached their destination, a woman would be waiting for them with their new ID cards, her name was Georgina and she was to be their liaison officer, she would help the girls settle in and would be their first point of contact if they had any problems or questions.

He explained that although they would be living and working in a high security zone, they weren't being confined and they were most definitely not prisoners, they would be free to come and go as they pleased.

The girls accommodation would be a spacious apartment in the grounds and they could use the gym facilities and on site spa, they would also be offered English lessons if they so wished.

Yelena of course had already been briefed about the reason why she had been brought to Portland and during the second week on site, she had been introduced to her peers and contemporaries where every single detail was explained in full by Georgina, who thankfully spoke fluent Russian

She learnt that Portland had a very serious problem and that her expertise was very much needed to help solve it. The project she was to be working on was called X12, the details seemed incredible at first, unbelievable even, and it wasn't until Yelena had encountered the problem first hand that she finally believed and accepted that such dangerous children could and do exist.

Two years passed, both girls attended English lessons and were soon talking the language. Yelena, was promoted to team leader on project X12 and the team had had some successes, and now thanks personally to Yelena there was a way to safely contain the problem as well as easing the strange children's suffering, but they still had a long way to go yet.

In July that year, project X12 was put on a temporary hiatus when an incredibly virulent toxic virus began effecting the farm animals on the island.

The virus was first detected in the carcasses of foxes and badgers and then in bovine on a farm near Southwell not far from the famous lighthouse, when all the farms cattle over two years of age suddenly died overnight, the surviving animals who were all pregnant cows, went on to give birth to mutilated and deformed young that died within a few days.

A week later the same thing happened half a mile away at Travis' goat farm in the old Suckthumb quarry. The virus spread exponentially, like wildfire, until 98% of all animals, domesticated and wild, on the island were dead.

Officials from the Trust tried to keep the outbreak quiet as their scientists battled to find a cure, until the MAFF (Ministry of Agriculture Fisheries and Food) over on the mainland, got whiff of it and immediately set up a cordon on Beach Road to hopefully stop its spread off the island.

MAFF scientists also began working on a vaccine but after eight months they were still as clueless as the

Portland Trusts scientists to what they had designate H9N41.

It was obvious that this situation couldn't continue, with no livestock on the island and none being allowed to pass the cordon, in or out, the residents began to suffer.

It was two days after the first suspected case of H9N41 was detected in a human that the Trust finally "remembered" that they just happened to have one of the worlds leading scientists in the field of animal microbiology already working for them, their oversight could possibly be forgiven though, because Yelena was enrolled in the Trusts covert Relocation Program, so her identity was secret to all but those at the very top and even then only on a need to know basis.

Yelena was immediately transferred to the H9N41 problem and her new team set about working on a vaccine.

Yelena's new team of six, seven if you included her sister Tatiana, who was employed as a lab technician, had many failures and knock backs over the coming weeks but at the end of the following month, Yelena Kushnova made the first major but ultimately tragic breakthrough, which came quite by chance.

'Tatty, can you get me a new box of testing solution please.'

Yelena stepped back from the microscope eyepieces and rubbed her tired eyes.

'Test on slide 134 completed and it's another fail.' she dictated into the desktop recorder, '66 to go.' she sighed heavily and inserted another slide under the scope.

Yelena had been aiming to test two hundred slides a day in her continual quest to find a vaccine for the terrible pathogen that was devastating Portland's animals, and more importantly, to try and stop any mutations that would allow it to become highly transmissible in humans, but so far the search had been fruitless.

There had already been one isolated case of H9N41 being detected in a human, but that person had underlying health conditions and a compromised immune system, which made them more susceptible, but even so, Yelena's findings had shocked her to the core and if what she suspected were true, then God help all of mankind.

She confided in her boss, Jonathon Coombs and told him of her suspicions, he promised that there would be a full investigation in time and to leave it with him.

Once Yelena and her team had discovered, through genome sequencing and genetic characterisation, using an adapted machine called a Mitchell narrow-beam phylogenetic detector (originally developed by another Portlander called Henry Mitchell), that H9N41was a hybrid avian and swine influenza strain, which had many mutated single-stranded Nucleotides. It was now down to testing samples of effected animals RNA with various anti-pathogen solutions that the team had developed.

The daily drill now was simple but exhausting, take a prepared slide of mutated animal RNA from the sterile box, add two drops of that days testing solution, view the slide under the microscope for any changes, record results on the voice recorder and repeat ad nauseam.

Yelena gave her tense muscles a quick stretch as she placed yet another slide under the scope.

'Still nothing? Don't worry sis, you'll figure it out in the end.' Tatiana said as she placed the new box of solution on the worktop.

'I just hope the *end's* not too late.' Yelena replied as she opened a fresh vial of solution and added two drops to the slide.

She thought about the first human death from H9N41 that had occurred the previous week, and her previous suspicions were re-ignited, *something is definitely not right here*, the thought terrified her.

'Test on slide 135 completed and its another fai...' she stopped mid sentence did a double take and rubbed her eyes again, surely she hadn't just witnessed what she thought she had, Yelena placed her eyes against the microscope again and peered at slide number 135, there were the green and pink cells with their twisted and deformed RNA strings, exactly as they had been time and time again on the tests already performed, yet this particular slide had definite signs of regeneration.

Yelena picked up the vial of testing solution that contained the substance she had dripped onto the slide and checked its identification label, but instead of the expected eight digit code number, there was only the word HH17 written in Biro.

Confused, she examined the slide through the eyepieces once more, yes without doubt there was regeneration of the damaged cell, in fact in the space of the twenty seconds she had spent checking the vial, more cells on the slide had began to regenerate.

Yelena scratched her head perplexed.

'Tatty, where did you get this box of testing solution from?'

It was Tatiana's turn to look confused.

'Out of the fridge why, what's up?'

'But did you prepare the solution yourself?'

'Yes, like I always do, why, is there a problem with it?'

'No, no problem, quite the opposite actually, this slide shows signs of biological regeneration which is amazing, but the label on this vial just says HH17.' she pointed at the little glass tube, 'It could contain anything.' 'Do you know what HH17 is?'

'Are you sure? The HH range is human haemoglobin and shouldn't be in that box at all.' then a sudden look of realisation dawned across her face.

'Oh my God sis, I'm sorry, this morning I had just finished preparing the Mandies and Dr Walsh came in and distracted me, I guess I must have put one of the Mandies in the testing solution box by mistake.'

'Mandies? What the Hell are Mandies?'

'The mandatory's, you know, the mandatory blood tests everyone has once a month for "health reasons", I draw all the bloods from everyone on-site, although I think they are to test for recreational drugs more than anything else though.'

The mandatory blood samples should have gone to a different lab for testing but it seems that the siblings error had been a Godsend.

Then a thought struck Yelena, this revelation could only mean that the blood of someone working for the Trust held a potential vaccine for this terrible virus.

'You wonderful girl.' Yelena hugged her sister

178

tightly, 'You might have just solved this bloody crisis.'

It took another two weeks of tests with the remaining human haemoglobin sample before Yelena could take it forward and develop a working vaccine that stopped the virus in its tracks.

Of course she had told her superiors about the anonymous human blood sample that had been the catalyst of the discovery, to which they had responded by getting everyone in the entire complex re-tested for a match.

The question now though was who exactly was that match, which of the employees at the Trust had such precious and valuable blood.

Two weeks later, almost three years to the day that Yelena and Tatiana had first arrived on Portland, they finally managed to have their first proper day off from their exhausting schedule, and they planned to make the most of it.

First they would go to the on-site spa and spend the morning in the sauna and jacuzzi unwinding, then a visit to the shopping center in Easton for some purse busting shopping, followed by an evening at an Italian restaurant and a visit to a nightclub to let their hair down, it sounded like a plan.

'Get the door sis.' Yelena called out at the sound of someone knocking on their apartment door and continued packing her gym bag, a few minutes later she entered the lounge and found Tatiana sitting on the sofa with Jonathon Coombs the sector head.

'Ahh here she is, the golden girl.' he stood and smiled.

'Hey it wasn't just me you know, it was Tatty's...

"oversight" that was the breakthrough.' she countered slightly miffed.

'I know I know and that's the reason I'm here, girls, I wanted to thank you both personally for your incredible help with this awful virus and to tell you that your achievements have been noticed by those higher up and they are pleased, very pleased with you both.' he lifted a bottle of Champagne that he'd held hidden behind his back and smiled some more before continuing.

'I know you're in a hurry to enjoy your free time but those upstairs have asked me to toast you both.' he didn't give them the opportunity to decline the gesture as he quickly popped the cork.

'Glasses?' he laughed as the fizz spilled out of the bottle.

As Tatiana rushed off to find glasses, Yelena quietly reminded Coombs about her suspicions over the source off the H9N41 virus, he whispered back that it was being investigated and everything that could be done was being done and not too worry.

Mugs had to suffice and Coombs made a big show of filling them to over-flowing

'Once again, congratulations girls on your incredible achievement, were all proud of you.'

The girls took a sip of the bubbly and giggled, they had never tasted Champagne before. Coombs watched over the rim of his mug as Yelena and Tatiana both finished their drinks in two gulps.

The sauna was scorchingly hot, Yelena and Tatiana had never been in a sauna before and they were loving it. They lazed naked on the wooden benches sweating nicely.

As the needle hit 65c, Yelena spooned another ladle of cold water onto the hot coals which sizzled and created a thick plume of steam, she relaxed again.

'This is the life eh Tatty.' no reply was needed and she closed her eyes.

The girls enjoyed the moment, lost in their own thoughts. Yelena remembered back to her ice cold flat in Petrekovia and the daily daggers of ice that she had to dodge on her way to work each day and shivered.

Five minutes later, Tatiana broke the silence.

'Yelena... Yelena... I uh... I don't feel so good... It's too hot in here, I think I'm going to...' Tatiana's head was spinning and her vision was darkening, she began to panic and looked at her sister for help, but Yelena was slumped on her side, her glazed eyes were wide open and a line of white foamy saliva ran down her cheek.

It's 2023 and not far from Portland Bill's famous red and white striped lighthouse, away from the tourist areas and out of view, is a large tract of land that's surrounded by two rows of electrified razor wire, signs affixed to the fencing state that beyond is private property and that trespassers will be prosecuted to the full extent of the law. This stretch of land abuts the southern end of the Sweethill complex but is far enough away from it that no one ever visits the area.

In the middle of this land is a small two storey white washed cottage surrounded by well tended rose bushes.

If you were able to cross the razor wire fences and visit the white washed cottage on a warm summer day, you might see an old woman sitting in a sun chair with a blanket draped over her knees.

The woman is very old now and her once blonde hair had long turned grey, she probably hasn't got long left on this planet and she knows it. If you were to speak to her, you might notice the slight Russian twang in her voice, that's if she replies at all though, she prefers not talking these days, she knows better than to talk to people.

Legend has it that somewhere on Portland is a secret hospital, if that secret hospital really did exist and you were to look in one of its mostly empty wards, you might come across a red haired patient that's in a permanent vegetative state and is being kept alive by a multitude of advanced machines that beep and ping constantly.

If the patient was able to speak she might tell you that she has very very rare blood, so rare that it is still used today as the main ingredient in a vaccine for never-ending virus.

A Curious Case of Twinacide

The smell of cordite assailed his nostrils as tendrils of smoke drifted from the sawn off barrels of his Webley and Scott 12 gauge, Eddie looked down at the lifeless body of his twin brother but he didn't feel bad about firing the shotgun at his head, it was something that had to be done.

He turned towards the sofa and looked at the two decapitated victims that his brother had placed there, yes he had been right, it *had* to be done, it was the only way to stop the killing spree.

Eddie reloaded the shotgun with two more Lyalvale Supreme cartridges and placed it on the dining table before walking to the kitchen where he calmly made himself a cup of tea, he sat at the kitchen table and tried not to look at the decapitated little girl sitting opposite him.

Eddie finished his drink, washed the mug and hung it back on the mug tree on a sideboard and headed back to the living room. He stood next to the dining table and looked at the remains of his brother again and remembered some of the good times from their childhood together when they were growing up here at Blacknor bunker, there weren't many and didn't he didn't shed any tears.

Eddie picked up the shotgun and and placed its still warm barrels under his chin.

Not far from the village of Weston over on the west side of the island is the area known as Blacknor, its mostly cow fields and the odd farmhouse but little else, there's also an old decommissioned military bunker complex sat right on the cliffs edge looking out to sea.

The eighteenth century bunker, built of Portland stone, was split into two parts, there was the single storey upper deck which was built at ground level and had a WWII gun emplacement constructed on its roof, it had once been equipped with a 6 inch Mark VII breech-loader for targetting ships far out at sea, the naval gun was removed at the end of the war when the bunker was decommissioned and turned over to civilian hands.

This part of the bunker had been been converted in the 50's into a more conventional abode with a kitchen and bathroom, a living room, three bedrooms and a study.

The lower part of the fort which had remained untouched, consisted of seven underground levels interconnected by a maze of tunnels, passages and a multitude of rooms and they remained an unlit damp and decaying labyrinth.

The outside of the fort which stood on a two acre plot surrounded by an eight foot high chain link fence, resembled more of a smallholding rather than a garden or yard, and over the years, a collection of ramshackle caravans had been collected and lined up along one side by the current owners, identical twins, Eddie and Gavin Stanford, both 79, the eldest being Eddie by three minutes.

The brothers lived together in the bunker complex sharing its facilities and tending to its grounds on the cliff tops. They lived a simplistic life growing their own vegetables in the unusually fertile soil and raising a handful of animals, water was drawn from the last remaining deep well on the island which was in the depths of the cellars and had to be pumped up to a storage sump on the upper deck via a hand pump once a month.

All in all the brothers were pretty much self sufficient and only left their domain a couple of times a year for a trip into Weston where they would stock up on the things they couldn't manufacture or grow themselves.

The brother's close lifestyle was a strange one considering that both men hated each other and they hadn't said a single word to each other in over fifty years. As with a lot of disputes, the origins of the Stanford brother's squabble was over some trivial matter that at the time could probably have been solved easily if the pair had just sat down and talked about it, but they didn't and the row escalated out of all proportion.

Now, years later, the two of them couldn't even remember what had caused the feud in the first place. Whilst the brothers hated the very sight of each other and avoided one another at all costs, they did have one shared common interest, and that was that they loved killing Kimberlins for fun.

They absolutely hated anybody that wasn't born and bred on the island and in their eyes Portland was for pure blood Portlanders only and woe betide anyone that they came across that couldn't prove their Portland lineage, luckily for the majority of Kimberlins, the pair hardly left their abode so they didn't come across many *foreigners* in their general day to day lives.

Their absolute hatred for all things non-Portland was so great that it meant that they had never stepped foot off the island in all their 79 years, not once.

This hatred of Kimberlins came to a head in the early 1980's when an up and coming young rock climbing enthusiast, while holidaying on the island, discovered the amazing cliff faces of the Blacknor area, he belayed the cliffs several times whilst enjoying his holiday on Portland and quickly realised that there was something quite special about those cliffs. It wouldn't of been so bad if the enthusiast had kept the knowledge to himself, but the young man also happened to be the editor of one of London's leading rock climbing magazines, and after an article appeared in his magazine extolling the virtues of the walls and crags at Blacknor, it wasn't long before climbers began visiting from all over the country.

The first time the twins discovered their newly found and unwelcome fame, was one early evening when a climber wearing a bright yellow helmet and climbing harness, strayed to far towards the bunker and his climb took him right past one of the partially bricked up old cannon ports which looked straight in

186

to the forts interior, the climber was beyond shocked to find a brick lined hole half way up a rock-face and he was even more shocked when Gavin launched himself out from the hole like a trapdoor spider pouncing on its prey, pulled the surprised climber inside and proceeding to stab him to death with his turnip knife.

When Eddie discovered what his brother had done that first time, he had helped him clean up the mess and disposed of the body deep down in the forts underbelly, he even went to the top of the cliffs and removed all traces that the climber had ever been there.

Five more climbers vanished from the Blacknor cliffs over the next few years by the brothers hands and they still hadn't spoken a word to each other.

Back in 1960, one of the the twins neighbours, a farmer called Evans, approached the brothers about the purchase of some land adjacent to both their properties, the land was being sold off by the Portland Trust, who owned most of the land on the island and had decided to sell off some unwanted plots.

Evans had wanted to introduce llamas to his farm and start breeding them for their wool and so some extra land was just what he needed, the only problem was that the parcel of land was just too big and expensive for him to take on alone, so he visited the brothers to put to them an idea he'd had.

Evans knew that the brothers could always use a little more land for their vegetables and livestock and hoped that if they went fifty fifty with him, and they bought the plot together, they could come up with some sort of arrangement about it.

The brothers liked the idea, it was true that they had been wanting to have some pigs and maybe a sheep or two, especially after the H9N41 outbreak a few years back, so more land was always welcome and a deal was quickly struck.

The understanding was that Evans and the twins would purchase the land together, with both sides paying exactly 50% of the asking price, a verbal agreement was made stating that each party would use their half of land in perpetuity until one of them wanted to sell, at that point the other party would have first refusal to purchase the others half of the land at the then current market prices, the men shook hands and everybody was happy with the deal.

Zoom forward 30 years and in 1997 farmer Evans had decided to retire, his llama business had long ago failed, it turned out that at the time llama wool was just too progressive for Portland.

Evans spoke to the brothers declaring his intentions to sell but added that he had already received a good offer for his part of the land from an off-island developer who had plans to build 75 houses on it, the twins were naturally horrified and reminded Evans about their gentleman's agreement, the conversation got a little heated but Evans was adamant, he was going to sign the contract with the developers the very next day.

That afternoon a note was pushed through the farmers door inviting him to the twins abode, it stated that they wished to apologise for their outburst that morning and now wanted to sign.

At 8pm precisely, Evans knocked on the front door of the bunker and was greeted by Gavin and a very big gun, Gavin wasted no time in pointing his shotgun at Evans, aiming low and firing both barrels at point blank range.

Mrs Evans who was waiting for her husband at the gate, unfortunately witnessed her man's body being ripped in half at the waist and promptly fainted on the spot.

Gavin was swiftly arrested and charged with first degree murder, he was locked in the cells in Fortuneswell to await a visit by the Portland Reeve who would set a trial date, but pure blood runs thick on Portland.

The Reeve sat alone in the cells with Gavin and they talked in depth in whispered tones for an hour before he left. Gavin was released on police bail by detective inspector Crowley an hour later and was driven back to the bunker.

The following morning Gavin went down into the bowels of the bunker to carry out the instructions he'd been given by the Reeve, he was gone for most of the day and when he finally returned to the surface, he murdered another three climbers that had strayed to close to the complex, one of them being a thirteen year old girl that had been on her first climb with her father.

It was at this point that Eddie finally decided that the Stanfords reign of blood had to end. Stopping it was a simple matter, he first took his favourite shotgun and sawed its barrels off, he then loaded it with two cartridges and sat in the living room waiting for his brother. Twenty minutes later when his twin entered the room, he stood up and spoke to him for the first time in years.

'Goodbye Gavin.'

And then shot him twice in the head.

Eddie had initially planned on killing his brother and then turn the gun on himself but just as he pressed the still warm barrels under his chin, he noticed that the soles of Gavin's boots were stained with a strange bright green sticky substance. Eddie knew instantly what had happened and his blood ran cold.

The rusting steel door opened with a hard shove and cool moist air blew in Eddie's face as he entered the huge cavernous cellar, he didn't bother closing the heavy door behind him, instead he walked in to the gloom.

The clawing darkness was thrust back by a bright Tilley lamp as Eddie navigated his way through the bottom most level of the bunker, he remembered back to the very first time that he went down there with his father.

'Remember son, it's your responsibility now, you and your brother are the keepers, just as my father had been before me.'

After a few minutes, Eddie arrived at the very same spot that his father had made his speech from and lifted the lamp high.

They were still there, they looked exactly the same as he last saw them some sixty odd years ago, the fifteen ancient lead coffins from another time, sentinels of the grotesque, sarcophagi of the damned.

Eddie stood for awhile just staring at the coffins, he knew that these coffins were not normal coffins and their contents were far worse than any decaying human bodies, these coffins were vessels of pure evil.

'You must protect them at all cost son.' his fathers words still rang in his head.

At the time he never understood why the boxes had to be protected but it hadn't been his place to question his families legacy, what had to be done had to be done, but now he knew, he knew that him and his brother hadn't been protecting the coffins from mankind, he had been protecting mankind from the coffins.

But it had all been in vain, he had failed in his mission, he knew it as soon as he had seen his brothers boots as he lay dead on the floor upstairs.

He had feared that this day might come one day, but he would never have guessed in a million years that the assassin would of come from within and been his own twin brother.

The Tilley lamp exposed the carnage, three of the coffins had been attacked with an axe and had large rents and gashes on their lids and sides which had spilled their contents of neon green fluid, splatters of it were everywhere. When it had come into contact with some of the nearby coffins, it had inexplicably caused their contents to react and explode like steam from a pressure cooker, causing more green fluid to splash and splatter everywhere, a chain reaction went from coffin to coffin until all fifteen of the lead boxes were now ripped apart and empty. There was nothing that could be done now, it was all over.

Eddie was arrested later that evening and locked in the cells at the Portland police station in Underhill, the Reeve made his customary visit and they gave each other a knowing nod before the Reeve set a court date and departed.

Eddie appeared at Portland's Crown court and pleaded guilty, he was sentenced to a minimum of twenty five years in prison for the murders of the five climbers and his brother.

He was sent to the Verne prison on his beloved Isle of Portland to serve out his sentence.

On the third night of his imprisonment, Eddie was dozing on his bunk in his solitary cell, he heard muffled whispers coming from outside his cell door and knew the time had come.

Four guards and a ginger haired civilian in an expensive suit, that he noticed had huge sausage sized fingers, entered the small room. Eddie watched but didn't say a word as the guards hurriedly made a noose out of a sheet and tied it to the bars set in the high-up window frame, he still didn't say a word when they made him stand on a chair and put the noose around his neck and promptly kicked the chair away.

The bunker complex at Blacknor was eventually sold to a couple from London who had the intentions of renovating it and living there, but the project was never completed and the couple mysteriously fled in the middle of the night back to the big city.

Now the bunker sits abandoned and has been boarded up by Portland town council, memories of the strange twins faded into folklore and the place became home to tales told by children of ghosts and murders and a place that lost pirate treasure could be found, but only if you had the balls to go and look for it.

A Tattoo Too Far

You could feel the music pounding in your chest long before you entered through the pubs doors, loud throbbing House music pulsated into the street from within The Sailors Return and reverberated around Castletown down by Portland's docks.

John Halliwell, part time cat burglar part time college layabout, and a pal called Casey, were leaning against the bar nursing a pint of Tennents each, Casey was getting deep into the groove and shut his eyes as "Your Love" by Frankie Knuckles dropped, this was his kind of Heaven. John was lost in space and stared into the distance, his thoughts elsewhere.

In the weeks that had passed since the ultra-bizarre incident involving the bird tattoo that had miraculously come alive and flew out of his bedroom window, John had tried to figure out the strange events from every possible angle but just couldn't get his head around what had occurred.

Eventually John came to the only conclusion that

he could, and that was that it never happened at all. There weren't any traces of him ever having had a tattoo on his arm, there were no marks or scars or lighter patches or skin blemishes, so it must have been either a crazy dream or a hallucination, either way, a tattoo of a bird on his left arm had NOT come alive and had NOT flown out of his bedroom window, that he was definitely sure of.

There was one thing that he couldn't deny though, and that was that the revolting looking tattooing machine really did exist as it was still lying in its mahogany box on his dressing table and proved its very existence every time he reached for a packet of smokes, but tattoos that come alive... Naah he wasn't having any of that bullshit.

John drained the dregs of his pint and signalled to the barman for a refill, it wasn't too busy in the pub tonight, just the usual gaggle of regulars and a handful of new faces that he hadn't seen before, holidaymakers most likely, but it was one of these new faces that quickly attracted his attention and pushed thoughts of that impossible night to the back of his mind, even if only temporarily.

This particular new face was attached to a very sexy blonde that was almost wearing a pair of red booty-shorts and matching stilettos, John being the red blooded male that he was, did what any other young red blooded male would do under the same circumstances, he vowed to find out what colour knickers she was wearing, and if he could get them onto his bedroom floor sometime that night.

He found out later, much to his surprise, that twenty one year old Tanya from London was actually

194

going commando as she hated VPL's.

Tanya was on holiday with her over middle-aged parents who's idea of a having a good time was to visit museums and crumbling churches, Tanya on the other hand had made it her mission to have as much fun as possible while the oldies were out site-seeing.

She explained to John, after he had bought her a glass of Lambrusco, that she had heard the pubs loud music all the way over at her campsite and had flipped a coin to decided if it was an early night-in watching EastEnders on the portable with the oldies, or locating the source of the music and having some fun, after five attempts, the fun option won and so here she was.

The rest of the evening went well, the twosome drank, danced, drank and danced some more, in the quieter moments the couple nibbled each others ears as they huddled in the recesses of the seating booths.

At one point, Tanya broke away from the mashing of tongues and sat back and studied John's face with a quizzical look in her brown eyes.

'There's something about you John, I dunno what it is but I'm strangely attracted to you.'

Well this was great news to John's ears, but she continued.

'You're not my usual type, I usually like good looking men, you know, with nice hair, a good fashion sense... actually the complete opposite of you.' she laughed a real girly laugh. 'But I dunno, there's definitely something strange pulling me towards you, some sort of animal magnetism maybe.' and with that she smiled wildly showing her perfect teeth and got back to sucking his tongue.

All too soon, last orders were called and it was

kicking out time, John gave Tanya a long wet toungey kiss, he didn't want to let her go but after Tanya's previous comment about him not being her type, he expected her to say her goodbyes and jump into a taxi and flee into the night, but it was her own suggestion that they go back to his place for some more intimate fun.

The wide grin on John's sweaty face said it all as he lay back on the pillow exhausted, he still couldn't believe it, John had always thought that he was a man of the world and pretty much knew all there was to know about sex but Tanya - Phwoar! she knew and did things to him that would have put the author of the Kama Sutra to shame, and he'd loved every single second of it.

The on-suite door clicked open and Tanya softly padded back into the room, the bounce of her ample cleavage was hypnotic, she climbed back into bed and rolled onto her side to face him.

'John...' she started. 'What's the horrible looking thing in that wooden box?' it was an innocent question but it caught him off guard, he hadn't realised that she had seen the mahogany box on his bedside cabinet yet alone had looked inside it, his face must of showed surprise at the question.

'I was... I was looking to see if you had any more condoms when you were in the loo and I looked inside the box.'

'Ahh that...' he had to think fast.

'It's just an old tattooing machine, styled on some alien movie prop or something, it ah... it used to belong to a goth tattooist.'

Tanya squeezed close, her face just inches from his.

'You're a tattooist?

'Uh yeah, I sort of... dabble now and then.'

She sat up eagerly.

'Do me... tattoo me... right here on my tit.' she lifted her right boob and pushed it towards him bringing a nipple temptingly within nibbling range.

'That'll really piss off my parents.' she added with a laugh.

John sat up next to her on the edge of the bed.

'Well I dunno I'm not that good really and...' he began but she cut him short.

'Come on John, after everything we've just done.' she pulled a sad face and doe eyes but held a cheeky smile, there was a heavy silence as he ran through his options in his head.

'I... Well I guess I could try, I'm not too sure if the machine is working properly though.' it was the best he could think of on the spur of the moment.

Tanya squealed with delight and clapped her hands excitedly then gave him a long passionate kiss, although he would have preferred to chew on that nipple.

Tanya nervously but excitedly sat on the edge of the bed with her right boob gently resting in John's hand, its erect nipple was burning into his palm and he had to fight hard to resist not giving it a friendly tweak. They had already discussed the design that she wanted and she had decided on a red rose with a long green stem that would coil around her entire breast.

'Wouldn't you prefer a nice little star instead or maybe a teeny tiny moustache on the side of your finger?'

'No no, it must be a rose because it goes with my name and I want it encircling my boob because life is full of misery, loneliness, and suffering.'

John raised his eyebrows confused by her logic but he eventually agreed to do the tattoo just as she wanted it.

What's the worst that can happen. he asked himself, e*ither nothing and I'll blame it on the machine not working properly, or she gets a crappy tattoo and I never see her again.*

With wary trepidation, John took hold of the tattooing machine and felt it throb gently in his hand, a warm glow instantly began to flow through his synapses and he shut his eyes, he felt the tattoo machines needle touch her soft skin, immediately a bright white light flashed inside his head making him grimace as a rush of intense power hit him full-on in the frontal lobe, he felt his hand begin to move on its own as if guided by some unseen force, while his mind filled with beautiful sensations and feelings, he swam in a warm sea of total bliss while eddies of pleasure washed over him and currents of ecstasy pummelled his heart.

After what could have been a lifetime, the sensations of ecstasy began to fade and clear, he had no idea how long the episode had lasted but he didn't really care, not at this moment anyway, he felt as though he had been on the best end of a thousand orgasms, his nerve endings tingled and fizzed, his mind was having a 'high' better than any illegal drug could produce.

'I really thought that it would hurt but I didn't feel

a thing,' Tanya trilled 'and it's totally amazing, it looks so real.'

John opened his eyes to see Tanya admiring the new tattoo that had appeared as if by magic on her body, he took a close look and she was right, the tattoo was a masterpiece, he couldn't fault it, the vivid red and pink hues of the rose petals shimmered with a moist dew, the long snaking green stem with its pointed thorns so sharp looking, the tattoo could have been a photograph.

Tanya couldn't sleep after that, she was far too hyped up, she kept admiring her new piece of art in the mirror and cooing over it until the sun lazily rose over the horizon.

John lay on his back, drifting in and out of sleep, still enjoying the after effects of the ebb tide of euphoria when a sharp scream brought him back to full consciousness. Tanya was sat on the edge of the bed with her back to him, she was staring in the mirror, she screamed again and John jumped to his feet.

'What's the matter...' he began as Tanya turned to face him.

The colour had drained from her sweet face and she looked close to fainting but no reply was required as he could see exactly what the matter was, Tanya's new rose tattoo had come to life on her skin and the long curling stem was slowly tightening around her breast, its sharp pointed thorns were piercing her skin making blood ooze from the wounds.

'Stop it!! stop it... please stop it.' she begged with tears streaming down her cheeks.

The poor girls hands flapped around in the air and

attempted to grab the plants stem but each time her fingers came away shredded to ribbons as the thorns punctured and ripped them, the long thorny stem tightened its grip around the girls pale flesh like a hungry boa constrictor and exposed yellow fat tissue from deep within her breast, John couldn't do anything, he just stood and stared at the horrific scene unfolding in front of him, he felt powerless.

Tanya gave an ethereal gurgle as the stem tightened its grip completely, causing the razor sharp tips of the thorns to meet and sever her entire breast from her body and it fell to the floor like a discarded dishcloth.

Tanya's body went limp and she fainted in a heap joining her amputated breast on the carpet at Johns feet.

 John stood paralysed and watched helplessly as the long stemmed rose with evilly sharp thorns, slithered its way up Tanya's body towards her neck.

The following two weeks passed like an endless nightmare for John, an endless nightmare full of guilt and denial and the constant dreaded anticipation of a loud knock on his door from that ginger haired bastard Crowley, he was known for helping people and then using it against them for his own personal gain.

John's heart had bled for Tanya, but slowly the memories of what had happened to her that night were being erased from his memory along with the terrible things that had happened afterwards, each time he tried to remember all he could see was a grey swirling mist that was punctuated by fading glimpses of flashbacks.

He could remember that he had met a girl at the local pub and had taken her home, then had given her a tattoo of a beautiful rose that had unbelievably came alive in front of his very eyes, but after that, nothing, except Crowley, and even his involvement seemed like a distant dream now.

John sat staring at the evil looking tattoo machine as it lay on its bed of black velvet inside its box, he accepted now that yes, he had given himself a tattoo of a brightly coloured bird which had became real and had flown out of his bedroom, and that it was as real as he rose had been, but he was totally baffled and clueless as to how it did what it did.

There were no obvious signs of power, multi coloured inks came from nowhere, he had no artistic talent whatsoever yet could create photo-realistic tattoos with his eyes shut, and the most scariest thing of all, the tattoos the machine created, came alive!

In the end, John eventually decided that he didn't really care, the tattoo machine did what it did, however it did it, besides, recently he had been feeling an overwhelming urge to use it again, to feel the delights and sensations that it gave him as he gripped it in his hand and it performed its black magic.

He tried to fight the desire but was he strong enough, could he resist the drug like addiction. Deep down he knew that if he failed and succumbed, it would write a new chapter in his life, a chapter so monstrous and foul it would change things forever.

Retribution at the Doghouse

You are cordially invited to attend The Doghouse in Castletown at 9pm tonight. The password is: Cunny

The gold edged invitation card was hand delivered by anonymous courier that very morning, the message was simple but effective. The small card was embossed on the bottom right corner with the acronym P.E.T in 12 point Times New Roman.

Jack Krocodile knew what that particular acronym meant, every pure blood on the island knew exactly what it meant.

The invitation was a response to a wedding shoot that had been booked two weeks previously, and luckily he had been in the right place at the right time, because the client who had booked the shoot for his daughters pending nuptials, had also hired him on the spot to make a video diary for his private men's club annual spring ball. Jack would be given unprecedented access to the evenings 'festivities' which he had been informed by the client in hushed tones, included lots and lots of sex.

The so named 'Doghouse' was Portland's largest brothel, it was run by Luscious Lips McGee and her two sisters; Tempting Pink & Precious Muff, the trio had operated the house of ill repute down by the docks in Castletown for as long as anybody could remember.

In years past, when the Royal Navy had been in town, the Doghouse had been a buzzing non-stop 24/7 shag central. In those days Luscious was running a hundred girls of all shapes and sizes, girls that would do anything with anyone, or indeed anything, to separate you from your hard earned cash.

Back then, the place would be full to the rafters on a weekend, especially when a new ship full of horny matelots sailed into port, and there would be so much fucking going on in the Doghouse that you could smell the spunk all the way up Fortuneswell.

Nowadays though it's a different story, those heady glory days of rum sodomy and the lash were long gone, in its infinite wisdom the Royal Navy de-commissioned the naval base on Portland and the ships sailed off into the sunset (Portsmouth actually), taking the sailors and their hard earned cash with them and they never came back.

The Doghouse, which was home to the infamous "ten shilling blowjob", was now only used by the locals and the occasional tourist that had happened to stumble upon the den of iniquity. The number of full time girls went down from around a hundred in its heyday to a miserly seven on a weekday, weekends weren't much better when there might be fifteen girls on duty to service around forty men, although the numbers did rise slightly when Luscious began inviting guest whores from Weymouth to come and perform one night specials.

Luscious Lips McGee was getting on a bit these days, nobody knew her exact age and nobody would dare ask, but the general consensus amongst the guys around the bar was that she had to getting on into her 70's by now. She was a short stout little woman and couldn't have been more than five feet tall, she had bright almost fluorescent blue hair that was so obviously a wig covering grey and she had the dirtiest laugh you have ever heard.

There was a large oil painting hanging on the wall behind the bar of a naked woman in her twenties stroking a greyhound whilst reclining on a yellow sofa, many a wager had been placed on whether the girl in the painting was Luscious in her formative years but as yet no one had received a payout. She was also a very astute businesswoman and no matter what your kink was, she would find you a girl that would willingly do it for you, or indeed too you, and on occasions the braying of a randy donkey could be heard coming from one of the back rooms, it all happens down at the Doghouse.

The last time Jack Krocodile had been to visit Luscious and her girls had been about five years previous, his visit then though hadn't been for pleasure, it had been purely business, or at least that's what he told himself.

Jack Krocodile, photographer by trade, asshole by vocation, had been there on that occasion to make a video of some of Luscious's most perverted whores, they had dressed up as dirty faced coalminers, sat in an inflatable paddling pool and were pissed and shat on by a bunch of men wearing Margaret Thatcher masks, Jack hadn't taken part in the debauchery himself unfortunately, but he had been the master of ceremonies and had videoed the whole thing and uploaded it to one of his many websites.

Hiring the girls, buying their costumes, the purchase of the paddling pool and a clothes peg for his nose for the evening had cost him a total of two grand, his website charged people fifteen quid a time to watch the video and in the first twenty four hours alone, Jack made over thirty thousand quid, who said porn doesn't pay.

Jack had often heard rumours about the wild crazy parties that happened at the private men's club annual spring ball to which he now held a prized invite and though he had never been privileged to attend before, he prayed that the evening would be as pervy as he had heard.

As the time neared, Jack more than once toyed with the idea of pulling out of the event, after all, he would be stepping into the unknown amongst complete strangers and Christ knows what might happen, he might even find himself out of his depth, but the pound signs spinning in his eyes pushed those thoughts aside and meant that he really didn't have a choice, he could see the mountain of cash that he could make from this upcoming video and he knew that everybody liked to see something weird occasionally, it was a curiosity thing, the nature of the beast as it were.

He crossed his fingers and wished that "weird" would definitely be on the menu tonight, luckily for Jack, his wish was about to come true.

Jack turned up nice and early at the Doghouse as he wanted to make sure that he got a ringside seat but he needn't have worried as there were only three people propping up the bar.

The old girl Luscious herself greeted him at the door with a shiny ill-fitting dentured smile, she seemed to remember him and offered him a quick toothless blowjob which Jack politely declined, uncharacteristically for Jack as he would never normally turn down a free gam, he had a freshly squeezed vodka instead, he was trying to cut back on the orange juice as it brought him out in spots.

As the clocked ticked towards 9pm, Luscious took Jack by his semi and led him to the top floor of the building to a room he had never been to before. A man in a leather gimp mask asked him for the password which he gave and he was ushered inside.

The room was a 1 star Trip Advisor special and nothing to write home about, it was all bare brickwork walls held together by greying cement and cobwebs.

The room was completely devoid of any furnishings except for a dirty stained mattress laying in the center which was illuminated by a single 100 watt light bulb dangling from the cracked ceiling.

This is great! he thought as he began setting up his equipment, *the décor will really add to the ambience and atmosphere, its got a nice "dungeons are us" vibe.*

He had just finished attaching a camcorder to a fluid head tripod (gotta be professional about these things) and framing the dank mattress for a good shot, when the door behind him opened and in traipsed a line of men wearing eye masks, pin striped business suits and black gloves, Jack counted seven in all.

He tried to put names to the noses lips and chins as they filed past him one by one and encircled the room but it was an impossible task, that was until the last masked man passed him, it was the bright ginger hair and sausage roll crumbs on his chin that gave him away, it could only be none other than the infamous DCI Gary Crowley.

The men arranged themselves around the edge of the room in a relaxed circle, leaving a gap by the door, nobody said a word or made a sound, there was no camaraderie or excited whispers like you would normally find at video shoots. The men stood silently, expectantly waiting.

The two minutes that passed seemed to stretch on and on but eventually the door re-opened and in walked a young platinum blonde female, she must have been in her early thirties Jack guessed, she wore a green bathrobe and not much else. Reaching for his handheld camcorder he pressed the record button.

The age of the woman surprised him a little, she wasn't too bad looking either, in his limited experience of this type of thing, the women involved were usually pretty haggard looking to say the least, old past their "sell by date" hookers and crack whores looking for easy money for their next fix.

Jack zoomed into the woman's eyes to see if there was any sign that she was smacked off her face, but her pupils weren't blown and appeared normal, he didn't really fancy the idea of doing this if the woman was there purely to get drug money, that didn't seem right somehow, even to him, if she was there by her own free will - then great bring it on.

The blonde dropped her bathrobe and was completely naked underneath, Jack slowly panned up from her red painted toes, past her slim waist to her face and then zoomed out as she lay down on the mattress.

This girl's a bit of a looker, he thought as his camera roamed across her lithe body, *how the hell did a babe like this get into this sort of fucked up shit. She's better looking than some of my professional models!*

The door opened once again and a silver-grey haired man carrying a small black case entered the room, he was wearing an expensive looking black mohair suit, possibly Prada, along with the same perfunctory eye mask as the others, he took his time and walked to the center of the circle before kneeling down next to the girl, he didn't seem in any sort of hurry as he pulled on a pair of blue latex gloves and opened the case that he'd been carrying.

Jack put down the handheld but left it recording and took up position behind the tripod mounted video camera and zoomed in for a closer look.

The inside of the case was lined with red velvet and laying on the red velvet was what appeared to be a set of surgeon's tools, a thin film of sweat formed down Jacks spine, *BDSM, I should have guessed.*

The first object in the case looked like a pair of stainless steel nutcrackers that glistened menacingly in the light, next to that was a small silver cordless surgical drill fitted with a large hole-saw bit, the type used for trepanning, a surgical hammer, assorted scalpels and various different nasty looking objects that Jack couldn't put a name too but that looked like they could inflict some serious pain in the wrong hands.

Jack zoomed back out to take in the entire scene. The silver-grey haired man picked up the instrument that resembled a nutcracker and weighed it in his hand as though he were contemplating if it was suitable for his requirements, he then lent forward and seemingly without a care in the world gripped the girls left nipple in its jaws and squeezed with all his might.

The blood curdling scream that ripped from the poor girl's mouth almost made a Jack grab his gear and leg it right outta there, but somehow he managed to keep his cool and continued shooting, after all, Jack was a professional.

The man in control of the girls screams twisted and turned the implement back and forth wringing every last ounce of pain from her nipple and by the time he put the tool back down, her nipple was a mutilated bloody mess.

Now you would have thought that at this point in the game the girl would have jumped up and got the fuck outta there herself, or at the very least would have shouted her safe word, but not this girl, though sobbing to herself, she slid a hand down between her legs and began masturbating, she was definitely enjoying this rough treatment. The man seemed to like this reaction and casually laid the blood covered tool back onto the red velvet then stood up and left the cameras field of vision, he walked to the circle of men and touched one on his left shoulder, this seemed to be the signal for the selected man to slowly walk to the mattress and kneel just as his predecessor had done.

This new man went through the same ceremony of deciding which of the evil instruments of pain was right for him, before deciding on a metal handled bone saw that had a particularly nasty looking serrated edge.

Oh Shit! Jack really began to panic now, *he's gonna cut her fucking feet off or something! I don't mind a little consensual pain now and again, but no fucking way am I gonna video someone cutting off a girls feet just for fun. I aint making no fucking snuff movie.* Jack reached for the camcorders off switch but felt a familiar iron grip on his shoulder.

He turned to see ginge shaking his head, the hand squeezed harder and Jack got the message, he turned back to the action and was relieved to see that instead of amputating a limb, bone-saw man had turned the implement sideways and was using it as a paddle to slap the girl's tits. Jack breathed a sigh of relief.

The makeshift paddle was brought down hard on the girls flesh time and time again, each blow getting harder, the blonde was groaning with pleasure as her other hand joined the first and buried itself between her legs. The loud *thwapping* of steel on flesh continued for ten minutes until the girls tits were a nasty dark maroon colour and blood was seeping out of every pore, then the man put the blood spotted saw back onto the velvet and retook his place again in the circle.

This whole process was repeated another five times as each man in turn, knelt in front of the poor woman (or ecstatic woman if looking from her point of view) and performed some horrible form of sexual torture on her body, but actually thinking about it, *was it torture?* Jack pondered, the girl definitely seemed to be enjoying the whole session, even when she was flipped over onto her stomach and the cordless drill was used to puncture holes into the meat of her arse cheeks, she seemed to have an endless supply of orgasms too, *I guess there's just nothing as weird as folk*, he muttered to himself.

Once all the men had had their turn with the girl, Luscious Lips McGee appeared out of nowhere and draped the bathrobe over the girls bruised and bleeding flesh, the two women smiled at each other before Luscious put her arm around her and they both left the room.

The fun was over for the evening, or so Jack thought, he went to switch off the camcorders and pack up his equipment but was again stopped by ginge, this time by the wagging of a sausage sized finger at him.

'There's more?'

Ginge nodded and a tinge of sexual excitement pulsed in Jack's groin, *if judging by the events I've just seen are anything to go by, then whatever happens next is gonna be totally fucked up,* he mused, *do I really want to witness this, of course I do.*

The suited men standing around the room began shuffling sideways as if acting on some pre-arranged plan, then linked hands and blocked the door, when they stopped moving Jack was in the middle of the room surrounded by a ring of masked Zorro's.

The silver-grey haired owner of the case took a

step forward, faced Jack and reached into his inside jacket pocket and pulled out what looked like a yarmulke, except it wasn't a yarmulke, this skullcap was black and had a large red cross in the center of an embroidered white circle, he placed it carefully on his head and then ceremoniously rotated it three times in an anti-clockwise direction.

Jack stood watching fascinated and wondered what the Hell was going on. Another masked man stepped forward out of the circle and picked up the handheld video camera from the floor and pointed it in Jack's direction, the stranger would of normally been on the end of Jacks sharp tongue for daring to touch his expensive equipment but he didn't get the chance as the man wearing the skullcap suddenly cleared his throat and spoke.

'Jack Orlando Krocodile.' he began in a clear booming voice. 'You have been tried in absentia for crimes against the good of the isle of Portland by all seven elected members of the Grand Synod. You were found guilty and your sentence has been set. You have been brought here tonight to receive your punishment.'

Was this some sort of weird joke, Jack chuckled and a puzzled look spread across his face.

'What the hell are you talking about? I've done nothing wrong. What's going on? Punished for what?'

Two more men stepped out of the circle and each grabbed hold of one of Jack's arms.

'Hey! now, this is getting stupid, I've done nothing wrong! What the fuck are you doing? Leave me alone!' Jack began struggling against the men as they forced him to his knees.

At this point Jack knew that they weren't fucking about, some serious shit was going down here and he was the victim.

'Get the fuck off me, I've done nothing wrong, let me go!' he demanded, a cold hard fear began spreading through him, he struggled to free himself from the strong grip of the men as he continued to plead his innocence. Ginge stepped in front and faced him.

'I know who you are Crowley, stop this shit right now, I'm telling you, I aint done nothing wrong!'

Ginge stared deep into Jacks eyes before speaking. 'Remember Sally Fletcher?'

It was all that was needed to be said, Jack now understood and realised what this was about and that he was totally screwed.

'Wait wait! That was just a bit of fun, I meant no harm... Ok, maybe I was a little harsh with her but but...' Jack stopped when he saw that the ginger haired policeman held in his right hand the bloodied nutcracker tool that had done so much damage to the girl's nipple, his bladder went weak and he felt hot piss running down his legs.

'Holy fuck no! get that thing away from me!' he squealed, he was genuinely terrified by now.

Another man left the circle and roughly pulled Jacks trousers and underwear down to his ankles.

'No please don't, I'm sorry, please no!' Jack began to cry, but his pleadings fell on deaf ears.

The pain was beyond extreme as Jacks testicles were crunched into a mush by the nutcracker, it really lived up to its name, and in minutes all that remained of Jacks family jewels was a bag full of gloop.

Jack passed out but was brought round by a hefty slap from Ginge.

The man wielding the stainless steel nutcrackers pushed his face close to Jack's, and waited for him to fully come to his senses.

'That was for my daughter, you bastard!' the man spat a thick wodge of phlegm in his face then retook his place in the circle.

Ginge stepped in front of Jack.

'Now you will receive the Synods punishment, the standard punishment for offending the great name of Portland.'

Two men clamped Jacks head tightly in their grip which although his limbs were weak, made him struggle like a caged animal, but he was nowhere near strong enough to fight them off.

Ginge leaned in and tried to get the nutcrackers into Jack's mouth but he met resistance when Jack slammed his jaw shut and sealed his lips tight for which he received a crack around the face that made his eyes spin in their sockets.

'Yield!'

Jack kept his jaw firmly clamped shut, another blow smashed into his face this time breaking his nose.

'Yield!' came the order again.

Jack screamed through his clenched teeth but another blow to his already shattered nose finally forced his mouth open and in an instant the silver tool was in his mouth and had gripped the tip of his tongue tightly.

Jack's vision blurred as the pressure increased, the pain was intense and felt like nothing he had ever felt before, it was even worse than the pain in his groin. He struggled with every fibre in his body but it was hopeless against the three men.

Ginge began pulling hard on the pliers and stretching Jacks tongue out of his mouth as far as it would go and held it there, suddenly another hand appeared in front of Jacks face, it wielded a glinting surgical scalpel which waved about in front of his eyes.

Ginge turned his head and looked to his left at the man in the skullcap who nodded his approval.

'Carry out the punishment'

In one swift movement, ginger haired Crowley, the bastard bent copper of Portland CID, grinned and sliced the scalpel across the back of Jacks tongue severing it at its root, in a splash of crimson blood, he lifted the three inch lump of bloody muscle and held it aloft as if it were a prize trophy.

The strong arms that were holding Jack suddenly released their grips and Jack slumped to the floor, blood spewed from his ghastly wound and filled his mouth, he began coughing and choking and as his vision began to fade and the room began to spin in front of his eyes.

Jack thought he saw Luscious and a couple of her girls rush into the room carrying a medical kit, the last thing he heard before he collapsed into blissful unconsciousness was skullcap man proudly announcing to the room that justice had been served, Sally Fletchers father stepped out of the circle, removed his eye mask and shook his hand.

The video of Jack's punishment that night ended

up on the internet just like all of his masterpieces did. The video was downloaded more than seven thousand times that first week alone and was passed around between different groups of perverts who all had a good wank and a laugh over the proceedings. Eventually the video ended up on the Dark web on a website called totallyrottenshit.co.org, where it can still be seen to this day for a fiver a pop.

The Elevator to Nowhere

Ello me old BoneChains, nice to see you this late in the evenin', it's lucky I kept me shop open or I might 'ave missed you. Mind you, I didn't really 'ave much choice about it did I, cuz I had a late customer rush in minutes before I was about to close for the day and he begs me to help him out.

Turns out the guys name was Ben and he'd busted up his works walkie talkie when he was doing something somewhere he shouldn't of been. Reckoned he'd be in a whole pile of doodoo if it wasn't fixed by the time he started his shift up at Sweethill in the morning.

So, what could I do right, I'm a nice guy, plus he offered to bung me a few extra squid if I could fix it right then, so I tells him ok, cuz I could always do with extra dosh, might even treat the missus to an evenin' at the Doghouse haha.

Anyways, this Ben guy gave me his radio handset and took a seat on me comfy sofa while he waited. I offered him a cup of java from me machine and a few spoons of me powdered milk and I started work.

It weren't long though that for no reason at all, the bloke started yabbling on at like fifty miles an hour, it was like he couldn't stop talkin', he gave me his life story and everything, weird chap, anyways, he went on to tell me this odd and a little scary tale about how his radio comes to be busted.

This what he told yours truly, by the way, I hope you aint just eaten ha ha.

I was working out at the old reservoir by the Heights Hotel, which we all know is really the main air inlet for the tunnels underneath the island right, when I get a call on me walkie talkie that there had been an "incident" over at Glacis, you know, the place up near the Ghost tunnels, the old WW2 radar station or whatever it is.

All I was told by my boss was that the incident involved two escaped teenagers from the Young Offenders Institute, or Borstal as it used to be called, over at the Grove, that they had broken into one of the buildings at Glacis and had trashed the place, so I was to stop what I was doing and get my butt over there pronto.

Mickey from the maintenance crew was waiting for me outside of the building when I arrived and he filled me in with some of the blanks.

Apparently the two youngsters in question, had escaped over the YOI farm wall and after skipping across a few fields and a quarry or two, had climbed the Glacis fence and had broken into one of the buildings there.

Maybe they were looking for food or just some shelter for awhile but whatever it was, they decided to smash the place up while they were there, typical yobs. Thing is though, that during their little rampage they only went and discovered the hidden elevator door leading down into the tunnels hadn't they.

Well these two lads, who couldn't have been over 19 seeing as they were guests of her Majesties YOI, managed to pry open the door, Christ knows how cuz it's a Knoxford security door and they are supposed to be impossible to break in to, but they did somehow and they went inside, only for the door to go and shut behind them. But as it happens, that was only the beginning of their troubles.

That particular lift aint been used in years, not since the dog kennels that used to be on that site had relocated anyway, and the electrics had been disabled for at least five years, so the lift weren't going nowhere in a hurry.

Christ knows how long the pair had been trapped inside the lift in the dark, it could have been weeks or months even, but when Mickey managed to re-open the door, he discovered what was left of them.

Mickey had been sent to Glacis by his boss who had received a call from a concerned member of the public who had been up there walking her dog and had spotted the damage to one of the buildings through the fence. Mickey told me that it was a horrible disgusting sight and he had hurled when he finally got the doors open. He reckoned that sometime during the weeks or months that the pair had been trapped in there, they had gone insane with hunger and had eaten each other to death.

The legs and thighs of one of the bodies had huge bite marks ripped out of them, right down to the bone he said, and the other ones guts had been pulled out of a long jagged tear in his stomach and what was left of his intestines were all chewed up and chomped, both the bodies were literally covered in individual bite marks and one boy had his throat ripped out. It looked like a pack of hungry wolves had been in their with them he said.

So anyway, that was when I got the call to go and clean up the mess and take the remains to those scary mofo's, Mr T and Mr S in the Chop Shop.

Mickey had been right, it was horrible in there, there was dried blood everywhere and little bits of flesh and skin all over the walls and floor, it was carnage, but luckily for me there weren't no stink left by then, too much time had passed I guess, which was great because there's no stink like a dead man's stink I tell ya, I heave every time that foul odour gets up me nose.

So anyway, I did what I'm paid to do and cleared up the mess. I spent the next hour putting body parts into blue sacks and loading them into the back of me van, then I hosed the interior with me portable water sprayer and gave it a little "pride" polish.

When the lift was spic-n-span again, I radioed in that I was all done and the lift cleanse was complete and I was heading off.

I was just about to start up my van when I realised that I had only gone and left me water sprayer on the floor of the lift hadn't I, so I went back in to get it but just as I had picked it up, the bloody lift sprang in to life and the door went and shut behind me.

My immediate reaction was to panic, I didn't wanna end up like those two YOI boys, but then I realised that I was being stupid because the lift now had power which must of meant that maintenance had reactivated it remotely, so all I had to do was to press the button to open the door right.

Oh if only life was so simple.

I didn't even get a chance to press the door open button when the lift suddenly gave a jolt and began to descend.

I dunno if you've ever been in one of the tunnel access lifts or not... naah course you aint, what am I thinking, anyway, those lifts only have three buttons in them, a door open button and an up and a down button. Well I started to rapidly press all three and not a sausage, they completely ignored me. Now this little predicament presented a problem.

The lift was probably just following some automatic reset routine hence it going down, but I don't have clearance for down there under Glacis and I could get... no, scrub that, I *would* get in to some very very serious shit if I was caught down there.

I know only too well how strict the suits are about people being in the wrong place without clearance, only last month old Billy Boy from maintenance was caught poking around one of the air vents up at Nicodemus Knob, he was instantly fired and lost his pension and was physically forced to emigrate to Weymouth, mind you it couldn't of happened to a nicer sexist, the twat!

I began panicking anew and started hammering on the buttons again but they still weren't having it so in the end I had no choice but to wait and twiddle me thumbs as it made its long descent.

Eventually after what seemed like a lifetime, the lift shuddered to a halt, went ping and the door slid open. I was half expecting to find a hoard of armed guards pointing rifles and guns at me, but was pleasantly surprised to see an empty corridor that led off in to the distance – Phew!

I tried pressing the up button so I could get out of there pronto but the lift had made a one way trip and was dead again.

The new corridor that was painted green, a right horrible shade it was too, anyway like I said, there was no one at all about so I followed the corridor to see where it went. After a few minutes of turns, blind endings and locked doors, the corridor opened onto a junction which had three others corridors leading off in different directions, on the floor of each corridor were these coloured lines just like there is at Sweethill. I normally have to follow the blue line which takes me back to my sector but there were no blue lines here, which meant I definitely wasn't allowed to be in this area, there was a red line an orange line and a brown line though, which I had a quick chuckle about because I was leavin' me own brown line in me underpants right then.

Anyway I knew that the red lines were for maintenance and orange lines were for scientists and technicians but I had never seen a brown line before, I dunno if it was curiosity or plain stupidity but as I felt some sort of affinity with it, I went and followed the brown one, yeah I know that if I followed either of the other two I would probably end up somewhere that I recognised and could have gotten out of there, but like

I said, it was a curiosity thing, I just hoped that it didn't do to me the same as it did to that damn cat.

The corridor went for about a hundred and fifty feet I guess before turning a sharp right and then it stopped in front of a door, there weren't nothing written on this side of the door so in I went and almost walked straight into the back of a woman dressed in brown overalls. My heart skipped a beat as I slammed on me brakes before I collided with her, I held me breath and prayed that she didn't turn around and see me or I'd be right in the brown smelly stuff and be charged with not only failing to have clearance but also for an attempted goosing.

Anyways, thankfully the woman went through a sliding door on her right without seeing me so I decided it best to keep going forward and around a corner ahead. Around that corner was an oblong room filled with metal clothes lockers, you know the type that they have in swimming pool changing rooms, well there were two doors here, the door on the left said "Nursery" and the door on the right said "Exit."

At first glance, when I read the word Nursery, I immediately thought that it was a plant nursery, then I thought naah maybe not, why would they be growing their own flowers and plants way down here, well they could I guess but it seemed unlikely.

I went to the door marked exit and was about to go through when that frickin' thing called curiosity grabbed my feet, turned them around and made me walk through the door marked nursery instead, the bastards. I was proven correct with my garden nursery theory though and there wasn't a single tulip to be seen, not even a Triffid which wouldn't have been

223

outta place down here.

I would say the nursery was about the size and shape of a cricket pitch and was decorated with white ceramic tiles on three walls while the fourth had a plate glass window running the length of the room, but that wasn't what surprised me, what surprised me was that the room was filled with baby incubators, yep, it really was a nursery, a nursery of the baby kind, hey wasn't that a movie, nah maybe not.

Anyway, there were about thirty of those transparent baby boxes like you see in hospitals plus all these medical looking machines like those automatic pumps that look like concertinas going up and down, I guess to help with breathing like.

I could see that most of the incubators were empty except for two that had little babies inside, they had tubes going up their noses and were connected to wires that went to different machines, I gave a shudder when I saw them and hurried on by. At the furthest end of this room were a pair of rubber double doors that had round portholes in them and through I went.

Inside this new area was what looked like a fully kitted out operating theatre but only it was in miniature, for operating on miniature things I guessed, like babies, I shuddered again.

There was another door here so that was obviously the way to go. I pushed the door open slightly with me foot and peered through the gap, only to find the millionth corridor of the day, it was also empty so with a sigh off I trot. There was only one door in this corridor and it was already open but at the end was a staircase that disappeared upwards, this was my new favourite kind of staircase, so with hope blossoming, I started walking towards it.

I guess I weren't thinking properly because without a single thought about it, I just walked straight passed the open door, I was halfway across the opening when I heard a voice from inside the room, I froze like a statue, I was terrified but there were no shouts or nothing so I guessed that I hadn't been spotted so quickly backed up and hugged the wall and held me breath.

I had only heard one voice coming from the room, so I hoped that it was one side of a phone conversation and prayed that whoever it was, was facing away from the open door, after a few deep gulps of oxygen to boost my nerve, I very slowly peeked my head around the door frame, but all I saw was the back of an office chair, wow was I lucky.

I took another deep breath and made a dash for it. As I cleared what seemed like an eternity of open space and made it to the other side I had to squeeze my chest to silence the sound of my heart because it was pounding a cha cha on the bongos.

As I leant back against the wall with my eyes shut tight, the voice resumed talking.

'Yes Stephen, of course I understand your worries, but like I've assured you numerous times, she has red hair and we've already cross matched her organs. No, that's a completely irrational thought so please forget it okay. Yes, she's 100% compatible... The donor, well that doesn't really matter Stephen, don't worry about that... No... Well all I can say is that it was a 17 year old female and... No Stephen not at all... Healthy, yes of course, we profiled her before selection just as we always do. Yes that right... from the Ghost Tunnels up at the High Angle Battery. Yes, they were having some sort of party or something... Yes of course, we have Crowley looking after that side of things, we will be extracting her juice this afternoon and we have two babies being prepped for the removal operation this very moment. Yes the empty carcasses will go to Tomalty and Spanglar as usual. Okay, now please don't worry, Sally will be fine, we are doing everything we can for her and once she's had the serum she will be okay. Yes will do, I'll see you at the club tonight. Yes, bye.'

My first thought was like holy fuck, what are these people doing down here, what I had just heard sounded like the script of a straight to DVD horror movie, I couldn't believe it. My second thought was to get the Hell out of there and off this screwed up island ASAP.

It was then that I remembered reading in the papers not so long ago about a red haired girl that had disappeared from the Ghost Tunnels, was the guy on the phone saying that they got her down here and are gonna be extracting her juice. Like what the fuck! *and* they are prepping babies for a removal operation, removal of what for God's sake! that's just like too fucked up for words, this was just mental.

My brain was completely scrambled at this point and I just ran for the staircase which I was soon tearing up three steps at a time, thankfully half way up there was a one-way door, you know like a fire door that only opened from the staircase side, anyway it led straight to level seven which was my level. I didn't hang around though, I immediately went to see my section head and told her that I felt sick and was going home for the rest of the day.

After thinking things through in my head with the aid of lots of whiskey that night, I thought fuck it I'm too old for his kind of weird shit and called my section head the next morning. I told her that I wouldn't be back and that I was gonna take early retirement instead, she was a bit surprised about my decision but accepted it and was congenial about it, she wished me good luck in the future all friendly like.

She called me back an hour later and her attitude was completely different, all kinda official like and all the friendliness was gone from her voice, she practically demanded that I take all my gear back to the Sweethill complex which included me tool belt, me overalls and of course me two-way radio, and that's what brings me here to you.

Somehow when I was down in that nasty place I busted the screen on my walkie talkie, which you are now hopefully fixing for me old mate, me bestest buddy, me... uh... what's your name again?

Well now, I put down me screwdriver and looked over the top of me work glasses at the bloke on me sofa, he was agitated and jumpy and his knee was bouncing up and down like he needed a pee.

'Andy.' I tells him.

'Yeah yeah Andy, that's it, that's your name.' he began giggling weirdly.

'Handy Andy... Yeah, Handy Andy Pandy, Handy Andy Randy Pandy.' some drool began running out the corner of his mouth.

'Yeah you're me bestest mate ever you are buddy...

227

Never was a buddy as matey as you Pandy... Fancy a shag?'

He was beginning to ramble and make me nervous, so I tells him I could fix his radio a lot faster if he went 'ome or to the pub or somewhere.

At first he was reluctant and kept saying he liked me coffee and could he have another cup or ten, but I had to lie and tell him I was all out. He pulled himself unsteadily to his feet and mumbled something about having the munchies and fancied a kipper, then promptly left me shop.

Phew what a rum do I tells ya.

Well mateys, what do you reckon to that. This Portland Environmental Trust place sounds scary as Hell if you asks little old moi.

Anyways, I've finished the blokes radio handset now, he'll be collecting it first thing in the morning on his way to work he said.

For some reason I fancy an extra large kipper meself now, so I'm off 'ome to see if I can gets me wifey in a fishy mood, I'll see you next time.

Adiós and all that.

Handy Pandy *always* Randy Andy

The Thomas Crimson Affair

It's June the 13th, 1661, Friday. The thirty six year old noted desperado and cavalier adventurer Thomas Crimson, born of Portland stock, had just stolen the English crown jewels from under the very nose of King Charles II.

Crimson, dressed as a parson, and his two fellow accomplices in crime, a nineteen year old gin soaked boy called Hunter and a thirty five year old Scotsman that went by the name of Wyke, undertook a bold and daring visit to that famed fortress and occasional Royal Palace, the Tower of London, which sits on the north bank of the river Thames in the greatest capital city in the world.

The Tower of London is often thought of as just a square tower in the middle of London, where as in reality what is known as The Tower of London is a whole complex of buildings and towers that are surrounded by high defensive walls and a deep moat atop a hillock called Tower Hill that overlooks the River Thames.

During this period in history, the crown jewels of England were kept in the basement rooms of a small inner building called Martins Tower which is situated just outside of the main White Tower (the famous bit) and it wasn't unusual for people from the upper classes and the more well to do in society, to make a payment to the custodian of the jewels and arrange an appointment for a private viewing, this act was quite normal and even had the consent of the King, it was under this pretence that our protagonist and his two companions, all of whom were disguised as men of the cloth, entered the fortress in readiness to carry out their devious plan.

Thomas Crimson was born on the Isle of Portland in the year of our Lord sixteen hundred and twenty five, his father Seth Crimson was a hard working mackerel fisherman that hailed out of the village of Chiswell, whilst his mother Sarah, like most women of the time, tended the family home and raised their three young children.

Thomas had two siblings, Jane and Zeb, Jane was a quiet blonde haired girl who pretty much kept herself to herself, she helped her mother out around the house with chores until she was fourteen, she then married her second cousin and flew the nest all the way to Wakeham. Zeb was a sickly child and had breathing problems for most of his eight short years on this mortal coil, he died in 1636 of the influenza, a common enough cause of death in those days.

Thomas on the other hand was as strong as an ox and could be just as stubborn. He began working on the fishing boats with his father when he was aged seven, gutting and de-scaling the haul of mackerel after it was dragged up onto the beach by the fishermen at the end of the day. He always seemed at his happiest when he was up to his elbows in blood and fish intestines.

At the age of eleven Thomas went to sea as an oarsman on his father's flat-bottomed clinker-built Dory where they would spend up to eight hours a day rowing around Hallelujah Bay dragging heavy nets behind them.

By the time he had reached fifteen, Thomas (who notably hated being called Tom) was bored of his life hauling fish and wanted to set out on adventures anew, he would have the chance to sate his appetite three days after his seventeenth birthday.

It was a Thursday that Thomas would remember for years to come and would often reminisce about it and his childhood spent rowing around the coastline of Portland, he had finished landing the catch for the day and had pulled his boat high above the tide line on the pebble beach, his mother had been to collect a sack of fish and he had made a few coppers selling some to the local villagers, the rest of the catch would be pickled and sent to market on Saturday.

After cleaning himself up in the sea he decided to walk to Castletown on the other side of the island where he would go visit "Odo Tarney's" the chandlers and purchase some new leads for his nets.

In those days there was only one dirt road into Castletown, it wound its way around Fortuneswell and the Mere before making a sharp right then snaking back around to Castletown, but he couldn't be bothered with all that palaver today, he just wanted to get there and back as quickly as possible so decided to take a little shortcut through Underhill, it meant having to climb down the crumbling cliffs of West Weares and down onto the rocks below, but he would have the fresh sea air in his lungs and it would cut over an hour from his journey, the path would also take him the back way into Castletown and alongside the deep-water piers of the harbour that were used by the occasional transatlantic clippers that would dock in port for repairs and supplies, if one of the massive ships were visiting it would be a nice bonus to his errand.

Fifty minutes later Thomas was strolling along the harbourside at the back end of Castletown, he wasn't in a hurry, the sun was warm and the breeze was light, he had his hands in his pockets and a smile on his face, it was a good day.

As he ambled along, Thomas admired all the boats that were docked alongside and he watched as they loaded and unloaded their freight, most of them were just local fishing boats and barges, small flat bottomed trading vessels that ran across the harbour to Weymouth and Poole just up the coast, there were also two 110ft Brigantines, a Collier that was unloading coal from the North, three South Coast Luggers and an ancient twenty five ton open Shallop.

One ship though stood out from the rest and they all paled in comparison, the Nancy Spooner, she was a massive 345ft, two thousand ton square rigged East Indiaman. It was the first time that the vessel had called at Portland, she and her one hundred and fifty crew had spent the last six months at sea sailing from the Spice Islands in Indonesia, she would have continued sailing up the English Channel and passed

Portland on by except that she was in collision with a one hundred ton French merchant ship The Philippe out in the Channel, the damage wasn't deemed that serious but the Captain, a stocky fellow called Edwin Stone decided it better to pull into the nearest port for a full damage report.

So here she was three days later berthed at the deep water pier in Portland harbour. The Captain had ordered that the cargo of spices, fruits and alcohol be unloaded to lighten her so that checks could be made below the waterline and the ships carpenters had repaired a section of the hull that had taken damage, now the Nancy Spooner was being made ready for sail on the next tide.

Thomas walked over to a large collection of wooden crates and barrels that had been stacked up on the docks in readiness to be reloaded into the hold, they were emblazoned with fascinating exotic words like Nutmeg, Cloves, Mace and Cinnamon, his mind raced with thoughts of far away countries and squash-buckling adventures.

Thomas sat on a coil of old rope and gazed up at the vast ship and watched awhile as the crew made her ready and shipshape.

A group of burly looking sailors were operating a traditional Portland hand crane and using it to lift a large pallet of crates from the dock and transfer it to the ship, with them were a handful of local buxom doxies that were laughing and flashing their wares hoping to make a quick shilling.

The sailors were taking it in turns trying to steal farewell kisses and it was obvious even to Thomas that their minds weren't on their job and that they were caught up in the moment with the flirting girls, it was then that Thomas saw that the winch-man on the hand crane hadn't secured its stabilising chain to the ground spigot correctly, Thomas used one of these cranes daily to winch his clinker above the shoreline so he knew all there was to know about them and right now he could see that the securing chain was slipping and that it could come loose at any time, he also knew that if the securing chain did come loose from its spigot the crane would be ripped from its mount sending its load crashing down, and at that very moment the load was dangling precariously above the receiving group of ten sailors on the deck of the Nancy.

In the next few minutes Thomas Crimsons life was to change forever, one second he was sitting staring, eyes wide, at the iron spike as the securing chain slipped another inch towards the end of the spigot, the next he had launched himself towards the ship yelling and shouting about the danger everyone was in, but nobody seemed to hear him and the sailors by the crane were still laughing and joking with the girls oblivious to his shouts, he switched direction and bounded up the gangway trying to board the ship and to warn those on deck but a few hands reached out to grab him and to halt the progress of this strange interloper invading their ship, he had managed to reach the top of the gangway before running straight into the arms of the boatswain.

Thomas yelped in agony as his right arm was twisted behind his back and he was thrust to his knees by the burly sailor, through gasping breaths he tried to tell the man of the impending danger but the words wouldn't come out.

'The the...' he stuttered, 'The crane!' he was silenced by a blow to the forehead from the boatswain's billy club, blood dripped into his right eye from a deep crescent shaped cut that appeared, the boatswain gripped his hair and held his head still.

'Stop flapping yer gums like a fish outta water and shut yer mouth for a second lad, take a deep breath and calm down.'

Thomas took a few gulps of breath and let his breathing settle.

'Now, tell me boy, what you doing trying to get on the Nancy like that?' the boatswain stared down at him with his club raised as he waited for an answer.

'Sorry Sir' Thomas swallowed. 'But it's the crane!' he pointed towards the docks. 'See the security chain? it's about to come loose, the crane will collapse!'

The boatswain peered in the direction Thomas was pointing, then his eyes widened, in an instant he had released Thomas and was sprinting down the gangway shouting to the winch-man as he went, this time the crew snapped to attention, he had their ears and they moved as one like a well oiled machine.

The doxies were long forgotten as the men took charge and began to swing the crane away from the ship, Thomas held his breath as the long boom slowly cleared the deck and its cargo swung out over the water just as a loud metallic rattling announced that the security chain had pulled free from its spigot followed by what sounded like a huge elastic band being twanged and a wooden cracking noise, in a cloud of wood-dust the crane collapsed in on itself and the cargo it was carrying dropped like a stone and plummeted harmlessly into the sea below.

Thomas was taken to the Captain's cabin by the boatswain who explained everything that had just happened and how Thomas had undoubtedly saved the lives of some of the crew and more importantly, untold damage to the ship itself.

The Captain, a middle aged portly seadog, shook Thomas' hand and couldn't thank him enough for his brave actions, the ship's doctor was sent for and whilst he dressed the cut above the hero of the hours eye, the Captain pulled the boatswain aside, the two men had a quiet exchange of words out of Thomas' earshot and then offered rums all round, after thanking Thomas once more the Captain made his excuses and left the cabin.

'Well young lad' the boatswain gave a toothy grin and looked at Thomas. 'You've certainly made an impression on Cap'n Stone, he likes you lad, reckons you got spunk so he does, I reckon I probably agrees with 'im too.' the boatswain walked to the cabin door and stopped.

'I've gotta go and lock that bloody fool winch-man in the brig now, the careless bastards always got tits on his brain he 'as!' he shook his head.

'So my young friend.' he looked back to Thomas.

'We got a vacancy on the Nancy if you reckon you can handle it?'

Thomas looked stunned.

'Mind you, after we drop the cargo in London and take on more supplies, we're bound for the Spice Islands and won't be back this way, maybe not for years, it's a long hard haul and the pays shit but we'll feed you well and the grogs free.' he laughed.

'Well what do you reckon son, you up for it?'

It was a no brainer, this is what Thomas had always wanted, a chance for some adventures in the Orient, sailing the high seas, fighting off pirates, bedding dark skinned beauties, a shiver of excitement ran down his spine and with a broad grin beaming across his face, he looked at the boatswain.

'Where do I sign?' he laughed.

Thomas Crimson spent the next eight years on the Nancy learning the ropes and sailing the high seas, visiting far away exotic places such as Ceylon, Indonesia, Burma and Japan, until she was scuttled by a Portuguese Man O'War at Maluku Province.

He then worked his passage around the Cape of Good Hope and made it back to Europe where he worked out of Cadiz for several more years and it was there that he fell in with a bunch of privateers and got into more scrapes than he could count.

Smuggling was his game these days and he began making quite a name for himself, especially with the Royal Navy and had many a run in with the Blue and Whites, he even managed to get a small, but modest, price put on his head for his troubles.

Eventually Thomas' luck ran out and he was captured in Cornwall unloading stolen barrels of rum from his ship the Abigail, he was to be hung on the gallows and would have had his neck stretched if fate hadn't intervened on his way to the noose when one of the horses transporting him threw a shoe and tossed him to the ground, he quickly had it away on his toes and escaped to the hills where he hid out for a few weeks until the dust had settled, when the coast was clear he decided that it was maybe time to try a different career in a different country for awhile.

Not much is known about the intervening years but it was said on the rumour mill that Thomas had signed on with a schooner and headed to the Jamaica's or that he'd joined a polar expedition and headed north, but no one knew for sure and it would be years before Thomas Crimson resurfaced and was once again seen on the merry shores of England, and this time as we now know, he was dressed as a Parson.

Crimson, Hunter and Wyke, accompanied by Timothy Edge, a seventy seven year old retired captain of the guard and now the official custodian of the Royal jewels in the Tower of London, spent a leisurely hour walking around the basement rooms of Martins Tower admiring the fine collection of crowns, sceptres, swords, rings, jewels and gold bullion that made up what is known as the Crown Jewels of England.

After much gapeseeding, over-zealous joyments and comments of wonderment suitable for use by men of the cloth, the little sojourn came to an end and it was time to leave the basement.

As was common at the time, the correct protocol was to view the famed royal jewels and then retire to the custodians private quarters one floor above in Martins Tower to take a tipple of port and make repatriations to him for conducting the tour, the three imposters had different plans though and as soon as the party had entered Timothy Edges quarters a wooden mallet was produced from under Hunters voluminous cassock and used to crack open the custodians skull.

As Edges body lay crippled and dying on the floor, Wyke purloined the keys from his pockets and they ran back down to the jewel room in the basement. The men knew exactly what their spoils were to be, Hunter grabbed the jewel encrusted St. Edwards Crown which was the official coronation crown used exclusively in the coronation of a new monarch, it was covered in four hundred and twenty two diamonds and pearls but due to an oversight it was too big to secrete on his person as planned, so Hunter flattened it under his boot, after all it was only the diamonds he wanted and he could pluck them from their sockets later.

Wyke took handfuls of gold rings and the Sovereigns Orb, the six and a half inch gold sphere studded with precious gems and diamonds, this he managed to successfully stuff down the britches he wore under his cassock.

It was left to Crimson himself to take the main prize, the St Edward's Sceptre which contained the largest known diamond in the world at the time, the 530 carat Cullinan Diamond. The Sceptre was promptly concealed under Crimsons clerical coat and now with their haul safely stashed upon their persons, the three men dusted themselves down and calmly walked out onto Tower Green.

They passed the Coldstream guard standing to attention outside with barely a drop of sweat shed between them and it would be a full eleven minutes before the body of Timothy Edge was found and a further eight minutes until the full extent of their dastardly deeds were discovered and shouts of *murder! Treason! The crown is stolen*, began to echo around the tower.

By this time Crimson and his men had made their way to their waiting horses at St Catherine's gate on the far side of the Tower and were approaching the drawbridge over the moat, when suddenly a few alerted Yeomen began firing upon them, Wyke took a musket ball to the back of his head and in an explosion of bone and gristle, he and the Sovereigns Orb hit the ground in a cloud of dust, the remaining two riders didn't look back and galloped over the drawbridge before turning left onto Tower Warf, all that stood in their way now was Iron Gate and once they had passed it they could lose themselves amongst the populace of the packed streets of London.

It is said that it was the confusion of the guards on duty at Iron Gate that aided the men to escape capture, when presented with the unusual sight of two churchmen hammering along the wharf on foaming nags they just didn't know what to do, it wasn't a common occurrence for sure, should they shoot at Holy men, were the alarm calls they could hear being shouted in the distance meant for someone else, so standing aside, they let the two riders pass through and ride away into the distance.

With the Tower of London quickly receding into the distance and now made invisible by the cover of other horse riders and carriages out on the streets, Crimson and Hunter slowed their horses and cantered through the crowed capital until finally ditching them and their clerical disguises in a dark alleyway in Whitechapel.

The plan was to meet up the following month at a pre-arranged flash ken just outside the City where they would sort the haul and divide it equally between themselves, so with a nod, both men then went their separate ways.

Glory was short lived for Hunter and he never made it to the safe-house, he was picked up in a tavern called The Nine Bells in Dulwich a week later hufty-tufty on gin. Hunter had been chirping merry to anyone that would listen that he was one of the daring fellows that had stolen the King's jewels right from under his very nose and how it was he who masterminded the brazen robbery, a groat was all it took for someone to pass that information on to the Yeoman at the Tower and a squad of soldiers were all that it took to apprehend him.

Hunter was still in a drunken stupor, leaning on the bar still spinning his tales when the soldiers arrived, he offered no resistance and once he was clapped in irons they took him back to the Tower for questioning. In the meantime Hunters rooms were thoroughly searched and the crushed St Edwards crown was recovered intact, all bar a single small pearl and was taken straight to the Palace goldsmiths to see if the damage could be repaired.

The following day, once sobered up and under the influence of thumbscrews, skin flails and eventually the rack, Hunter confessed to everything, he named his accomplices as Wyke, whose body now rotted in a ditch outside the Tower gates, and Thomas Crimson. He told his interrogators where and when the loot was to be divided and he also admitted to removing the missing pearl from the crown and selling it for two guineas to a Frenchman in the city. Hunter spent a total of two weeks in the dungeons of the Tower in the hands of professional torturers and once they were satisfied that they had gleaned all the information they could out of his wrecked body, he was sentenced to death.

Hunters crimes were so heinous that no trial was needed, treason against the state and murder most foul could only be dealt with by the greatest and most grievous punishment available.

Three days later Hunter was taken to Tyburn gaol where he was hung until he was half dead, then and only then, he was taken down from the gallows and within sight of his own eyes, his genitals were cut off and thrown onto a fire, if he hadn't died of shock by this time he then had the pleasure of watching himself being disembowelled. Once these acts were done, he was finally beheaded and his body was cut into four quarters, his head was sent to the Tower for par boiling in brine whilst the pieces of his body were mounted on spikes along the roadside outside to deter other would-be-traitors.

It was 7pm and as usual during the British summertime it was pissing it down with rain. The early evening clouds throbbed and pulsed as they watered the landscape below them, the torrents of rain had turned the mud track that ran up to the farmhouse on the distant hill in to a swampy quagmire of brown slop, it was the kind of evening that you would prefer to have been snuggled up in front of a cosy log fire with a loved one, not the kind of evening that you wanted to be hiding under a bush up to your eyes in mud, at least that's what twenty year old private Archie Jones of the Kings Own was thinking at that very moment - *A roaring fire, a mug of hot rum and the pleasure of an even hotter woman.*

Archie had only been in the regiment for five months and he hated every single minute of it, army life definitely wasn't for him, but what could he do, it was this or gaol, mind you gaol was looking a lot more better than being under the bush right now, he scooped up a handful of the thick sloppy mud and stared at it, it reminded him of the food back in the barracks, he went back to thinking about hot women.

Two squadrons of soldiers, sixty men in all, lay in wait secreted in a loose circle around the crumbling farmhouse that was four miles out of London on the Woking road. Express orders had been given by the King himself to take Crimson alive and on no account should he be killed, his majesty wanted the scum to pay.

The plan was simple, stay well hidden until Crimson had entered the building and then quietly close the loop and strangle off all exits, the troops would then make their presence known and the overwhelmed Crimson would know it was a lost cause and would surrender without a fight, it was a classic ambush.

The soldiers surrounding the farmhouse had been waiting since first light and were totally and thoroughly depressed but they wanted this bastard as much as the King did, this was personal, nobody but nobody strolls onto their turf and walks out with their jewels, this was a matter of pride, there was shit to be kicked tonight and they were wearing their best size

11's.

The seconds took minutes to pass but at almost 7.30pm word went around from man to man that Crimson had been seen by the lookouts entering the area.

The 2nd lieutenant colonel made a final speech and told his men to keep it quiet and wait for the blaggard to enter the house as per the plan, there were going to be no mistakes and that was an order.

At 7.48, dressed in dark waterproof leggings and jacket and a huge Sou'wester pulled down over his eyes, Crimson finally rode up in the shadows and dismounted his horse outside the front of the building, he tied the black and white filly to a tether ring that was bolted to a wall and took a quick glance around to make sure the coast was clear then entered the building shutting the door quietly behind him.

The inside of the farmhouse was in darkness as he knew it would be, he took a furtive glance up the staircase to his right and began slowly walking along the corridor towards the kitchen doorway at its end.

The 2nd lieutenant colonel silently drew his sword from its scabbard and signalled his men to begin the advance towards the farmhouse.

Inside the kitchen Crimson struck a match and lit a tallow and placed it on an oversized table in the center of the room, he placed his loaded pistol next to the tallow, took a seat and waited for Hunter to arrive.

At the rear of the building the soldiers began lining up along the wall either side of the back door like schoolboys waiting in the dinner queue, they drew their swords. Young Archie Jones peered through a grimy window and spotted Crimson sitting at a table staring at the floor and as the word went down the line that their foe was just inside, more and more troops began crowding around the door, all eager to be the first to grab him.

Crimson reached into a pocket and produced a small silver flask of ha'penny rum, took a slug and grimaced as it burnt its way down his throat, a sudden creak of the stairs pricked his ears, was Hunter already here, had he been waiting upstairs.

Too many soldiers were cramming around the back of the building, soldier after soldier piled into the cramped space and bodies began to be jostled and ribs were elbowed, a serious crowd control situation was rapidly developing and the more soldiers that entered the area the more the ones in the front were being crushed against the wall and rear door, it was inevitable that something bad was going to happen, yet still more soldiers poured into the scrum.

Archie Jones suddenly had his right arm pinned to his side and there was no way that he could raise his sword in the melee of soldiers, but there was also no way on this planet that he was going to go face to face with a murdering bastard like Crimson unarmed, so after a panicked struggle he managed to drop his sword and draw his pistol from his belt.

The kitchen door rattled in its frame and made the desperado look up from his seat at the table, someone was outside.

'Who goes there? he called through the door. 'I hope tha.. '

A loud splintering of old wood echoed around the room as the rear door burst inwards nearly taking it off its hinges. Standing there on the threshold with a

pistol in his shaking hand was the young soldier
Archie Jones, his eyes wider than dinner plates, there
was a seconds pause as both men stared at each other
in disbelief, their minds raced. As quick as a flash the
older man's hand wrapped around the grip of the
pistol lying on the table and raising it towards the
soldier, he pulled the trigger, a single shot rang out.

A lone figure dressed in a long woollen overcoat
stood in the shadows of a small copse of trees
alongside the main road to London and watched in
silence as sixty weary soldiers on horseback rode
from the dirt track of the old Padgett farm and pass
him by.

Maybe they had caught Hunter he mused, the
bastard definitely hadn't shown up at the safe house as
they had planned that was for sure. He had even
waited an extra hour after he thought he'd heard him
upstairs at the farmhouse but it turned out to be just
rats.

The rear of the cortège of dejected looking soldiers
was closely followed by a horse drawn cart and
Crimson was surprised to see the body of a man
lashed to its bed, he tried to see if it was Hunters
corpse as it passed but whoever it was no longer had a
face and was totally unrecognisable, he knew though
that old Padgett himself wore similar waterproof
leggings and jacket, so it could be that the alcoholic
farmer had a tumble with the soldiers and came off
the worst.

Crimson was just pleased that the troops hadn't
gone to the next farm over and tumbled him instead.
He shuddered at the thought and pulling his collar
high, he about turned and disappeared into the dense

trees.

The limp unconscious body of Private Archie Jones hit the hard flagstone floor of the stockade to where he had been taken after the 'Unmitigated cock up.' as the 2nd lieutenant colonel had called the night's operation.

Archie lay in a heap of twisted limbs, already his eyes were swollen shut and were a nasty dark puce colour, dried blood clung below his shattered nose and had splattered the front of his tunic.

'The stupid fool's lucky not to be dead.' the colonel looked down on the comatose soldier.

He was lucky that the colonel had only hit him in the face with the hilt of his sword, it could easily have been the bullet from Crimsons pistol.

The colonel had been livid when he found out that Jones had killed the blaggard scum, *What the Hell was he playing at the young idiot.* he knew that the orders had specifically said that their foe be taken alive. The King would have his sweetbreads on a plate for this mess that's for sure. *Mind you, it was a bloody good shot from twenty five feet* the colonel thought, *a single shot straight in the kisser - Blew Crimsons whole damn face off.* He gave an admiring and respectful nod to Archie and dropped a coin on to his prostrate torso.

'Buy yourself a mug of gin when you recover soldier.'

The years ebbed by as they do, Crimson was all but forgotten about, except by the King himself, he had been completely outraged by the audacity of the

247

robbery plot and it had stuck in his craw, how dare these thugs try and steal from him, how very dare they.

Publicly the operation to apprehend the culprits had been announced as a complete success. The official line was that Crimson had been shot dead and brought to the justice that he rightly deserved and all the stolen treasures had been restored to the Tower of London where they belonged.

In private the King had told his advisors that the faith of the nation should be restored at all cost, even if it meant covertly replacing any missing jewels with replicas.

So that the people of England would know that no one could ever get away with stealing the Crown Jewels again, the age old custom of paying the custodian of the jewels for private viewings was stopped forthwith, the Crown Jewels themselves were moved from the basement rooms in Martins Tower where they had been housed for the past two hundred years, to an armoured strong room in the Main White Tower itself, and it would be almost twenty five years before the public were allowed in to see them again.

So in a way, Portland born and bred, Thomas Crimson, can be thanked as the man that improved the security of one of the nation's greatest assets, but I don't think we will be seeing his face on a bank note any time in the near future.

The Wheelchair Killer of Portland

Have you ever heard the phrase 'Bobs your uncle?' Yes of course you have, I bet you even have a relative called Bob and he's an uncle to someone. Most Bobs are quite amiable guys, or girls, as in the case of the Bob I used to date back in college, she was definitely one of the amiable Bobs woohoo!

To me, the name Bob conjurers up happy jovial fellows, the kind of guys that when you were a child would buy you a Mr Whippy even when your mum had said no.

Unfortunately this story isn't about one of those types of Bob, this story is about Bob Stoner the notorious Wheelchair Killer of Portland. Just to clear up any confusion before we get started, I would like to explain that the non de-plume "Wheelchair Killer", doesn't actually mean that the guy would go around killing wheelchairs, as if, the Wheelchair Killer didn't even go around massacring people that use wheelchairs, no, in this case, Bob Stoner was the one in the wheelchair and he also happens to be a serial killer.

You can blame the local press for the confusion, as we all know the papers love to put a tag on things and give them names, you've got "Jack the Ripper" of course, the "Granny Killer" and you've even got the "Boston Strangler" over in America, if it was me, I would probably have called him "Wheels the ripper killer", or then again maybe not.

I first met Stoner not long after I left college, that was what, some fourteen years ago now, he had a pair of legs back in those days and travelled sans a wheelchair, and I must admit that they were quite nice legs too, in a "I've found my inner woman and I'm quite happy with my sexuality thank you very much", kinda way, but they were a bit hairy for my liking as I do tend to like my suitors legs to be waxed at least.

Our first meeting came on the day that Bob walked into my place of employ. As I just mentioned, I hadn't long left college where I had received a diploma in I.T. with first class honours, so was working at McDonald's in the high street, burger flipper extraordinaire that was me, well there I was, Ben Sorbet (Yep that's my name, Sorbet, just like the ice cream, only a little less umm... creamy), up to my elbows in fried minced cow, and who should walk into the kitchen, none other than Bob Stoner, he was wearing a brand new freshly pressed Maccy D uniform which was a little too short for his six foot three frame. For some reason I remember that he was wearing red ankle socks, isn't it weird some of the things that we remember.

Bob grunted a greeting to me and I shook my

burger flipper in his direction splattering his nice clean shirt with a large dollop of grease. At lunch we sat at the same table and both munched on double cheeseburgers and drank diet cokes, we had so much in common.

We didn't say much that first lunch date, he concentrated on eating his two meat patties and getting melted cheese all over his chin, while I stared over the rim of my diet coke at the hordes of young lovelies that walked in through the door, which was one of the perks of the job, more tits and ass walked in through those double doors at lunch time than there are on an 18 to 30 holiday let me tell you, sometimes during the summer months when the girlies were all scantily clad in bikini tops and short shorts, I would get so hot I could have cooked burgers in me underpants – Sizzleishious!

When the shift was over on Stoner day (That's what I like to call the day that I first met him - *Stoner day*), I was out the back of the restaurant near the bins, I was filling a carrier bag with unsold burgers and fries as I always did at the end of my shift (saves a fortune on buying groceries), I was studying the contents of the bag in earnest and wondering if I could also squeeze in a thick shake or two, or three (yeah ok, I'm a fat bastard), when Bob walked up behind me, I think he must have been standing there a few minutes just watching me before I noticed him.

'You ever kissed a black man?' he asked, his spotty face deadpan, for real, that's what he said, "You ever kissed a black man?".

I looked him up and down a bit curious as to why he had asked the question and watched as one of his acne spots erupted like a mini volcano.

'Uh no, I don't think so.' I replied, I was pretty sure that I hadn't, I hadn't kissed any man come to think of it, I did think that this was a strange question at the time, especially as neither he nor I were black, did I detect a bit of racism in his voice, naah, but I did detect a bit of a twat standing in front of me, he then lent forward and gently took the thick shake out of my hand, it was strawberry as I remember.

'Do it like this.' he told me and he removed the plastic lid from the cup and proceeded to pour the shake into the carrier bag coating my burgers and fries with pink gloop, wow! I mean like totally wow!! the guy was a genius, dinner *and* dessert in a bag! how come I'd never thought of that, it would even save on the washing up, that was the turning point in our relationship, I was now in awe of Bob Stoner.

I can hear you all muttering under your breath, 'Tell us how he lost his legs! – Tell us how he lost his legs!' Well I'm coming to that so bear with me.

At this period in my life, I was living on Portland, I still do actually for my sins, and it turned out that so did Bob, although I had never seen him around the island. Apparently Bob lived at home with his mum in a flat at East Weare, you know East Weare, the place to be avoided like the plague unless you don't mind getting gang raped by a bunch of twelve year old psychopaths.

His mum, so he told me, was a junky and she hated him, but he hated her too so it was all fair, he told me how he had wanted to kill her and that he'd come up with some amazing plans to fulfil his desire.

He had already tried three times to commit

matricide but she kept foiling his plans – the bitch! Bobs first attempt at murder was when he used a screwdriver and some wire to covertly connect his mother's computer keyboard directly to the 240v mains socket, unfortunately the damn fuse blew when she switched it on and she didn't receive even as much as a tingle, she called in an engineer to take a look at the computer and he discovered what the problem was when he replaced the fuse and got an electric shock that blew the fillings right out of his teeth.

Bob's second murder attempt came when he climbed inside the tumble drier on washday, the plan was to wait until his mother came to fill the machine later that day and then launch a full frontal attack on the surprised woman and smash her head in with a ball peen hammer. So he squeezed himself into the drier and waited, and waited but typical of Bob he went and fell asleep, eventually his mother arrived with a handful of damp clothes but found the drier door already closed and the load indicator already lit, thinking that she must have already filled the machine she switched it on and tumble dried the snoozing Bob.

For thirty five minutes Bob span around and around slowly cooking and all the while the hammer was clonking him all over his body, Bob confessed to me that he had actually enjoyed his tumble in the drum and even found it quite an exciting adventure, that was until the heat of the dryer caused his underpants to shrink so much that they severed his left testicle, and that he could never forgive her for.

This brings me nicely to how Bob managed to lose his legs. (see, I told you it was coming), the third and final attempt on his mother's life came when Bob brought home a viscous Rottweiler that he had stolen from a twelve year old drug dealer down the road.

He successfully managed to hide the animal in his bedroom wardrobe and starved the poor creature for a week to make it go crazy with hunger, his infallible plan was to wait until his mother fell into one of her drug induced comas, sneak into her bedroom and smear her face with dog food, he would then release the ravenous beast from the wardrobe, lead it to her room and close the door behind it, as a back up Bob had also taken to poking and prodding the animal through a hole in the wardrobe with a large sharpened stick that had a photo of his mother sellotaped to it just to make sure that the k9 hated her as much as he did.

The day of execution arrived and after a pre-celebration of a Pop Tart and coke, he sat in his bedroom with an open can of Pedigree Chum in his hand.

Bob waited for the sound of his mother entering her bedroom and gave it another thirty minutes for her to shoot up her junk, just to be on the safe side, all this time the dog in the wardrobe was going insane from the smell of the dog food, it snarled and it hissed and flames shot out of its nostrils, Bob giggled to himself that he had created a true Hell beast.

Unbeknown to Bob though, his mother wasn't in the land of nod or wherever it is that junkies go to when the pass out, she had in fact been off the hard stuff for two weeks now and she was at that present time sat in her bedroom listening to Rammstein through headphones.

As Bob's ears strained for the sounds of his mother

zonking out, he sneezed and accidentally tipped the can of dog food on to his lap leaving a big patch of sloppy, stinky, goo all over his crotch, the smell of the freshly spilt dog nosh wafted up through the poking hole in the wardrobe and entered the dogs flaring nostrils, everything went quiet.

Confused at the sudden silence, Bob stared at the wardrobe door just as it shattered open and the most evil of evil dogs sprang out, before he even had a chance to think, the snapping and snarling Hell hound bounded straight for the food spillage on Bobs lap and began to rip into it with its razor sharp teeth, the dog wasn't satisfied with just the pet food though, it didn't calmly eat and say thank you very much it was nice meeting you, before finding the nearest lampost, no, the crazed rabid fiend opened its dripping jaws wide and clamped its fangs deep into Bobs thighs and groin where it happily ripped away at the flesh and muscles of his lower body, the dog would have happily continued tearing away large bits of Bob if it hadn't finally choked to death on Bobs plastic testicle implant.

Unfortunately the dog's demise came too late to save Bobs legs, they were now nothing but gleaming bone and were forever trashed.

I expect that Bob was a little bit pissed off at how events turned out that day but as he never spoke much anyway it was a bit hard to tell. In total he spent four months in the hospital intensive care unit plugged into beeping machines and fluid drips. Eventually though he was deemed fit enough to leave and so the doctors unplugged him, plonked him in an NHS wheelchair and sent him home with a packet of Aspirin in his shirt pocket.

I went to visit Bob for the first time a month after 'dog day' and found him alone in his flat waddling around on his new stumps.

His mother was nowhere to be seen, apparently while he was in the hospital she had fallen in love with the dog and they had gone to live in Brighton.

When I saw Bob that first time without his legs I couldn't help but laugh, he reminded me of ET the extra-terrestrial from that movie, I laughed even more at the way his solitary testicle dragged along the carpet as he moved but he forgave me for it when I gave him a carrier bag full of burgers and fries from work. I told him to look on the bright side because at least now he didn't have to buy any new shoes, Bob gave me an odd look and clambered up onto the coffee table and started rocking back and forth like one of those nodding head dogs you see in the backs of cars and began tucking into his burgers, I sat on the floor and played with a dried up baked bean that I found on the dirty carpet.

I fell asleep at some point during that evening and when I woke in the morning I had a big sticky slime trail running up the right leg of my jeans to my groin as though a giant slug had been partying on my crotch, I looked over at Bob who was naked and asleep on the coffee table, his lone bollock winked back at me.

At about lunchtime, Bob told me to put him in his wheelchair and push him to Fortuneswell. While he pulled on some clothes and tied knots in the trouser legs, I pocketed my newly found baked bean (you never know when a dried baked bean might come in handy) and we left the house.

Bob told me to push him into the Co-op supermarket where he instructed me to buy a huge stainless steel carving knife but to make sure that it had a yellow handle 'The biggest they got' he ordered.

We left the shop, turned right and continued on up the hill, Bob gave me directions by casually poking a finger in the direction he wanted to go and we turned into an alleyway by the library, we rolled on for a few more minutes until we reached the end of the alley where an auburn haired woman sat on a bench reading the Daily Mail, Bob signalled for us to stop.

'Bring her here.' he suddenly announced, I don't know why he wanted her but I suspected it was because she was a Mail reader. I approached the woman and caught her attention and apologised for disturbing her.

'Could you please give my friend a hand?' I pointed to my helpless buddy in his wheelchair.

She eyed him up and down a bit and probably felt a little guilty at his predicament, then putting down the paper, she walked over and stood in front of Bob.

'My feet.' he said as he nodded at where they used to be, a quizzical expression appeared on her face and she crouched down and stared at the footless space.

Bob leant forward and plunged the knife into the side of the woman's exposed neck. For the first time since the day I met him, I saw Bob smile, the woman didn't, her face turned as white as a sheet of paper as she realised what had just happened, her jaw dropped open and she flopped forward into the space where Bobs lap used to be.

Bob thrust the blade in again, this time you could hear a crunching noise as the blade severed the vertebrae in her neck, it was a strange sound and I don't know if I liked it or not but Bob obviously did and he began a sawing motion, he sliced through muscle and cartilage until finally the woman's head was only attached to her body by a few remaining sinews, he gripped her auburn hair in his left hand and made one last slice, her head came away cleanly from her shoulders and Bob placed it between his legs stumps.

We left the scene of the crime and returned to Bobs flat through the back streets of Portland, it was lucky that no one saw us as Bob was soaked in blood and people tend to get a bit suspicious of blood soaked people.

Once behind the safety of the front door, I gave Bob a bath to clean him up which only took a half a bottle of Matey bath wash to remove all the red stuff, probably because he only had half a body to wash. It was an ultra weird experience as I've never given another man a bath before and at first he screamed when I scrubbed his scuffed bollock with a loofah, but then he eventually relaxed and began enjoying himself.

That night Bob took the woman's decapitated head to bed with him because he said he was lonely and wanted to talk to it, and I slept on the floor in the corner of the living room again, but not until after I had found another dried baked bean that matched the first.

For two weeks Bob seemed sated with whatever pleasure he had gained from the killing of the woman but he was soon performing his nefarious deeds again.

This time he was more prepared, he still used the same big stainless steel carving knife with the yellow handle as he had before but this time he wore a waterproof poncho and leggings even though he didn't have any legs to go in them, he also wore an adult sized Pampers nappy underneath which may have been to protect his scabby bollock, I don't know.

Bob told me that he wanted to go to Portland Bill so that's where I pushed him, which was damn hard work up all those hills. His victim was a middle aged man that was sat in his car in the car park, it was early in the day and there were no other cars about so we wheeled up to the man's blue Renault and I asked him for his help getting Bob out of the chair, the man was only too happy to help and as he bent down to hoist Bob up, the shiny knife blade entered his right eye, watery blackish eye juice squirted out and ran down his face which made him look like he was wearing mascara in the rain, I don't think the man really knew what was occurring as it happened so quickly.

The blade squelched as Bob removed it from the eye socket and then calmly sliced it across the man's windpipe making him gurgle as blood flooded into his lungs drowning him, once again Bob smiled.

I think that Bob might have been practising his knife skills because the man's head came off really quickly, one minute it was there on his shoulders just like a head should be, the next it was under Bob's blanket just where a head shouldn't be.

Bob had me wheel him out and around the island quite a few more times that summer to collect his bloody trophies, although I'm sure that he must have gone out alone once or twice without me because the newspapers were reporting that there had been twelve headless corpses found so far, and I'm pretty sure that we never went out that many times, but you never know, I do have a bad memory sometimes, especially since the headaches I had been having were getting worse.

The last time I ever saw Bob was the day that he told me he wanted to go and get himself some new legs.

We were in the park at Fortuneswell on a Sunday I think it was, Bob had been feeding frozen fish fingers to the ducks in the little pond which they weren't too impressed about. He said that we shouldn't travel too far from his flat as it would be difficult getting the legs back without them being spotted by a nosey busybody.

We were going to take a roll up to Easton to see if there were any suitable suppliers up there but there was no need in the end as Bob quickly saw a nice pair of legs that he liked not far away from where we sat, the prime suspects were attached to a young woman in her twenty's that was lying on a towel getting a suntan nearby.

At the time I thought it a bit curious as to why Bob would want female legs when male legs would suit him much better but I didn't like to say anything to him and appear that I was legist. I wheeled Bob over to the young woman and asked her if she wouldn't mind giving us a hand (well I couldn't really ask her if she could give us a leg), isn't it strange that people always seem ready to help the infirm, no questions asked.

Once again the sharp stainless steel carving knife did its job and the woman's neck gushed blood like the Trevi fountain, two quick deep slashes and a bit of sawing and off popped her head as clean as a whistle, he was clever was Bob, he had the art of head removal down to a T. Bob then did something that surprised me and I had never seen him do before, after he had placed the head in his lap he used the knife to cut out the woman's tongue, I think he did that just for fun though because he put the severed tongue between his own lips and made it wiggle and flap for a few seconds then he threw it in to the pond, weirdly it appears that ducks prefer human tongues to frozen fish fingers.

Now that the woman's head had been removed, Bob tossed it unceremoniously onto the grass and proceeded to slither out of his chair, he landed on the woman's stomach which was a little messy as it caused thick blood to squooze out of her neck just like when you squeeze the end of a toothpaste tube, Bob pierced the knife into her stomach and began slicing sideways, he seemed to struggle slightly as he cut through her spine and he tutted a loudly a few times, but eventually the blade made it through to the other side and the legs came free from the woman's torso.

At Bob's command I picked him up and placed him back in his comfy chair then put the legs on his lap covering them with his blanket, it was quite a funny site to see Bob sitting there with these legs poking out from his wheelchair and I must admit I sniggered a little bit because the bright green flip flops on their feet clashed with his tartan blanket, it wasn't just me that thought so either because we got a few funny looks as we wheeled home, some people have no respect for the disabled.

Once back inside Bobs flat he told me to *carefully* put his new legs on the coffee table, he said that he was going to clean himself up and then waddled off towards the bathroom, but to be honest, in retrospect, I don't think that he really went to the bathroom because I never heard any running water or other sounds coming from there.

I made myself busy scanning the carpet for more dried baked beans to add to my collection when the next thing I knew there was an almighty crash from the direction of the front door and loads of policemen came rushing into the room, I think Bob must have known they were coming and had abandoned me, that would be typical that would, I make a new besty and he runs off on me at the last moment.

For some reason the police grappled me to the ground and I remember a big ugly ginger one with sausage sizes fingers smirk as he stomped on my head, that was when everything went black as I passed out.

Well that's pretty much my story told, plus I have to go, I have an appointment with the doctor anytime now, he's bringing my tablets and he doesn't allow me to do any writing, that's why I'm having to use a broken pencil lead to write this on a roll of loo paper.

Mind you, he *says* that he's a doctor and yes he wears a white doctors coat and has a stethoscope around his neck, but I'm not too sure and have my doubts to his authenticity, after all, why would a genuine doctor walk around accompanied by an armed guard, and thinking about it, why is my door

262

always locked from the outside. It's most peculiar, but I can't complain really, at least I don't have to wear that stupid straightjacket anymore and they've stopped trying to convince me that Bob was just a figment of my imagination..

I hear the keys rattling in the lock so I really must go now, thanks for taking the time to read this. By the way, if I ever manage to get out of this place I'll come and visit you, I also have a weird feeling deep inside my head that Bob will finally turn up again very soon, and I'm sure he would like to make your acquaintance.

– Toodle pip

The Why Files

Ello me old Rubik's Cube swallowers, your buddy Andy 'ere again.

Who would of thought that Portland had its very own serial killer eh. Makes me wonder if the "Muddy Hand" incident was anything to do with the Wheelchair Ripper too.

Did I tells you about the Muddy Hand incident, was a bit of a rum do it were, no mistake.

It was little Sammy Tune that found the yucky thing. Him and a few pals were up at Rip Croft quarry with their air rifles, shooting dem damn long-eared furry things, like you do, when he spies a mobile phone poking up out of the mud, just standing there it was like, that black monothingy from the film 2001 A space odyssey.

Well Sammy goes and pulls the phone out of the sloppy stuff and it comes free with a slurp, complete with a human hand still attached to it.

The police were called and they took the hand

away but not before Sammy had pocketed the phone, the little scamp.

And that's how old Andy here got involved, cuz he couldn't get it to work and brings it to me to work me magic on.

After the phone was all fixed and working again I had a little peekeroo around on it, well I was bored weren't I, and I came across some voicemails which kinda shocked me they did and I didn't know what to make of dem.

Me being the electronics genius that I am like, I decided to extract the voicemails and transposedagated them onto paper before giving the phone back to little Sammy.

I still got the paper here somewhere, have a gander and let me know what you reckon.

Sender: Michael James Clarke
Receiver: Jake Frederick Hallett
Hey Jakey boy, how's things?

It was a most excellent Friday night I gotta say. You put on an amazing party, fuckin excellent music too – Aciiiiiid!! I luv that retro shit.

I hope your head recovered and you made it to work on time in the morning, nah I don't, I hope they fired your arse you fucker lol. With the amount of booze and pills you put away I wouldn't be surprised if you didn't surface until next Wednesday, oooh your so hardcore ya cunt lol ;-p

That Sandra girl I was with was a bit tasty no? OMG she should change her name to Electrolux cuz nothin sucks like an... yeah yeah you got it lol, she didn't come up for air for about two fucking hours, me knob was as sore as fuck in the morning, I even have teeth marks on me bellend to prove it lol. Hey those Goa trance toons you were spinning hit the fuckin spot man, I gotta hear some more of that stuff, do you have any CD's I can borrow? - Course you do, your Jakey the fuckin man lol.

Have you heard from the Wilson twins? Mandy belled me this morning and said that she ain't heard from them since that night, she said she was worried cuz Ady had a job interview which he missed, now she's getting letters from the social warning that they is gonna stop their benefits, I reckon he's with 'Gail the Goer' from Weymouth and he's still round her gaff shagging her ass off, lucky cunt.

Hey, now I'm thinking about it, the twins might have been caught up in that church shit... Holy fuck! Yeah the church shit, I forgot all about that, fuck man! How could I forget about that? What the fuck was all that about?

That's right I remember now, I seen you and Chelle walking through the graveyard about two in the morning just before all hell broke loose, hope you two made it ok. Me and Sandra was in the church when the roof started caving in, I seen Zimo take a huge lump of brickwork to the head and never saw him get up, but we was too busy legging it the fuck outta there - Christ yeah! There was Tommo too, that fucking huge stained-glass window came down on him, shit, I saw his head explode in a cloud of fucking blood and coloured glass man.

Seriously! What the fuck is going on? How could I have forgotten all that shit? I'm sort of remembering bits of it now but for fucks sake!

266

Me and Sandra had been on the dance floor non-stop for about an hour so we decided to go and chill for a bit, we went outside to the graveyard for a joint. That's when I saw you and Chelle walking away through the grave stones, yeah I remember that cuz I said to Sandra that I bet you two were off for a shag.

We finished the smoke and went back inside the church, whose fucking idea was it to have a fucking party in an abandoned church anywayz? Good bass response my fucking ass! Good fucking kill ratio more like it! And what was that fucking noise?

Yeah that's right, I remember, there was this huge fucking bang and the amp system went up in smoke, that's when everybody started screaming, then there was that fucking ear piercing high pitched squeal, my fucking ears started fucking bleeding, and that green fucking strobe light! It weren't from the lighting rig cuz all them lights went out just after the toons went off.

Ah shit man, I remember, the green light was coming from under the floorboards! Fuck! It was then that the fucking windows blew in and that bunch of girlies, Marie, Bella and her mates all got cut up, little Bella had blood pumping out of a hole in her fucking neck. Fuck fuck fuck! OMG yes... She had been talking to Gaz Williams when that happened, Gaz's face! His face! Oh fuck, his face was sliced off, I seen it on the fucking floor being trampled by everyone as they scarpered, little Bella was screaming and fuckin well slipped over on it!

Oh God. This is a fucking nightmare!!

I remember Sandra grabbing my hand and we ran to the door when those guyz... hang on a fucking minute, those guyz? Who the fuck were those guyz that came bustin' in through the main door? Sandra dragged me down behind them pew seat things that we stacked up before the party.

Shit that's right! When the fucking guyz burst in they was dressed like the fucking army or something except their uniforms weren't like normal soldiers and they had these badge type things on their sleeves that looked like a red cross in the center of a white circle, and OMG yeah, the fuckers had fucking guns man!

We was hiding behind them pews and I saw this girl, remember that blonde that we saw when we arrived, the one that was wearing that real tight white dress and her nips were standing out like organ stops? Well the dress weren't white any more, it was red, red all over, and her fucking arm was gone man! Just a fucking ragged fucking stump with all this… all this fucking blood pumping out all over the fucking place.

And fuck me yeah, those fucking soldier guyz burst in, about fifteen of them there was, they… they… they just stood there and started fucking shooting man, oh Fuck! They were shooting at anything that fucking moved man!

I seen a bunch of people go down in a spray of bullets, and there was this one guy, never seen him before, but I seen his fuckin eyes explode and his brains erupting out the back of his fucking head man, OMG OMG, that's when Sandra pulled me out through the rear door, I could still hear all the shooting and screaming from inside. I remember we ran down to Chiswell like the fucking devil was after us, I was fucking terrified man I don't mind fucking telling you. Sandra said we should clean all the blood and gore off us by jumping in the sea, I said no, that we should call the cops first, but she insisted that we had to get cleaned or *they* would be angry with us, what the fuck did she mean, who the fuck are *they*?

We stripped off and dived in from the rocks, I remember the sea was fucking freezing and that Sandra was laughing at me cuz me dick had shrivelled up, she didn't seem bothered about the fucking shit-storm happening back at the church!! Then we walked around the coast to her gaff up on the cliffs and she gave me some of her dads *special* whiskey as she called it, that's when I started feeling dizzy and groggy. I woke up on Saturday afternoon back in my own gaff!! WTF! Seriously... What The Fuck man!! OMG. How the fuck could I forget all that shit?

This is totally fucked man.

Get back to me ASAP. We need to talk.

Big Mick

Sender: Michael James Clarke
Receiver: Jake Frederick Hallett
Jake where the fuck are you man?

I just been up to the fucking church, you never guess what? there's no sign that anything happened up there at all. Everything's back to normal just like we found it on Friday, even the fucking stained glass windows are back in place, I saw them fucking windows destroy Tommo for suck sake! Am I going mad??

Call me NOW!

Sender: Michael James Clarke
Receiver: Jake Frederick Hallett

This is all too fucked up. I went to see Sandra at her gaff earlier, she denied all knowledge and says she don't even fucking know me, has never set her fucking eyes on me man! I told her what happened on Friday night and she called me fucking crazy. She said that her uncle was the head honcho of Portland CID or something and that if I didn't piss off immediately he would come and fuck me up big time, probably even get me sent to prison.

This is so seriously fucked up man.

What should I do? Do I call the cops? My heads totally fucked up with all this.

Where the fuck are you!!!

Sender: Michael James Clarke
Receiver: Jake Frederick Hallett

Well I'm totally fucked now you fucking bastard. I called Sandra about an hour ago and begged her to help me figure this shit out, it's doing me in man, but she didn't want to fucking know, told me I was insane and called me all these horrible fucking names.

I started to fucking cry man! Can you imagine that? Me, Big Mick - *THE* fucking face! Me, fucking crying! She told me to grow up and stop being a pussy and that she had had enough and was getting her uncle, the CID dude, to come around my place to sort me out once and for all. So like I said, I'm totally fucked now. I asked around about her uncle and he has a fucking reputation bigger than King fucking Kong's dick! Even his mates call him the ginger cunt!!

Fuck! There's the fucking door bell. That'll be him. Fuck, I'm so fucked.

I don't give a flying fuck where you fucked off to,

you fucking fucker - Fuck off!

Sender: Michael James Clarke
Receiver: Jake Frederick Hallett

Hey Hey Jakey Jake McJakeson, ignore all my previous messages ok. It seems like I was too fucked in the head when I sent them. Everything is sorted now though, thank fuck for that. I gotta visit from Sandra's uncle the ginger haired copper guy and he persuaded me to go and visit his doctor up at Cheyne house, I didn't even know that there was a doctors up there, but still. They did some tests and it seems that I was under the influence of some uber high powered hallucinogenics when I saw and experienced all that shit up at the church, or didn't see and experience all that shit up at the church lol. The doc told me it was too crazy to be true anyway and I guess she was right, wow it was totally fucked up and seemed so real lol. Anyway, this morning I got a surprise invite to a rave up at the High Angle Battery, you know the Ghost tunnels where all the young-uns go partying, dunno who sent the invite though cuz it was hand delivered, but it says they got some top hot DJ's on the tables so I think I might go even if its just for the toons. I hope they play some aciddubz. I'll see if I can get you an invite too cuz I gotta feeling that its gonna be the shitz man. Green glowing lights and armed soldiers, fuck I feel like a complete twat now lol.

Anyway take it easy dude, laters and all that – Big Mick (*THE* Face lol)

Weird no? But I guess that's Portland for you in a nutshell - Weird!

271

Well I must dash, I'm expecting the Philpot sisters any mo, they're twins you know. Anyways, they phoned me earlier and are coming to drop off a mysterious personal intimate item, they said, whatever that is, you got any ideas cuz I don't have a clue, the girls want me to work me magic on it apparently.

So I'm gonna refill the java machine and stock up on powdered milk for when they arrive, it could be a long night.

Tatty bye byes for now.
Ever ready Andy

One Rasher or Two?

If there were two names that would scare the shit out of most Portland pure bloods it was Tomalty & Spanglar, they were names only said in hushed circles and then only by the very brave, mothers fed up to the hind-teeth with their unruly children might suddenly tell them that unless they behaved themselves Tomalty & Spanglar would come and get them while they slept, the warning worked every time.

Locals all know the stories, have heard all the tales and rumours about the the job that Tomalty & Spanglar do, they know that there's no bull involved – they know there's no pig involved either come to think about it, but sometimes a blind eye is needed to be turned and in the case of the two grey haired septuagenarians, it was best to turn your eyes 180 degrees in the opposite direction, pull them from their sockets and put them in your pocket for safe keeping.

The two old men that look so alike they could pass as brothers, work for the Portland Environmental

Trust in what was officially titled Sector K but was more better known as the "Chop Shop".

Some people will try and tell you that the Trust was initially setup to help the islanders overcome a serious typhoid epidemic in 1844, but in truth they went much further back in history than that. As mentioned elsewhere, the Trust had evolved from a much earlier secret society based on Portland that originally called itself the Insula of Calx Scientia Statio and had famous names such as Newton and Flamel as its patrons.

The Trust had survived and developed over the generations and now ran almost every aspect of daily life on the island from water manufacture and production to artificial insemination services for pure blood Portlanders, even if the pure bloods weren't actually aware of it themselves.

The Portland Environmental Trust had its main headquarters in the Sweethill area heading out towards Portland Bill although they had many satellite units scattered all over the island, each of which undertook different operations and aspects of the Trust.

Portland being an island has kept itself to itself over the years and has tried its best to stay segregated from the mainland and it had pretty much been able to remain isolated in one way or another. The islanders were completely self-sufficient, they grew all their own crops, bred & raised all of their own animals and even had their own water supply via numerous artisan wells scattered around the island.

Over the years Portland has seen some good times and has definitely seen its fair share of bad times, more than most some would say. The good times are usually forgotten but the bad times are always remembered and so it was with the winter of 1843.

It began when a "perfect storm" of disaster struck the island, first there was a massive typhoid outbreak which was swiftly followed by an outbreak of foot and mouth in the animals.

By mid March that year, the first Portlanders began to die, by the time July 1844 came around the outbreak had become an epidemic and over fifty five percent of Portland's inhabitants were dead or dying from the disease.

The dire situation couldn't continue, Portland was dying and there seemed no end to it.

The islands elders held an emergency meeting and decided that they had two choices, either go cap in hand to Weymouth on the mainland and beg for help, or to make contact with the Portland secret society of genius boffins, the so called Insula of Calx Scientia Statio. The latter was chosen.

When first contact was made, by the brothers friend of someone that knew the uncle of one of the society's members, the Insula of Calx Scientia Statio, being like all covert organisations, denied their own existence, and it wasn't until their own members began dying that they agreed to help, but their help came with the proviso, that they would not put their official name of the Insula of Calx Scientia Statio to any help they provided, and instead they would form a new off-shoot wing which they would call the Portland Environmental Trust, which was just as well as nobody knew how to pronounce the former anyway.

The first thing that the newly named "Trust" did was to spray the entire island with a special chemical powder that they had developed in their labs at Sweethill to kill off every single bug, insect, germ and bacteria, good and bad, island wide, they also boarded up all the public drinking wells on the island and removed their pump handles to stop the public drinking contaminated water from them.

These combined measures successfully stopped both the typhoid and foot and mouth in its tracks, but it was a double edged sword as it also wiped out every animal on the island and meant that there was no fresh water for Portlanders to drink.

The drinking water problem was easily resolved by the development of a new water substitute which they called HydroPrep™ and was initially delivered to street corners in large bowsers until a reservoir was built near New Ground at the top of the island and pipework was laid connecting it to the existing water pipes.

The fields were then replanted and reseeded but it would be months and months until new farm animals could be re-established and even longer for animal life to return to sustainable rates.

It was then that the Trust labs began working on a meat substitute, something to keep the islanders going until the first harvest at least. It took a few weeks but before long a breakthrough was made and new meat replacement was developed which they named it B-Aconospore Saphilasis after a small green fungus discovered in the caves of Portland.

Pure blood Portlanders were swiftly issued with special ID cards and shipments of the substitute began immediately to the church halls around the island where everyone could go and receive a weekly ration for free.

At last it seemed that everything on the island was going to be okay. It wasn't until another three months had passed that people began getting side effects associated with the new super food. As it turned out, B-Aconospore Saphilasis was highly addictive and it caused pregnant women to go into early labour and their babies, if not miscarried, were born with terrible deformities and birth defects. That first year alone, seventy six babies were taken into care by the Trust's scientists for studying, it is not known if any were returned to their parents.

The B-Aconospore Saphilasis problem continued without a solution for years, although the substance was now highly restricted and no longer given away free, its addictive qualities made it a big revenue maker when it went on sale in the local butcher shops a few times a year.

The solution eventually came via a most unlikely source.

In 1976 it was brought to the attention of Trust's executives, that a convicted serial killer was living on the island, the man was a Mr Samuel Goldstein a tailor of Needlers Walk in Fortuneswell.

The tailors true identity came to light when a new customer turned up at Goldstein's bespoke tailors shop for the fitting of a handmade suit he was having made for his grandsons wedding to a Portland girl, incredibly and against all odds, the customer was a survivor of Gardwald labour camp in Germany during WWII and as soon as the tailor held out his tape measure the customer had recognised the unusual blackwork tattoos on his hands and the tailors missing little finger. How could he ever forget, the tattooed hands that had forced a large Satan tattoo on his chest under pain of death.

The customer contacted the authorities as soon as he got to a phone and the tailor was swiftly taken into custody by the local police. Bizarrely, by his own admission, Goldstein straight away admitted that he was indeed the murderer known as Leon Bergman and that he was a convicted German serial killer.

Goldstein/Bergman's original court files were sent from Germany confirming the tailors story, that he had indeed been found guilty of multiple counts of murder and cannibalism but surprisingly added that he had been hung, yet here he was, living and breathing on the isle of Portland.

As there was no records of Bergman having done anything nefarious while he was living on the island, the shocked authorities decided to have him deported back to Germany and to let them deal with him, that was until the scientists at the Portland Environmental Trust came forward and declared an interest.

The Trust said that they had developed a way to analyse the human brain and extract all of its thoughts and memories, even its most hidden secrets buried deep in the subconscious, such information could be very beneficial to their future projects they said, and they wanted to test the procedure on Bergman.

So forms were signed and Bergman was transferred to a secure holding cell in the Sweethill laboratories.

A week later the tailor was sedated and underwent

the new procedure, every single detail of the revolting individuals past life, from birth until the present day, was recorded and stored on huge Winchester computer tape drives from where the information could be studied at the scientists leisure.

Unfortunately for Bergman, the procedure completely fried the man's brain and he was transformed into a person with the mental capacity of a cold bowl of custard, so after the signing of another form, the man's cerebellum was removed and dissected and his body went to the furnaces underneath the Sweethill complex, a fitting end to such an evil monster no doubt.

Bergman's small tailors shop that he owned under the alias of Goldstein was cleared out of anything relating to him by the authorities, and as no one in their right mind would want such a tiny shop in the miniscule Needlers Walk, it was just left to rot away and to be forgotten in the annals of time.

The problems associated with a meat substitute that wouldn't be addictive or cause birth defects in newborn babies was eventually solved using the vast reams of data that was sucked out of Bergman's head, and this is where Tomalty & Spanglar enter the picture.

The two stalwarts of the Portland Environmental Trust, Mr Algernon Tomalty & Mr Hastrup Spanglar of Sector K, who's official job titles were joint heads of recycling and meat production, ran all aspects of their job from an underground facility five levels under an area of Portland not far from an area called The Grove and was actually underneath the local football pitch.

It had been the task of Mr T and Mr S, amongst other things, to solve the B-Aconospore Saphilasis problems and they did it using the data gleaned from the German serial killer head, although the exact details of what the data was and how they used it is highly classified.

Sector K (the Chop Shop) was the department that collected and recycled the dead bodies of all pure blood Portlanders that die on the island. Once informed by the Portland doctors service of a pure bloods demise, personnel from Sector K, under the guise of a local undertakers called Thrumptons & Brash, would collect the body from grieving relatives and take it to the underground facility at The Grove where it would undergo specialist treatments involving various chemicals and procedures.

If a replacement corpse was required to fill the empty coffin, well there was always a plentiful stream of holidaymakers available for the job.

Once the body was at Sector K, it would be first stripped of all body hair using industrial heat lamps and placed into a tank of a specially formulated acid and salts solution which was bubbled through with nitric oxide. After a few hours in the brine, the flesh and bones would have dissolved leaving a thick genetic soup, which after the addition of some special compounds, a souson of a peculiar neon green fluid and some vitamins, would then be filtered from the acid solution and sent onto the next section for further processing.

This involved removing all traces of DNA from the soup and so making it genetically inert, this was achieved by using another special compound developed by the Trust and a set of Mitchell Micromeshtex filters. The final step in the process was to solidify what remained of the soup and press it into one metre square blocks ready for slicing and butchering.

The Trust now had a cheap viable way to feed the masses of Portland without any risks of birth defects, it also solved the bed blocking problem that was rife at Portland hospital.

As well as being the joint heads of Recycling & Meat production, Tomalty and Spanglar had a lucrative little sideline going which was overlooked by everybody including the Trust's chiefs, why - Because even the Trust's chiefs loved its results.

Deep inside the bowls of Sector K, fifty meters under the football pitch at The Grove, there is another special processing plant, it's hidden away behind double sealed security doors that no one but Tomalty and Spanglar can access.

Inside you will find something that resembles a small abattoir, and in fact, most of the equipment has actually come from a slaughterhouse.

As you walk through this area the first thing you will see is the holding pen, next is the restraining gate where the "animal" is stunned by either a 240v 60 amp electric shock to the temples or Mr Spanglar's favourite toy, a captive bolt pistol to the front of the head.

A little further along the line you will see two rows of sharp metal hooks suspended from the ceiling by a pulley system, this is where the fresh carcasses are suspended upside down by a stainless steel hook through the posterior inferior tibial ligament on each ankle. The two carotid arteries in its neck are quickly severed to drain the blood and whilst the blood is draining, the digestive tract is removed from the abdomen to avoid cross contamination with the meat.

Today, all but two hooks are empty, their occupants are the bodies of a heavily tattooed biker and a very tall thin albino that once sported long pure white hair.

The next station along is the pre-processing stage where the animals head and skin are removed, these two parts will be sent on for DNA removal and destruction as they are not of pure blood breed and are unwanted, unless Mr Tomalty fancies some "special crackling" or when the skins are occasionally used to make the leather for Tomalty and Spanglar's shoes. Finally you reach the massive walk in freezer where the carcases are frozen to a chilly -26c.

On the second Wednesday of every other other month, Mr Tomalty and Mr Spanglar like to put in a little overtime in Sector K. Once all the other members of staff have finished work and have left the building, the couple ride their little golf cart through the double sealed security doors then strip completely naked and don heavy leather aprons. They each remove a frozen carcass from the large deep freezer, lower the bodies onto steel gurneys and push them to the steam powered defrost machine.

Whilst the headless bodies are thawing, which takes no longer than an hour, Mr Tomalty inserts his favourite CD into a player and as the dulcet tones of Mozart's Piano Concerto No. 21 echoes around them, they take each other's hands and perform a slow naked waltz around the room.

Once defrosted and marinated in a vat of special, if not dubious, liquid smokey bacon flavouring of their own design for another twenty minutes, the two grey haired men push the gurneys over to the processing area where Mr Tomalty picks up his favourite blue handled filleting knife and hones it on a sharpening steel, he looks at his compardre.

'Shall we?' he asks with a smile.

'Yes I think we shall.' Mr Spanglar replies.

The two strange men then spend the next few hours slicing and chopping, de-boning and filleting the carcases into an assortment of different cuts.

Rump and loin, ribs and shoulder will be wrapped and boxed, the belly and hocks will go into the infuser to be infused with more than 57 special herbs and spices, and the belly meat will be further processed and sliced into exquisite, yet highly addictive Portland bacon rashers and sent straight out to the butchers shops of Portland. The pancreatic sweetbreads and testicles, when available, will be wrapped separately in wax paper and string and taken home as a little butchers treat for themselves.

So remember, if you ever visit Portland and you see a sign appear in one of the butcher shop windows announcing that there's been a delivery of Real Portland bacon, you may want to think twice before tucking into that nice juicy BLT sandwich, unless of course, you've already acquired the taste.

The Lost Treasure of Blacknor

Ello me little Bone Machines, welcome back again, it's your your friendly fun lovin' tv repair guy Andy 'ere.

Did you just see Stan leave the shop? You must of passed 'im on the pavement outside, mighty pissed off he was, he came in to collect his ginormous flat screen telly, he paid his bill and then.... well see that pile of twisted metal, plastic and broken glass there in the corner. That were his newly repaired tv that were, he only went and dropped the bloody thing, a total write off, poor chap, I mustn't laff but...

Anyways, as it's gonna be Halloween sometime during the next 12 months, I thought I'd tell you a scary tale for a change and as a bonus its totally true, I know because I... well you'll see later.

As you already know, and if you don't then shame on you haha, I was born on this funny little island called Portland and as I grew up there was a rumour among all the kids that there was treasure buried at

Blacknor bunker.

I dunno where this rumour first started but we all believed it to be true and some of us even tried to find it, the myth was that the treasure once belonged to a famous pirate called Crimson who used to haunt these parts way back in the 1600's.

It was the thoughts of pirates having their buckles squashed, sword fights and buried treasure that was such a lure to Cole Samways and his buddy's, that one weekend they decided that it was their turn to have a go at finding it.

Blacknor Bunker, as the name implies, is a combine harvester, just kiddin' haha, it's really a military bunker complex built hundreds of years ago over on the west side of the island near the village of Weston. Not much is known about the bunker except that it was used by the military during WWII and placed in civilian hands afterwards.

All the island's kids knew though that the bunker was once owned by two crazy brothers, who ended up killing each other during a quarrel about a secret hoard of treasure that they had found buried in the depths of the bunker.

When the brothers bodies were discovered, a search of the bunker took place and the police found the bodies of some missing rock climbers that had all had their noggins chopped off. The kids also knew that the bunker was haunted and that ghosts had chased away a couple of Kimberlins that had recently moved in, they fled back to London in the middle of the night and never returned, the bunker has been left abandoned ever since.

The story of the mass murders alone was enough to

put most of kids off from attempting to enter the now boarded up bunker complex, but a few of the fearless amongst us, cough Mark (Smiffy) Smith cough, would enter through holes in the rickety fencing and tag the bunkers exterior walls with graffiti and run amok in the above ground buildings, but even they never had the bollocks to enter the miles of dark wet tunnels that run underneath it, and if you believed Smiffy that his sisters ex boyfriends brothers mate had once been dared to stay in the tunnels overnight and was never seen of again, you'd understand why everyone was so reluctant to explore there, that is until Cole Samways finally managed to persuade his two mates to take on the challenge.

'Come on guys, let's go to Blacknor and find the treasure.'

Cole Samways the fourteen year old ex Brummie Kimberlin and newby to island life, stood up and rubbed his hands together as he tried to invigorate his two friends.

The trio were sitting in Cole's back garden at Easton just lazing around doing nothing in particular, although Dave Morris and Shane Peters were both watching Cole's sixteen year old sister Kirby sunbathing on the patio.

It was coming to the end of the long summer school holidays and they had done everything that they had planned during the break, now they spent their time just lazing around being bored.

'Come on guys, lets go explore Blacknor.' Cole kicked aimlessly at the dry sun baked dirt.

Shane nudged Dave and giggled as Cole's sister turned on her beach towel and exposed a bit of side boob, they weren't so bored.

'Come on, It'll be fun, just think of the treasure, we'll be rich and famous and be on tv, they might even make statues of us.' he was beginning to sound desperate now.

'Id rather think about your sister Cole.' Dave laughed.

'Pervert!' Cole laughed back, 'Mind you she does have nice tits.'

Both Dave and Shane looked shocked, 'Eww, she's your sister dude, you're the pervert you perv.' In unison they launched themselves on their friend and began rolling around the garden as they play fought together. It was Kirby that stopped their fun.

'Will you little boys be quiet, I'm trying to get a tan here.'

Egos bruised and taking umbrage, the three lads came to rest.

'Blacknor guys? Treasure, fun, excitement, come on lets go... or are you scared of the ghosties?'

'Cole, how many times we gotta tell ya that there aint no treasure. It's all a load of bull.' Shane tried to explain to his young buddy. 'Just like there aint no ghosts in there either.'

Cole might just about believe that there wasn't any treasure he supposed, cuz kids always liked to pretend there was buried treasure all over the place, just like the time when Sonny Richards said he found a solid gold woman's foot buried under the pebbles up at Church Ope Cove, but there was no way he would believe that ghosts weren't real because he'd seen one himself when he and Chumps Williams broke into the creepy old church in Weston looking for his missing brother Gaz, and saw a spooky green glowing ghost rising up from under the floorboards, besides, he knew Tommy Jenson whose brother had got into Blacknor and seen a ghost of a soldier carrying a rifle, and Tommy was nineteen so he wouldn't lie.

'Aww come on lets go, it'll be fun, or are you chicken?' Cole began clucking and scratching his foot on the ground in a bad impersonation of one of Colonel Sanders favourite animals.

Shane looked at Dave who had gone back to staring at Kirby's side boob.

'Come on Dave, we might as well go, he'll never shut up unless we do.'

Kirby rolled onto her front ending Dave's fantasising. 'I suppose.' he said with a disappointed tone in his voice, although he was secretly pleased because he'd always liked exploring around Portland and a good treasure hunt was right up his street, but he'd just turned fifteen and it wouldn't be cool to let the others know it right.

After a quick rummage around Cole's house and shed for essential treasure hunting tools like torches and rope, plus of course the requisite shovel to dig up the treasure, the three amigos set off on the thirty minute hike over to Blacknor bunker on the cliffs at Weston.

Unless you are climbing up the two hundred foot cliff face on the sea side of Blacknor, the only way into the bunker is along a twisting and turning muddy track that runs off at an angle half way along Wide Street, at the end of the track you are faced by a huge chain link barricade that was erected by the council years ago, but thanks mainly to Smiffy, there were a few holes and breaks for the lads to squeeze through.

Once inside the compound the three lads surveyed their new surroundings, the place was an overgrown jungle of waist height weeds and shrubs that obviously hadn't been touched in years, they passed what looked like the burnt out remains of some caravans and headed in the direction of the bunker structure nearer the cliff which they could see had been boarded up with steel cladding and was covered in years of graffiti.

The lads scouted around the building looking for some sort of entry point but it looked like it was sealed as tight as a drum. For ten minutes they searched without any luck, it really was sealed tighter than the proverbial mackerels arse and the friends were on the verge of giving the whole thing up as a bad job and going home, when Cole, who had clambered up onto the roof of what looked like an old chicken coop, shouted down that there was a way onto a flat roof and he could see a skylight and was going to investigate further.

The glass skylight window looked as though it had been smashed years ago but the hole helped Cole shine his torch into the gloomy depths below and he could see that someone had positioned a table below to make easier access in and out, but judging by the amount of mould that covered its surface, no one had stepped on to it for a very long time, possibly years. He went back to the roofs edge and shouted down to his two pals that he had found a way in and to come up and join him.

'Here we are lads, the entrance to Aladdin's cave.' Cole pointed at the smashed skylight. 'Dave, find somewhere to tie off the rope, it'll help us get out later.'

Whilst Dave secured the end of the rope around the guttering, Shane and Cole shone their torches into the ominous looking hole.

The room below was covered in mildew and green mould from years of rain pouring in through the open skylight, it gave the room an eerie green glow under the torchlight and Cole remembered the creepy old church in Weston, maybe he had been a bit too hasty in talking the others into coming here to explore but it was too late to back out now, his street cred depended on seeing this through.

The drop through the skylight was easy enough and went without a hitch, it was only twelve feet to the table below but the green slime on its surface had made it slippery and Dave's foot skidded out from under him causing him to nearly break his neck as he shot off the table and landed in a heap on the floor, luckily only his pride was hurt.

The flaking Magnolia emulsioned room was some sort of utility room and against one wall stood a Zanussi washing machine and matching spin dryer, that although both were coated in lots of dust and a sprinkling of mold, looked to be almost new, the wall opposite had a long worktop running its entire length on which stood the crumpled remains of a few large sized washing powder boxes and a pile of what could once have been folded clothes but now resembled a flattened fibrous mass.

At each end of the room was a door, the nearest door on the right was double glazed and was obviously the door that originally led to the exterior and through the dirt on its top glazed half, you could see the sheet steel that had been erected to block access from the outside. The door on the left was a simple unpainted pine affair that was half open and led deeper into the bunker.

Shane being the eldest and having the largest gonads, led the way through the door and into what was once the lounge area, the three boys shone their torches around in the darkness and were surprised at what they saw. Although the room was some thirty feet long by twenty feet wide, it was still fully furnished, running along the far wall was a green stained sofa and armchair that could once of been blue, the opposite wall had two wooden Ikea type shelving units which were still covered in niknaks and trinkets including some framed family photos, in one of the corners of the oblong room stood a relic of a tv set on a matching stand and in the center of the room was a small table that had two cups containing what looked like dried up green tinged coffee sitting on it. It looked like whoever had lived here before had left in a big hurry.

The three teens didn't linger in this eerie looking area and quickly moved on through the door opposite them on the far wall. The next room they came to after walking down a short corridor was stranger still, it could have once been a study or something and like the room before, it was still furnished, except this time all the furniture had been pushed aside and piled up around the walls leaving a large empty space in the center. Dave spied an old computer system lying on its side under an upturned chair and noted to check it out on the way back, just because computers were his thing and he loved to tinker, in the middle of the cleared space somebody had put four stained and manky looking mattresses in a rough circle and in the middle of that circle was a large scorched patch of carpet and the remains of burnt wood and ash, Shane aimed his torch at the ceiling and they saw that it was covered in black soot.

Around the perimeter of the mattress circle were a scattering of crushed beer and cider cans and discarded fag packets, some well thumbed porno magazines that dated back to the early nineties, which Dave began leafing through excitedly, one man's sized Reebok trainer and a pair of girls filthy knickers that were spotted with mildew, Cole laughed and commented that how come you always only find one shoe and where does the other one go, which raised a few chuckles.

Shane kicked a few beer cans around the room and tried to score a goal into the fireplace while Dave slipped one of the porn mags into his back pocket for perusal when he got home.

There was nothing else of interest in this room except some marker pen graffiti on the wall near the boarded up window where some joker had written in neat handwriting: Julie Conway swallows for a quid, to which another hand had replied underneath, Hey that's my mum! whilst a third wit had added: Is that why you get it for free?

They moved on and out through the only other door in the room which led onto another hallway, again like all the other rooms in the building, the hallway was in darkness but their torches illuminated yet another doorway halfway along and a quick check showed that this one led down into the bunkers underbelly and its maze of tunnels and passages.

'Well guys, we're here, this it.' Shane stood on the threshold and shone his torch down into the darkness. 'Are we doing this?' he looked at the faces of his companions 'Or are we chicken shit?'

'We do it.' Dave stood defiant.

Cole looked shamefaced at his mates, 'I'm chicken shit.' he croaked '...seriously guys, this looks scary as Hell.'

Shane placed his free hand on Cole's shoulder. 'It'll be ok dude, I'll look after you, we've come this far, we can't turn back now, you know what you're like, if you leave now you will regret it forever... and you'll be begging us tomorrow to come back.'

Cole knew deep down that his buddy was right, he pointed his torch down the stairwell. 'Okay, but I'm going in the middle!' they all laughed and following Shane they headed down into the unknown bowels of the building.

The descending staircase turned three times before it finally levelled off onto a long stone corridor. Through the powerful glow of their combined torches they could tell straight away that this was definitely the underground part of the bunker complex as the ceiling and walls of the corridor (or tunnel as it should be more aptly called), were made of undecorated aged Portland stone.

'Bloody Hell it's cold in here.' Dave's voice bounced off the walls and echoed in their ears which made them laugh and eased the tension somewhat, and for the next few minutes the lads began making daft sounds and calling silly names as they listened to the echoing around them, but they soon bored of the childish game and continued their journey.

The tunnel ran for some sixty feet into the distance and all along its length were doorway after doorway, each door was made from iron or steel and was heavily rusted, most of them stood open but one or two remained shut, the boys shone their torches into the open doors as they passed, empty, empty, full of junk, empty and so it went on until they came across one room that looked like it had once been a kitchen.

They entered. Again like the rooms upstairs, this one was still furnished but this one seemed like it belonged to a different era, heavy wooden cupboards adorned the walls, an old double industrial type sink was bolted to one wall and a large oak farmhouse table stood in the center.

Shane and Dave began opening cupboard doors looking for anything interesting that they could get their hands on until Dave let out a yelp as he came face to face with an object that looked like it had more in common with a voodoo ceremony than a military bunker.

On the shelf in front of him was a large stone bowl that was filled with some foul waxy looking substance, in the center of the waxy substance somebody had inserted what looked like a pair of chicken wings complete with feathers, and they in turn had been coated in a red substance that looked just a little too much like blood for Dave's liking, he studied the bowl closer and in more detail, around its edge was carved Gothic looking symbols and an inscription that read "praepara animam tuam ad abyssos", he had no idea at all what the inscription meant but it was far too spooky for his liking and he slammed the door shut with a look of disgust on his face, he turned to Cole to tell him what he had found but Cole was standing by the side of the large table staring at a dark patch on the floor by his feet.

'Hey Cole, what ya gawping at?' there was no reply so Dave walked over to see what had caught his young pal's interest.

Cole suddenly pointed at the stain.

'It's blood!'

Dave was about to say that it could be anything and is probably just paint but Cole continued, 'This is where those brothers killed all the climbers, they chopped them up on this table.'

They both stood and stared at the discoloured patch on the floor, lost in their own thoughts, in his mind Cole could see the mad murdering brothers dragging their victims down here from the surface, laying them on the large table and chopping them up into pieces before burying the bits in the cellar, and Cole just knew in his heart of hearts that that's where all the treasure was buried and that's why no one has ever been able find the treasure because its protected by blood and bits of chopped up body parts and guts and brains and and and …

'Cole! Snap out of it dude! You were miles away then.' Dave could tell by his friends pale face that he was scared, he gently put an arm around his shoulder and whispered in his ear

'Don't worry dude I'm scared too, we'll protect each other ok.' he smiled warmly at his mate then flushed with embarrassment.

'Hey look see what I found.' Shane quickly

pointed his torch at an open door that no one had noticed before.

'There's another staircase, probably goes down into the cellars or somewhere.' he rubbed his hands together excitedly.

'This is it boys, we're gonna be rich very soon.' He didn't wait for a response, instead he followed his torch beam and skipped off into the gloom leaving Cole and Dave staring at his disappearing figure. They looked at each other and raised an eyebrow in unison and then quickly darted after him into the darkness.

Shane descended four more flights of stairs, each one twisting around on itself like a spiral staircase, the lower he went the damper the walls and steps became so he slowed his pace being careful not to slip, he imagined that he had been descending for miles and miles deep into the earth's crust, he imagined that he was on a Jules Verne quest for the center of the earth and was on his way to discover giant mushrooms and lost civilisations. He turned another bend in the staircase and suddenly stepped out into a small arched atrium that was blocked by a huge metal door preventing any further access.

Shane illuminated the massive door and contemplated his options, the door was set in a massive metal surround that had large rivets running around its edge, the door itself had a rusting metal wheel in its center which made it look like it should be in a submarine not in an underground tunnel, he put his ear to the cold metal and listened.

'This is it... This is the way to the treasure, I just know it!' He said aloud to himself, all thoughts of returning to the surface were now forgotten.

Shane was busy trying to turn the wheel on the metal door when the other two finally caught up with him, he didn't acknowledge their presence but had heard them coming.

'Give us a hand turning this bloody thing will you.'

They all grabbed a handful of wheel and gave it a yank, it didn't budge.

'Again!' Shane ordered, it still wouldn't move.

'Looks like that the end of that then.' Dave sighed,

'I'm getting hungry anyway, let's go home and get some grub, anyone fancy a Big Mac?'

'No fucking way!' Shane almost shouted, the pitch of his voice raised, he pushed the others away and gripped the wheel anew, the sinews in his neck stood proud as he strained with all his might. He heaved and tugged, yanked and pulled, his face turned red and his eyes bulged in their sockets until slowly, almost unperceptively, the wheel let out a creak and jolted and inch, Shane took a deep breath and strained even harder if that was possible and with a screech the wheel turned another inch, the two lads watched in awe at their mates strength then hurriedly rejoined him at the wheel and added their muscle to the fray, the wheel shifted again, a whole three inches` this time.

'Come on boys, we got this bastard!'

With their new combined efforts the wheel suddenly gave up its rusty grip and began to spin freely. They all cheered as Shane spun the wheel around and around on its spindle until all of a sudden there was loud clank and the door was finally unlocked.

Shane rested while the other two used their shoulders to get the door open wide enough for them to squeeze through and eventually all three passed the obstacle and crossed the threshold on to the other side.

A gust of cool air blew in their faces as they crept through the doorway and shone the torches around to get their bearings, they appeared to be in large cavernous room that was so big their torch beams couldn't reach the other side, all there was was stone stone and more stone.

The floor was of rough flagstones, the wall behind them was of large stone blocks and even the vaulted church like ceiling of this huge room was made from stone. Dave had the horrible sensation that they were in a crypt.

'Come on.' Shane waisted no time and followed his torch beam in to the darkness ahead, Cole and Dave quickly caught up with their pal and they all walked together in silence for a few minutes until Cole's light beam pinpointed something strange ahead and to the left, *Shit are those coffins??*

All three lads felt icy fingers run down their spines as they peered at what most definitely looked like fifteen ancient coffins, the six foot long oblong boxes were covered in dirt and grime and thick dust-webs and lots of dried green mildewy looking stuff, they could easily of come straight out of a Hollywood vampire movie.

'Holy shit guys, no one said anything about coffins and dead people.' Cole stammered as he shone his torch around half expecting to get attacked by vampire bats, 'Seriously guys maybe we should get outta here now!' he was really beginning to panic, he was terrified and started to retreat towards the way they had came but Dave called him back.

'Its okay look, look, they're empty.'

Some of the scary looking coffins did indeed appear to be empty, but on closer inspection they saw that the lids had all been attacked by some heavy tool, possibly an axe, the sight didn't help reassure Cole, especially when he saw that the other coffins had large ragged holes on them, which gave them the appearance that something had burst out from the inside.

'Oh great, not only have we discovered a bunch of vampires coffins but they've all been attacked by some raving lunatic who's probably running around here somewhere with an axe looking for some heads to chop off!'

'Well it looks like it happened a long time ago, look.' It was Shane, he had cautiously approached some of the strange green liquid that had pooled on the ground and kicked at it with his DM boot.

'Its completely dried up and soaked in.'

The puddle of green stuff had collected and then run like a little streamlet, meandering across the flagstones and away into the distance like a glowing green snake, Shane's torch followed the fluids trail.

'Come on, lets see where it goes.'

'Are you completely bonkers? You think I'm gonna follow that weird stuff into who knows where?' Cole was shocked at the very idea and he knew his mate Dave would back him up on it.

'I'm right ain't I Dave?' he turned to face his friend but Dave was already heading off in the direction of the green trail.

For two more minutes the lads wandered in silence around the huge room as they followed the line of green, each of them lost in their own thoughts. It was Cole that spoke first.

'Over there!' he whispered in a hushed voice and pointed his torch towards what looked like some sort of raised dais growing out of the floor, the green liquid had collected around the edges of the six inch high stone platform and then disappeared through one of the many cracks in its base.

With a wary trepidation in their step, they carefully crept their way towards it.

'What do you think it is?' Dave asked as they stood facing the raised stone plinth.

'What do *you* think it is?? It's a bloody double decker bus aint it.' Shane laughed as he hopped up onto the platform.

'Hey look, there's a manhole here, right in the middle.'

Dave's light shone on what looked like a rusty square metal plate that had an iron ring handle on one side.

'That's not a manhole dickhead, it's a trapdoor.' Shane countered as he and Cole joined Dave on the dais.

Everyone stared at the trapdoor like it might bite them until Shane asked the question they had all been fearing.

'So... who's gonna open it?'

They looked at each other in turn.

'I think Cole should do it, this was all his idea.'

Shane tapped his foot nervously, all his former bravado now gone.

Cole wished for the second time that day that he hadn't thought of the idea of coming here, but Shane was right, this had been his idea, also his street cred had to be defended.

Shane and Dave looked surprised when without further a word Cole bent down and took hold of the dirt covered ring in the trapdoor and pulled. Cole was just as surprised when the metal door lifted with hardly any effort, he had been expecting to have to tug and pull for all he was worth to shift it, but it almost glided open and in seconds it had pivoted 180 degrees and come to a rest with a loud echoing clang.

So this was it, finally their two and a half hour trek and exploration of the horrible dirty scary bunker complex had finally come down to the wire.

'Get ready boys, in three minutes time we're gonna be millionaires, you'll see.' Shane announced with excited anticipation in his voice.

The trio aimed their torches in unison into the murky depths of the artisan well but there was nothing to see except for the green fluid that had dried on its walls, all there was was a cool calm blackness and a long drawn out silence from the disappointed friends.

'Guys... where's the treasure?' Cole's voice sounded as sad as it sounded desperate, 'The treasure guys!.. It should be here... right here!... Guys?'

The three friends continued staring into the dark hole saying nothing at all, then Shane's eyes suddenly widened.

'What the...'

Dave noticed Shane's reaction first and quickly followed his gaze and stared into the depths of the black abyss, his jaw dropped and his eyes bulged.

'What is it guys? Tell me what you see... is it the treasure?' Cole had also noticed his friends reactions and directed his beam at theirs in the blackness. 'What the Hell is in there?' he said, throwing the beam all around the insides of the well, 'What are you looking at?' nobody said a word.

An eerie silence drew out for a few seconds before Shane spoke in a strange deep voice that was barely audible.

'There's...there's a...' he pointed stiffly in to the depths,

'There... There's..." he repeated and turned to Cole, his eyes were on stalks. 'There's... *NOTHING!!*'

Shane shouted it as loudly as he could and then doubled up laughing.

'You knobend Cole, it's empty just like we said it would be.'

Shane and Dave hi-fived each other as Cole again peered into the depths.

'Yeah very funny guys ha ha, that was so funny I pissed me pants.'

Secretly Cole was so embarrassed that he wanted the ground to open up and swallow him whole.

As Shane and Dave continued laughing and joking at his expense, Cole really did notice something in the gloom near the bottom of the well, *what was that?* he peered harder and aimed his torch trying to see it clearer.

'Hey guys, there really is something down there, right at the bottom.'

'Course there is Cole, it's the boogieman coming for you.'

Shane and Dave laughed and hi-fived again.

'No there really is... look.'

The thing Cole had seen at the bottom of the well shifted slightly, now it was no longer just a thing, it was a shadow, almost a shape.

'Look look, there it is again!'

'Cole we just did that one, you can't pull it off again, it doesn't have the same effect the second time around.' Shane laughed.

The shadow that was almost a shape moved again, it began slowly rising up towards the mouth of the well getting faster and faster as it neared the top.

Cole's face turned pale.

'I aint shittin' you guys, look, there's something down there and it's moving this way – fast!'

Shane was losing his patience.

'Cole there aint nufin down there except manky water.' he shone his torch back into the hole.

'Holy shit!' he saw the shadow shape too.

Dave saw the change in expression in his mates faces and also peered into the dark hole.

'What the Hell is *that?*' he said aloud.

As all three boys stared in disbelief into the old artisan well, the shadow shape thing burst forth from its hiding place and enveloped them in a swirling mass of black and green streaked fog.

In a tangle of screams and shouts that reverberated around the walls of the huge cavernous room, the black and green shadowy thing span like a mini tornado, around and around it went until you could no longer see the boys or hear their screams at the center of the maelstrom, moments later the black and green tornado began to slow down until it was just an idly turning cloud rotating on the spot, then just as fast as it had appeared, it disappeared back down into the depths of wherever it had come from.

All that was left in the cavernous room were three spinning torches and a shoe laying on the ground.

Barry Flan stood amazed at what he saw, he had worked for nigh on fifteen years as the curator of Tout Quarry Sculpture Park and he knew the place like the back of his hand, each and every day for those last fifteen years, Barry had walked through the park on his way to the sculptors workshops and could give you a detailed description on every single piece of carving there, including the sculptors name, when it was sculpted and what tools were used to sculpt it, he was, you could safely say, a walking encyclopaedia on Tout Quarry Sculptor Park, but he was completely stumped and baffled at what he was looking at this morning.

Ello mateys, its me, Andy again, sorry for the interruption but I just wanted to let you all know that me big moment is coming up, me 15 mins of fame as it were haha, ok sorry continue.

'Howdo Barry' a voice called out from behind and footsteps approached but Barry didn't need to turn his head, he recognised the voice instantly, it was Andy from the repair shop in Fortuneswell.

.'What do you make of this then Andy?'

Andy stopped and looked.

'Well now... it's just a guess and I could be completely wrong mind, but I think what you have there Barry is...' he paused and tilted his head in different angles. 'Yep, I would say that what you got there is definitely, what we call, without doubt... a statue.' Andy chuckled as his poodle cocked its leg on the bright white Portland stone composition of three young lads standing on a six inch high dais with what looked like a trapdoor in its center.

'Well gee! - I guess your right about that Andy.' Barry replied with a chuckle, 'Only thing is, this statue weren't here this mornin'!'

Barry rubbed his stubbly chin and pondered the strange manifestation awhile before the two men and the dog walked away in the direction of the Eight Kings for some liquid refreshment and a pork pie.

Well there you go mateys, I hope you enjoyed that one, a teeny bit scary no? Did you see me make my special appearance? Anyways I must run, I got Miss Andrews the guitar teacher coming this evenin' to tune me strings, I likes it when she gives 'em a good old pluck, but don't tell the wife.

TTFN

No autographs please – The now Famous Andy.

The Raymondo Effect

Ello me Beautiful Maladies, welcome back, Andy 'ere again, sorry if I seem a bit sad today, it's because the Co-op 'ave only gone and run out of chicken tikka sarnies aint they. The girl working there says I should try 'ealthy food instead and recommends some stuff for me, well I guess you gotta try these things aint ya, so anyways, I goes and buys a tub what she called posh salad, *posh salad!* like what the 'ell is posh about a salad.

Anyways, lets see what delights I got in me little plastic box, quinoa, chickpea, pomegranate and something called green Tahini dressing, never 'eard of any of 'em, well that lot can all go in the bin I reckon, I'll 'ave a packet of crisps and a Mars bar for me lunch instead.

So, me old mud slingers, you aint come 'ere to listen to old Andy wiffle waffle about 'is lunch, so get comfy, I've got a long one for you, 'ere 'ere stop giggling in the back!'

Well I've seen a lot of strange things with me job as you all know, but one of the strangest things that I've come across was all to do with them so-called witches down in Chiswell, you've heard of the Witches of Eastwick of course, well they're pussies compared to the witches of Portland, pesky little blighter's they are, they're always causing trouble, complete pains in the arse they be, if they aint out worrying the sheep, goats and chickens with their black magic sacrifices and stuff, then they're 'aving orgies down on the beach in Hallelujah Bay.

They're the same bunch of witches that got that priest chap, the Rev Dougal Dodds I think his name was, in trouble back in the 1800's, well obviously not *the* same same witches, cuz that would make them pretty old, I mean like the descendants of the original witches.

The story goes that the witches had a nice little coven thing going on in Conjurers Lodge down in Chiswell and at that point in time they had about thirty members, they used to do all them witchy type things that witches are supposed to do I guess, like having raging sex orgies in graveyards, scary black masses where they conjure up the Devil, reading the bible upside down while standing on there heads and eating children for breakfast, all that sort of thing you know.

Well the local churchgoers in the area, Methodists I think they were... hey a quick spot quiz - Who was it that said 'Never trust a Methodist if he owns a two legged sheep?', answers on a postcard please. Anyways, these churchy types didn't like the witches having all that fun whilst they themselves were on their knees grovelling to the man upstairs every Sunday, so they called their bosses, maybe it was the Pope or maybe even God himself, I don't know, and made a complaint about them - typical busybodies huh.

Well the church bosses decided to send their best anti-witch guy who I guess was the modern day equivalent of the WitchFinder General of the middle ages, to stop this witch nonsense once and for all, so they sent the Reverend Dougal Dodds to go undercover and infiltrate the coven.

The Rev was one of those all starched knickers and brimstone type religious fanatics that you read about sometimes, to begin with, he made his weekly reports on the witches activities just like he was supposed to do but then after a few months the reports suddenly stopped coming, so the bosses thought it best to go and find out what had happened to their man, they feared the worst and was expecting to find the poor guy nailed to an inverted cross or some such, but what they actually found was the dirty old Rev up to his elbows in witches knickers and having a right old time of it, not only had he disowned his own church and joined the coven, he had persuaded twenty three members of the Portland's Methodist church's congregation to join him.

Well obviously his bosses couldn't be having none of that, fun was illegal as far as they were concerned, so the Rev got struck off and was de-Revved or whatever they call it, not that he cared one iota because he was busy shagging the witches in the graveyards around Portland undercover of the dark.

As far as I know those witches are still doing their

witchy things in Conjurers Lodge every Wednesday night even to this day.

I dunno why I mentioned all that because it hasn't anything to do with this tale, well it does slightly but not much, you will see what I mean later.

Ok so let's get this tale of woe started - So there was this lad that lived in East Weare, Raymondo was his name, he absolutely hated being called Ray or even Raymond and he would completely blank anyone using anything but Raymondo, I'm not too sure of his surname but it could have been Brown, Black or Blue, something like that, it was defo a colour anyway.

Well young Raymondo was a Kimberlin, his mum was a pure blood but his father was Turkish or Chinese or Brazilian or... well he was foreign anyways, his mum got up the duff when she went on her hols and came back with more than a stick of rock in her suitcase.

Eighteen year old Raymondo, like I've said, lived at East Weare in one of those communist bloc looking apartments that they got over there. He was a nice lad, a bit of a loner and only had one real friend, a girl called Becci that he had gone to school with, they were both semi-goths and both had the same interests in music and horror movies, especially the classic 1922 Max Schreck vampire sucktacular, Nosferatu, and in Raymondo's case (but don't tell anybody) the glittery skinned vampire series Twilight.

Deep down though, Raymondo was troubled, not having had a father present during his formative years and a mother that was either constantly working or asleep recovering from long hard hours, and having no other family or friends except for Becci, meant that he was lonely and felt totally unloved, but he knew that everybody had their own crosses to bear so he never said anything more about it and just got on with his life the best he could.

Raymondo's favourite hobby was exploring weird places and there was nowhere weirder to explore than Portland, he must have traversed this little island a hundred times or more during his past explorations and he himself had witnessed some real weird shit in his time, but they all paled to insignificance compared to the weird shit that began on a Saturday morning one July.

That Saturday was the day that Raymondo decided to go and have a look around the ruins of the old church up at Church Ope Cove, you know the one, St Andrews, where all the pirates are buried, you ever been there. It's a strange place no lie and if you ever want to see some genuine pirate headstones with skull and crossbones carved into them, then that's the place to go.

So there was Raymondo, wandering around the grave-markers, he could have been taking rubbing's or something I don't know, when he came across this little stump of a wall, which was probably the remains of a side wall of the church that once stood there on that site or something. For some reason only known to Raymondo, he decided to climb over this stump of a wall and have a rummage in the bushes on the other side, it was there that he discovered this thing, and *thing* is a good word for it I think, I've personally seen it and can't think of a better description myself.

Imagine this, take a football, just an ordinary one,

no need to go for the match ball or nuthin, just one plain football will do, now inflate that ball so its twice the size that it should be (don't be kicking it around though because it will probably explode), once you have this double size ball, cut it in half and you will now have the rough shape and size that this thing was, like half a double sized football, I could have just said that couldn't I really, oh well.

So, take this half-ball and coat it in a dirty yellowishy browny, green concrete and let it set until its hard (gas mark 7 for 45 minutes - just joking), when the concrete has set, remove the plastic ball part and you will be left with a bowl type object, now you got to get some beige reddish green coloured yucky stuff that stinks to high-heaven and pour it into the middle, when the icky stuff has solidified in the bowl type object go and kill a pigeon, no don't really! just imagine that part ok, and pluck off its wings, follow this by dipping one of those wings into some fresh (or stale - take your pick) blood and then press the wings into the horrible stuff in the bowl so that they they that stick up like a boats sail and hey presto, one ugly thing just like Raymondo discovered in the bushes behind the stump of a wall at St Andrews Church.

Now Raymondo being Raymondo, thought that there might be some money to be made with this "thing", maybe he could sell it to a gallery up in London or even Harrods, some people will buy anything if someone tells them that its art, so he slings the thing into the rucksack he always had on his back when exploring, and takes it home with him. There was something that Raymondo didn't know though - how could he, there were no instructions or anything with the weird bowl shaped thing, there was some Latin words etched around the rim though, but who reads Latin these days (and I guess that this part leads us right back to them pesky witches down in Chiswell again), the thing that he had discovered wasn't just a weird bowl shaped full of stinky icky stuff no - it was in fact a 'human oil sacrificial bowl' - nice sounding name eh.,I think I preferred calling it the weird bowl shaped thing.

To the witches of the Portland coven, this object wasn't just a thing or even a weird shaped bowl thing, it was in fact a super special sacred object that they had lost over seventy five years before, I've no idea how they came to lose the bowl but I like to think it was those damn Methodists that stole it and hid it in the bushes on the other side of a stump of a wall at St Andrews church in Church Ope cove.

According to the witches' bible (what do they call a witches bible – Is it an elbib, think about it, nah never mind). According to the witches bible, this bowl contained real human essence (in reality it was human fat that they had rendered from some long forgotten victims of their evil debauched witchery), also it's said that the bowl had magic powers and would give its possessor the thing that they most desired in the world - scary stuff eh.

Whether any of this is true or not is up to you to decide, but those witches believed it, and so did Raymondo after he took it home and dropped it in his kitchen.

Raymondo wasn't too impressed at having to clean all that icky slimy human juice off the floor before his mum came home from work and by the time he had finished he had it all over his hands and arms up to his elbows (Now here's a thing, can you tell me why it is that every time you get icky slimy human juice all over your hands and arms up to your elbows, you always get a real big itch on the end of your nose).

Anyways, there was Raymondo trying to scratch that itch without getting the icky slimy human juice on his nose but not making a very good job of it, in the end he had it all over his hands and arms up to his elbows, all over his nose, streaked over his cheeks and in his hair, not a pretty sight I can tell you, I bet he stank something rotten as well, it was probably just as well that at the time he was unaware that the icky slimy waxy stuff was human juice.

From that moment on, life began to change for young Raymondo, not much happened that first night, except that his mum was in a really good mood when she came in from work (which was unusual in itself as she worked hard and all she would want to do for an hour after work was to collapse in her Parker Knoll which was fair enough), and she made him his favourite grub, Andana Kebabi loaded with yummy garlic, she didn't even mind when he said that he wanted to stay up late and play on his PlayStation which again was very unusual as he had college in the morning and he was a right bugger for getting up in the mornings as it was.

It was the next day though that things stated getting a little weirder (scratch that), it was the next day things started getting a lot weirder.

Raymondo was never the most popular lad at college, he had some strange ways about him and it wasn't just his multiple piercings which included a labret, uvula, frenulum and septum (don't ask me) among others, they seemed to put people off him slightly, some people are just so prejudiced, but not today, today Raymondo was Mr popular.

The first incident that took him by surprise was when he was in the study hall with his nose buried in a book and he felt something tickling the back of his neck, well he brushed it away like you do thinking it was just a fly or something buzzing him but the tickling continued, he turned around and there was Alice Baldwin, who's only *the* sexiest girl in his tutor group, well there she was blowing gently on his neck, can you believe it.

She giggled and quickly leant around and gave Raymondo a little peck on the lips, well now - what about that, talk about being stunned, there was Raymondo struggling even to get the class nerds to talk to him, and up pops hot Alice Baldwin and gives him a kiss for no reason at all, well he liked that obviously, what red blooded male wouldn't, but Raymondo being Raymondo, he was too embarrassed to follow it up, he just blushed and turned away back to his book (he also had an erection but he didn't like to admit it in polite company).

At lunch he sat on his usual table in the canteen munching on a sarnie, cheese and tomato I believe, when Sue Clarke came over and sat down next to him, she didn't say anything, just sat there staring at him, she didn't even have any lunch with her. Raymondo looked at her to see if she actually wanted anything because there was no way on this planet that a female would normally sit next to him without having an ulterior motive, Sue smiled and put her hand under the table and gave his knob a gentle squeeze through his Levis, 'Holy Sh-it!' is exactly what Raymondo thought about that, Sue smiled again and gave him a full breath stealing wet kiss on the mouth, the day was getting better and better. It did cross his mind that the girls were playing some sort of game with him and taking the piss like girls are prone to do but he looked around and couldn't see any phones or cameras lurking nearby, Sue whispered something in his ear taking her time and making sure she poked the tip of her tongue into his ear hole as she did, he tingled all over, and do you know what she said, go on have a guess, don't forget thought that Raymondo was the college weirdo that no one really wanted anything to do with and tended to shun on a daily basis, so what did this hot girl whisper in his ear. ok give up, well I'll tell you, she said, 'I want you to fuck me!'

If Raymondo had been drinking a cup of coffee or a can of coke at the time he would have splurted it all over Mike Cooper sitting at the next table in front, but luckily for Mike he didn't, Raymondo just sat there blushing like a traffic light stuck on stop, Sue giggled and walked off leaving him sitting there stunned, nay, shocked, at what had just happened.

That wasn't the end of the weird things that happened to Raymondo that day either, when college kicked out at 3:15 Raymondo was approached by no less than five other girls at the college gates, they all kissed him in turn and whispered in his ear some seriously sexy things that made the jammed traffic lights appear on his cheeks again (at this rate he was gonna need factor 180 suntan lotion to cover the burn on his cheeks), he didn't even know three of the girls that snogged his face off, but this was just the start of the seriously weird shit.

When he got on the bus to get back to Portland, the female bus driver blew him a kiss and refused to take his fare, the bus itself was packed as usual and he had to sit next to an old dear that was at least 300 years old, she smiled a toothless grin and gripped his knee with one hand while running a wrinkly fingertip in circles over her cardigan where her nipple would be with the other, it was enough to scare the bejeezus out of Raymondo and he jumped off at the next stop.

Totally bizarre, he thought as he began a two mile walk across the Portland causeway. After five minutes of minding his own business, a middle aged woman coming in the opposite direction stopped in front of him and gave him a big hug, he tried to ignore her and hurry on but she grabbed his leg and wouldn't let go so he had to half drag her for a hundred metres before she lost her grip and lay on the pavement sobbing to herself.

When he had finally made it across the causeway he looked back and saw that there were at least ten more women following him, he felt like the Pied Piper of yore, the women began wolf whistling and telling him to stop for a kiss, one even complimented him on his dress sense and asked if he fancied a shag.

Now this was definitely getting too weird for words, in fact it was beginning to get a little scary. As Raymondo turned into his street at East Weir and began walking towards his flat, more women began to follow him, they even came out of houses and crossed the road to join the procession that was trailing behind him, he sped up and walked faster and faster as more women joined the pack until he was at full trot and at last reached his front door, slamming it quickly behind him, he peeked out the window, outside was a huge crowd of women milling around waiting, so Raymondo went into the front room hoping to find his mum, but she wasn't there, instead it was his next-door neighbour, old Nosy Nora, the 80 year old had a key courtesy of his mum for emergencies but she had never let herself in before.

'Hello little Raymondo, how are you doing today?' she croaked.

Raymondo sighed and wiped a bead of sweat from his forehead.

'It's been a very odd day today Nora, I've had women chasing me and making lewd inappropriate comments and suggestions, it's been unbelievable.'

Her reply shocked him.

'Well I'm not surprised, dress sexily like that and you are asking for it Raymondo.'

Nora came and sat next to him on the sofa making sure that her leg pressed hard against his. What she said next terrified him.

'Let's go upstairs, I'll make a real man of you and give you the ride of your life.'

Raymondo jumped to his feet and backed away.

'Come on Raymondo, you know you want me, you know you want it really.'

He ran up the stairs two steps at a time and locked himself in his room, but he could still hear Nora shouting at him from downstairs.

'You slut! you're all the same you pussy-teasers!'

Raymondo remained hidden away cowering beneath his bedsheets for three hours before praying that the coast was clear and ventured out. Thankfully there was no sign of Nora or the women outside the house now.

He breathed a sigh of relief and walked off along the road but had only gotten about thirty feet when the driver's door of a parked car opened in front of him and this big bruiser of a guy stepped out onto the pavement and blocked his way.

'Oi you!' he grunted as testosterone dripped from every pore on his face, 'You the guy that all the women have been going crazy about?'

Well Raymondo didn't know how to answer the question so he just blushed some more.

'Well one of those women happens to be my wife!' bruiser scowled, flexing his muscles which made car alarms to go off all along the road.

Raymondo gulped, now he was for it, bruiser stepped closer and Raymondo almost shat his pants, he was about to find out what it felt like to have an irate husband knock ten bells of the proverbial out of him, he shut his eyes and waited for the punch, but it never came.

'I can see why the wife's got the hots for ya lad.' Bruiser leant forwards and kissed him on the cheek.

Raymondo shrieked like a little girl and sprinted off down the road as fast as his thin little legs could take him, it wasn't that he wasn't in touch with his feminine side but he would of preferred it if it was a woman doing the kissing rather than a seven foot wide man with muscles the size of an elephants thigh.

Ten minutes later Raymondo was panting in the Co-op leaning over the cheese twists with his hands on his hips.

'What the hell was all that about?' he gasped to no one.

As he recovered his composure Raymondo bought himself a Mini Milk lolly and left the shop, but not before the grey haired guy behind the counter winked at him and asked if he was doing anything later. Poor young Raymondo was horrified, seriously, like what is going on here, first women are falling over themselves to get at me and now men are doing the same.

To prove his hypothesis correct, two lads outside the shop came up and put their arms around him and asked if he fancied a quickie behind the bus stop, once more his spindly little legs carried him off down the road like a greyhound chasing a pork pie, he didn't even stop to pick up the half-sucked lolly that he'd dropped.

Next morning Raymondo was a nervous wreck, should he risk college today, what would he do about all those crazy people that wanted his body, what would he do if those crazy people got it, it didn't bare thinking about. Then he had an idea.

Raymondo got dressed in black leggings and a hoody, making sure that his face couldn't be seen and then after checking out the window to make sure the coast was clear of women *or* men, he ran all the way to college.

He needn't have worried though, no one took a blind bit of notice of him, no women jumped out on him and no men blew him kisses, no car drivers stopped to accost him and no pensioners chased him on their Zimmer frames.

By the time he had reached his destination,

Raymondo had come to the conclusion that whatever it was that had attracted people to him had now passed and everything was back to normal (silly boy).

Deeming it now safe, Raymondo lowered his hoody and entered the college building, surprisingly he had been completely correct for a change, everything was back to its dull normality, he was back to being Raymondo the nerdy weirdo once again, that is until lunch time.

As it was Wednesday, half day in the college world, Raymondo took a leisurely stroll into town to visit the amusement arcades and play the video machines just like he always did on a Wednesday afternoon. He had just turned the corner out of the college road when he saw a cat stuck in a tree, always the good Samaritan, Raymondo stood under the tree and tried to coax the poor cat down but as he purred and cooed into the branches, he felt something rub against his legs, looking down he saw that another was cat winding itself around his ankles,

'Hello little cat, you waiting for your mate to come out of the tree?' the cat purred and continued winding.

Suddenly the cat in the tree leapt out and landed on the pavement in front of him.

'Here he is, your mate has come to see you, now off you go.'

Pleased with himself, Raymondo moved off along the road but the two cats followed him, when he reached the next corner he looked back and there were now four cats trailing behind.

'No not again!'

Raymondo took up a jog and glanced behind him to see eight cats and three dogs with their tails wagging in unison hot on his heels.

'This can't be happening to me.' he cried, 'What
have I done to deserve this?' no answer came but
another two dogs did, they trotted out of some gardens
and joined their four legged brethren in the chase.

By the time he had reached Aladdin's Cave
Amusements on the seafront, there was a menagerie
of forty seven assorted cats and dogs trotting after
him. The security guy on the door of the amusement
arcade refused to let him in telling him that pets
weren't allowed, so Raymondo gave up and decided
to jump on the nearest bus and flee to the safety of
home.

As the number 1 bus bounced its way along the
roads, Raymondo watched nervously out of the back
window as every cat and dog in the vicinity turned in
his direction and gave chase, poncey poodles were
snapping at their owner's hands so that they could
join in the chase and little old lady's were being
dragged along the street by excited Great Danes.

Once again Raymondo slammed his bedroom door
and hid himself away until the next day.

Thursday came all too quickly for Raymondo, his
head hurt and he felt sick to the bottom of his
stomach, so when his mum called up to him that he
was going to be late for college he told her that he
didn't feel well enough and was going to take the day
off.

He spent the day pacing the room as thoughts ran
through his mind, *what is going to chase me today?*
he could imagine goldfish & koi carp flippering
themselves along the pavement trying to get to him.
He kept trying to think of a logical explanation to

what had happened over the last 48 hours but couldn't think of a single thing, *it must be animal magnetism* was the best he could do.

Around 6pm Raymondo's mum came home from work and soon had his tea ready for him. As poor liddle Raymee waymee *(*as she always called him when he was poorly), had been feeling under the weather, she had made his favourite Andana Kebabi and brought it up to him on a tray, she knocked on his bedroom door and entered. Raymondo who had been relaxing in his deckchair (purloined from Blackbarge beach) suddenly started to have a really bad hot flush and he felt himself begin to drip with sweat, as his mum came closer holding the tray in her hands he started to hyperventilate, he had the urge to get away from her as fast as he could and with every step she took towards him his heart thudded harder in his chest,

'No mum! Keep away!' he yelled, she stopped with a shocked look on her face, he didn't know why but he was suddenly terrified of her and the thought of her getting nearer was sickening, she took another step towards him and it felt like someone had stabbed him in the head.

'Back mum!'Back away, please!'

Raymondo's mum tutted and told him to stop being a drama queen, placed the tray on his dresser by the door and left the room, instantly his heart began to slow and the pain eased in his head, he wiped the sweat from his brow. *Christ now I'm scared of my own mum! What the hell is going on with me* he mumbled not for the first time in the last few days.

Feeling slightly better now his mum was

downstairs, Raymondo went to pick up the tray of his most favourite ever food *mmm Kebabi* he drooled, but as he closed in on the tray the pain in his head returned, he felt sick and nauseous again, with every step he took towards the plate of steaming loveliness, the pain increased, the sweating returned, his face burned and his heart throbbed so much that he thought it was going to exploded right there and then. He staggered back to the bed clutching his head in his hands and the pain eased, he tried again to pick up the tray, because he really was starving and hadn't had a single bite all day, but once again, as he neared the tray, the agony returned, *hang on a mo* he thought as the pain ebbed on the verge of unconsciousness, he tried a quick experiment, taking one step towards the tray made the pain increased a level but he could handle that, he took another step closer, the pain doubled, an irrational fear spread through him and his heart began to pound, he paused and waited but it didn't subside, he took another step closer and the pain and nausea went up three fold, he yelped and stepped back, the pain eased slightly.

Raymondo stared at the tray over on the dresser and felt scared of it, he didn't know why, why should he be terrified of his favourite food all of a sudden. The smell of all the garlic in the Kebabi made his mouth water but at the same time it dawned on him that it *was* the garlic that terrified him, even the thought of the word garlic wanted to make him heave.

He backed away to the other side of his room and the pain and sensations vanished completely, as quick as a flash he suddenly thought 'garlic!' and his head almost exploded, *my God I've become petrified of garlic*, his head panged.

Raymondo called down to his mum who reluctantly came back upstairs and he told her that he was still feeling sick and couldn't eat the scrummy Kebabi, so could she please take the tray away, she didn't like the idea of her son not wanting his favourite food and told him so.

'You're as thin as a stick as it is, get any thinner and you will snap, just like your father did' she tutted but eventually relented and took the tray back downstairs He felt as right as rain as the garli... the tray disappeared out of the door.

A depressed Raymondo put his headphones on and crawled into bed, he had had enough for the day, he only hoped that tomorrow would be better.

The day dawned nice and early like it always does and Raymondo jumped out of bed. Even though he hadn't eaten at all yesterday he felt raring to go and he bounded down the stairs and plonked himself down at the breakfast bar. His mum was cooking some scrambled eggs on the stove.

'Good morning mummy, how's my favourite parent today?' he said to her, his voice far too jolly for that time of day, she turned to look at him and stopped with a strange look on her face.

'Are you all right there son?' she asked, 'You look as white as a sheet you do.' Raymondo stood up and looked at the mirror on the back of the door and almost fainted clean away, he didn't have a reflection, none whatsoever, *this definitely can't be right, the mirror has to be broken* he thought, slowly, he slid his head in from the side of the mirror to see if he could catch it out, but nope, there definitely wasn't a reflection of his face there, all he could see was his mums back as she stood at the stove, he peeked again but quicker this time, still nothing, a horrified thought flashed into his head and slowly he raised his hand and wiped a finger across his incisors, he breathed a sigh of relief to find that they weren't an inch long and pointed *hmm, oh well.*

He shrugged his shoulders, having no reflection wasn't the worst thing in the world, plus he felt really great so what the Hell, he jumped back onto the stool by the breakfast bar and asked his mum if she had any steak and if so could he have it tartar, he got scrambled egg on toast with a loud tut.

College that day went without a hitch, although he did get some strange looks and people kept asking him if he was feeling ok because he looked so pale, almost white, some people said, he shrugged it off and continued as per usual.

Later that day, once college had finished and he had returned home, Raymondo remembered that the following day was "donor day", this was the day that occurred every few months when he and his one and only friend Becci, would go to the Mason's Hall in Victoria Square and donate a pint of blood, this was something of a ritual that they had both done since leaving school, they felt good about doing their thing for the nation and were both in demand because they both had A Rhesus negative blood, which was semi-rare apparently. A quick call to Becci confirmed that she was still going and arrangements were made to meet at the hall in the morning as soon as they opened.

Nine thirty came and saw the mates being

welcomed by the nurse at the blood transfusion portacabin in the Masons hall car park and they both took up position on a bed each, the nurse did her premed checks, sterilised their arms and then inserted the needles that led to the blood collection pouches.

The two friends had been nattering to each other for five minutes and Raymondo was regaling Becci with the odd events over the last few days, when the nurse reappeared to give their bags a squeeze and a shake and make sure everything was going ok, when it came to Raymondo's turn a puzzled look spread across her face and she turned her back so he couldn't see what she was doing, suddenly she quickly skedaddled from the room and left them alone, Becci laughed and said that perhaps his blood had turned mouldy. Raymondo strained his neck to look where the nurse had gone and he could see through a semi shut door that she had picked up the phone and was making a call, the nurse looked up and saw that he was watching and quickly shut the door with her foot.

At the end of the hour donor session, the nurse returned but never said a word about the strange incident, she gave them each a custard cream, thanked them both for coming and quickly ushered them outside, as the portacabin door shut behind them the nurse hung the closed sign up and they heard her bolt it from the inside, they didn't even get their free "I've donated blood" stickers.

For the next two days Raymondo kept himself to himself and locked himself away in his bedroom playing Grand Theft Auto 5 on his PlayStation, around lunchtime on the third day his mum shouted up the stairs that there was a phone call for him, *unusual* he thought as he went down to answer it, on the way he had a quick peek in the hall mirror and noticed that he still had no reflection but he was getting used to the idea now and thought it was quite cool.

The phone call turned out to be a woman who explained that she was from something called the Portland Environmental Trust medical section and that she wanted a quick word with him. Raymondo gulped and tried to think if he had ever gotten a girl pregnant and if so how much of his wages would he have to hand over to her, he sighed a big sigh of relief as he realised that he was still a virgin, plus he was a poor student so didn't actually have any money to hand over to anyone.

The woman on the phone told him that the Portland Environmental Trust were involved in medical research and that they had been contacted by the blood donor service regarding the donation he had given recently, she explained that they had found a small anomaly in his blood, and although it wasn't anything to be worried about, they would like to take a peek at it themselves and would it be possible for him to come to the lab that afternoon and give a drop or two. Raymondo didn't really fancy the idea and told the woman so, but when she said that he would be paid £200 for his time, he asked for directions.

An appointment was made for Raymondo to visit the lab that very afternoon at 3pm, he was told that the lab was at Cheyne House near Southwell on the Top of the island and was given specific directions on how to get there.

Two thirty came and found Raymondo standing

outside Cheyne House eager to get his hands on the two hundred quid. The building was an imposing place, there wasn't another like it on the island, it was a large white building that stood alone near the cliffs with no neighbouring houses to be seen anywhere.

He hunted around for any direction signs to show him that he had the right place but there were none to be seen, the place just looked like it was a normal house not some sort of medical research center. Raymondo was about to give up when a woman wearing a white lab coat appeared out of nowhere and asked him to follow her.

The inside of the building was just as imposing as the outside, it was decorated in a Gothic revival style that was all dark woods and red velvet furnishings complemented by a black and white chessboard floor, it still didn't look like any medical center that Raymondo had ever seen.

The woman introduced herself as Professor Strokes and thanked him for coming, a *Professor no less,* thought Raymondo, *I'm getting the royal treatment huh.* The woman went to a metal door across the large hall from where they had entered and inserted a small plastic card into a slot, the door swished open to reveal an elevator.

Horrible cheesy music played as they descended in silence until there was a ping and the doors reopened to reveal some sort of waiting room filled with rows of modular seating, they passed through the room and went through another door and into a plush looking office where Raymondo was offered a seat, the professor sat opposite him in a small chair in front of a heavy mahogany desk and exposed a healthy length of stocking topped thigh then began to explain exactly why he had been invited there.

'Firstly thank you for coming Mr...' she checked a clipboard laying on the desk in front of her, 'Brown or is it Mr Blue? Pink maybe? He was beginning to feel like he was in a remake of Pulp Fiction.

'Anyway, thanks for coming this afternoon, why we have asked you here today is like I explained to you on the phone, we have found an teeny weeny anomaly in your blood donation, now don't get scared but as it's quite a rare anomaly we would like to examine your blood further.'

Raymondo had been too busy staring at the profs shapely legs and hadn't heard a thing she had said, so she had to repeat it once more.

'Can I ask you, have you noticed any strange things happening to you lately?' she continued.

Raymondo nodded.

'Anything out of the ordinary? Something that seemed weird and unusual?'

Raymondo nodded.

'Any changes in the way others react to you maybe?'

Raymondo nodded once more like one of those bobble head dolls.

'Well I just want to run a few little tests right here and now if that's ok?' she opened a drawer in the desk and removed what looked like a small version of a tradition doctors bag.

'Now there's nothing in here that can hurt you, I just want to watch your reactions to them ok?' she slipped her hand into the bag and held it there awhile before slowly removing it again, she held her hand in

329

a fist and offered it to Raymondo.

'Don't forget, nothing can hurt you ok.' the prof quickly opened her fist to reveal a clove of garlic.

Raymondo hissed like a snake and leapt out of the chair as fast as his bony little legs could move, a seriously nasty pain erupted in his head and his heart almost went supernova, he cowered by the far wall squeezing his temples and sobbing to himself. The professor put the garlic back into the bag and the pain vanished just as fast as it appeared.

'It's okay it's gone, sorry about that, it won't happen again, please retake your seat.' she made a few notes on the clipboard and put her hand back into the bag.

'I promise no more garlic okay.' she smiled a reassuring smile then slid her hand out again slowly, once more she held her hand in a fist and offered it to him. She turned her hand and opened it, Raymondo looked at the object lying on her palm.

'What's that?' he said, then the realisation dawned on him like a cricket bat between the eyes, he screeched and hissed and jumped from the chair and batted the object from her hand but in doing so his own hand came in to contact with the object and it burnt like acid, he hissed again.

'It's gone, it's gone, don't worry, your safe now.' she made some more notes on the clipboard as Raymondo studied the red burn mark on his hand.

'So we know you don't like garlic and crucifixes then.' she chuckled ignoring the perplexed look on Raymondo's face.

'Only one more object and that will conclude the tests okay.' this time when she brought her hand out of the bag and offered it to him he just sat and looked at the object, *That's not so bad* he thought - *I can handle this,* he gingerly took the little vial of clear liquid from her offered palm and held it to his face.

'Cool, no problem with this.' he proudly announced all smug like, happy that his reaction had spoiled her tests.

'That's good because it's only water, no harm there eh?' she smiled yet again.

'Tell you what, why don't you drink it, I promise it's only water.'

Raymondo glad that the tests were now done, shrugged, pulled the stopper and poured the water into his mouth, but the liquid never passed his lips, somehow whilst he wasn't watching, a stranger had crept up behind him and put a lit blowtorch to his gums and held it there, or at least that's what it felt like, the pain in his mouth was the most excruciating and terrible thing he had ever felt in his life, it was even worse than when his Prince Albert went septic and he had to spend a week pissing out of a tube stuck down his bell end. He howled in agony and rubbed at his flaming lips.

'Here rub this on.' the professor handed over a small tube of green paste which he rubbed on as quick as he could, the pain eased immediately.

'I'm sorry about that' she said as she made another note on the clipboard.

'Okay, so that's the tests definitely over now, there's no more surprises, I promise.'

Raymondo was going to ask what the Hell she thought she was doing getting him to drink acid when she announced that the cream he had rubbed into his lips was made from a mixture of Wolf bane extract and unconsecrated grave soil.

'It's the perfect antidote to Holy Water, I think you will agree?' she then got up and walked to the door.

'Now if you will follow me'.

As they left the room and he followed her along the corridor, he asked if he could leave now that the tests were finished, to which she informed him that she just wanted to get a little drip of his blood and he could be on his way, her little laugh didn't ease Raymondo's nervousness much.

They entered another room and this time it looked more like a laboratory, there were medical tubes and flasks of bubbling liquids pouring from one container to another, there were those Bunsen burner things that he remembered from school when he had set Jane Munroe's hair alight by accident and there were various computers and other interesting looking machines scattered around on desks, some of them even went ping!

The professor showed him to a chair and he sat down then she began placing large thick straps around his wrists, then she did the same to his ankles.

'They don't strap you down like this at the blood donor portacabin in Victoria square.'

'Well we want a little more blood than they take down there.' she smiled.

'How much blood do you want?' he asked, 'Don't forget I just gave a pint, aren't you supposed to leave it for a few weeks before donating again?'

The professor chuckled and said that it wasn't a problem for them.

'Well how much blood are you going to take

exactly?'

'Oh, just all of it.' her reply was as casual as if she'd just told someone the time of day.

This wasn't good news, Raymondo didn't like the sound of it one bit, he wanted to keep his blood or at least enough of it so that he stayed alive and he was about protest when she continued talking.

'You see Raymondo, you have been infected by a... how shall I put this... a virus, yes, a virus. It has, as you have probably guessed by now, turned you into what we call in the medical profession, a homosapiens homovorus'

'A homo what now??' Raymondo was more than stunned.

' A homosapiens homovorus, or what's known as a raging blood sucking he-beast... a vampire Raymondo. Now we're all nice chaps down here and we want to help you, so what we are going to do for you is...' she checked over her shoulders to make sure no one was eaves dropping, not that there was anyone else in the lab to eavesdrop.

'What we are going to do for you young Raymondo is remove all that nasty horrible vampirey blood and replace it with some nice new shiny stuff, we will even let you keep it.'

Now that didn't sound too bad to Raymondo, he liked blood flowing around in his veins so was pleased to hear that they would give him some to replace it, although deep down, he guessed that he didn't really have a choice in the matter, they were gonna take it with or without his permission.

The Professor inserted a cannula into a vein in Raymondo's right arm and connected it to a long tube that ran to a large glass bottle mounted on a stand, she then stuck him in the other arm with a needle that led to a tube running to a large machine parked nearby, she crossed over to the machine and began flicking switches and tweaking dials which caused a neon green liquid to flow along the tube and towards his left arm.

'What's that stuff?' he cried as he watched the green disappearing into his vein.

'Oh that's your new blood, the stuff we are giving you free of charge.'

'But it's not red like it should be.' he said with a worried tone in his voice.

'Its ok don't worry Raymondo, it's a special recipe synthetic blood that we manufacture down here, it won't hurt you.'

Where had he heard that before.

As the green stuff gurgled in to his left arm, so his own lovely red stuff squirted out of his right and sped along the tube and began to pour into the glass bottle, *bye bye beautiful blood* he sobbed inside.

'This procedure won't take long, maybe about two hours, you'll feel a little dizzy and faint as the blood is swapped but don't worry the sensations won't last long.'

Famous last words and all that.

Raymondo woke up nine hours later. He felt as sick as a dog that had just had its hind legs removed without anaesthetic, in fact he felt like he had just had a fight with a ride-on lawnmower and had lost, then the ride-on had called all its little Hover mower mates and they had all given him another good seeing to just for fun.

The room that Raymondo woke up in looked like a hospital ward, there were twenty beds lined up against two walls but as far as he could see he was the only patient. He lay on the bed trying to fight off the pain that wracked through him when the door of the ward opened and in walked the Professor with the sexy legs.

'Hello Raymondo, I noticed that you were awake.' she looked in the direction of a CCTV camera fixed to the corner of a wall.

'I bet you feel pretty awful at the moment, here swallow this.' she handed him a small yellow pill and a tiny cup of water that wasn't even enough to wet his whistle but he gulped it down anyway.

'The blood transfusion was successful I'm glad to say, you slept for quite a while, longer than expected but you're awake now, that's all that matters.'

Raymondo rubbed his temples and looked quizzical,

'Exactly how many people have you given this green blood to before me?'

The Professor looked at her clipboard and did some mental arithmetic and counted on her fingers awhile before telling him that actually, he was the first ever.

'But enough of this idle banter, what I came to tell you is that we're quite happy with your progress and you can go home in a few hours.' she smiled her now famous unreassuring smile which made him very nervous indeed.

The Prof then told him that she would be back to collect him later in the day and left the ward.

Happy about the latest update but realising that it

could be quite a few hours before he would leave and go home, Raymondo began to relax a bit and that's when he first noticed how ravishingly hungry he was, so decided to go and find something to eat, he figured he'd go and look to see if there was a MacDonald's or a Burger King in the vicinity, *you can normally find one every twenty feet so there should be one around here somewhere* he mused to himself, but first he wanted to try an experiment.

Raymondo sat on the edge of the bed and gave his muscles a quick shake followed by a side to side neck crunch, he cleared his throat and gave his knuckles a crack, when relaxed and ready, Raymondo shut his eyes tight and spoke quietly.

'Garlic.' he whispered and hunched his shoulders in readiness for the onslaught of pain, but nothing happened, he tried it again, a littler louder this time and with his eyes wide open, 'Garlic.' still nada.

'Garlic! Garlic! Garlic!'

A big grin spread across his face, he was cured.

Joyed by this new revelation, Raymondo jumped to his unsteady little pins and turned towards the wards exit.

It was then that he noticed that he wasn't the only patient in the room after all, in the furthest bed at the end of the ward lay a sleeping young girl with beautiful long red hair, he quietly walked over and took a closer look.

The girl was around twenty years old he reckoned judging by her face and the size of her boobs, not that he peeked or anything of course, there were no outwards signs of what was wrong with the patient but she was plugged into several machines. There was a clipboard hanging on the end of her bed so he picked it up and began to read which caused his eyes to widened and shards of ice to quickly replace the marrow in his bones, by the time he'd reached the bottom of the page, where there was something written in Russian, he decided not to bother with a Big Mac and medium fries and possibly some mozzarella sticks, and to just get as far from this place as humanly possible.

Outside the ward were three doors, the first door he tried was a store cupboard which wasn't much use unless he was planning on sweeping the floors or doing some frantic polishing, door number two led to another corridor which was a much better option than the cupboard, so off he went.

At the end of the corridor was an elevator but that needed a card like the one Professor stockings had used when they had entered the building earlier, there was no other way to go, so he backtracked and went through the only other available door, door number three.

This time he found himself in another corridor, slightly longer this one, it had a large plate glass window running along one side which of course Raymondo peered through, it was full of baby incubators, not that surprising really seeing as though he was inside a hospital. There was another door opposite the large window so through it he went.

In front of him was a spiral staircase that led upwards, a*ha!* u*pwards and outwards, sounds good to me.* Raymondo began climbing the stairs which seemed to go on forever, until he eventually came out into another corridor, this one was painted pale blue and had a myriad of doorways leading from it, these doors though had signs on them which he read as he passed by, Consultation Room 1, Consultation Room 2, Storeroom, Supplies, yada yada yada.

All the doors were pretty useless to him and it wasn't until he came to the seventh door that things started looking up, the sign on the read "elevator" but best of all there was no card slot, just a button, Raymondo quickly decided that this was his favourite kind of elevator and he gave the button a prod.

To his surprise the door immediately swished open so he quickly hopped inside, unfortunately though he noticed that there was a distinct lack of buttons for him to choose from, in fact there was only one, and it was labelled GO.

Hmm now what button shall I choose, he mumbled to himself, *I think I'll choose… this one!* he clicked the GO button, the door slid shut and the lift began playing horrible cheesy music.

There was no way he could sense in which direction the elevator was going but whichever way it was, it was taking one Hell of a long time to get there. The horrible cheesy music had looped through twice before he felt the elevator slow and then the door slid open with a ping.

This isn't right! he said to himself as he stepped out into what looked like a tunnel that had been hewn out of solid rock, *where's the hospital gone?* He was about to step back into the relative safety of the elevator when the door pinged again and quickly swished shut, he could hear the cheesy music begin playing as it disappeared back to wherever it came from.

338

The tunnel was lit by a string of glass bulkhead lights, the kind you see dangling from your car bonnet when the mechanic has his head buried under there to fix your fan belt for a very reasonable price of just seven hundred and fifty quid plus VAT, the bastard! but the lights offered enough of a glow for him to see that the tunnel went on for quite a way in to the distance.

With no other options Raymondo headed off into the semi-darkness of the unknown in front of him. The tunnel twisted and turned a few times before it eventually came to a heavy metal door with the most cryptic sign he'd ever read in his life screwed to it:

"Please DO NOT feed the children."

Well this is a most curious sign to read in a dark tunnel somewhere underneath Portland, Raymondo thought to himself, but as there was no other way to go and he didn't have any food on him to feed any children anyway, he pulled the large lever that acted as some sort of locking mechanism and entered inside.

Raymondo stood still and took in his new surroundings which on first glance appeared to be a dark dank cave, he studied this new vista for awhile and yes it definitely was a dark dank cave, it had everything it needed to qualify as one, it had cavey type walls and it had an uneven cavey type floor with stalagmites all around, he was sure that if he looked upwards he would also see a cavey type ceiling covered in stalactites as well. While he was studying what he now knew 100% definitely was a huge cave, he didn't notice the door behind him silently gliding shut, he noticed it though when there was a loud clang and it re-locked itself afterwards.

Raymondo was dismayed to see there was no handle on this side of the door or any other way to open it, so with his options limited to walking further in to the cave system or walking further into the cave system, he nervously chose option C and walked further in to the cave system. He hadn't travelled far when he realised that although he had no torch and there was no artificial lighting system like the bulkhead lights from earlier, he had no problem seeing anything, it was as though his eyes had switched to night mode.

This is definitely good, I can make use of this skill. he wondered if he could activate God mode too and give himself an extra life or two.

As he travelled deeper in to the cave, his nostrils started to twitch and flare as an odious pong began to invade them, he couldn't quite put a name to the nasty niff, but it smelled musty sweet, dirty and clean all at the same time, it wasn't unpleasant although he could live without it, a bit like a Liberal Democrat he thought.

It didn't take too long to discover where the olfactory assault was coming from because as he rounded a curve in the cave he came to a field of little green fungi, there were literally thousands of them covering the rocks and the cave floor creating a funky carpet of glowing greenness. Raymondo stooped and plucked one of the luminescent mushrooms and took a deep sniff, *yep it's definitely these little fellows causing the pungent whiff.*

'Hey! Leave that alone.' a voice rang out of nowhere.

Startled, Raymondo dropped the toadstool and looked up to see a little girl walking towards him.

'How would you like it if I played with your food?' she asked him like it was perfectly normal for two people to be standing in a dark cave picking green fluorescent mushrooms.

'I uh... I'm sorry, I didn't realise' he began.

The little girl, who he reckoned must have been around ten years old and had the greenest hair he had ever seen on a person, picked up the little mushroom from the ground and quickly popped it into her mouth and began chewing it. As she munched on the fungus Raymondo asked her her name.

'I'm called Eden121.' she replied.

What an odd name he thought but didn't like to appear rude so didn't press her about it, instead he asked her what was she doing in the cave and wouldn't her parents be looking for her, he asked her all the usual type of questions that you would ask a little girl that you found in a cave.

'Don't be a silly billy.' she said 'I live here.'

Raymondo looked aghast.

'You live here? What live *here* in this actual cave?'

The girl giggled.

'Of course I do... we all do.'

As if those had been magic words, myriads of young children began appearing from behind rocks, out of alcoves and through gaps in the cave walls.

All the children looked to be under sixteen years of age and were all dressed in the same type of clothes which looked like an 80's jumpsuit made from a shiny flexible metal material, most strikingly they all had the same shade of green hair. The girl spoke again.

'Are you our parent?'

'Your parent? No sorry, I'm not.'

The girl looked sad.

'So you have come to play with us? her eyes questioned him.

'I... uh... no sorry.'

'Please say you will play with us.'

Before he could reply again, the girl took him by the hand and led him through the mushroom field to where the throng of other children were massed. He noted that her little hand was ice cold.

The children crowded around asking him questions and excitedly laughing amongst themselves, it was like Father Christmas had arrived with a sack full of presents.

Suddenly a hidden klaxon blared out a warbling oscillating tone and the children fell instantly silent, they seemed mesmerised by the sound and all turned together as one to face its direction. The droning faded but the children remained silent and all facing the same way as a shadow appeared on the ground in front of them quickly followed by a figure dressed in what can only be described as a spacesuit straight out of NASA's wardrobe.

The figure stopped at the far edge of the fungus field and beckoned him over with a padded glove, instinctively Raymondo obeyed and walked towards the urban spaceman.

'Please don't go, stay and play with us, please.' the children began crying and wailing as Raymondo increased the distance between them. The little girl Eden121 ran in front of the spaceman and faced him, she looked up at the wide mirrored face panel with big sad eyes.

'Please parent, please let him stay with us, we love him, please!'

The figure rasped a few Darth Vader breaths, ignored her, turned and began walking back the way he had come with Raymondo obediently in tow.

Before long, Raymondo found himself being led through another metal door and back into the familiar confines of the hospital that he had first started out in, but this time he was led into an unfamiliar room and left alone as the space cowboy, who hadn't uttered a single word the whole journey, departed.

The grey painted room was devoid of any furniture at all, not even a seat to sit on, the only object in the room was a massive steel door on the opposite wall from the one he had entered, its frame was decorated in black and yellow hazard tape. Raymondo stood staring at the large ominous door trying to figure out what could be behind it, knowing this place and some of the crazy and bizarre things he'd already seen and experienced over the last few days, he wouldn't of been surprised to find a portal to another dimension, but he gave up on trying to figure it out after an hour as it made his head hurt too much and he began pacing the room like a caged bear.

After an hour of pacing he gave up on that too as it made his scrawny little legs ache too much so he sat down in the corner of the room. Slowly his eyes began to shut as the arms of doctor sleep began to embrace him in their grasp.

'Raymee, waymee, wake up Raymee.' a familiar voice called out to him through the fog of his dreams.

'Mummy! Is that you?'

343

'Come on Raymee, wake up now.' the dislocated voice sounded calm and it soothed him.

'Mummy?... Where are you, I can't see you! I've had a terrible dream.'

'Wake up Raymee... open your eyes.'

'Mummy! Why are you wearing those sexy stockings??? Mummy! Mummy!...'

'Raymondo it's me, Professor Strokes, wake up now.'

Raymondo's eyes slowly opened and saw that unfortunately it hadn't all been a horrible nightmare and that he was still in the bare grey room.

The voice came again and he looked around for the mouth that it came from but no one was there, it must have come from a hidden speaker somewhere.

'Why am I being locked up like this?' he asked the no one.'

There was a long pause before the voice spoke again.

'Oh Raymondo Raymondo, what have you done? We were going to release you after you felt a little better, but now...' the Professor sighed heavily, 'But now... You went into the containment area didn't you? You met the children!' she sighed again.

'Listen Raymondo, those children are in there for a reason, a very good reason.'

Raymondo suddenly started to get angry, which shocked himself as he never ever got angry.

'What bloody reason could you possibly have for keeping children locked up in a cave?'

'They're dangerous Raymondo, very dangerous to everybody.'

'Dangerous? They're just kids, how the hell can

they be dangerous?'

'They are… different, different than you or I, they have… I don't know… it's difficult to explain.'

'Just try, I'll figure it out.'

'Well the children have been here a long long time, much longer than me and I've been here twenty five years.'

Raymondo was confused.

'But how can they have…'

'Listen Raymondo!' she cut him off. 'The children have different… metabolisms than us, we can't let them go because they will infect us.' she paused for dramatic effect. 'They'll kill us Raymondo! All of us. Everybody that comes into contact with them dies within minutes!'

'But… but…'

'Listen, the children were created a long long time ago and for reasons we still don't understand, they emit a neurotoxin through their skin, we have been trying to find a cure for years but nothing seems to work, so we keep them contained where we can monitor them and keep *them* healthy and *us* safe until the day we can cure them.'

Raymondo was trying to get his brain around all this information when a flaw in her explanation dawned on him.

'Ah but, I've been in contact with the children and I haven't died, how do you answer that one then?'

A static silence echoed around him, until the disembodied voice came back.

'We don't know Raymondo and that's what interests us, we think it's something to do with Serum KP345.'

'KP What now?'

'The green synthetic blood that we transfused you with, it must have something to do with you not dying, we just don't know how, we have so many questions and no answers at all.'

'So you mean that I'm immune to them?' he sounded hopeful 'And I can go home?'

'I'm sorry Raymondo, you've misunderstood me, you aren't immune, you have been infected by whatever it is that the children have, that's why you haven't died - you have become like one of them.'

It was Raymondo's turn to be silent now.

'Until we can figure out what it is that's stopping you from dying we are going to have to keep you here, we have no option Raymondo, I hope you understand, if we let you go you will infect everybody down here and everybody in the outside world and we will all die.'

There was an electronic click and a slot opened up in the far wall.

'Take these special clothes, they're thermal and will keep you warm.'

'But I'm not cold and my clothes are fine thanks.'

The professor sighed once more.

'You still don't get it do you Raymondo, it will be cold where you have to go, the children's body temperatures are so much more different than ours, they have to be kept at a constant seven degrees above zero or they hurt.'

The realisation finally dawned. 'You mean I have to live in there with them?'

'Sorry Raymondo, it's the only way.'

A buzzer sounded and the heavy steel door hissed

as its air tight seal was opened.

'If you would please go through the door, we will…' she couldn't finish the sentence.

'Go on,' she prompted warmly, 'go through the door Raymondo.'

He felt like he should say something at this point but nothing came out of his mouth, he stood and stared at the open door for awhile and sighed and then with a deep breath he walked through.

The heavy steel door hissed and clunked as it shut behind him and his new life began.

So there we go me old Glockenspiel Tuners, what do you think of that. Poor Raymondo, all he ever wanted was someone to love him, but I guess he found that in the end.

What are we to learn from this tale? Well I'm not sure what you learned but I definitely learnt that if I ever find a half ball shaped dish full of beige, reddish green coloured yucky stuff, I'm gonna give it a very wide berth thank you very much.

Well it's time to shut the shop for the day, I've decided that 'ealth food don't agree with me, so I'm gonna grab a take out chicken Tandoori with extra popadoms on me way 'ome.

TATA.
Super healthy, no diet needed, Andy

A Tattoo Too Far Two

Friday the 7th of October was John Halliwell's twenty fifth birthday, it was only two thirty in the afternoon but he was alone and propping up the bar in the Sailors Return in Castletown.

He had been hitting the alcohol more and more in the last few months, he had been fighting a losing battle with his internal demons, the desperate longing to use the hideous tattooing machine again, had been hard to fight and he had sunk into a deep dark depression that left him feeling empty inside, it was as though something was missing, that he had become an empty vessel waiting to be filled with some unknown force.

John raised his glass of bourbon and in a voice that was beginning to slur he toasted himself a happy birthday. A noisy commotion from behind made him turn his head in the direction of the pub door and he watched as three leather jacketed bikers stumbled over the threshold and entered.

The trio, were playfully punching and shoving each other towards the pool table where the shorter of the three fed some coins into its slot and began racking up a game while the other two continued towards the jukebox.

Forty minutes of Zeppelin, Nazareth, Motorhead and Iron Maiden passed without any incidents, the bikers were a little rowdy but they kept themselves to themselves at the pool table racking up games and taking it in turns to play against each other.

John was massaging Jim Beams ego for the forth time that day and minding his own business when one of the bikers mis-cued the white ball and it bounced from the table and rolled towards his feet, the group laughed and shoved each other about for a few seconds then one of them called out to John.

'Oi ye poofter! Ye wi' th' fancy jaekit.'

John slowly turned his head in the direction of the beer laden Scottish voice.

'See th' wee white baa ower thaur? Pick it up an' brin it haur!' It wasn't a request, it was an order. John looked down to the ball at his feet but remained sitting.

'Dae it noo ye feckin' poofter!' Scottish stood up erect and puffed out his chest, 'Whit ur ye waitin' fur, a burst mooth?'

To John, this whole one sided conversation could have been taking place on the moon or under the sea, he didn't understand a word the biker had said in his thick Scottish drawl, he looked back at the ball on the floor again.

'Awe right pal, a burst mooth it is.'

The biker casually came around the table and

walked towards him, pool cue in hand, and stopped inside John's personal space so close that their chins touched. John stared into the biker's fiery eyes, a second later he was staring at the ceiling as Scottish landed a perfect headbutt and John dropped like a sack of spuds.

Minutes passed in a daze of distorted vision and raucous laughter from the bikers but eventually the distorted Scottish voice rang in Johns ears.

'Hey poofter, while yer doon thaur can ye lok tae see if there's a feckin' tattooist coz thaur sure isnae oan on thes feckin' islain.'

Even though still groggy, Johns ear pricked up at the question, he had no idea why or how or where it even came from, but he heard terrifying words coming out of his own mouth.

'Yeah me... I'm a tattooist.'

The result was if somebody had just flicked a switch, the mood instantly lightened as leather clad arms hoisted him to his feet and tattooed knuckles dusted him down before manhandling him to the seats by the pool table. Scottish belched out some sort of apology for the headbutt and gave his shoulder a friendly punch before sparking up a big phat joint and handing it to him.

'Yer oor new best mate pal... see we hae bin lookin' tae gie new tattoos.' Scottish told him between deep tokes of the blunt, 'An' ye pal, yer th' jimmy is aff tae dae thaim'.

A fresh round of drinks was bought and paid for by the bikers who then went on to explain what tattoos they each wanted, Scottish went first.

'Ah want a Leatherface, ye ken th' camel blower

frae 'at movie Texas Chainsaw Massacre? Ah want heem holdin' a fuck aff big chainsaw, ah want it reit haur at th' top ay mah skinny wee arm', he removed his leather jacket revealing a bicep the size of a boulder and pointed at a blank space amongst the other assorted tattoos that he already had.

'Scrote ower thaur,' he pointed at the shortest biker, 'he wants a necklace of razor blades oan his neck, and Pukeball haur,' he thumbed at the last biker, 'he wants a Grim Reaper oan his huge belly... Reit troops?' The others grunted 'aye' and nodded in the affirmative.

'Sae here's th' plan, we will tak' ye tae gie yer tattooing gear an' 'en we will tak' ye tae uir camp up top ay th' islain en ye can dae yer magic awe rite.' again this wasn't a request which Scottish confirmed it with his next sentence.

'An' listen mucker, ye fuck onie ay these tats up an' we will rip aff yer arms an' legs an' use them tae kill ye wee mammy with... awe rite?'

Perfect!

John smiled inwardly to himself and nodded in compliance at the terms, this was exactly what he had wanted to hear.

The little gang drained their pints and escorted John outside to the pub car park, a quick argument followed over who would take him pillion which Scottish solved with his right fist, and they all rode off in a rumble of rat bikes up Victory road towards the top of the island, they stopped only once for John to collect his tattooing gear and they soon arrived at their destination, Bottomcombe quarry in Easton.

The HellsBlades MC were a patch wearing gang of

351

nomad bikers, their numbers fluctuated depending on how many were in prison or hospital at any particular time but on average they numbered around two hundred. The club originally hailed from the Midlands area, they travelled the music scene moving from festival to festival and adding to their numbers as they went, their last port of call had been the Stonehenge free festival where they had been on the wrong end of police truncheons during the Battle of the Beanfield. Now they had arrived on Portland and had set up camp at the disused Bottomcombe quarry just outside the village of Easton.

The quarry comprised of a two hectare hole blasted out of the limestone bedrock by Portland quarrymen over a period of two hundred years, its fifty metre high rock sides made a natural secure boundary and its one access road in and out made it the perfect location for the HellsBlades to camp and set up a new free festival.

The entrance road to Bottomcombe quarry was blocked by a well placed fallen tree which was chained to a big Harley trike that gunned its engine and hauled it out of the way as the newly formed band of brothers approached and let them through, they announced their arrival with lots of revving of their V-Twins as rode into the compound proper.

John could see from his perch on the pillion seat of the lead bike that the HellsBlades had been busy and had transformed the quarry, the once bare limestone rock walls that encompassed it were decorated by huge graffiti, murals, slogans and rock band names, the right hand side of the quarry floor had been roped off and had been turned into a parking area which currently held over a hundred motorbikes and a scattering of assorted vans and trucks which looked as though they had been converted into living accommodation, behind the parking area nearer to the rock face was a rainbow sea of canvas tents of all shapes and sizes, some had campfires burning outside and had small groups of leather clads sitting nearby either drinking and chatting or making their own entertainment.

Most of the action though seemed to be coming from the direction of the old maintenance shed which took up the entire left side of the quarry, the vast enclosure which was once home to the massive rock cutting machines that had been used in the quarry over the years was now the beating heart of the bikers encampment.

The three motorbikes roared into the huge building through its large hangar sized double doors to cheers from the crowd already present, cans of beer and lit joints were handed to the welcomed heroes as the little entourage rode at walking pace through the melee.

The inside perimeter of the football pitch sized building was lined with numerous large canvas marquees and smaller portable tents, each one had a different purpose, some were advertising hot and cold food, some advertising beer and alcohol and even a few with spray painted signs outside advertising hash, cocaine and speed. A dj booth had been setup in one corner of the building and was currently pumping out Breaking The Law by Judas Priest to which thirty or so male and female bikers rocked out to.

In the very center of the maintenance shed, a

makeshift stage had been erected out of scaffolding poles and planks upon which various musical instruments sat awaiting their players, tall stacks of Marshall speakers towered above the stage on either side and a lighting rig made from more scaffolding poles hovered above it.

The bikes slowly weaved through the throng towards the largest marquee at the back where they parked up and dismounted and once off the bikes John was led inside.

'Awe rite sit yer crease doon thaur.' Scottish kicked at a ripped and stained sofa with a boot. 'Gie yer tool an' nae weel gang first.'

John correctly translated this to *Get your tattoo machine out and I'll go first,* so he joined Scottish on the sofa and opened the wooden box that contained the tattooing machine.

'Whit th' fuck is 'at gross lookin' hin'?' Scottish stared at the machine with a look of utter disgust on his face, 'Urr ye taking th' pish or whit ye fud?... Ah will bite yer boost 'oaf n' jobby doon yer neck if yer, ye fud!!'

'No no, it's cool, this is my tat machine, I had it specially made by a white witch from Glastonbury a few years back, it looks a bit weird but it works beautifully.'

Scottish ignored him and turned to one of the other bikers and laughed.

'Hey Scrote! It looks loch yer dick.' the gathered watchers erupted into laughter, headbutted each other and collapsed in a fit of weed aided giggles. Scottish straightened up and offered his bare arm to John.

'Awe rite noo gie oan wi' it, ye ken whit I want.'

John rubbed the sweat from his hands and took a firm grip on the tattoo machine, it pulsed and throbbed, he hovered its sharp bone needle over the Scots arm and took a deep breath.

What the fuck am I doing. he lowered the machine and it began to buzz.

It took just over thirty minutes to complete all three tattoos that he had promised the bikers back at the Sailors Return, all three of which were completed without any hitches or complications and as with the previous tattoos that he had done, intense sensations had rocked his brain while his hand had gone into autopilot and drew its pictures on the bikers skin.

John sat back feeling satisfied, the feeling of emptiness he had been feeling lately was now gone. Scottish and his two compardres were more than impressed with their new pieces of artwork, they agreed with each other that the workmanship was 'feckin guid' as Scottish put it, they each took turns in studying each others new pieces of skin art and seemed to forget all about John and didn't notice when he quietly slipped out of the marquee and joined the masses outside.

The air in the maintenance shed was thick and yellow, the stench of hash and alcohol hung heavy and it had to be at least 90% proof.

Loud music was still pounding out from the DJ area and it looked like the party was warming up nicely, John kept his head down as he wandered around trying not to make eye contact with anyone, he weaved in an out of the crowd making sure not to jog any elbows or make himself stand out, and after a few minutes he came to the make-shift stage where a group of dancing females were in the process of getting naked, aided by a crazy looking long bearded compère who leapt around them wildly and emptying the contents of a bucket of water over them. John stopped and was watching a big brunette peel off her wet t-shirt to roars and cheers from the crowd, when a stiff finger poked him in the back.

'Oi poofter, there's someain 'at wants tae meit ye.' Scottish had reappeared and had tracked him down, but he didn't seem annoyed that John had slipped out of the tent, he even smiled slightly showing brown stained teeth.

'Follaw me.'

Scottish walked into the crowd with John following like a little lost dog, he had no idea at all at what was going on now, he began to get worried.

They headed back towards the marquee but continued past it and stopped outside a native American teepee where a lone shades wearing biker stood guard over its entrance, he unblocked the way after Scottish whispered something in his ear and he let them both pass.

It was uncomfortably warm inside the tall tent which was being heated by a small brazier filled with glowing embers in its center, its acrid tang of smoke drifted up and out of a hole in the canvas roof while a yellow haze filled the teepee with a strong smell of some exotic herb. John took stock of his new surroundings, one part of the teepee appeared to be a sleeping area made up from an inflatable mattress that was covered in a stiff and greasy black animal fur and various sized cushions, next to the mattress was what resembled a large sugar bowl on a stand, it was half full with a white powder that definitely wasn't sugar, on the other side of the teepee was an upturned beer crate with an ominous looking machete and a handgun sitting on top, at the far side of the teepee was a stack of ten large cellophane wrapped blocks of more white powder that John instinctively knew was cocaine, a damn lot of cocaine.

Muffled voices suddenly came from behind him and the teepee's door flap was brusquely pushed aside as a giant of a man entered, unlike the bikers, the nearly seven foot tall stranger wasn't wearing any leather, instead he wore black drainpipes a black button down shirt and a pair of Ray bans, long pure white hair hung down past his shoulders framing his paper-white, almost translucent face and even in the teepees reduced light John could see blue veins under his skin. In the man's left hand, the odd looking stranger held a dog lead which was attached to a studded collar around the neck of a naked brunette woman, he stopped a foot in front of John and held his gaze for a few seconds until Scottish broke the silence.

'Snowman, this is th' fud ah tellt ye aboot, hes a bawherr handy wi' a tatty machine.' Scottish nodded in John's direction. 'Poofter, meet the boss, meet Snowman.'

The white haired man lifted his sunglasses to reveal the pinkest of pink eyes and stared hard at John who felt like they were dredging his very soul, before he opened his thin lips revealing big gaps in his teeth.

'So...' he began, his voice was as thin as his lips 'So you're the one that my boys have been raving about?'

John was surprised, he had expected a deep commanding booming voice but it had a light airy tone to it and sounded well educated.

'It seems that you have a talent Mr...' he waved his finger in the air as though he was trying to remember his name.

'Poofter Boss, we jist caa heem poofter.' Scottish leaned forward and chortled.

The tall man mulled this info over for a few seconds,

'That may well come in very handy for what we have planned for you later.' he chuckled to himself at the thought of some untold joke.

'I'm going to make you an offer Mr...'

'Poofter Boss.'

Snowman scowled at Scottish putting him in his place.

'You can stay here in our lovely camp as our guest...' he paused for effect before continuing. 'and tattoo every member of my little family, or...' he paused again. 'Or we kill you now, outside there on the stage, but as I'm not an unfair man, I will give you time to mull over my generous offer, you have, what...?' Again he waved a finger in circles in the air, 'You have ten seconds to decide.'

Any normal person would have possibly felt hot urine streaming down their legs by now but not John, he took it all in his stride, ever since the weird tattoo machine had come in to his possession and he had performed the first tattoo with it, he had felt a surreal sense of internal gasconade, he felt as though nothing could phase him, not even this earth shattering announcement, he didn't need the ten seconds thinking time.

'Of course I accept your kind offer of hospitality, it's a no brainer really' he smiled back at Snowman.

The boss's pink eyes narrowed to slits and the corners of his lips curled slightly, he didn't like his scare tactic failing.

John was told to make himself comfortable on one of the dirty cushions and was then informed by Snowman that he was to ink a Nazi stormtrooper in full military regalia holding an oversized Sturmabteilung dagger on the back of his almost white neck. Snowman added that when he'd finished the tattoo, he would be taken outside to another tent where he would begin tattooing the rest of "the family".

It took the best part of fourteen hours to complete the 200+ tattoos. John had made a spectacular job on Snowman's neck, once again the tattoo was photograph quality and looked incredible, the detailing on the Nazi uniform was exceptional and the huge oversized dagger looked razor sharp and all but glinted in the light.

After finishing the boss's tattoo, john had been escorted to a smaller tent near the DJ area, fed and watered before a long queue of eager bikers began to form outside.

First in line was a short biker with lots of black wiry hair that they called Pube, he wanted a green dragon on his upper back with flames coming out its mouth, the job was finished within ten minutes, next was a man that was more hair than actual man, he said that his name was Yeti and he wanted a picture of his namesake on his thigh.

'Make it really fierce looking with fuckoffing big claws he instructed. A vampire, a Templar Knight with sword and even a small cartoon of Pinnochio, asked for by a dainty little biker chick called Scrag, followed.

Eventually the last of the human canvases stood in front of him, it was a young lad that couldn't have been more than sixteen named Elf, he explained that he wanted a long zipper running down the whole length of his back, it was to be open half way along its length so that it looked like his spine was being exposed to the elements, with a heavy heart, John complied with his wishes.

John collapsed against the back of the tent and slid to his haunches, he was exhausted, it wasn't so much all the tattooing that he had performed, that had been the easy part what with his hand being on autopilot, it was the mental stress on his brain that almost destroyed him, the incredible visions and sensations that tore through his mind as he inked each tattoo had been so intense he felt as though his occipital lobe had been dipped in batter and deep fried, he rested his throbbing head in his hands and had tears in his eyes when he finally fell into a deep yet troubled sleep.

The sun was still low in the morning sky when John jerked awake, his back exploded like glass in a spasm of cramped muscles as he got to his feet and stretched, he re-boxed the tattooing machine that lay at his feet and with slow drunken like steps, he stumbled out of the tent.

The massive maintenance shed was almost silent now last nights partying was over, a big bonfire that had been lit near the stage had now been doused, rubbish and items of discarded clothing lay scattered around the vast echoing building but there were no bikers to be seen, even the guard that had been standing on sentry duty outside of Snowman's teepee was nowhere in sight. John peered in through the half open flap and saw exactly what he needed, a sealed bottle of water and within moments he was inside and gulping down the refreshing liquid.

Thirst now quenched, John made to leave when he heard voices approaching from outside, he had to hide quick or Christ knows what would happen if he was caught alone in here. He darted towards the stinking black animal fur that was piled on the bed and buried himself under it the best he could, the voices stopped on the cusp of the teepee, half in and half out and continued talking, Johns ears pricked up when he recognised the voices.

'You get the merchandise when you pay the 20k, its as simple as that.'

'Come on Snow, how long have we been trading? You know you can trust me for it.'

John heard Snowman laugh, 'Trust you? Trust a bent copper you say?' he laughed again, then sighed loudly before he continued.

'Like I said, it's 20k on delivery... Now fuck off, I'm sure you got some speeding tickets to hand out.'

John heard feet moving away outside the tent but waited another five minutes under the rancid fur just in case and was about to make a move when he heard a couple of long deep sniffs as Snowman snorted a line or two of coke, he hadn't left as John had thought and he'd been in the teepee all along, Johns balls tightened, he thought he was busted for sure.

Guid jobby aye gaffer... Mynd if ah hae a bawherr toot? Scottish was back on the scene.

'Help yourself. Then tell the boys that we're packing up and shifting out tomorrow, this place is beginning to stink worse than that crook Crowley.'

'Och aye boss, dae ye want me tae sort heem?'

'No not yet, killing a cop right now would cause too many questions and we don't need the filth poking around while we have all that nose-candy stashed in here, wait behind for a few days after we leave then have some fun with him.'

'Och aye will do boss.'

The sound of footsteps followed by the sound of the teepees door flaps being opened proceeded one last sentence from Snowman.

'But you can get rid of the tattooist, let him stay for the party tonight, he's earned one last night of fun, then cut his throat and dump him out at sea.'

This was not the kind of news that John wanted to hear, he gripped the fur covering, his knuckles turned white and he held his breath for as long as he could, but he was sure that the two men could hear the pasodoble that his heart was doing in his rib cage.

Several minutes passed before John had the nerve to exhale, several more minutes passed until he had the nerve to finally break cover and to slip out the tent.

Being murdered wasn't on top of John to-do list, he had an aversion to dying and there was no way that he was going to be sacrificed by some weird albino gang leader, he had to get out of there, the question was how.

The coast was clear outside the teepee and there

was still no sign of any activity so John began walking towards the maintenance shed doors, that part was easy and he passed through without seeing a soul. It was then that he decided that as he'd gotten that far he would just try to blag it and carry on going, he wasted no time crossing the compound, he kept his eyes glued to the ground in front of him and prayed. Casually John strolled towards the exit road leading out of the quarry hoping that he wouldn't be spotted and he almost made it, his prayers went unanswered though and as he neared the fallen tree barricade a barrel chested biker holding a baseball bat appeared seemingly out of nowhere.

'Sorry pal you can't leave yet, you're the star guest at the party tonight, didn't you know?' he chuckled, 'Oh and thanks for the tat', the biker showed a tattoo of a cut throat razor dripping with blood on his lower arm, 'Now go back down there and grab a few beers, the fun starts at eight so don't be late.' he laughed as he emphasised the baseball bat by cracking it hard against the barricade.

Bikers came and went all day long, they brought in beer and food and other supplies by the van load and as the day wore on an excited buzz began to fill the compound.

John tried to keep a low profile and keep himself to himself but occasionally a group of staring bikers would pass-by sniggering amongst themselves like there was some private joke that he wasn't privy too. In the afternoon John tried getting into some of the vans parked on the hard-standing but all the vehicles were locked tight with shiny padlocks, he also tried the main gate again, but the bikers guarding it were on the ball and there was no way they were going let him through, if he was going to escape with his life, he needed to come up with the plan to beat all plans.

John had been sat near the back of the main compound for a few hours just kicking up dirt and watching more and more motorbikes arriving, he'd been wracking his brains for a plan of action but had so far drawn a blank, the situation looked dire.

It was nearing seven o'clock and the sun was down to a blaze of light on the horizon when finally a plan entered his head, it was a crazy plan and would require all of his cunning but it would be his only chance and he knew it.

The music that had been filtering out of the maintenance shed for most of the day suddenly ramped up in volume and began drawing in the bikers that were milling around the compound like moths to a flame, it was time for John to put his idea to work.

He had gone over his plan hundreds of times in his head, and he figured there probably wasn't a cats chance in Hell that it would work and he'd need the Gods of luck on his side, but if he wanted to live longer than the next few hours he was gonna try it, no matter what.

Black Sabbath were getting Paranoid on the sound system as John casually strolled into the large shed and began meandering through the throng of happy bikers, most of them seemed to be off their faces already on either drugs or booze, a few came up to him and patted him on the shoulder thanking him for their great tattoos to which John feigned smiles and quickly hurried on by, the last thing he wanted was to make a show of himself at this point.

He neared one of the tents selling booze and picked up a bottle of lager, the biker in charge just nodded and didn't ask for payment, then he wandered inconspicuously as he could around the perimeter of the building. When he was as far as possible away from snooping eyes, he quickly smashed the bottle on the concrete floor and pocketed the sharpest piece of glass, he then continued on until he neared Snowman's teepee where he sat in the shadows and waited and watched.

It was thirty minutes before the Gods of luck finally lent a hand and Snowman appeared from within his tent and spoke to the guard on duty and then disappeared into the crowds, John wasted no time and as quietly as he could he sidled along towards the rear side of the teepee which stood against the maintenance shed wall, if he could get there without being seen he might, just might, be able to cut through the canvas and gain entry.

The plan went better than John could of hoped for, the guard was more interested in swigging from a bottle and talking to two females than anything that was happening at the rear of the teepee, and he managed to make a slit with the broken glass shard and squeeze through.

Once inside, John quickly put the second part of his plan into action, he took the smelly animal fur and the dirty cushions from the inflatable bed and piled the lot over the stack of cellophane wrapped blocks of cocaine, then he went to the closed door flap and using its ties he secured it in place, he also placed anything movable in front of the flap to create a trip hazard, anything to slow down any wanna be heroes.

John stood back and admired his handiwork and when satisfied, he dragged the brazier full of glowing coals to the flammable pile he'd just created, with a sharp kick of his boot the brazier tipped and emptied its contents on to the greasy black fur, *come on... come on burn!* John tried using thought power to will the red hot embers to catch, *come on!!!* Slowly after what seemed like three lifetimes, the fur started to flame and once the flames had taken hold, fuelled no doubt by the grease on them, they took on a life of their own.

Happy now that the fire was quickly becoming a blaze, John slipped back out the tent the same way that he had entered and didn't stop walking until he had reached the maintenance shed doors where he turned and waited.

Within a few minutes he could see thick white smoke start billowing out of the top of the teepee which at first went unnoticed by anyone else, but after a few more minutes, flames began to lick the canvas and appear on the outside of the teepee, that's when the bikers began to realise what was happening.

John could hear some individual shouts of alarm coming from the crowd but soon a chain reaction had begun, the shouts went from person to person as quickly as the fire became a raging inferno, the smoke went from white to black and bits of burning teepee began raining down on the assembled bikers.

It was time for him to leave. Panic and pandemonium quickly ensued as bikers began running towards the exit where John mingled with them and headed out into the night, the compound was quickly filling up with coughing and spluttering bikers but

John didn't stop there, he quickly moved towards the quarry entrance and thanked God that the guards were nowhere to be seen, having presumably left their posts to try and help their comrades, freedom loomed.

John approached the fallen tree barrier, a few more steps and at last he was out of the biker camp, he could have dropped to his knees and kissed the hard tarmac he was so relieved.

A loud voice boomed out from just behind him that made the hairs on the back of his neck stand up and his balls go in to hiding, John turned to see the albino called Snowman standing astride the back of a speeding trike like a Roman gladiator riding a chariot into war, his long white hair streaming out behind him.

'Stop right there!!'

John didn't hang around and started to sprint up the access road but as he neared the top four motorbikes appeared ahead of him coming towards the quarry, it was impossible, he was fucked.

The quartet of bikes stopped in front of him and one of the late-to-the-party bikers called out to Snowman.

'You lost something boss?' and laughed.

John slowly awoke from the blackness, his head was throbbing from the battering that Scottish had given him, his face felt stiff either from caked on dried blood or nerve damage taken during the beating. He tried to move his hands but they were fastened securely behind him with a cable tie.

Painfully John opened his swollen eyelids and his blurred vision slowly cleared to a sea of staring faces in front of him, not a sound could be heard from the two hundred odd bikers that had assembled around the stage in the center of the maintenance shed where John was now slumped in a chair, he could feel the anger of the cold hard stares, but not one of the bikers made a sound.

The stench in the shed was terrible, it had a nasty acridness to it from the fire but it didn't seem to bother anyone, a full three minutes passed before John heard slow heavy footsteps mounting the steps at the rear of the stage and Snowman came into view, he stopped at the edge of the stage and faced his audience then held his arms wide, the crowd went wild, screams and yells and cries of adoration rang out around the building for a full minute until he put a finger to his lips and they silenced as one.

'Brothers, friends... and their filthy whores, we are gathered here tonight because of this creature...' Snowman pointed briefly at John.

'We invited this... this thing, into our family and showed him our hospitality, he ate our food and drank our beer, and what does he do to repay us. He betrays our trust and stabs us in the back!' the albino pointed towards the charred mess that was once his teepee.

'This man must be shown the error of his ways brothers and friends.' the crowd hissed and cheered, he raised his hands and silenced them again.

'I... your leader and master, have decided that this filth shall receive the ultimate punishment.' the crowd went into a cheering frenzy at the news.

'The mighty HellBlade will slice the meat from his bones for his betrayal and we shall feast on his flesh!' the screaming and shouting became frenetic, Snowman let the crowd enjoy the moment but raised his voice.

'The sentence is to be carried out immediately.'

Johns muscles weakened and he fell forwards from the chair to the floor but was hoisted to his feet by two bikers that appeared from behind.

The short biker chick that had received the cartoon Pinnochio tattoo came walking up the short flight of wooden steps that led to the stage and crossed over to Snowman, she cradled something in her arms that John couldn't see. The agitated crowd began straining their necks to get a glimpse at whatever she was carrying as she handed it to Snowman.

'Brothers, friends and assembled bitches' he held the object with both hands and lifted it aloft, the crowd fell silent once more. 'Bow your heads to the mighty HellBlade' there was 100% compliance.

'We thank you Dark Lord of all things foul, for bestowing on us the HellBlade so we can do your bidding.' Snowman faced John giving him his first sight of a massive razor sharp knife.

'We thank you Dark Lord for your hatred and revulsion that has allowed us to see this man for what he really is.'

Johns sphincter tightened as his eyes fell upon the most evil looking knife he'd ever seen, the two foot long weapon looked like the bastard love-child of a Japanese Tanto and a Gut hook, it must surely have been forged in the Devils arsehole itself.

The knife had a leather wrapped two handed grip and a long serrated hooked blade that gleamed with evil intent, along the blades thick top edge were large shark-teeth like protrusions that would rip out internal organs as it was pulled out of a wound, the thing looked like it could fell a tree with one blow and grind it to sawdust on the back stroke.

'Dark Lord, let the first kiss of the HellBlade make this creature feel the pain of the sins he has committed against us.'

Snowman calmly walked over to John and gently placed the sharp honed blade against his right thigh, his pink eyes glowed with evil and in one swift movement he drew the blade backwards towards himself, the knife effortlessly sliced through Johns jeans, through his skin and muscle and only stopped when it hit bone, resulting in an ear-piercing blood curdling scream as a white hot lightning bolt exploded and shot through John's entire body, the blood thirsty crowd lapped up the sight and began cheering and clapping while chanting *more more,* Snowman was only too happy to oblige them.

'Oh Dark Lord, let the second kiss of the HellBlade show this man the error of his ways.'

This time Snowman placed the blade against John's left thigh and pulled, the searing acid pain that wracked through his body felt like molten lava was roasting him alive and he let out another blood curdling scream, the crowd cheered and clapped even louder.

'Brothers, friends and their stinking sluts... Listen to me!' the excited bikers fell silent once more.

'Time has come for this turd of a man to pay his debt to us in full, watch now as our Dark Lord gives me the power to split him in two from his head to his feet, we will then sate our bellies by feasting on his organs and drinking his hot fresh blood!'

The cheering and clapping became a wild roar of

excitement at this news, cameras began flashing throughout the crowd as they prepared to capture the moment for posterity.

Johns eyes flickered open, his legs were on fire, sweat was pouring from every pore and his breath came in shorts spurts but somehow he managed to stay conscious and watch in dread as Snowman turned to face him and lift the blood soaked blade in readiness of the fatal blow.

John was light headed and pin pricks of light danced in front of his eyes, he felt sick and almost gagged on the bile being forced up from his stomach, all the while his head span and his legs throbbed in agony.

The cold edge of the steel blade was placed gently against the top of his head causing a bead of blood to run down his forehead, Snowman grinned and the room fell silent. The knife was raised to its apex and hovered motionless above Johns head like his own personal Sword of Damocles, he squeezed his eyes shut tight and tensed his muscles ready for the blow that would end his life, an eternity passed.

Snowman's eyes suddenly widened and a look of confusion spread across his face, he grunted a sound of bewilderment which quickly became a strange liquid gurgling noise.

To gasps from the crowd, the HellBlade dropped from Snowman's hands and fell backwards, clanging to the stage with a loud metallic echo. Confused, John re-opened his eyes and watched the unbelievable scene that unfolded in front of him.

From the exposed skin on the front of Snowman's neck, just above his Adams apple, a pointed lump appeared, the skin stretched menacingly and then split open as the glint of shiny steel appeared, the steel wiggled rapidly from left to right and back again widening the cut, before a tiny hand appeared through through the gashed skin and grasped the edges of the wound, the hand belonged to a miniature Nazi stormtrooper wearing full military regalia who proceeded to haul himself from the gaping hole in Snowman's throat, the little uniformed soldier carefully balanced himself with a jackboot on each side of the fresh cut and using the oversized Nazi Sturmabteilung dagger, began hacking at the albinos throat and neck, the only sound apart from the sound of Snowman drowning on his own blood was that of his severed head as it bounced onto the stage.

The bikers stood agog at the hideous unbelievable scene, those closest to the stage could have sworn that they had seen the boss's newest tattoo, the stormtrooper on the back of his neck, come to life and decapitate him, others only saw a fountain of blood mysteriously spurt from the bosses neck and then his collapse. Astonished cries and shouts began filling the air, total chaos ensued.

Scottish ran onto the stage and knelt at the dead man's feet then looked up at John, pure hatred raged in his eyes, he opened his mouth to speak but stopped and looked at his own arm, his eyes widened as his fresh tattoo of the Leatherface character from the movie, The Texas Chainsaw Massacre peeled from his skin, inflated itself and became sentient, it gave a few sharp tugs on the starter cord of the huge chainsaw it was holding and plunged the buzzing tool deep into the Scotsman's chest, Scottish gave a high pitched girly scream as Leatherface weaved the chainsaw back and forth as though he was carving ice and within seconds a large section of skin and bloody ribcage fell away revealing the Scottish bikers still beating heart, there was a quick flick of the chainsaw and Scottish watched as his own heart splatted to the floor with a bloody squelch, two seconds later his lifeless body joined it.

The little Nazi stormtrooper hopped from the Scotsman's corpse and landed on Johns upper thigh, John stared incredulously at the little figure who returned and held his gaze for a few seconds, for some inexplicable reason, the Stormtrooper didn't attack him, instead, with a shout of *lang lebe die Fuhrer*, it leapt off of his leg and disappeared into the screaming crowd.

A greasy haired man near the front of the crowd that John recognised as one of the bikers from the Sailors Return, watched in horror as his bikers necklace of razorblades began slicing long strips of skin from his neck and face giving him a newly mown striped lawn effect and then sliced off his eyelids nose and lips, as he fell, the razorblades cut into his neck and disappeared inside his head.

The biker that had had a green fire breathing dragon on his back screamed as it crawled onto his shoulder and snorted red-hot flames into his face igniting his hair and as the skin on his face began to melt, he ran screaming into the throng.

Another biker did battle with a small war-hammer wielding Viking that was using it to smash a hole in his skull, when the hole was big enough and his brain was exposed, the Viking jumped inside and disappeared from view, the bikers eyes span in their sockets a few times before his puréed brain began dribbling from his nostrils and he gave his last breath.

A middle aged female biker was pulling at a pair of white turtle doves, one of which had a nipple firmly clamped in its beak, the other was pecking at her right eye until it popped in an explosion of pink and black watery pus, as the woman screamed in agony, the doves flew into her mouth and wedged themselves inside her windpipe, she died gasping for breath.

John watched stunned as all the tattoos that he had created suddenly and brutally came to life and turned on their hosts, it was carnage, blood and bits of bodies were flying everywhere and as soon as one tattoo had finished off its owner it jumped to the next available body.

A group of bikers battled with ten or more tattoos at a time, they didn't last long and went down in a bloody and torn mess. Through the maelstrom, the young lad called Elf, the one who had had the tattoo of a long zipper running down his back exposing an image of his spine, was using his bloodied hands to try and pick up his skin which was laying in a pool of blood, he had been completely skinned, his misery only ended when a nasty looking six inch high grim reaper jumped onto him and scythed through his windpipe.

A girl biker was spinning around on the spot pleading for someone to help her as her arms scrabbled at something behind her back, she had already ripped off her t-shirt and John saw that the large tattoo of her own face was biting into her back, with a loud crunch her spine was severed and she collapsed to ground, she couldn't do anything as a large green Incredible Hulk tattoo jumped onto her shoulders and twisted her head 180 degrees producing a loud cracking sound but she did had the pleasure of witnessing her own face sniggering at her as it sucked the spinal cord out of her backbone.

John had seen enough and began struggling with his bonds, he had to get out of there but the cable tie that secured his hands and bit hard into his wrists was attached to a long chain and he wasn't going anywhere.

A screaming female darted onto the stage and collided with him sending him flying to the floor, her face was a mass of dripping liquefied skin, two H.R Giger styled aliens were perched on her shoulders spitting acid at her head.

John struggled more.

To one side of the stage a fat biker was grappling at his mouth as a miniature Harley Davidson motorbike forced its way down his throat only to erupt from his stomach seconds later in an explosion of guts and intestines.

A female was running past the stage when suddenly her entire upper torso separated from her legs and both parts skidded to the floor as her barbed wire 'slag tag' encircled her waist and ripped her in two like a wire saw on a piece of balsa wood.

John lay on his front and watched as the head of the biker called Scrote rolled to a stop in front of him, its dead eyes still wept.

From out of nowhere, a flock of tiny prison style tattoo sparrows swooped down on John and landed on the cable tie that bound his hands and began pecking.

A biker with blood spurting stumps instead of hands collapsed to his knees as Darth Vader used his light saber to slice off bits of his face while Luke Skywalker made good work of cutting out his eyeballs, Obi Wan Kenobi shouted encouragement from the bikers right shoulder and told him to use the force.

The bloodshed went on and as the piles of bodies grew higher, the air became thick with the tangy iron stench of death.

Suddenly John was free, the pecked cable tie released his wrists and the tiny flock of birds flew towards his face, they hovered for a few seconds as they looked into his eyes, then with a chirp, they flew away.

The pain in Johns legs was intense but somehow he managed to stagger to his feet and lurched off the stage, and step by agonising step, he stumbled and crawled his way through the bloody carnage that lay scattered across the maintenance shed floor.

Bodies lay all around, some of them were still twitching and shuddering in their death throws and some were still in the process of being mutilated but with the agonised screams fading in his ears and the bikers numbers rapidly diminishing behind him, John heaved himself across the threshold and out into the sweet refreshing Portland air.

The early morning light was rising in the distance by the time John had managed to get his wrecked body to the fallen tree blockade, he sat panting and turned to look back at the biker encampment, all was still, not a thing moved and not a sound could be heard. He sat awhile just watching, it was then that he realised that he had lost the tattooing machine somewhere back there, he sighed, it was probably a good thing. John hauled himself back to his feet and slowly but very painfully began walking up the hill towards the warm morning sun.

John woke up three days later in Portland hospital, he was shocked to find that he was plugged into various machines that were standing guard over his health because he had absolutely no recollection of anything at all, his last clear memory was him sitting in the Sailors Return in Castletown on his birthday.

The doctors explained to him that he was lucky to be alive and had been found unconscious at the side of the road near Easton by a man out walking his dog, he had some serious lacerations to his legs and had lost a lot of blood. They kept John in the hospital for three weeks as they repaired his wounds. He spent the initial days blissfully pumped full of painkillers but at night his dreams were filled with torturous nightmares of blood, death, motorbikes and a strange albino giant. As the third week of Johns stay in hospital passed, the doctors gave him the all clear and signed him out of their care, they gave him a stockpile of pills and medicines and told him to see his GP in a month to get the stitches removed and then booted him out of the door, but he was still none the wiser about the events that had put him there in the first place.

A weel later, saw John at home in his kitchen, he was loaded up on painkillers and was making himself a cup of coffee when there was an urgent rapping on the back door, he opened it to a familiar ginger haired man wearing a suit.

'Ah Mr Halliwell, I'm glad I caught you.' he gave

John a sly grin before continuing.

'DCI Crowley of Portland CID.' the man flashed an ID card and nodded over Johns shoulder.

'I smell coffee.' he didn't wait for a response and edged past into the house.

'How's your legs doing John? You don't mind me calling you John do you, I hear they were pretty cut up, 120 stitches each leg, that'll give you a nice war wound.' he sat down heavily on a kitchen chair and placed a white plastic carrier bag that he'd been carrying on the table, then lit a cigarette and exhaled nonchalantly, he didn't take his eyes off a John and continued staring.

'You've, caused us a lot of trouble you know John.' he spoke matter of factly.

John tried to speak and ask how exactly, but Crowley continued.

'Listen. I don't know what the fuck went on up there at the quarry and to tell the truth I don't want to fucking know,' he looked blankly at John. 'but I will say this, it was like fucking Vietnam all over again up there.' he stopped to take another deep drag on his fag.

'Two hundred and eighty fucking seven bodies, or what was left of them.' he flicked his cigarette ash on to the floor. John didn't know what to say so stayed quiet.

'To tell the truth, just between me and you...' he leant forward and summoned John closer with one of his sausage sized fingers.

'I heard on the grapevine that,' he paused, 'well it don't matter what I heard, but I think somehow I owe you, and as a thank you, I think we can say that we're even about the girl incident, what was her name again,

378

Tanya?' he sat back in the chair again and gave a dry cough.

John continued saying nothing.

'Anyway, those bikers were becoming a pain in the arse and we had plans to remove them ourselves, but I guess you saved us a job.' he stood up and walked to the door and stopped.

'Something stinks about this whole fucking thing that's for sure, and know this Halliwell, I'll be keeping my fucking eyes on you son.' he opened the door and stepped outside before turning back to face John.

'Oh and I believe that that... that *thing*, is yours.' he pointed to the carrier bag he had left on the kitchen table, 'I recommend that you get rid of it ASAP son.' the ginger haired copper grinned again and casually walked away whistling to himself.

John shut the door and scratched his head, *what the Hell was all that about?* he was totally baffled, he went to the plastic carrier bag on the table and peered inside where he found a scuffed dirty wooden box, he gave it a quick clean with a damp cloth and saw that it looked as though it was made of a mahogany type wood, the wood seemed thick with a deep lustre, the corners were protected by a brass corner pieces and on its front was a small keyhole in the middle of an engraved brass scratch-plate.

John tried lifting its lid but it was locked tight, curiosity peaked, John went upstairs to his bedroom to fetch his lock picks.

So Long, Farewell, Adieu

Psst! Over here!, guess who this is, go on, 'ave a little guesseroo...

Wrong!

Me fake moustache fooled you eh? Well it is I, your buddy and mate Andy the tv repair guy.

Sorry for the disguise like, but you just never know right.

Anyways, I just thought I'd let you know that I'm shuttin' me shop down for me summer hols so I won't be able to give you any updates on the weird and wacky things that go on on this odd island for awhile, thank Christ for that you say, aww you hurt me feelings now, haha, nah not really, thick skinned is Andy, well I gotta be aint I, livin' 'ere and all that.

I just wanted to tell you before I go and packs me suitcase that I had this strange bloke in 'ere yesterday morning, dressed in bright orange overalls he was, anyways he comes in looking for one of those new-fangled recordable iPlod things, well I told 'im that if he wanted any of that futuristic stuff he would ave to go over the water into Weymouth (spit), anyways, he says he wanted an iPlod so he could replace his broken tape player and he goes and pulls this mangled looking thing out of his overalls pocket and puts it down on me counter top, I reckon he's been playing footy with it I does, ooh what a mess it was.

He starts telling me that it was imperateeff that he gets the info off it and on to digital media, I just kinda stares at him when he says that, *digital media*, like what is it even. I was about to tell him that maybe they sell digital media at the florists down the road when suddenly the door of me shop bangs open real 'ard like and that ginger haired twatpot Crowley comes storming in, you probably know about him already, he's a copper that's so bent he can suck his own farts without turning his head, he's in cahoots with Armstrong the drug lord, who just 'appens to be me landlord so I can't says too much about him.

Anyways, me and Crowley goes back awhile and he kindly lets me be on nodding terms with him, but he completely ignores me this time and goes and grabs this fella in orange all rough like and puts his arm behind his back before snapping a pair of handcuffs on him and frog marching him out me shop without a word like.

I was thinking to meself that it was a right rum do when I notices that the fella had left his little tape player on me counter, well I sees it there and I knows all about these things cuz I used to supply and fix them for those boffins up at Sweethill, dictaphones they's called, ooh look at me talking all posh haha, anyways I picks it up and... well not that I is nosey or nufin, but you just gotta press the play button on somethin' like that when you see it aint you.

Anyways, so I clicks the little play button and listens to what he's got recorded on there. Well bugger me, you wouldn't believe what I 'eard. It was some chap having a talk to another guy and he was explaining about... hang on, I'll switch it on and you can listen for yourself like, some of it's a bit technical mind and even me, Andy, the high tech guy don't know some of the things they is talkin' about, but here goes, get your listening tubes on this:

Click... static... silence... *phone handling noise...* Collins, department twelve has just updated me about project Quellar. The latest borehole tests indicates that the limestone under the Osprey area is just too unstable and that if we pump in seawater at the planned 4000 psi, it will undoubtedly cause serious fractures in the rock. If we then pump liquid gas into the voids it *will* vaporise and leak to the surface through the fractures.

We could be looking at an 97% mortality rate in the Fortuneswell and Chiswell areas if it does... and Collins, I don't need to warn you about the catastrophic consequences that would occur if liquid gas came into contact with the little ones down in the... *muffled...* now do I?

(New voice) *Nervous cough...* Do you mean the children Mr James?

Of course I bloody well mean the children you idiot, I'm not talkin about damn beefburgers!... AND I needn't have to warn you yet again what wou... wait, who's that, what are you doing in here? *muffled voices... click...* recording ends.

Well now, whadya think about that then. All a bit scary and dubious aint it. That's when I decided that old Andy needed a little 'oliday, so I called the travel agents and booked meself a cheap last minute deal to a place called Pripyat in somewhere called the Ukraine, they said the holiday was cheap cuz it's a bit hot there at the moment, so I'm takin' loads of coconut butter and me skimpiest trunks to get a good all over tan.

Anyways matey, I'll be back at some point, if the bastards aint gone and blown Portland to bits by then.

And by the way, it might be a good idea to keep out of that cockwomble Crowley's way for a bit.

Wanna buy a used moustache? only one previous owner.

TTFN and stay safe.
Your pal, soon to be sizzlin', Andy.

A Stranger Called Christmas

The Isle of Portland hasn't changed much over the years, in fact it's hardly changed at all, the houses are a little bigger than they used to be, the roads are now surfaced with tarmac and are a little wider than years ago but in essence, things on Portland are still pretty much the same as they have been for century's, one area in significance that still looks as it did when the latest mode of transport was the pack horse and each man had to carry a longbow by law, is the village of Wakeham.

If you follow the road down through the village towards Portland lighthouse you will eventually come to a large sweeping bend, on the left-hand side of this bend is Pennsylvania Castle built in 1800 by John Penn the grandson of William Penn, the guy that founded the State of Pennsylvania in the USA.

Immediately before you reach that great castle you will see two small Portland stone cottages, these have since been knocked into one and are now the Portland museum, but back in the 1600's one of them belonged to the eccentric Mr Christmas Mono.

Christmas Mono, Mono, or even Chris M as he was known locally, was as strange a fellow that you would ever meet on Portland. No one knew much about the man but it was said amongst the locals of Wakeham that he was well over seventy at the time of his death in 1687 but it was all conjecture and no one really knew for sure, it was hard to be certain as his long grey hair and huge bushy beard and moustache covered most of his face and on most days you could only ever see his green eyes peering out from amongst the fuzz, if the wind blew in the right direction though, you could sometimes catch a glimpse of a heavily wrinkled weather beaten face and if you looked close enough you might also see the faded crescent shaped scar above his right eye, a souvenir no doubt from some adventurous escapade in his former years.

Chris M wasn't a pure blood Portlander, or so he told people, *'I just 'appened on the island and can't remember ow I got ere'* he would joke if asked, if you were to believe any of the wild tales that he often span in the local tavern you would know that he had undoubtedly once been a seafarer by trade, *'Spent many a year, Cap'n of me own rigger, sailin' the trade winds round the 'orn'* he would say after a few flagons of ale. One thing that everyone could agree on though was that Chris M could spin a good yarn whether it be true or not.

His small cottage in Wakeham was filed to the rafters with sailing memorabilia and souvenirs from far flung countries with exotic sounding names, on the walls hung various sized helmsman's wheels, ships lanterns and chunks of old knotted rope, on various tables scattered around the two room cottage were charts & maps, many with quill scrawl and the occasional red x marking the spot written on them, a brass astrolabe, a nocturnal and a cross-staff sat on oak shelves affixed to the wall by the cottage door whilst even more assorted seaman's tools like a mariner's quadrant and a traverse board were scattered around the floor, in one corner of the room near the staircase was a rack containing many vicious looking knives swords and other nasty looking cutting implements but taking pride of place right in the center of the room was a large brass free-standing thirty two point compass rose that looked as if it had been hauled straight off the deck of a grand ocean going galleon.

Christmas Mono never seemed short of a bob or two, not that he would ever flaunt it in front of anybody, but he never went short of food or a bottle of rum and he always had money if he needed it for any "emergency" that might occur.

There was one such occasion a few years previous that was often attributed to him although no proof was ever found, not that anyone looked very hard, but he was the only person in the village of Wakeham that owned his own house outright and wasn't under the thumb of the landlord, that alone stood him in good stead as prime suspect number one.

The incident involved an old Wakeham woman called Aggie Pritchard who lived just up the road from Chris M.

One winter, Aggie fell foul of her landlord Mr H

Gent, never had such an inappropriate name been given to a person, for he was a right rum fellow and definitely no gent, bald headed and hooked nosed, Gent who owned most of the cottages in Wakeham carried a gnarled wooden club with which he would hammer on your door every Saturday come rain or shine, his modus operandi was five hard blows on your door with a shout of 'Rent man! Pay up or your out by the morning' and he meant it too, if you missed his call it was your responsibility to find him and pay your dues before sun up the next day or his boys would frog march you out of your home and will have burnt your belongings in the street by midday, he took no quarter did Mr Gent.

Mrs Pritchard's husband of 48 years, Gabriel, had recently passed away after a rockslide at Rip Croft quarry, a bunny had been seen in the quarry that morning but he had refused to obey the superstition of never working in the quarries if a bunny was seen, and he had paid the ultimate price. Four days later was rent day and as usual Gent came a rapping at her door, only this time instead of demanding the rent money he offered his condolences for her loss, this alone was so out of character that it should have triggered alarms bells straight away, never in the forty years that she had known Gent had she ever seen him to show compassion towards a single soul.

'Don't you worry your pretty little head about the rent Mrs Pritchard', he sleazed with a thin toothy grin.

'I'll make sure everything's ok.'

Aggie Pritchard felt a sense of relief as she was now penniless, Gent stared her in the eyes without blinking as he continued.

'So just let me in and make me happy for an hour and you can forget the rent.' the thin toothy grin appeared again.

At first she was horrified shocked and disgusted but as she looked back into his eyes she knew that she had no choice, so she stood aside and let him in. This sick arrangement continued each Saturday for the next three weeks until Gent stopped calling on her and she believed that he had kept his word and taken care of the rent for her just like he had promised he would, how naive of her.

A full year passed by, Mrs Pritchard was still wearing her widows weeds but had managed to find work as a Purefinder, collecting dog turds from the streets to be used in softening animal skins at the Portland tannery in Easton, the work was filthy and stank but if put food on her table. On the occasion of Aggie Pritchard's 70th birthday, there was a familiar hammering on her front door, it was Gent.

'Ah Mrs Pritchard, I just thought I would let you know,' he started, 'I'm here to collect your back rent.' the familiar thin toothy grin reappeared on his his bony face.

'So pay up or you're out by the morning!'.

The bombshell nearly floored her and she gripped her chest as a panic attack ripped through her frail body, there was no way she could afford such a sum, even if she owned her cottage and could sell it, it wouldn't cover the £12 10s 6d owed, she was so distraught that she wanted to throw herself off the cliffs at Church Ope.

It didn't take long for the sad story to get around the community, everyone was livid, but what could they do, no one had enough money to help the old woman even if they pooled their finances and they couldn't confront Mr Gent himself, after all he was their landlord as well and they might find themselves out on the streets alongside her.

The following morning saw a terrified Aggie Pritchard and a handful of friends and neighbours anxiously waiting in her parlour for Mr Gents boys to appear and throw her out on the street. She didn't know what to do or think, all she knew for sure was that she had no money to pay her landlord and she would be homeless very soon.

Boom boom boom boom boom, Gents wooden club came a knocking. It was time, Aggie sat awhile just staring at the door and then steadied herself and dried her eyes, if she was going to be evicted she was at least going to be evicted with some dignity, she slowly opened the door and there he was, the bastard Gent, his face showed no emotions and his eyes gave nothing away, the pair stared at each other for a few seconds before he spoke in almost a whisper.

'Mrs Pritchard... £12 10s 6d owed... and £12 10s 6d has been paid, your debt has been fulfilled.'

Without further a word Gent about turned and marched off down the street. No one could believe what had happened, the entire village was stunned, *who had paid Mrs Pritchard's back rent, who was the generous mysterious benefactor,* nobody knew and no one would ever find out.

That's not the end of the tale though because two weeks later the lifeless body of Mr Gent was found at the bottom of Rip Croft quarry, his tongue had been cut out at the root and a jagged sail makers knife was discovered alongside the corpse, the cause of death was a traditional seafarers revenge.

Eventually the story became just another mystery in a long line of mysteries that happened on Portland.

Amongst Mr Christmas Mono's apparent obsession with all things nautical he had another little quirk, this one was no secret and the entire village knew about it. At that period in history personal hygiene was a bit dubious to say the least, the closest a lot of people came to having a wash was either a quick dunk in the sea or a trip to the public bath house in Fortuneswell once a year if they had a penny spare, but Chris M was the polar opposite, he loved a good bath and had an unusual bathing ritual.

Once a month without fail, he would take it upon himself to visit his "special" bathing place which was not far from his cottage and just behind where Pennsylvania Castle is now.

Tucked away in the undergrowth there was a relic from times past in the shape of an old Roman reservoir which was fed by a natural spring in the vicinity, the spring has now long since dried up, but back then the fresh running water constantly kept the reservoir topped up. Its original Roman use is unknown and lost in the annuals of pre-history but whatever its purpose is irrelevant, because in 1687 it was used for the sole purpose of hosting Chris M's personal bathing ritual and come rain or shine, without fail, he would take a stroll down the winding dirt pathway that led from the back of his cottage to the small wooded area at the top of Church Ope Cove, there he would strip down to his long john's and take a plunge and would lay there all afternoon with the fresh spring water up to his chest in the quiet shade of the oaks.

Portlanders have a very long history with the Kings of England. The island has always been a Royalist stronghold and the men of Portland have always fought on the side of the King in defence of their country, and it was this loyalty to the throne that led to Portland being issued with its own Royal Charter which is still valid to this day. This *special bond* was further enhanced when Christopher Wren specified the use of Portland stone in the rebuilding of St Paul's Cathedral and many Royal residencies in and around London after their destruction in the great fire of 1666, this one act alone would provide work for the Portland quarrymen for hundreds of years to come and it was also because of this special bond that William III the successor to not long dead Charles II, was visiting Portland in July 1687, he was coming with his entourage to give thanks to his loyalist of loyal subjects.

Chris M was dismayed when he heard this news and if he were 20 years younger he would have jumped on the first ship out of port and headed east, but he was beyond all that now, he was too old to keep running and hiding and too old to stand and fight but he knew that the ransom put on his head by Charles II was still valid and even though the old king was dead, his surviving courtiers and entourage that now followed King William meant that the risk of being captured was high, it was a risk he didn't want to take, being hung drawn and quartered just didn't appeal.

Mono stripped off his muddy clothes, even his long

john's this time, and lowered himself into his beloved outdoor bath turning the water a murky brown colour, he made himself comfortable and after a few seconds of what seemed like a studied reflection of his life, he heaved a heavy rock that he'd placed on the side specifically for this last act and placed it on his chest, the weight of the granite lump instantly forced him fully under the water, he didn't fight it, he gazed up through the bubbles at the distorted tree tops above him and as the air in his lungs seeped out of the corners of his mouth he smiled a contended smile, he was happy, he had done all the things he'd ever wanted to do with his life, he had sailed the high seas, he'd fought with pirates, bedding dark skinned beauties and he'd had squash-buckling adventures in far off exotic places, his spirit for adventure had finally been quelled, he could at last die a contented man.

Two hours earlier as the sun started to rise in the sky and had just begun to burn off the early morning dew clinging to the damp grass, Mr Christmas Mono or Thomas Crimson to give him his correct moniker that we now know, stepped out of his little cottage for the very last time and inhaled the sweet tasting morning air, of all the many many countries around the world that he'd visited, nowhere did the air taste as sweet as on the Isle of Portland.

He'd had a hard but fun and adventurous life but had no regrets, well maybe he would have liked to have kept in touch with a few of his offspring around the world but such is life.

He took another deep gulp, rubbed his freshly shaven chin, a chin that hadn't seen the light of day for over thirty years, and gripped a waxed paper object he held in his hand.

Normally at this time of day the old pathway that led to his bathing area would have been busy with people making their way from the Ope to Wakeham and vice versa but not today, today was the day that the whole of Portland had been excitingly waiting a whole year for and was to be a very special day in the lives of the islanders.

For weeks now, islanders in the villages from Chiswell to Southwell had been baking extra provisions, washing their best clothes, cleaning the outsides of their cottages, sweeping the streets and even hanging bunting across the roads, nothing less was worthy for the King of England himself, King William III was coming to visit.

Thomas Crimson wandered down the inclining path towards the old Roman reservoir with a resigned but resolute look on his face, he didn't particularly want to do what he was going to do but it had to be done.

If you or I were to walk down that same steep wooded path leading from Wakeham village to Church Ope Cove that Mr Christmas Mono now trod, we wouldn't be blamed for walking right past the old Roman reservoir, it's tucked away on the left hand side of the track half way down, you have to squeeze between ancient oaks that are almost surrounded by foliage and if you manage to pass through this natural barrier you will find on the other side a much smaller path (almost not a path at all) that winds its way between the trees for some fifty feet then opens out to a shaded clearing and the Roman reservoir.

At first glance the reservoir itself looks nothing special, it's a low squat pedestal probably five feet in height made from local Portland stone, a small worn stone staircase on the left takes you to its top which is made from solid granite and it's this granite slab that has been carved into a deep bowl that the natural spring empties into and had become Crimson's bathtub, but it's not the bath itself that was his concern at the moment.

With a long drawn out sigh, the ageing seafarer approached the stone edifice but instead of climbing the steps as he would usually do, he pushed his way through the surrounding bushes to the back of the pedestal and stopped by a particularly thick gorse bush, behind that particular bush, obscured from view was a small narrow gap in the stonework that allowed access under the structure, he brushed aside the greenery and entered.

It was almost pitch black inside but he didn't need much light for this particular task, he entered and trudged through the thick sticky mud that covered the floor, the roof of this "cave" was supported by thick man-made pillars of Portland stone that took the weight of the granite slab above, he walked to the furthest pillar in the darkest area and dropped to his knees in the wet sludge and proceeded to dig a hole with his hands, once happy, he took the wax papered object that he had treasured ever since his daring raid on the Tower of London all those years ago, had one final peek at his good luck charm, the enormous 530 carat Cullinan Diamond, gave it a kiss goodbye and smiled.

The Last Tattoo on Portland

The frail old man groaned as his joints popped and a spasm of pain shot down his sciatica ravaged legs, old age didn't agree with him, not one bit.

He stood at the window and stared out over the drab rooftops of Underhill. The grey slates of the decaying buildings matched the feelings he felt in his soul. He was lost, his very essence was doomed to eternal damnation and he knew that he deserved every second of it.

His mind rewound back through the years reliving memories that he wished had remained hidden to him. He had had total recall six weeks ago when the dark protective veil of false innocence that had shielded him from his past horrors had suddenly lifted, he had been torturing himself everyday since.

The man groaned again as his gnarled arthritic hand picked up the phone and he dialled a number. Today was the day that he had put off for so long, if only he'd had the courage to do it before now, but he knew he was a coward.

The dial tone was replaced by a familiar voice, older for sure but it was still as brutal as it had ever been even though over fifty years had passed since he had last heard it.

'Crowley here, what?'

'It's John Halliwell.' The caller swallowed hard and paused before continuing.

'We must talk.'

It was enough to grab the full concentration of the man on the other end of the line, and the two men talked for almost five minutes before John hung up and sobbed his heart out.

Early the next morning the now 76 year old John Halliwell put on his coat and dragged his tired body to the overgrown allotment he kept in Queens road, nothing had grown there in years, not since he and Crowley had *dealt* with the girl, her name came back to him again, Tanya! yes, poor innocent Tanya, she hadn't deserved what had happened to her, what HE had done to her, him and that rancid tattoo machine, what he, with Crowley's help, had done to her after her death, she at least deserved a proper funeral. The memories of that terrible night filled the old man's thoughts and he sat down and sobbed again.

The ground at his allotment was dead, contaminated with evil and although nothing had grown there in years he still kept up the monthly payments on it, he had to, he couldn't risk the chance of what was buried there ever being discovered.

It took John nearly two hours to finish digging in the dirt and to get to the meeting place that he'd arranged with Crowley. The final descent down the steep hill to the field in what was once Bottomcombe quarry was total agony on his old body and he almost passed out twice, but the pain was deserved and it seemed a fitting place to finally end the nightmares, a fitting place to finally put to rest the ghosts, the ghosts of so so many people.

The old quarry maintenance shed where he'd once been held captive had long gone now, it had been demolished years ago, not long after the tragedy. Some years later a supermarket had been built on the site and had lasted for ten years, but it had failed and eventually shut its doors, several other businesses tried their luck on the site but they also failed in the end, nothing seemed to thrive there, the land was tainted, cursed, it was only fit for cattle now.

John slowly walked towards three grazing cows on the spot where he remembered the stage and lighting rig had once been, the same stage that he had been tied to by his hands and had helplessly witnessed all those awful things happening, fighting back tears he hung his head and closed his eyes and prayed for all the lost souls.

The sound of a car pulling up and parking at the top of the hill announced that Crowley had arrived and it was time.

John reached into the carrier bag he had been carrying and removed the mahogany box with brass corner pieces that he'd not long ago dug up from its secret hiding place at the allotment next to the girls grave, his hand trembled in pure abject fear as he opened the lid and stared inside.

The repulsive device looked exactly the same as the last time he'd seen it all those years ago, the sight of it sickened him to his core but he felt a sudden desire to hold it again and to feel its power, it drew him to it like a rat to a piece of shit.

Gently, almost lovingly, John picked up the tattooing machine and gripped it tightly in his hand and enjoyed its warm fleshy feel, it almost felt alive.

Crowley gave a low growl as he started walking down the hill, *the bastard had to choose this place! Why couldn't he pick a flat car park or something.* He could see Halliwell away in the distance, it looked like he was praying, *the pussy!* he grumbled.

It felt so good holding the tattooing machine again after all these years, John had a sudden urge to find new living skin so he could begin laying down more ink and savour the sensations that the device would give him as it worked its evil black magic.

Crowley's sudden shout from half way down the hill resonated in his ears and brought John to his senses, what had he been thinking, he had almost succumbed to the heinous Devil inside the wretched device. Shaking his head to settle himself John pushed aside the desires being forced on him, he had to do what he'd come to do, he had to finish it once and for all and pay penance for his sins, it was the only way out of this nightmare and he knew it.

He approached the largest of the three grazing bovine that stood a little way from him, the device in his hand throbbed, it wanted to draw, it wanted to tattoo and above all else, it wanted blood.

John Halliwell raised the tattooing machine from Hell high above his head and paused.

'You want blood? Well have blood.'

In a sudden swift motion he brought the needle of

the machine down against the thick cow hide and it immediately began to throb and vibrate in his hand, he closed his eyes.

Crowley neared the bottom of the old overgrown quarry access road, he was sweating profusely and he wiped the few thin wisps of ginger hair that remained from his eyes.

'What's that old fool up to?'

Johns mind filled with nightmare images and a blaze of coloured light that swirled around inside his tired brain, the hand holding the tattooing machine began to move as though it were guided by some unseen force leaving behind it a thin black line of ink on the skin of the cow.

Crowley finally reached the flat of the quarry and approached the spot where he had just seen Halliwell standing but there was no sign of the old man, just three cows happily chewing the cud.

'I'm getting too old for this kinda bullshit Halliwell.' Crowley snarled. 'Where the fuck are you?'

A loud creaking sound emanated from the far side of the largest of the three of cows, it sounded like a rusty door shutting.

'What the Hell are you doi...' Crowley stopped mid question.

Did he really just see what he thought he'd seen. No! he couldn't have, it was impossible. The ginger haired, long-retired policeman's eyes fell to the ground at the the cows hooves and saw an open mahogany box fitted with brass corner pieces lying on the grass. He recognised the box as the same box he'd found at the scene of the biker massacre all those years ago. When he'd forced it open in his car and examined its contents, the sense of pure abject fear that he'd felt as he looked at it caused him to slam the lid shut immediately and he hadn't even dared to make a guess as to what the revolting object was. He also remembered that he had seen that exact box before, in John Halliwell's bedroom the night he had sorted out the mess Halliwell had made with the girl Tanya. But now, as he looked at the source of the strange creaking sound, he finally realised that what John had told him was true.

Crowley watched in stunned silence as John's gnarled old hand reached out from the inside of the cow, grabbed a small tattooed handle on a small tattooed door and pulled it shut.

And with that, John Halliwell and his evil nefarious tattoo machine disappeared forever.

Crowley looked at the unperturbed cow as it chewed happily on the grass, all signs of a tattooed door on its side were now gone. With a sad confused look on his face, he tucked the empty box under his arm and began the long trudge back up the hill towards his car.

The Cost of Doing a Good Deed

JJ Phelps honed his butchers knife to a gleaming edge on a long leather strop that hung from a hook high up in the abattoirs rafters and grumbled to himself.

The nineteen year old could have been partying, getting pissed on cheap Spanish booze and shagging the lads and lasses with his Uni mates in Ibiza during the summer break, but no, his father had been short handed on the farm and JJ had stupidly offered to help out, how was he supposed to know that the old man would accept his offer, the bastard!

It might not have been so bad if all JJ had to do was feed the animals and drive the tractor around the muddy fields, but here he was, in the small abattoir processing cows and worn out old nags.

The metallic rattle of stainless steel chains and hooks announced the arrival of the next carcass that needed his personal attention. The current intake of animals were old milkers and lame horses destined for pet food which made his life easier as the safety inspectors stamp wasn't required, but it was still a messy job.

The carcass of a cow came to a stop in front of him, its still warm body had already been bled-out, all he needed to do was slice the animals underbelly, cut out the guts with his razor sharp blade and collect them in a large white plastic container, but as he soon discovered, this particular beast was rotten to the core and its internal organs were nothing but a thick, black and red streaked, stinking sludge, that sploshed in to the container below with a sickening watery squelch.

JJ grimaced and pulled a face and dry heaved, but something caught his eye, what was that amongst the foulness, some sort of weird alien gun, a prop from a horror movie perhaps. Whatever it was, it shouldn't be in the guts of an old cow.

JJ crouched down and cautiously fished the strange looking object out of the detritus of organic slime and held it in his hand, his initial thought was to lob it straight into the biohazard waste box for incineration, but as he studied it more, he began to change his mind.

'You know what?' he mumbled to no one as he turned the find around in his fingers. 'The guys will love this horrible nasty looking thing, in fact everyone at Uni would love it, it's just the sort of thing to interest those freako's.'

So he decided that he would take it to campus with him next term, he might even be able to sell it and make a few quid.

Suddenly the rancid looking object throbbed and buzzed in his grip, JJ clamped his eyes shut tightly as visions of pure ecstasy erupted in his brain and waves of never-before experienced pleasure rippled through his body, he immediately ejaculated in his boxer shorts and sighed contentedly.

ABOUT THE AUTHOR

Saxon's claim to fame is that he's ridden his Triumph Bonneville 650cc twin to every country in mainland Europe, and he's planning to tackle the rest of the world as soon as possible.

When not plotting to conquer the world astride his British iron, Saxon lives at home with his African Grey parrot called Sharon, in a little cottage on the South Coast of England where he has a prime view of an old 18th century Victorian coastal defence fort, and sometimes, when sitting in his "found" deckchair in the garden, he swears that he can still hear the strains of melancholic bagpipes drifting on the zephyrs of the late summers evening.

Printed in Great Britain
by Amazon

23201924R00225